EXILE
OF THE
PAN ARCANUM

THE INCURSION CHRONICLES

EXILE
OF THE
PAN ARCANUM

ERIC N. LARD

4 Horsemen
Publications, Inc

Exile of the Pan Arcanum
Copyright © 2024 Eric N. Lard. All rights reserved.

4 Horsemen
Publications, Inc.

Published By: 4 Horsemen Publications, Inc.

4 Horsemen Publications, Inc.
PO Box 417
Sylva, NC 28779
4horsemenpublications.com
info@4horsemenpublications.com

Cover by CD Corrigan
Typesetting by Autumn Skye
Edited by Joseph Mistretta

All rights to the work within are reserved to the author and publisher. No part of this publication may be reproduced, stored in a retrieval system, or transmitted in any form or by any means, electronic, mechanical, photocopying, recording, scanning, or otherwise, except as permitted under Section 107 or 108 of the 1976 International Copyright Act, without prior written permission except in brief quotations embodied in critical articles and reviews. Please contact either the Publisher or Author to gain permission.

All characters, organizations, and events portrayed in this novel are either products of the author's imagination or are used fictitiously.

All brands, quotes, and cited work respectfully belongs to the original rights holders and bear no affiliation to the authors or publisher.

Library of Congress Control Number: 2024943089

Paperback ISBN-13: 979-8-8232-0628-0
Hardcover ISBN-13: 979-8-8232-0629-7
Audiobook ISBN-13: 979-8-8232-0631-0
Ebook ISBN-13: 979-8-8232-0630-3

DEDICATION

I'd like to acknowledge God, family, and friends in general—all played a pivotal role in the creation of this story. Specifically, I'd like to call out K.C. Reiter for approaching my work the way he does all things; full speed and with reckless abandon. S.K. Marre for her in-depth and ever-insightful analysis. As well as Chase Gamwell and Sean Rowland for their honest and unfiltered (at least I think they're unfiltered) insights. Last but by no means least, my mom, for her unceasing encouragement, and my beautiful wife for her support and mostly gentle reminders that the first three things on this list need to be nurtured at least as much as my writing.

TABLE OF CONTENTS

CHAPTER 1	MOP UP	1
CHAPTER 2	BURIED	11
CHAPTER 3	BLACK FLOOD	19
CHAPTER 4	NOT SO EASY	31
CHAPTER 5	MAYBE THIS WAS A BAD IDEA	38
CHAPTER 6	THE ASPECT	46
CHAPTER 7	THE HANGOVER	57
CHAPTER 8	HOPE NOT LOST	73
CHAPTER 9	THE DEFILER	86
CHAPTER 10	PELL-MELL AND BERZERK	95
CHAPTER 11	THE DEBRIS FIELD	104
CHAPTER 12	THE ARCFIRE	112
CHAPTER 13	ORBITAL DECAY	125
CHAPTER 14	SOME RANDOM DRONE	139
CHAPTER 15	WAHR-ZEN	148
CHAPTER 16	HELL ON EPRIOT	155
CHAPTER 17	THE INITIATE	165
CHAPTER 18	THE REMNANT	174
CHAPTER 19	INTAKE	189
CHAPTER 20	HOPE RE-IGNITED	198
CHAPTER 21	THE RESISTANCE	209
CHAPTER 22	BREAKING IN	217
CHAPTER 23	SPIRES AND THE RIGHTEOUS FURY	229
CHAPTER 24	THE GATHERING OF FIVE	240
CHAPTER 25	BETRAYED	247

CHAPTER 26	CHANGE OF PLANS	253
CHAPTER 27	GOING DOWN	257
CHAPTER 28	ASCENDING	263
CHAPTER 29	RUTKER AND THE OTHER REMNANT	266
CHAPTER 30	MACQ & SERAF	273
CHAPTER 31	THE CIRCLE OF FIVE	282
CHAPTER 32	THE OUTSKIRTS	291
CHAPTER 33	REALITY ZERO	299
CHAPTER 34	CHRONOSHIELD	309
CHAPTER 35	RUTKER AND 'ZERK	322
CHAPTER 36	SERAF AND THE VOID	329
CHAPTER 37	THE CRASH SITE	339
CHAPTER 38	HOPE AND THE HERETIC	353
CHAPTER 39	THE ANCIENT	361

BOOK CLUB QUESTIONS 365
AUTHOR BIO 367

CHAPTER 1
MOP UP

Epriot Prime, Preta Compact (Southern Continent), Western edge of the Monther Accord
[Two Weeks After the Third Invasion]

Galas's hands were bone cold, but her palms prickled with sweat.

She wasn't nervous, exactly. Well, she was, but that's just how she got before a firefight. Even when she felt good about the odds.

But seven to one?

No one should feel good about odds like that. However, Galas just accepted certain things. One of those things was that shit just keeps coming. And another was that in many ways Galas was like a chainsaw. Things might not look pretty, but in the end, Galas could handle some shit.

She shook out her hands for about the third time to get the circulation going again. Good thing she didn't have to fuss with the still unfamiliar manual controls of the alien mech she was piloting.

She allowed a smug smile to creep onto her face.

Recently liberated from the ill-fated Delvadr armada, she thought to herself with deep satisfaction. She flexed her fingers again and cracked her neck side-to-side.

Still not comfortable...

What was bothering her? She scanned the undulating corduroy of dusty gray and yellow hills spread out before her. The aerial view from the flyer drones made them look idyllic and relatively flat. From ground level, it was a brutal slog through choppy, dusty hard pan that seemed as though it had been tilled by the very hand of Maker himself.

She drew her legs up into a cross-legged position in the pilot's chair before rushing through a set of breathing exercises.

"Still not working," she growled under her breath.

After a moment, she retrained her focus on the SortieNet. Its tactical and operational imagery splashed in a near-constant deluge of data across her corneal implants. Something she was used to and just took for granted.

It was dark in the captain's module. In the reflected light of a blank display screen, she could see her pupils and irises glowing gold as she perused the virtual dashboard with all the mech's operational and armaments data.

That might sound pretty cool, but what she was seeing was anything but. The mash-up of alien weapons, operational tech, and her native Epriot version didn't mesh well. Raph managed to make it workable, and that was the important thing. Galas knew he was doing a metric ass-load of computational adjustments behind the scenes to make the interface between her neural hardware and the stolen mech work right. But that was the sort of thing he was good at.

Trust.

See? I can do it.

She sat there for a moment longer and then palmed her forehead.

"Ughh!" She hit it a couple more times for good measure and then massaged her temples in frustration. It was Seraf's birthday.

"That's what's got me all twitchy."

She blew a warm, shuddering breath into her freezing hands. *It's gonna be a rough day.*

"Raph!" she barked. "Sweep again for anomalies. I know what we're seeing on the scope isn't everything these bastards brought to the sandbox." She blew into her hands again. "And do something about these damned environmentals. I'm freezing my bony ass off in here."

She scanned the broken hills as she continued to try to put a bridle on her churned-up emotions. What stood out were two blacked-out Delvadr Elite mechs. Top-of-the-line Thune hardware, just like the unit Galas had heisted. They bristled with weaponry, and their sleek muscular forms oozed deadly effectiveness. They were vaguely humanoid in appearance, but there was no head, just a canopied crew compartment in the middle of a wide torso with ample space atop the broad shoulder platform to mount rockets, lasers, plasma cannons, chain guns, rail guns, and a whole host of other weaponry. The arms, too, were guns and likely hid chain or plasma blades in foldout compartments.

That wasn't all. Elites were jump mechs, meaning they had boot- and pack-mounted repulsors that could be used for short flights. And if that wasn't bad enough, they also had active camouflaging, which made them temporarily invisible to the naked eye and to most sensors.

Badass didn't even begin to describe the feeling of power that came with piloting a mech of that capability. Up until a few weeks ago, Galas had always made do with Epriot gear. Now, she might not be able to go back.

Two elites. Okay.

She breathed through the mounting fear. There were more mechs out there. Galas spread out her flyer drones to augment the visual data coming from the Epriot's woefully impaired satellite network and easily picked out five more.

The saving grace was that these were standard mechs. Smaller, graphite in color—with none of the fancy black-on-black detailing—and thankfully, lacking both the stealthing capability and the enhanced jump characteristics of the elites.

Still, the fact that she could see those two elites at all was a tell. There were more out there, hiding beneath their active camouflaging.

I know you're baiting me...

With a thought, she maneuvered through the SortieNet dashboard, expanded the drone's sweep pattern, and tweaked her mech's energy consumption to reduce its sensor footprint.

She'd tracked the Delvadr this far. Wiped out three squads of the stranded invasionary army. They were all headed to this location. Some sort of rally point.

Good luck, she thought. *Your armada is nothing but space dust in Epriot's low and middle orbit and you're sixty-five light years from home, you pompous pricks.*

I'm gonna find you. And I'm going to kill every last one of you.

Anger was a great tool for distracting herself from feeling uncomfortable emotions.

Still...

She tried to focus, to force her daughter's memory out of her mind. Tried to compartmentalize it until later, when she could process things appropriately without risking the lives of her two-, or technically three-person crew.

It was a gray area, personhood. Raph, her former mech's AI, wasn't *exactly* a person. At least not an EDC-acknowledged one. But to Galas, over the course of the Arcfire mission, he'd become something more than just a neural interface to the SortieNet. *Time to get to work.*

Her brain was going in eighty different directions. Situation normal. But this was too much, even for her. She huffed out an anxious breath, brushed an errant strand of auburn hair back under her cap, and snugged it back down.

Baby, I'm coming. It's been a really long time, I know, but I just have to take care of a couple things first.

Seraf was seventeen today. That was the problem.

At seventeen, Galas was parentless and solo-piloting her first mech, a reconner named Skinny Boy. She had no idea what Seraf was up to or had suffered through, or even what she looked like. Other than the casual observation that she "looked just like you."

She shook her head and flashed a thousand-watt smile. It was forced. A fake-it-till-you-make-it sort of thing. She tried not to let her eye twitch as she did it.

She wanted nothing more than to go find her baby girl, whom she'd believed dead for well over a decade. Nearly the entire span between the second invasion and this most recent, and thankfully final, one.

Galas had missed so much.

She *would* find her. Hell, she'd forfeit her soul to do it if she had to.

Galas's scattered thoughts smoothed out as she drew nearer the inevitable moment of contact with the enemy. It'd be soon. She navigated slightly away from the edge of a gorge but noted the distance precisely, even as she peeled back one of the drones to build a high-res model of the terrain within the gorge and within a half-klick radius around her.

The Delvadr were stranded here because she, Raph the AI, and Jinnbo, her Cycarian co-pilot, had reactivated the Arcfire—a planetary defense system left behind by a race of people who'd disappeared millennia before humans arrived in the Epriot System. That ancient weapon eviscerated seven interstellar supercarriers and most of the shuttles and dropships that were falling to the surface of her home planet in the first waves of what was going to be the coup de grâce. The culmination of a four decades-long invasion.

Humanity had lost billions. And she had personally taken the lives of millions of Delvadr in return.

Unfortunately, that still left hundreds of thousands of enemy troops and thousands of mechs to mop up here on the surface. It was going to take everyone left on Epriot Prime to do it. And every one of these genocidal alien bastards she killed was one less to get in the way of her seeing Seraf again.

"Yes, Ma'am," Raphael responded, what seemed like minutes later but was only a few seconds. He wasn't just the AI for Galas's current, pirated mech, an elite unit they'd heisted in an elaborate Trojan drone scheme. He was Galas's personal AI and virtual wingman after she'd been forced to scuttle her previous mech, Betsy, and take him onboard her battle armor as they'd perpetrated the remainder of the Arcfire mission.

"However, as successful as I've been in subverting each of the mech's command systems, convincing the environmental scrubbers to back down with such a large contaminant source has proven to be beyond even my significant capabilities."

That ejected Galas from the maelstrom of thoughts and emotions swirling in her head.

"Contaminant? What do you mean? Am I going to catch some sort of alien STD from these bastards? After all I've been through? One final, filthy, F-U from these... these..." she stuttered as she pulled her arms up to her chest and stared dubiously at the pilot's chair she'd been lounging in.

"Not likely. According to the scrubbers, the contaminant is you. *And* your co-pilot."

"Oh, that makes sense," she responded, nodding absently and relaxing a little.

A new voice rose into the audio circuits as a fur-scaled face flashed across her virtual dashboard. It looked like a fox-faced monkey and it had taloned bat wings for arms.

"Capt. Galas, any commands for meeeeee???" The buoyant inquiry came from Jinnbo, her Cycarian co-pilot. The image panned out to show him in his typical uniform: a faded purple and yellow tropical print shirt that he manifested on the lightly furred scales of his alien skin. The outfit had no pants, just a pixelated blur where his gender-specific bits were located. Galas shook her head. Such a weird little being...

"Sorry. Didn't mean to leave you out. Still getting used to this 'relying on other people' thing," she replied. She turned her focus again to scanning and sorting the typical avalanche of data provided through SortieNet's virtual BattleSpace Model.

She'd grown up in a battle mech and was the most experienced and most effective pilot in the whole of the Epriot Defense Collaborative. Of course, with an average mech pilot life expectancy that barely exceeded that of a swamp midge, it wasn't saying much.

Jinnbo, for his part, had been next to worthless as a co-pilot until only recently when he'd gone catatonic, formed a cocoon, birthed an evil twin, and vanquished him by the narrowest of margins as part of a previously unknown Cycarian rite of passage. That evil twin had almost ended Galas's life through sabotage and, incidentally, was where they got the idea for the trick with the virus-infected drone since he'd used it so effectively on Galas's own power armor.

But that was near-ancient history, and the defeat of that horrible creation proved to be quite the confidence booster for Jinnbo. More than that, it had induced a tsunami of hormones that continued to unlock new and sometimes useful attributes, as well as the occasional psychopathic rage rant.

Other than that, things were pretty good with her crew. Minus the part where Galas suspected that Jinnbo had been assigned to her as part of an interstellar witness protection program. Details.

"Excuse me, Ma'am," Raphael interjected, "but suddenly, we appear to be even more outnumbered than before."

Galas watched the 3D BattleSpace populate with close to a half dozen new targeted red cursors across the tortured terrain. She inhaled sharply.

Finally...

Her muscles tensed and then her heisted alien mech sprang into action, launching into the air and unleashing a hellfire barrage of rockets, plasma, and laser weaponry.

She wasn't surprised they were there, just that there were so many. Only Delvadr royalty could afford the obscenely expensive stealth armor with its active camouflaging capability. Apparently, the Delvadr had a surplus of 2nd, 3rd, and even 4th-born sons. And daughters. And some other gender she hadn't quite sorted out for the roughly humanoid invaders.

Little matter. They didn't appear to discriminate on who to send to be fodder for her cannons. And she didn't either. That was one thing she appreciated about the alien scumbags who'd been perpetrating a four decades-long campaign of genocide upon humanity.

The whole of the sprawling landscape before her erupted in fire as a return barrage issued from every square meter of vegetation ahead. Her mech fell back toward the ground, it twisted, bursting like a struck pinata with confetti-like countermeasures before slipping out of sight into a narrow crevasse. *Thank you, mapping drone.*

She hit the mech's boot-mounted repulsors hard right before landing and turned that downward momentum into a sprint along the bottom of the gorge. Light and sound erupted everywhere above her, caving in the walls of the gorge behind her and throwing up a huge plume of dust. *Perfect.*

The mech's active camouflaging kicked in and suddenly the white outline that represented her position in the BattleSpace faded to gray. She kept pushing toward the end of the runout gully, putting as much space between her last known location and herself as possible.

Some of them would buy the ruse, but the more experienced warriors among them would not.

More rockets impacted the area where she'd disappeared, and she gave one last push to the end of cover.

"Jinnbo, target just the closest elites. Focus on one at a time. Burn out their shields with the plasma cannons."

"Good as done, baby mama."

"That's not how this works. You don't get to call me that. And besides, I don't think you know what that means," she hollered even though her voice carried through the intercom, the SortieNet, and the fact that he was only meters away in the unfamiliar layout of the stolen mech. She made a mental note of this unnecessary effort while focusing on the maneuver at hand.

"Aye-aye, Cap'n."

"Better."

Cadian Galas was actually a Captain Major, but right now she wasn't going to stand on formality. Besides, she'd been informally promoted to colonel based on the success of what had been considered the hail mary of all hail mary missions: the Arcfire.

Suddenly, the mech burst from hiding. Its stealthing dropped to hurl another massive barrage. Rockets streaked out like angry hornets as at least four Delvadr standard mechs erupted into fire. Galas knew a weak spot in their shielding, thanks to Raphael's massively supercharged processing speed, a benefit of running on the vastly more powerful Delvadr platform. Her mech needed a name.

Betsy II lacks imagination, she thought while analyzing the virtual model and tweaking a slew of normally off-limits reactor parameters to increase the mech's performance. Her mind just worked like that.

The mech plummeted toward the ground again, this time in a parallel gorge to the first. This area had several of these gashes in the natural landscape, which suggested some recent seismic activity—which was a little alarming, but honestly, the people of Epriot Prime had other things to worry about.

Meanwhile, Jinnbo had success with two elites, burning out their sheilds, but he wasn't quite able to deplete their body armor. Still, he'd done exactly what Galas had asked. It was going to take a minute to get used to this new, useful Jinnbo.

Again, enemy rockets closed in and Galas engaged a metallic and RF cloud of countermeasures before shunting down to the bottom of this new gorge.

Her peekaboo attacks had been effective, but that gambit was providing diminishing returns. A pony without tricks is destined to become glue. As if to emphasize this fact, the main force of elite mechs had pressed forward and found new cover. Additionally, the remaining standard mechs had split ranks and were now working a pincer maneuver—flanking from either side.

Things were about to get dicey. *So much for colonel.*

"I've got 200 Xandrs on the other team," Raphael offered.

"Raph, is that your way of trying to tell me the odds without actually telling me the odds?"

"No ... but the spread is—"

"Can it. Besides, the exchange rate between Xandrs and Galactic Standard Reserves is too volatile to make that bet even worth it," she cut him off, as all the elite cursors went gray and then disappeared. A growing sphere with dotted lines depicting possible movements spread out from each as the SortieNet struggled to maintain the positioning of each of the stealthed-out mechs.

A squat form dropped into the gorge before her. She turned her sprint into a flying, two-footed kick and hammered the repulsors just as she made contact. The smaller, Delvadr Regular exploded back, smashing into another that had the misfortune of joining the fray at just the wrong time.

Galas flared rockets from both shoulder nacelles. Half of them flew at the tangled mess of armor ahead, and the other half arced through a quick 180, before ripping down the gorge behind her, where two more standards had just dropped in and were spraying a wall of laser and plasma fire. They took the barrage flat-footed and blew backward in a yard sale of parts. Raphael's precision guidance was paying off in spades.

Still, he was on the right side of the bet as far as Galas was concerned. Regardless of currency. There was no way this was going to end well. She'd seen the trap and waltzed right in. Victory favors the bold or something like that, she'd been thinking at the time. But there was a thin line between bold and stupid. She'd crossed that line.

No going back now.

Galas's yet-to-be-named mech dove for the tangled armor before her. Slicing with forearm-mounted plasma blades, just to be sure the second mech was toast, she hit the ground, stealthed-out, pulled the bodies on top of her, and riffed a rocket into the hillside above.

Galas was a ballet dancer wearing a 60-ton power suit.

A wall of rock and dust engulfed them. The avalanche roared outside as the mech bucked and jolted before silence and darkness ensued.

"Galas? Are we dead? I don't feel dead."

"Shhh."

"Oh, good. We're not dead."

Galas shot a thought-to-text to her confused co-pilot.

[Galas: No. We're not dead. Now, please shut up so I can figure out where the rest of these bastards are.]

[Jinnbo: Blink-Blink] he texted back.

CHAPTER 2
BURIED

Galas wiped her brow with the back of her forearm while waiting impatiently in the humid darkness. A few random lights glowed like beacons scattered across the cockpit, giving the sensation of being swallowed by some foreign valley on an alien moon.

With the mech shuttered and power reduced to near zero, it was hauntingly quiet. It would almost be peaceful if it wasn't so hot and if the stillness wasn't pregnant with a sense of impending doom. She cursed herself for being so reckless. Destroying an entire armada had gone to her head.

And then there were the hordes of psych-bugs she'd slain in her power armor with just the chain maces she'd fashioned from the suit's grappling lines and some random stone blocks. And also defeating the creepy-as-hell demon god, Sun-Thurr. The list of monumental achievements was lengthy and yet ... somehow hollow.

She shivered and shook off the memories. It was a lot to process and, in typical Galas fashion, she'd forged ahead, forever running from the metaphorical bear. A lot had transpired to get her to this place of slowly dying from either suffocation or heat illness, while buried under a thousand tons of rock with a squad of alien mechs hunting her down.

They would kill her. If she was lucky. And if she wasn't?
Can't I be allowed this one tiny miscalculation?
Her inner legion of critics responded as expected.

A boom reverberated through the silence. The heat was continuing to build with the mech's active sinks disengaged. Sweat dribbled down her face and she wiped it away with a shaky hand. Adrenaline. She was still way-juiced from the fight. She needed to zen out to think straight.

Breathe ... three, two ... breathe ... one, zero ... breathe. She whipped her biometric charts into the SortieNet dashboard playing across her corneas, shook her head at the results, and tried a different breathing exercise. She took one long breath through her nose and exhaled slowly while imagining herself being pulled into a black triangle in her mind's eye. Darkness flowed from the outer dark to the complete void within the triangle. She repeated this while listening to the activity outside of her self-imposed mausoleum of rubble.

[Jinnbo: Are you sure we're not dead?] Jinnbo texted again.

She ignored him and focused on her breathing. The jittery tension in her diaphragm began to lessen and her pulse began to slow.

Silence followed for another couple of minutes and then a dull thudding started up, one after another, but from farther away. *Something* was going on.

[Galas: Raph, can we get an eye on what's happening?]

They'd called in all of their flyer drones just as the fight began. The Delvadr used precious few compared to Epriot mechs and they couldn't be used to augment the functionality of the mech like Epriot units did. She fumed over the handicap. It was something she planned to rectify, just not now.

[Raph: I'll send Flyer Three. From its present stowed location, it has the best access out of the rubble. I'll have to engage limited systems to do it, though.]

[Galas: Do it. But don't turn up any systems that'll give us away.]

[Raph: Duh?] the AI provided by way of ending the conversation and reminding Galas who was the super-computer here.

She nodded to herself, grudgingly admitting that it was an irritating and unnecessary addition. She really had to work on this *team-player* thing. She was used to being in charge, but just not being in charge of anyone worth commanding. Her style of authority amounted to doing everything herself and then making sure everyone was still alive in the end. That wouldn't fly as a colonel. One thing at a time.

In Galas's former paradigm, Raphael had just been an interface to the tool that was the SortieNet. Now he had become something more than just a part of the crew. And Jinnbo? The jury was still out, but more and more it seemed like he'd managed to upgrade himself to a worthy, if still annoying and unstable, co-pilot.

Of course, they were still all probably going to die. Maybe Galas didn't have to worry about that pesky 'growing up as a person' thing after all.

Flyer Three wiggled its way through cavities in the rock and bullied through the last few meters of loose rubble before it broke free. It shot up toward a ceiling of thin, scattered clouds but stopped short at 1,000 meters. It started scanning the battlefield while deploying its own version of stealth technology to fool the other drones into thinking it was part of the Delvadr Superlink.

Everything that the Delvadr did was super-this, elite-that … ultra-something-or-other. Galas smiled as she thought fondly of all the super-burned-out mech carcasses scattered across the southern continent. And of their supercarriers bursting into super pieces in middle orbit. It warmed her cockles, even though she had no idea what those were or if it was anatomically appropriate for her to have them.

Imagery from the flyer splashed across her corneal implants. She cocked her head in confusion. The hills were littered with the broken and burned-out husks of elites and regulars alike. But many more than there should have been from her recollection of the battle.

She pulled down a window in her virtual dashboard with a thought and replayed all the action in 3D at high speed. She allowed a broad smile to raise the corners of her mouth as a buoyant sensation of pride bubbled up inside her. A few missed opportunities here and there but, overall, quite a respectable showing.

However, her conclusion remained. The bodies didn't add up. There were more than half again, as many as there should be.

Typical, she thought. Many of the Elites had hung back and waited for others to do the hard work, only dropping their stealthing when it looked like a sure victory.

But, if it wasn't her that waxed them, then who did the fighting?

Movement, a shimmer and pop like water flicked across hot grease, caught the drone's attention. Half a click away to the northeast, black figures surged across the terrain, blinking in and out of visibility, spurting forward at completely unreasonable speeds.

Another elite, heavy with bolted-on armaments, materialized before them, launching a barrage of rockets from its back, chest, and shoulder-mounted nacelles. The rockets shot into the turmoil of bubbling black rolling across the hillside, but the dark shapes disappeared and reappeared as the rockets exploded on empty earth.

What is that? A power armor regiment? But the way they move ... She absently rubbed her face and then propped her forehead up on short-trimmed fingertips.

Flyer Three zoomed in as the melee continued. The black shapes now appeared humanoid but monstrous in form, like half-human, half-wolf creatures made of blackest night. There was no reflection, no visible weaponry but talons, fangs, and incredible speed. This was no armor. These were legitimate monsters.

The creatures, fifty-strong, ate up the ground as they disappeared and reappeared meters away in a sporadic, blinking tsunami of wicked fangs and talons.

Galas noted their movements. They seemed coordinated.

They act like cavalry, fighting in fluid formation.

And then, despite the chaos of rockets and plasma fire, the wavelike formation crashed against the mech, slashing and ripping it apart savagely.

Galas sat straight up and zoomed in on the action.

They slipped right past its shielding. A chill ran down her spine. *So much for the perceived benefit of roaming around in 60 tons of armor.*

She thought the frenzy looked like a herd of demon squirrels attacking an inebriated polar bear but less comical and more, well, terrifying. She didn't feel bad at all about the crew but watched in fascination as the elite mech smashed and hacked itself to pieces.

Serves ya right.

Still, it was disturbing. The creatures were relentless, jumping in and blinking away with only a handful of casualties. The few that did get caught burst into a blaze of light and then poof ... nothingness. No bodies. No nothing.

Galas had never seen anything like it. She was glad to see the Delvadr getting their tail ends handed to them, but this was an alarming turn of events. Where had they come from? Who were they? What did they want? And even more importantly, how many more of them were there?

"Ma'am. Highlighted quadrant," Raphael provided, no longer worrying about texting.

"Oh, I see it," Galas responded, her attention focused on a gold cursor around a shimmer in the air that, if she'd been feeling particularly imaginative, would have looked like a rip in reality. As she spoke, a second contingent of the creatures easily a hundred strong entered the field. No imagination necessary.

"Oh. Not good. We should exfil and let Command know about this."

"What's EDC High Command going to do?" Jinnbo asked in an oddly chipper tone. But the question was right on.

"I dunno, but something. Something needs to be done," she continued as she watched retinue after retinue enter the field and the battlespace model before the rip in reality grew dark.

It extended roughly 50 meters into the air, shimmered, and blinked out. In its place, a blackness hung. So black that the light seemed as though it was being sucked into it. The hair on Galas's neck shivered.

"What is that?" Jinnbo asked in awe, echoing her own internal dialogue.

"Yeah," she whispered. "What in the galactic frag is that?"

She thought the command and Flyer Three whooshed in closer but even as the blacked-out space grew in definition so she could see that it was made of thousands upon thousands of spindly black arms, one of those arms whipped out and snatched the drone from the air and crushed it.

Static filled the viewscreen that overlaid what she could see of her darkened cockpit. She knew tons of rock and rubble lay just beyond the plasteel viewport mounted high-center of what was her mech's chest.

The destruction of the drone was a clear message of intent.

"Time to go."

Galas twisted the mech, worked her repulsors, and muscled her way out of the pile of rubble and armored body parts.

Dust and rocks poured over the images from various cameras and then as daylight emerged through her dust-streaked cockpit plas, a massive flash blinded her and glitched all the images out, "What in Skleetrix was *that*???" Galas cursed.

"An anomaly. I believe it's similar to the rift we saw earlier," Raphael supplied.

"An anomaly? That's less than helpful," Galas pulled the BattleSpace model into her visual dashboard with a thought and sure enough, a golden cursor highlighted a new area farther east from where the blackout creature still hovered in the air. Its contingents marched northward as new contingents of the ground forces sprang into the space around the new rift.

She deployed the remaining three drones, and they shot into the sky to cast a wide net of surveillance—well enough away from the floating blackout beasts to avoid a similar fate as that of Flyer Three.

Not wanting to draw attention to herself, she crept along the gorge when a scattering of blue cursors washed across the battlespace.

"Now what?" she asked in exasperation as thick splotches of blue sprang up even farther to the north.

"I have a bad feeling," Raphael offered.

"Ditto," Jinnbo's voice issued over the audio, suddenly devoid of mirth.

Galas shook her head, blinking away confusion.

She peeled out Flyer One and instantly regretted it. Below, a horde of small to medium-sized mechs stomped across the terrain, leaving bubbling black and orange goo in their wake. From this vantage, the whole ensemble looked like a creeping sore.

"What're *they* doing here? I've never seen so many," she asked in shock to collective radio silence. It seemed both Jinnbo and Raphael were just as stunned as she was.

Deathhound mechs were notorious across the planet as hunter-killers. Once a bounty had been placed, they stopped at nothing and could never, ever be shaken off. Galas was the only person she'd ever heard of who had survived an encounter with a pack, let alone evaded a bounty entirely.

Of course, she had to scuttle Betsy, her mech, and slink off in just her power armor to do it. And, even then, she still ended up going head-to-head with the Deathhound leader to finish the task. She didn't know what happened to the rest of the pack, but she could only assume that he'd wiped them out when he went rogue and came after her, despite Sun-Thurr's command to the contrary.

As it was, they were both dead, and she couldn't be happier. But now, here an entire army of Deathhounds had materialized on lands she thought only had to be liberated from the straggling Delvadr.

Another blast of light squelched her electronics.

"Don't tell me."

"Uh-huh."

"Dammit Raphael, I asked nicely."

"Sorry, Ma'am."

"It's more of the black thingies," Jinnbo provided, heedless of Galas and Raphael's dialogue.

"We know," Raphael and Galas scolded simultaneously.

"Sheesh."

"Sorry," Galas sighed out, rubbing her face with her hands, trying to get her brain cells all going in the same direction after this sensory overload, "Delvadr. Blackout thingies. Deathhounds. What is going on around here?"

"I haven't the foggiest idea, but we definitely need a better name for those void-like creatures than Blackout Thingies," Raphael suggested.

"You're right. Void it is," Galas agreed.

"Void?"

"I rather like Blackout, but Void works too," Jinnbo added.

"Yeah. Either. Both. Whatever. Rift Rippers are the big, spindly things, Savages are the creatures that make up those packs. Log it."

"Okay," the other two echoed, just as the new monikers plus "Deathhound" populated the virtual BattleSpace next to all the blue and gold cursors.

Galas noted that all the formerly red cursors of the Delvadr were now gray. She knew there were more out there, probably pissing themselves under their stealth armor. She'd need to be careful. Stepping into a 10m-long plasma blade would be a silly way to end her career.

Besides, Seraf was out there somewhere and she had every intention of seeing her daughter again before fate finally caught up with her.

CHAPTER 3
BLACK FLOOD

Galas maneuvered her heisted mech through a series of gorges well away from where the two alien armies were about to clash.

After seeing what she'd seen of the Savage hordes and what they'd done to the Delvadr, she wasn't sure what to expect from the Deathhounds—even if there were an absolutely obscene number of them on the field.

Galas edged the mech around a corner, skirting along the shadows of the ravine. Mechs that had stealthing were mostly invisible to sensors and optics, but that didn't mean they were silent. Except for specifically designed sniper units like the Novak Long Rifle, mechs made a hell of a racket. But even the Long Rifle had its own issues with cooling that she'd never wanted to contend with. Dying from overheating while hiding from the enemy didn't sound like her kind of gig. It did have a very big gun though.

So regardless of having her stealthing on, she moved slow and low in the elite mech. It was the only thing that saved her when at the last second she spotted an Amorphous Visible Disparity. The barely perceptible shift in the visual feed was directly ahead of her.

AVD's were something like a mirage. Mirages meant stealthing. And stealthing? Well, it was pretty obvious what that meant.

She shot, thought-to-text to Raph and Jinnbo as she quickly but quietly brought the mech to a halt.

[Galas: Don't make a sound. Big danger.]

Jinnbo started to respond but Galas grabbed his snout and held his lips shut. She'd slunk out of her chair while piloting and texting, slipping into the copilot's cockpit, expecting just this kind of response.

She put her finger to her lips while she continued the text.

[Galas: Stealthed-out elites. Fifteen to thirty meters. They can hear us inside our mech if they've got their sensors up.]

Jinnbo nodded slowly, eyes like saucers. She nodded back and let go of his snout, but only slightly, just to make sure he wasn't going to blurt something out accidentally.

An ultra-low boom from somewhere far off caused the mech to lurch. The visual feed of her SortieNet showed streams of rocks pouring from the walls of the gorge. She cringed as the excruciatingly long and drawn-out flurry clanked and thudded against the mech's armor.

Then, as she watched through the feeds, massive dust-shrouded silhouettes materialized where the AVD mirage had been. Three elite mechs just ahead. Which meant she was just as visible as they were.

Purple plasma crackled from her mech's forearms as she lashed out at the closest one. Its shields blurred the air as they were coming up when the blade plunged into its chest, burying the full ten meters of raw energy into the crew compartment, intentionally missing the reactors. Molten metal bubbled and spurted from around the blade.

The other two spun, but they were flat-footed and too close for rockets. She withdrew her blade and used that momentum to spin into a back kick with a blast from her boot-mounted repulsor that knocked the third mech clear off its feet while she let loose her plasma cannon on the second. Just as he unloaded his.

Both she and the other mech flew backward from the barrage. Their shields crackled with ball lightning that splashed out, gouging channels in the gorge walls and the ground around them.

"So much for keeping a low profile," she growled, letting loose a volley of rockets now that they were a suitable distance apart.

The third mech had just pushed up to its feet when the barrage hit him and blasted him back again.

"Jinnbo, take out his shields!"

A long stream of plasma bored into the enemy mech as it tumbled back, causing the shields to glow molten orange before disintegrating into nothing. Galas had already launched another missile volley and was readying her laser cannons when the second mech sprang from cover, launching his own volley of missiles and lasers. This was the veteran of the bunch.

Galas twisted to her right, dropping into a side roll, and came up just behind the first mech she'd disabled. It was hunched over, collapsed on reverse-jointed knees, and leaning against the wall. The barrage from the veteran's mech blew the ravaged mech into her. Galas's shields rippled with hissing energy at the contact, washing the whole gorge in a purple-white light that squelched her forward-facing feeds.

She switched views in her SortieNet to the battlespace model, disengaged shields, and used the ravaged mech as an old-fashioned meat shield. Galas lurched forward, the disabled mech before her taking the brunt of the veteran's barrage. This could only last so long before the unshielded mech blew up and took her out with it. In fact...

"All weapons on the burnt-out mech in ... three ... two..."

She pushed it ahead and jumped into a two-footed kick with her repulsors slammed to full. The mech blew forward, smashing into the vet. Galas kept her repulsors pegged, whipping her own mech through a backward somersault that brought all her weapons to bear as she touched down.

"...one."

Her mech erupted in missiles, laser, and plasma fire; all aimed at the disabled mech. The vet was ready. He shouldered his fallen comrade off in a burst of shielding. The mech fell flat, right between himself and the other elite. Galas's barrage hit the dead mech. A fraction of a second later, its reactors ignited.

The gorge erupted in fire. Galas saw her mistake in slow motion, stumbling backward. Then everything went black.

Dim, red light washed the cabin. Galas tried to shake the fuzzy thoughts from her head, but shards of piercing white light rattled around behind her eyes.

She grabbed her head and moaned. That wasn't going to work. After a moment, she hazarded a squinting glance at her surroundings from just one eye and then the other. And once deemed safe, both, but slowly.

She realized she'd failed to strap into her pilot's chair before the encounter with the three elites. She'd been simply holding onto the bulkhead near Jinnbo's copilot chair while performing all of those ridiculous combat antics. Webbing and padding lined the walls and every angle throughout the interior crew space, so there'd been plenty to hold on to—until the explosion.

The taste of iron on the sides of her tongue and the smell of it in her stuffy nose told a familiar story. Then she realized her face felt slick and tacky. She adopted the typical routine, probing gently with fingertips, first her nose, then her forehead, and then working up into the hairline.

Ouch. There it is.

A good-sized lump and plenty more of the sticky wet stuff she couldn't quite manage to keep on the inside of her body.

"'Zevrybodyogay???" she mumbled, staring at a leg that was twisted up in the corridor webbing. Her stomach clenched as she tried to decipher the angles. They weren't quite wrong. She shifted to relieve the weight on it and it didn't scream at her. She let out a breath she didn't realize she was holding. And shifted some more to work herself free.

"Come again?" asked Raph.

"Zevry. Buddy. Ogay?" she said again, louder and slower, while squinting against the throbbing in her head.

"We're fine. You, on the other hand, are mildly concussed. You should find your way back to your pilot's seat, or, better yet, slip into the power armor where I can administer nano-enhancers and rebalance your vitals," came his patronizing reply.

Galas tried to think about it, but it hurt to do so. Instead, she pushed herself up to her knees and the whole compartment started swimming. It didn't look right. She remembered that her power armor was stowed in a half-recessed wall cubby in the main corridor, but her pilot's chair was ... she looked around again. Things still didn't look quite right. Then she realized the mech must be lying on its back because she was currently kneeling on the back wall of the corridor. Her knee *was* tender but okay. And she was practically on top of her power armor.

Galas tapped the face shield. It recognized her biometrics and slid up. Then the torso split from chin to crotch and the thigh sections split open after that. A body-shaped cavity of beige and black hex-panel cushions greeted her.

"Well. Okay then. As good as anywhere, I guess." She slipped her feet in through the upper thigh openings, then gingerly poured the rest of her body into the snug quarters. The armor buttoned itself up and within seconds, she felt a cool wash of chemicals tumbling through her insides.

"Oh. That's nice."

"Don't get too comfortable. We're still loitering in an active battle zone," Raphael reminded.

Galas was enjoying the supportive lift from the chemicals and was just beginning to softly groove on some low-fi island music that kicked on when that boom happened again. The one from before that caused the avalanche of loose rubble that started all the drama.

Galas reduced the volume with a thought. "There's that noise again. What *is* that?" She scanned what feeds were available, which weren't many. Most were looking at dirt. Much of the rest was covered in dirt. Only a couple were clear of obstructions and looking up at a flat gray sky bordered top and bottom by the rock walls of the gorge.

"Raph, where are the drones?"

"Umm, have you looked at the BSM?" the AI asked.

She quickly pulled up the model. "Yeah. What?"

"You see that big golden cursor in the middle?"

Thankfully, the cursor flashed because she was struggling to find it.

"Oh, got it. Yeah?"

"It's new," Jinnbo whispered in rapt fascination, "One of those blackout thingies."

"Shit. For real?"

"Yee-up," Jinnbo confirmed, still whispering.

"So, where are my drones? The ones that are left, anyway?"

"See that golden cursor?" Raphael provided identically to before.

"Yeah, we just went over this."

"That's where they *were*."

"Double shit."

"Yee-up."

She noticed on the BSM a small horde of golden cursors that had broken off from the main pack. They were headed in their direction.

"Is anyone else concerned about that pack of Void Savages right there?"

"Yes. In fact, we are very concerned about that. We were just going to talk to you about it, but you were incapacitated. We think we should leave," Raph concluded.

"Yeah. Good thinking," she said, feeling suddenly sober. The inside of her head felt like a crisp winter morning. The kind that stings your face and aches in your lungs. The chems and nano-enhancers were doing their job. She switched the island music to something decidedly more urban. And angsty. She cranked it up a few notches and then zoomed into the BSM, pulling an ETA herself though she could easily have asked.

"Ninety seconds." She whistled. "Cutting it close."

"Yes. We thought so too. Jinnbo was going to have to drive."

An odd, guttural whimpering sound came through the audio circuits.

"Jinnbo?"

Silence. She was pretty sure he was having one of his inconvenient bipolar meltdowns. He was so close to being dependable. Just... right there...

Another massive boom like distant thunder shook the mech.

"Dammit, what *is* that?"

"Oh. Usually, I don't participate in wild speculation, but I'm going to go out on a limb here—"

"And say that it's that massive blue cursor in the middle of the BattleSpace?" she asked, suddenly transfixed by the improbable data showing up in the model. Something that big couldn't just appear. She zoomed around it in the virtual model, approaching from every angle, but nothing materialized. Just an empty cursor. A very, very large, empty cursor.

"Exactly," Raph said, agreeing that's precisely what he was referring to.

"But what is it?" There was silence. "Raph?"

The cursor bumped out even more, but there was no visual feed to accompany it. Then it doubled again. Her breath caught in her throat. It was now large enough to encompass hundreds or even thousands of the Void creatures she was referring to as Savages. A hollowness began to grow in her stomach. Then her attention was drawn to the part of the field where the Deathhounds were just clashing with the Savages. She tried to focus on the BattleSpace model, but it glitched, struggling to keep up without any of the drones to fill in the gaps from what her sensors could provide. It was amazing that it could piece together anything at all, really.

She needed to know what was going on, but she also needed to not get caught by the regiment of Void creatures closing in on her position.

"Jinnbo. Get ready with the plasma cannon. You need to target those things individually. Rockets did next to nothing."

More whimpering.

"Jinnbo!"

"Hmmm...?" came his ineffectual reply before it was choked out by something that sounded like a sob and a burp at the same time.

"Nevermind. Raph?"

"Already on it."

An EDC mech wouldn't allow AI control of weapons systems. But this was a Delvadr Elite. Galas's AI had rewritten all the programming anyway to force synchronize the EDC SortieNet with the alien OAS—Operations and Armaments Systems. She didn't mind that he'd aired on the liberal side in terms of following EDC protocols.

Galas rolled the mech over and pushed it up to its feet. Twenty seconds remained on the BSM's eta. She was still strapped into her power armor, which was, in turn, strapped into the berth in the main internal corridor of the mech. But she had everything she needed right here thanks to her hacked Delvadr ops systems and her own neural hardware that was, if a little well-used, still pretty much top-of-the-line.

I am due for maintenance soon, she realized. *Later.*

"Hold on tight," she broadcast through the power armor and the SortieNet's audio.

The mech burst forward and, within five or six strides, was sprinting down the bottom of the gorge. She turned and leaped with repulsors blasting at the top of the wall, away from the incoming horde. As she cleared the escarpment, she got her first full view of the enemy. "Oh, damn." Her stomach dropped.

It looked like a flood of inky black crashing over the scraggly foliage and scrub brush of the southern continental plain.

She goosed the back-mounted repulsor pack 2x over max to clear the edge and turn that upward momentum into a flat-out sprint as soon as the mech's feet hit the ground. Behind her, the stampede of Savages blinked down into the gap and within only a few seconds reappeared at the edge of the gorge behind her.

A stream of plasma lanced out as Raph strafed individual targets within the boiling mass. She rifled out a dozen rockets at the escarpment's edge. The first wave of Savages evaded easily, but the ones behind didn't have a chance.

A dozen of the creatures vanished in the explosion and didn't reappear. Galas's mech pounded across the terrain, boosting over the next gorge and putting a little more distance between them. Her attention was on the terrain and on the creatures racing after her, but she still needed to know what that massive blue cursor was in the middle of the battlefield.

"Raph, do we have spare drones in this thing?"

"We have redundancy on all peripherals."

"Prime please?" referring to the common language of the solar system. Although no humans lived anywhere in the system but Epriot Prime anymore. The Delvadr had seen to that.

"Four. Each of our four drones had a replacement."

"Well, get 'em airborne. We need eyes on whatever that blue cursor is before we bug out of here. And frankly, I don't feel like lollygagging."

"That part I can't do."

"What do you mean?"

"They're locked up. They need to be physically removed from the equipment locker and then let out through one of the ports. I am many things, but corporeal, I am not. It's gonna have to be a meat bag."

"While we're running a high-speed, fighting retreat? And by the way, I prefer meat *person*." Galas was running a thousand operations in her mind. Piloting a mech was not a normal human skill set. The AIs existed for a reason. Galas just happened to be mentally challenged in all the right ways, she guessed. Still, her newfound chemically induced clarity was fading.

"Noted. But I'm afraid it still has to be a body that does it."

"Jinnbo?"

Still nothing.

"Ugh. Fine. But you're going to have to share the load here. Muh brainz is killin' me."

"So you are human, after all. I'll inform the press," he said, ending with a mock disappointed tsk.

Galas was already on to the next dilemma. Get out of the suit and risk further head trauma? Or try to pilfer the equipment cabinet while in her power armor? All while piloting the mech.

Option two. She'd gotten pretty good with the Targe IV suit over the Arcfire mission. Exceptional would probably be more accurate. With no one there to see it, except Raphael. Even Jinnbo had been MIA for most of that, what with being caught up in battle for survival with the evil twin he'd birthed out of his chrysalis after having gone catatonic from ingesting too many acid frogs. She decided she could forgive him that one tiny indiscretion.

"Raph, can you disengage the suit restraints? I can't find them in the SortieNet menu."

"Yeah, that was one of those things that didn't have a counterpart in the Delvadr programming. Power suits don't just get unstowed while the mech is in operation."

"First time for everything. Make an override."

"Gimme a second."

She ran through all the system startups. The gel couches applied gentle pressure to her legs, arms, and torso, snugging her in even more tightly. The suit's microreactor purred to life and there was a quick hiccup in the environmentals as it shifted from shore to onboard power. The SortieNet imagery that splashed across the inside of her visor burst with warning after warning as the suit had to reconcile being inside an enemy mech.

"We don't have time for this," Galas disengaged the suit's HUD and let the feed continue to play out on her corneal implants, "Might wanna tell the suit we're not the enemy, hotshot."

"Working on it. You're not the only one multitasking."

That was an understatement. Even with the vastly superior Thune-built processors in the alien mech, there was a lot of data that needed parsing.

The retainers snapped open with a clunk and Galas was free to move, but free to move in a mech that was sprinting at full speed was less than optimal. She made use of the webbing as she navigated the corridor down to the equipment closet in the ops module one level down. There were a lot of different spaces inside a mech, none of them very large. The Delvadr units ops center shared a wall with the galley, another with the cargo bay, and still another with the fab.

It was a layout that wasn't all that different from most EDC units so Galas had no problem navigating the VR overlay to find and unlock the surplus equipment storage, which was made up of floor-mounted cabinets that extended up into the ops space when unlocked.

Galas slid the mag chairs away and a 1.5 by 1.5 meter cube slid up from the floor. The far side housed the drones, along with handheld flood lights and various replacement optics and sensors. She grabbed what she needed as the mech bobbed right and left. Her Targe armor had storage in thigh and abdomen compartments and she split the drones between them. These were similar in appearance to EDC drones, but the EDC ones were vastly superior in Galas's opinion as they could be used to augment or sabotage other equipment. Plus, the EDC used them in the dozens rather than just four at a time.

She missed Betsy for a number of reasons, but this was one of them. It made her feel like she was handicapped, like fighting with one hand caught in a bubble of ceramite.

"Okay, now what?" she asked. She was still splitting her attention between this task and piloting the mech as it raced across the plains. Luckily, there were few obstacles, but ahead, things looked like they were about to get dicey. The flat terrain broke up as it descended into a dry river valley. Ridges fanned out like interlocking fingers, causing deep gaps between rock outcroppings and steep sandstone walls. These convoluted ridges tumbled down to a shelf and then another and another before finally reaching the valley floor.

"Ugh, that's going to suck."

"You should probably hurry up."

"Thanks. So much help," she said by way of reply to the AI. Then to her co-pilot, whom she hoped was finally out of his dirge of emotional dysfunction, "Jinnbo? Buddy? How ya feeling?"

"Better," came his sulky reply.

"Feel like driving this bad boy?" though she was pretty sure it was a lady. She just had feelings about these things. Plus, with the exception of her first mech, a reconner named Skinny Boy, she'd only ever piloted ladies.

"Well ... okay," he said, perking up a little.

"Okay, let me know when you're ready to—"

The mech lunged to the right and then over-corrected to the left, stumbling to a knee and an arm before bounding off repulsors and landing in a run again.

"Skleetrix waxing Jinnbo! What the f—

"Sorry. Sorry, just ... getting things... Just remembering where ... all the bits..."

The mech lurched to the side again before righting itself just as the crumpled terrain opened up beneath them. Her stomach jumped into her throat as she floated, weightless, before the mech hit the ground in big bounding leaps.

"Maybe slow down?!? Maybe? Take it," she breathed a shuddering breath, "a little, ya know, easy?" She found herself praying, though she couldn't rightly say to whom at that moment.

The mech slowed and the cadence of right to left and back to right again became a little more even. *Okay, that's better. Let's just get this over with so I can drive again. And remember to never, ever, do that again.*

She checked the BSM. They were getting very far away from the action. The golden cursors of the pack of Savages were still hounding them, but there was a little gap now. They needed to correct course if they were going to get the info they needed before making their way back to High Command on the northern archipelago continent, known as Articles Corwin. All geography on Epriot was named after its founding documents.

"Jinnbo, cut north. We need to stay close enough to get eyes on whatever that thing is before we exfil."

"Heh, heh, heh," came a deep, husky voice over the comms.

"Jinnbo?"

No response. Of course, he would have to swing to the far side of the emotional spectrum.

"Just don't kill us, please."

"I shall ... not."

"You shall not what? Kill us or obey an order from a superior officer?"

"Heh, heh, heh. Verily."

Galas face-palmed her helmet. *Just get this done. Just get this done. No one has to die. No one... Well, maybe someone has to die but, not right now. Things to do. Focus. Focus. Focus.* She talked herself through stowing the equipment shelf while not losing her footing.

Galas pinged the SortieNet for the path to whatever access port she could utilize while lurching and bounding across broken terrain with an insane co-pilot at the helm. The cargo access was just on the other side of the back wall of the ops module she inhabited currently, but the entrance was from the main corridor and then down a hatch.

That'll work.

She slid past the fab wall. It was humming, making more missiles like it was supposed to.

Good thing. We're not out of this yet.

She made her way along the cargo webbing, her feet flailing out from under her several times along the way before she reached the hatch.

Okay, down we go. Let the drones out. Get eyes on the bad guys and then haul ass for the Articles. Easy.

CHAPTER 4
NOT SO EASY

The port hatch didn't work. Galas bounced off the door as the mech lurched back and then violently forward.

"Grrr... Jinnbo! Take it easy, ya think?" she snarled as she fumbled again with manual controls. The VR controls wouldn't even materialize. Some roving glitch in the system, according to Raph. Something about Delvadr programming and its similarity to loose stool. He kept trying, but so far had zero luck. She bounced off the door again, only this time it gave.

Galas tumbled forward, staring at the ragged terrain sliding by as she caught the last bit of cargo webbing with her trailing hand.

"Shit. That was close—"

Suddenly the mech slammed through an outcropping of rock and she was ripped free, tumbling through free air until she hit the far side of a ridge and glanced off an exposed boulder, sliding over an escarpment and wedging between two columns of rock.

Her power armor took the brunt of the blow, but her body buzzed all over and her brain, still rattling loosely within her cranium from her previous concussion, felt like the greasy side of an over-hard egg.

"Jinnbo! For Cyclopedae's sake, you overgrown monkey-bat, piece of cycarian—" she caught herself. In his wildly oscillating emotional state, she just never knew how he'd react. He might suicide himself and her mech and Raph along with him. Or he might just curl into a ball and not talk to her for a day or two. The second option wasn't so bad, but there was a full spectrum of possibilities between them. None of them were good in an active battle environment. Especially not with... *Oh no. Where's the pack?*

When she had Jinnbo cut north to keep within visible range of the massive anomaly in the middle of the battlefield, they'd effectively given up some of the distance they'd placed between themselves and the enemy horde—that and the fact that the broken terrain was slowing them down. And, with Jinnbo at the helm rather than Galas, things were ... not running quite as smoothly as they could have been.

The fact that she was now outside the relative safety of her mech and wedged between some rocks somewhere in the very worst possible kind of terrain to evade creatures that could just blink from place to place and didn't have to run, jump, or climb like Galas did—well, "easy" just went out the window.

"Jinnbo?!?"

"I'm trying to negotiate with him now but he's being..." Raph provided.

"Difficult?"

"Yes. Q-Q-Q-Quite."

"What's that? What's going on with your voice?"

"C-c-comms array. Mashed. I-I-It's really better when y-y-you d-d-d-drive."

"Raph?"

Silence.

"Raph??? Shit." She struggled against her pinned arm and torso. Her head was downhill, with her legs up and one arm pinned above her.

"Don't worry. I won't leave you hanging. I'm still your wingman."

"Raph! Oh good. I thought I was going to die alone."

"Let's see what we can do about the not dying part. I'll do what I can with my limited onboard functionality."

"Oh, so we're cut off from the big mech. This is your lite version using the Targe IV's processors then?"

"Yes. Unfortunately."

"Okay. We'll work with it." She scanned the BSM. In the background of the data, she could see her irises light up gold as they reflected off the interior of the face shield. Raph already highlighted the horde and had established the ETA to her position as well as one to the mech as it moved away to the north.

Dammit, Jinnbo. If your mood swings don't even out sometime soon...

She watched as a dozen or so of the Savages split off from the main body pursuing the mech.

"Of course. No way they could have missed the person in the power armor falling out the ass end of the mech."

"It would seem so."

Galas navigated the VR environment of the suit with ease now that it was disengaged from the insides of the alien mech. She tried to open the two storage compartments, but only the thigh compartment was accessible. Two of the drones spilled out. Rather than whisk away into the sky to do something useful, they tumbled down the rocks and wedged themselves in amongst the rabble of calved granite.

"Raph? Explain."

"The replacement drones don't appear to be taking the startup protocol."

"And...?"

"Well, it's going to take me a minute."

She desperately scanned the battlespace model but the info coming back was garbled, "The BSM is glitching out. I can't tell how far away the enemy is. We're kinda fragged up here with our collective ass to the sky and no way to move."

"Lemme see what I can do."

"Yeah. Do ... something. I'm going to work on getting us out of this, but I could really use some eyes on the bad guys and maybe, I don't know, something behind us?"

Galas wiggled her arm underneath her. She had the grappling lines. Useful those. At least they had been in the caverns beneath Braex, Xiocic, and Daxn as she battled multitudes of the Makrit acolytes' pet psych hoppers. *Those were the good times*, she thought as she considered how to deal with this new threat.

She shot a line from the forearm-mounted grappling device but heard it bounce off of the rock without anchoring. She reeled in the cable, adjusted her arm, and fired again. The line clanged off her left boot this time.

Careful. Don't shoot yourself in the foot with a grappling line, you idiot.

The line went slack. Again, no purchase. She reeled in, huffing out a breath of frustration, all the while watching the chrono tick down until she'd have interdimensional wolf soldiers gnawing on her nether parts. *Nether parts ... who talks like that?*

"Galas. I think I got 'em" Raph was saying when the visual feeds sprang onto her SortieNet dashboard.

Gully. Galas's ass end (a little on the thick side in the power armor, she had to admit). Then sky. Then ... *frag.*

She shot the grappling line again, desperate for it to connect. She heard it bounce, but then it stuck somewhere else. *Good enough.* She reeled in the line, pushing against the rock with her free hand.

The drones had split up, one hanging close to the top of the escarpment and the other shooting up to a default 500-meter altitude. The view from above seemed like all of those cool military vids dramatic landscapes, a fast-moving hostile force bearing down on the good guys' position. She watched as the dozen or so dark dots, highlighted in gold cursor, blipped toward the edge of the plateau.

The live feed from the ground-level drone was something else entirely. Terrifying was a good descriptor. The pack of blacked-out wolf creatures with burning red eyes bore down on Galas's location in a lurching, stuttering wave. Savage was right.

Galas ripped free, shooting back toward the cliff wall just before the wave of creatures flashed overhead, several springing off the very rock formation where she'd been trapped just moments ago. She thought they might just carry on in hot pursuit, but then, as their target didn't present itself, the pack fanned out. The last couple, a short distance ahead. Galas watched in growing horror as the last remaining Savage waited at the top edge of the cliff, not five meters from where she was pressed in against the rock.

She whipped the closest drone right between the two drones ahead of her and down the tumbling rock hillside. They tore off in pursuit. The last Void Savage did not.

She pushed the second drone out over the escarpment to keep all the creatures within its visible field. The one above her stood up on two legs like a man and appeared to sniff the air. She was transfixed by this action. *These things are hunters.*

She pushed thought-to-text for Raph to guide the others away with the remaining drone as she tried to adjust her position to fight if it came to that.

The great thing about power armor is that it's armor, and it has armaments and it amplifies the user's own physical strength three to five times, depending on the quality and how you tune it. Galas could jump from a third-story deck and land without so much as a twisted ankle. She could tip a three-ton transport onto its lid if she felt especially motivated, and it came with a pretty "okay" AI if one was lucky. And she was. But the Targe IV armor was also pretty damn heavy.

As Galas shifted her weight, the sandstone beneath her cracked and ground beneath her boot. She didn't even see the movement before the creature had blinked off the edge and was crouched before, midway through a swing with its huge, clawed hand that would take her head from her shoulders, armor or no.

The crackling purple glow from a plasma blade split the space between them, and that claw never reached its target. Instead, an explosion of white light blinded her and her sensors, leaving Galas stumbling to find her footing in the uneven terrain. She found the wall behind her before stumbling over the edge, falling down the mountain and into the thick of the pack.

"You probably can't tell, but the creatures are headed back this way. They lost interest in the drone when you killed one of their buddies."

"Can't I catch a break?" She cried, her voice sounding canned and distant in the helmet's audio.

Then she heard another one of the big booms coming from back up on the plateau. Not the deep resonating one that happened when mind-numbingly massive, city-sized Chareth-Ul mech stepped, but the punchy, rending boom that happened when the blackouts ripped a hole in her dimension. She didn't need to confirm the visual feed.

"It's another one of those big blackout thingies, isn't it?"

The Battlespace Model confirmed it. No glitches. Big as day.

And with it, two regiments of Savages. If she had any thoughts about evading the group that had been chasing her, they were gone.

Now, the only way to safety was *through* them.

Galas bolted forward, her impaired vision barely up to the task. She launched to the top of her least favorite outcropping and let her own point of view mesh with the imagery provided by the drones and the virtual model. Ahead, the terrain blistered with bad guys, heading her way from all points below. She ejected the other two drones from her side compartment and slung them high into the air.

"Get these working. I'm going to need very high resolution to make this happen."

"Done. Now that I have the proper codes—"

She wasn't listening, she was moving. Repulsor-aided leaps, with well-placed grappling lines, swept her down into the mix and then out of the way at the last second. She whipped across the terrain as she riffed out rockets to corral her quarry. Because that's what they were now.

Her attention snapped to one of the creatures nearby as she skated across a wall of rock, sparks trailing behind her. She could tell by its positioning, instinctually reading its body language, that it was watching her. She may not know these creatures, but she was fluent in the universal language. Warfare.

It leaped into the air ahead of the others, appearing talons extended right before her. If there'd been an expression to read on its face, it would have been shock, as it ate her blade and went supernova in front of her. She already had her visor's active attenuation tuned to keep from being blinded again, which was good because this was going to happen. A lot.

"Two down ... twelve—

"Thirteen," Raph interjected.

"...thirteen to go," she amended with a cavalier lilt just as two more blipped into her path.

She'd already loosed a flurry of rockets. One at these newcomers and a handful to disperse the masses converging on her, when suddenly her cable gave, sliced clean through by one of the Savages. She'd been watching the one that'd done it too...

Galas was supposed to veer away at the last second as her airborne enemies exploded, using the blast to boost her along on her merry way. Instead, she flew right at the growing ball of fire and was swatted violently in the wrong direction. Galas flailed, spinning end over end through the air before hitting a scree-filled gully like a meteor and then continuing to rag doll down the hillside.

CHAPTER 5

MAYBE THIS WAS A BAD IDEA

E'rth, Unknown Location
[Before the Construct]

To say that D'avry and Rutker's relationship had been anything but prickly thus far would have been a gross misrepresentation. D'avry, the young mage from another time stood a few feet away from Rutker, the grizzled pilot from another planet. Flexible versus rigid. Mystical versus militant. They couldn't be more different.

And D'avry, admittedly, had been toying with the man. He could have been a little more forthright, even though he, himself, was only receiving information doled out in measured parcels by the enigmatic magic known as the Astrig Ka'a. Being its sole chosen vessel didn't seem to come with the privilege of unrestricted access. To power, maybe. To knowledge? He was having to work for that.

D'avry took his eyes off the bright spot in the night sky that was the focus of their concern for just a moment. The man to his right's normally crisp military posture was noticeably weighed down with the fatigue of 48-plus hours of mech fighting and evasion. His foes were no slouches either. Exceptionally, no ... suspiciously, well-equipped pirates and mercenaries against one tiny little sniper mech. And that, just as likely to kill its pilot as any of the other, more overt dangers with its history of overheating with its baffles cinched down tight to eliminate thermal leakage.

He felt for the man. Crash-landed while on a diplomatic mission. His wife and two sons were still aboard the downed ship defending it against external threats, all while knowing that someone on the inside had given them up and stranded them on this unknown rock. Meanwhile, here was D'avry, spouting insanity upon insanity to the military man from a non-magical planet. And to make things worse, D'avry had to ask him to do the unthinkable—leave his family behind and face an unknown foe of unspeakable strength.

D'avry looked back up to the sky to a dot that was actually a ship larger than anything he could comprehend. He was from a simpler time, when people barely navigated across the seas let alone an ocean of stars and galaxies. It was a lot to take in, but then again, he was the flexible one. The fickle magic system he was subject to made certain of that.

D'avry pulled the edges of his hooded long jacket tight around him as the wind tugged at it and the fine, dark blue fabric of his loose-fitting pants.

He and Rutker were an odd pair. Neither were where they should be but fate, or more accurately, D'avry's obscure form of magic, had brought them here to do a task. And the Astrig Ka'a was always right. So now it was time to find out who the enemy was. This entity, who was supposed to mediate a truce, had played both sides against each other for a purpose that was still a mystery.

D'avry didn't know what this had to do with Rutker's world, but he understood that it meant everything to E'rth. A machine was going to be built. And it would enslave humanity for epochs and millennia to come. And he and some of his newfound friends were going to stop it. Or at least that's what he deduced was supposed to happen. The Astrig Ka'a didn't really illuminate his pathway as much as pin him on three sides with unspeakable danger, guiding his flight toward whatever end it had in mind.

He placed the elegant fingers of his hand across his mouth, contorting the blond-stubbled skin, and then rubbed his face with both hands. He let out an anxious sigh and tried not to wonder at what he intended to do next. It was no small thing.

Before them, the towering Thune-built dropship jutted out of the floor of the chalk flat like an aging citadel, right where it had crashed down fully loaded only a couple of days prior. It cast long shadows from the light of the two moons hanging low on the horizon. Four out of the five mech cargo bay doors were retracted in their upright position. The one remaining bay lay extended like a beckoning drawbridge except that it barely hung onto the superstructure. But it would likely support a small mech the size of the Novak Long Rifle, the aging sniper mech nicknamed the widowmaker, resting a few meters away.

D'avry didn't understand much about the differences between spaceships and dropships but one key difference was that dropships, ones like this one anyway, were fully automated, meant to insert massive battle mechs into an active war zone. The important element here was that they didn't have any seating for extra personnel. Maybe sometimes they did, but this one did not.

That meant that D'avry and Rutker would have to make the roughly five-hour flight from E'rth to the alien flagship—currently sprawling in outer orbit—by riding in the Long Rifle which was, of course, a single-seater.

There was no way that either man was going to suffer the other riding on their lap.

A solution was required.

After a brief but terse discussion, Rutker raced off in the agile mech kicking up ghosts of chalk dust that rose and faded away in the urgent desert breeze.

He returned thirty minutes later, dragging that solution behind him—the jettisoned crew cabin from one of the pirate mechs he'd destroyed within hours of landing on this planet. He dragged it up the tottering dropship ramp and lashed it to the corrugated flooring of one of the bays. It didn't sit flat, but it did still have an intact environmental seal and functioning scrubbers. Something he'd been told would be needed on their journey through first the atmosphere of E'rth, and then the ruthless void of space beyond.

Of course, first, something had to be done about the body...

D'avry tried to block out the lingering smell of blood and other fluids choking the cockpit. The transport vibrated relentlessly.

Maybe This Was A Bad Idea

Violent winds ripped past shorn ceramo-metallic edges to create a shrieking wail to rival even a banshee choir. And D'avry would know, he'd met some banshees.

As memorable as these interactions tended to be, one in particular haunted him, and this roaring wind was uncomfortably reminiscent. He even had a souvenir from that near-fatal experience. It was called the Puerch'k Talles or Soul of the Mountains and it revolved around an infinite space just below the gold-veined glass of a lantern door that was set in his otherwise normal-looking, human chest. It was an Astrig Ka'a thing. A weirdness, of which there was an endless supply.

The lantern door had appeared in his chest after a harrowing flight down a storm-swollen river while being chased by an undead orc warlord. This too was an Astrig Ka'a sort of thing. But the gold-veined glass and ornate framework wasn't just jewelry. It housed things. Certain artifacts that he was compelled to find. Supposedly, once he found them all, he would have what he needed to defeat the great mechanism that he called simply, the Construct. This alien ship had something to do with it.

That was his working theory anyway.

The Astrig Ka'a moved within and around him at all times. It was through its influence that he found his companions, the people who were helping him find the artifacts, each from wildly disparate epochs in E'rth's history. They all had one thing in common too, humanity was on the verge of complete collapse each and every time.

This was the cycle; slow build, magnificent collapse. And it wasn't all just self-inflicted drama, as any casual observer of the human condition might surmise. It was managed. An inside job.

He looked up, imagining being able to see through the cabin of the destroyed mech, through the ceiling of the dropship hangar, and out into space where the enemy waited.

His hand drifted to trace the edges of the lantern door beneath the fabric of his tunic. He jerked and jolted in his seat as his current accommodations threatened to rattle free and go tumbling about the cavernous interior of the alien craft now flying pilotlessly *away* from his home planet.

"It's gonna be okay, it's gonna be okay. You've been through worse. Okay, maybe that's not entirely true but, you've seen some stuff. You can do this," He mumbled nervously against the dull rumble reverberating through the repurposed cockpit.

Bile rose in the back of his throat. He was pretty sure he was going to be sick. Then he was. Everywhere.

"Ugh…" he moaned, wiping his mouth on his tunic and then staring dejectedly at the little bits of leftover dinner. Sullenly, he wished that maybe he'd been something else's dinner on the way here, the same way this bit of trout had been his.

He searched for something to divert his attention from the smoky, acidic taste in his mouth and his gaze rested on the fifteen-foot tall, mechanized armor that was the Novak Long Rifle. *That'll work.*

The idea of mechanized armor was something he was still trying to wrap his mind around. People traveling between the stars in ships big enough to hold all the cities of E'rth was another idea that he'd just relegated to the corners of his rational conscience until he could grapple with it more thoroughly.

There was a goodly amount of crap occupying that space. *Like, who was the alien being they were going to meet? Scratch that. What is the alien being?*

He didn't know how he knew what he knew, but this apparently was an important distinction to the Astrig Ka'a. D'avry just accepted facts as they floated into his mind. Certain things resonated inside him and they were as good as fact. This alien entity was a what. *Duly noted.*

Continuing on the theme of distraction, D'avry sorted through a long list of unanswered questions in his mind. Such as, what was Rutker's relevance in the dilemma that ensnared all of humanity? Or that of D'avry's companions who were hunting down artifacts in far-distant timelines of human history? D'avry didn't know the specifics of what he was dealing with, just that human civilization was somehow trapped in a perpetual cycle of crescendo-and-crash, unable to get out of it.

His own time and place was hovering on the brink of all-out war between human and orc-kind. And every window into humanity's history the Astrig Ka'a had carried him through seemed to be caught up in the same throes.

And then there was Deven, the stunning brunette—a crippled soldier from another era—who he'd accidentally saved from creatures that looked like they were made out of pure void. He'd inadvertently brought her back to his own time, only to have those same creatures burst en masse through a rift in space caused by a meteor strike.

To say that D'avry's life was anything but a picture of absolute chaos was an understatement. Yet, even *he* was having a hard time processing all of what had transpired.

The vibrations continued, even as the roar of the wind slowly diminished. Were they getting closer to the outer edges of the planet's atmosphere? Rutker said this would happen. Panic threatened to take over, so he focused back on his memories as if they were a lighthouse beacon in a raging storm.

He locked his mind around the last battle, where the meteor had cast the sky and everything beneath it red before it struck the mountain to its core. Then there was the rift beast, a massive light-sucking tangle of blackness and chitinous tentacles that erupted from the gash, rending a hole between its dimension and theirs. There were so few companions left and they'd suffered dearly.

D'avry's mind was drawn to the epic finale when he'd compelled the fighting priest, Gemballelven Farn, to strike the final blow that defeated the beast, only when all was said and done, the man, and the beast, were nowhere to be found. He'd been so certain of that decision.

The weight of that loss, the guilt, wore heavily on D'avry's heart.

The cabin went quiet except for the thrum of some sort of engine propelling them through airless space to an unknown destiny. He had hours still to go. He rested his head back, hoping he'd adequately cleaned that spot but wasn't willing to check. It wouldn't change anything and he already felt dirty, so it didn't much matter.

The dull thrum and vibrations reminded him of the airship he'd brought from yet another era to that final battle on the mountain, The Eleven Sevens. It, along with its crew of mutant mages, had bridged the gap between his beleaguered team and the blackout beast and its minions.

And then he realized where his mind was going with this little diversion. Deven was on it, traveling the skies in some far-off 'other' time-place, hunting still more of the artifacts he'd been so compelled by his magic to seek out.

The Astrig Ka'a had brought them together. And now it had torn them apart. In this moment, he could get lost in the memory of those emerald eyes.

Right then, he realized he was weightless. The harness Rutker had insisted he wear was doing its job. Little yellow gobs of vomit were now floating freely about the cabin. One floated toward his face and he blew it gently away, grimacing.

What am I doing here? I'm clearly not ready for this.

His thoughts drifted again to the artifacts revolving within his chest. He focused on the feeling of power within him. He needed the reassurance. Normally, there was a great tension, like light and dark colliding inside of him. Normally, it was a barely bridled power emanating from beneath that door. Normally, it vibrated in his fingertips, swelled in his chest and in his mind. Now it seemed docile. Subdued. And yet, with each passing minute—

His stomach dropped with a realization he never imagined possible. His power was dwindling. Until now, he'd barely been able to contain the rushing torrent of growing power that accompanied the addition of each artifact. But now...

D'avry's eyes snapped wide with concern. His hand flashed up to his face, fingers dancing in wild manipulations of shapes and gestures, and the result ... a poof and the faint smell of a snuffed-out candle.

He swallowed and did it again even as the cabin's environmentals whisked away the remnants of his former failed conjuring. Again, nothing. Again, and again, and again, and...

D'avry ripped open his long jacket, fumbling with the overlapping hems of his tunic, and grimaced down at the gold-veined crystal and finely wrought metal door heaving up and down in his chest.

Within it, he could just make out shapes of the two artifacts there: a tiny book with a flaming arrow thrust through it and a dazzling blue gem. Two points in a five-sided shape, ever spinning in a shared orbit. Only now, that rotation, which had always been in motion, was slowly grinding to a stop.

"I'm losing my magic," he whispered in disbelief, his eyes drifting to where he knew the massive otherworldly ship awaited them. "We're doomed. This was *a very* bad idea."

CHAPTER 6

THE ASPECT

E'rth, Far Orbit, The Gefkarri Flagship

"You think?" Rutker growled as he pounded again on a door that was harder than it had any right to be. It *looked* like wood.

"I left my family behind on that Maker-forsaken rock to follow you up here on this cockamamie recon mission to 'find out who our enemy is' or whatever," he spat, shaking his hands and body in an approximation of mystical buffoonery. It was an uncharacteristic display, but he could forgive himself the outburst. He was operating on less than three hours of sleep in the last fifty-two, no ... fifty-three ... no, fifty-two.

Damn, my brain feels mushy as day-old protein goop.

He pinched the bridge of his nose and then rubbed his gritty eyes. They felt like they were packed with sand. His muscles felt sluggish and flat and this witch doctor from a backwater planet—a kid, really—had led them directly into a trap.

He was an officer of the Epriot Defense Collaborative, and not given to laying blame on others. But this was definitely D'avry's fault. All of it. And Rutker was rightfully pissed about it.

He could also be grumpy because he hadn't been able to take a proper shit in all that time. Space travel always messed him up. And then fighting well past dehydration in the Long Rifle with the baffles on most of the time. He was sure if he did hit the head, it'd feel like passing a ten-pound hunk of ceramite. And that would still be an improvement on how he was feeling right now.

He came up abruptly against a wall, turned, and paced across to the other side. His jaw hurt from gritting his teeth. He forced himself to stop and focus on the imagined sound of gently crashing waves on the pink sand beaches of Tola Huway. He counted to ten. The mage was *still* yammering on about something.

"To see the face of our enemy, I think is what I said," D'avry provided, but he appeared to be only half listening. The lion's share of his attention was on a slender hand he was waving around before his face, looking much like he was grasping at invisible cobwebs.

"Yeah, that's what I said," Rutker replied, turning on his heels and then stopping to stare at the bizarre antics of his even more bizarre counterpart.

The large space echoed with his movements and then fell into silence as he stopped, with only the faint sounds of his own breathing and the whoosh of fabric as D'avry continued to play with the invisible web.

The barren chamber was tall, maybe three times the height of a man, and equally wide and deep. All of it appeared to be fashioned of some sort of wood that was harder than any metal that Rutker had ever come across.

He couldn't stand it any longer. "What ... are ... you doing?" he burst out.

"It's odd. It's like, I can feel something ... that isn't there," D'avry responded, seeming genuinely perplexed. Rutker turned away to face the wall and decided to count to ten again.

He couldn't get past one. For not the first time, he wondered if the kid wasn't mentally challenged in some way. He stretched his neck and something twinged. The whole of his upper back felt like it was trying to cramp up into one solid mass. He stretched harder, grabbing his head and pulling it down to coax the tension out of his shoulders.

"No, I couldn't die down on the planet..." Rutker muttered to himself. "I couldn't go out in a blaze of glory against Kergan interorbitals, or mashed to pieces by that Osiris heavy. I have to die here, with Waldo Wanderlust, the imaginary magician!" he snarled and spun back around to see D'avry hovering in midair. Albeit not well.

D'avry crashed to the ground and rolled lithely to one foot, balanced for a moment before setting the other down. He dusted himself off and looked to Rutker with a bemused smile.

"What was that?!? I thought you said you'd *lost* your magic?" Rutker demanded, crossing the short distance to stand eye-to-eye with the thin young man, as he pulled his shoulder-length blond locks back into a leather thong.

D'avry managed a strained smile. It was unassuming and irritatingly charismatic. Rutker could almost let himself like the kid if he wasn't such a colossal pain in the ass.

"Well. I had. But, I think—"

"There's another source," supplied a voice from across the room.

The two spun. There, inexplicably inside the cell with them, was a woman of sorts.

She was slender, elegant of form, and hauntingly beautiful.

Her skin was pale and supple, like stripped Ashwood and her eyes glowed softly with an unspecific light. It was impossible to tell from where or how they were illuminated.

The light in her eyes reminded D'avry of the Queen of Storms. The banshee who commanded hordes of the dead inside the mountain. The one tied to the Peurch'k Talles. His hand drifted to the hem of his tunic resting just above the lantern door in his chest where the artifact resided.

Suddenly vines burst from the woman's hands and body, rippling through the air, engulfing him and ripping him to her. In a flash, he was face to face with those glowing eyes, and those haunting lips twisted into a mildly amused sneer.

"Be careful you don't hurt yourself."

The way she emphasized 'hurt' sent a clear message. And if that didn't do it, the trick with the vines did. She was the one with the power here. Even if he could touch it, she *controlled* it.

"Wh-who are you?"

"You may call me Seda. I am an aspect of the Gefkarri Pentarch. A seedling of the tree that is the root of all worlds."

"That's a very long name," he whispered.

The Aspect

They were still inches from each other. Rutker, on the other side of the room, sighed and crossed his arms.

"So, the ... Gef ... um, Gefkarri? Is it?" D'avry stuttered.

"Yes."

"Um. What, exactly, is it you want with E'rth?"

Seda's eyes narrowed, which D'avry was thankful for since the light had been somewhat uncomfortable to look at for so long and so close.

She cocked her head slightly to take in Rutker standing a few meters away and then turned her attention fully back to D'avry. Apparently, Gefkarri didn't understand about personal space. His stomach was twisting with unease and he couldn't quite tell what was causing it—fear, intrigue? It was a heady cocktail of emotions. And the foreign magic that was somehow elusive and energetic at the same time...

Her lips curved into that amused smile again. "Your E'rth means nothing."

"You might know it as Gellen-III, I think it was called. It doesn't show up in the star maps," Rutker chimed in.

Seda ignored him.

"It's you. And your kind," she said, nodding toward Rutker, "that we find interesting."

She drew even closer to D'avry, close enough that he could feel her breath on his face.

He swallowed. It smelled faintly of birch and peach blossom and in a pleasing way of freshly tilled soil. D'avry struggled to clear his mind and focused intensely on a spot just between the glowing, pale sapphire almonds of light that were her eyes. They cooled in intensity, almost turning to a milky jade.

Her gaze dropped, and her attention focused now on his chest, where the lantern door was hidden by the crossed hems of his tunic. One pale, exquisitely feminine hand rose up to touch it and he stumbled back abruptly, chuckling nervously as heat rose in his cheeks. He shot a nervous glance at Rutker, who just looked back with raised eyebrows as if to say, 'Don't look at me...'

A shadow flitted across Seda's face as her eyebrows knit together. Then she vanished into a tangle of vines that sank into the floor and then disappeared entirely.

D'avry sucked in a deep breath and let it out.

"What ... was ... that?" he asked, searching Rutker's face for answers.

"Haven't the foggiest, kid."

"What do you mean? You meet aliens all the time, don't you?"

"Some. But nothing like that. I don't think that's the real thing. This Gefkarri is classified as a super-entity. It's an interconnected forest of trees as big as a small planet. This, Seda, is an emissary. Just a fraction of the whole. I think that's why they call it a Pentarch. Though I can't think of anything more unnerving than having four others of these things running around mucking about with the galaxy."

D'avry listened, fascinated, still reeling from his encounter with Seda the aspect.

"The Gefkarri was supposed to preside over the peace talks between the Epriot people—my people—and the invading Delvadr forces," he sucked in a tense breath and pressed a pained smile onto his face.

"And that's where the double-cross with your Colonel Dexx came in? Sending you on a snipe hunt for diplomatic packages that had nothing in them and nothing to do with any sort of truce."

"Yeah. Apparently so. I don't know what the Gefkarri Pentarch is playing at, but I saw a Delvadr Elite down on that rock you call E'rth. Clever name, by the way. Might as well call it D'rt."

"Ah! You make jokes now. Very good, very good," D'avry said, pacing contemplatively, his left hand swishing about in arcane gestures once again. Suddenly, fire shot across the floor and halfway up the wall in front of him. He jumped back, shaking his hand as if burned, his eyes saucer round.

"Yeah, I enjoy barbecue as much as the next guy, but maybe don't do that around me," Rutker said, relaxing from a ready stance to something a bit more casual, but not much.

"Hmmm. Yes. Tone it back," D'avry said, still massaging his hand and looking at it contemplatively before continuing, "Um, so the Gefkarri sabotages the peace talks between your people and the Delvadr, and then what?"

"Exactly. I don't know. The aspect—"

"Seda."

"Yeah, her. She said they don't care about E'rth or Gellen-III, which I realize now is a false name and why it didn't show

The Aspect

up properly in the star charts, but they *do* care about humanity. And about you, in particular, I gathered. Why do you think that is?" Rutker asked, suddenly fixing D'avry with a penetrating stare.

D'avry stepped back self-consciously. "If I had to guess, I'd think it's about the magic. I'm just trying to formulate an idea, but I *felt* my magic, the Astrig Ka'a, diminishing as we left my world behind us. I think magic may be tied... no, no, no," he shook his head, concentrating, "...focused by our planets." He looked up with certainty, "Yes, that seems right. I practiced another magic before the Astrig Ka'a chose me. I could invoke neither form here before I felt this new intangible, *flux*," he danced his fingers before him and little sparks chased their movements.

Rutker's curiosity was piqued. "Wait, what do you mean the Astrig Ka'a chose you?" His suspicion slipped into a less threatening form of curiosity, for which D'avry was thankful. Secretly, D'avry feared the man's temper and had been very uncomfortable, forcing his way through most of their prior interactions. Though he had to admit, he did enjoy goading him a bit.

"Well, I was, actually I and my former betrothed had run off to wed. And then something happened."

"You were married?"

"No," he shook his head, staring off, focused on some unspecific point. "Almost. The crown princess. Well, she wouldn't have been if she'd married me. Crown, that is. Although now, I'm pretty sure she *is* the queen after all. Or so I've heard anyway," he blurted out and avoided looking in Rutker's direction.

"What happened?" Rutker asked, softening a little. D'avry realized he was a married man and his wife, whom he clearly loved, was still grounded on the planet—D'avry's planet—below.

"Well, we were about to recite our vows before the priest, which was a little awkward since I myself was a brother of another sect—"

"The point, D'avry?" Rutker interjected, again pressing a smile onto his face that was clearly not comfortable there.

"Um, yes, well, that's when I was teleported to a pig stall on another continent in the middle of a hurricane."

Rutker squinted a little and shook his head ever so slightly. "That's how the Astrig Ka'a *chose* you?"

"Yes."

"How do you know that was some new form of magic and not a curse from some other magician, or maybe someone hired by the King? I imagine the king would have been not pleased that you had plans to elope with his daughter?"

"No. That was just the beginning. After that, I would show up somewhere new, be compelled to do something peculiar, usually completely daft actually, and then I'd just blip off somewhere else. No rhyme. No reason. No heroics. Just months and then years of completely random troll bollocks.

"That is until Gearlach's crew showed up and the lantern door appeared," he said, tapping the crystal glass beneath his tunic.

"I'm sorry. Who's ... Gearlach?"

D'avry explained how the lantern door came to be and about the void creatures and how D'avry was compelled by the Astrig Ka'a to acquire various artifacts and people from different times throughout E'rth's history for some unknown purpose. And that the build-up and subsequent crash of human civilization over and over again appeared to be managed and that his investigation into this matter had led him to E'rth's prehistory, to Rutker, and now to this ship.

Rutker did the thing where he just stared at D'avry in quiet judgment.

"You don't believe a word of this."

"Nah. Not really."

"Okay." D'avry clapped his hands together as if ready to get to work, but then got distracted when tiny tornados whipped away into the air in several directions. He shoved his hands into the pockets of his long jacket.

"Okay. Forgetting all of that, the point I'm trying to make is this. I think the reason they're interested in humanity has to do with magic. But I don't know why that's important."

"It's important because no other alien race we're aware of can do what you can do."

The two jumped back, snapping their heads to focus on where the voice had just come from.

"You've gotta stop that," D'avry exhaled in a rush.

Rutker just looked annoyed. "What do you mean, no other race can do what we can do?"

The Aspect

Seda glided closer. Her legs moved like she was walking, but her bare feet never seemed to break contact with the ironwood floor.

"Humans appear to be non-mundane."

"Great!" Rutker replied with faux enthusiasm, "What does *that* mean?"

D'avry jumped in. "A term we use is paenarcanum. *All magics.* I think she's saying we can use magic regardless of its source. And that source is usually focused around a planet. If I'm making the correct assumptions?" he asked, looking from Rutker to the Gefkarri aspect.

Seda nodded. Her eyes blazed cooly as she considered him. That feeling in his stomach bubbled back. All of his masculine urges welled inside him. They were so strong and sudden that it caused him to pause.

Was she manipulating him? Of course, she was. She presented herself as a woman, or maybe she actually was the Gefkarri equivalent of the feminine form. In either case, she was most certainly trying to manipulate him.

The hairs on the back of his neck prickled as he recognized the source of that manipulation as magic. *Sylvan.*

An echo of a memory from the many texts he'd scoured over the years he'd spent in the cloistered halls of Academie whispered as much.

Sylvan was a term used for woodland magic. Something ancient, and subtle, but still very much wild. And sometimes dark.

He chewed his lip as he considered this detail when his attention returned to her. Only she was already staring back.

"Um, Seda? What are you—"

Vines crept from where she stood, snaking across the floor, and then began working their way up his legs. They wrapped around his thighs. "Um, Seda?!?" his voice rose an octave.

More and more vines burst from the floor, wrapping around his torso and his neck, tangling in his hair, gripping every part of his body. He tried to scream but couldn't. And then there was just darkness.

Rutker sprang forward as vines engulfed the mage. He turned in time to see the Gefkarri aspect melt into the floor again. Rutker battered the vines with his fists, but to no effect. They swallowed him up and began subsiding into the floor.

He clawed at the tangle of rock-hard tendrils, straining to pull the larger ones away but with little luck. He was still clinging to one of the vines when it melted completely into the floor, nearly taking his fingers with it.

Rutker pulled back and fell on his ass, breathless.

"Shit," he huffed, slapping his hands on the floor, and cursing again. "Some recon mission."

His thoughts ripped to Katherynn and the boys, stuck with that traitorous bastard Dexx, back on the *Xandraitha's Hope*. *What a joke,* he thought darkly.

What did the Gefkarri want with them? Or worse yet, what did they want with humanity? Also, and he hadn't put any thought into this, what were humans doing on Gellen III? *E'rth,* he corrected. As far as anyone knew, humans only existed in the Epriot System. Was this a time thing? D'avry kept rambling on about time and place. Did he really mean it?

Time? Rutker had just assumed that, just like everything else, was just the rambling of a madman. He was mad, right? What were orcs anyway? And these dimensional creatures, what did he call them? Void? It had to be nonsense, but then, D'avry had little knowledge about the greater cosmos. For all intents and purposes, he was an E'rth native. That was the most likely conclusion.

Okay, so in the future, the Epriots apparently survived and populated that little backwater planet, E'rth.

That could be used as a working hypothesis, anyway.

There was something in the mix that didn't feel quite right. This business with the Gefkarri double cross. And the Delvadr. What was their role? The Delvadr may be devious, but they really weren't all that bright. Their saving grace was that there were a lot of them and they had the GSRs to buy top-shelf gear. But what they lacked in brainpower, the Gefkarri could certainly fill in. Still—

And then it clicked.

The Delvadr aren't on the inside. They're stooges just like us.

That meant it was Epriot Prime that the Gefkarri wanted. They had let the Delvadr waste away resources, probably all while fronting the trade with the Thune, building every mech and every ship, and then, when they were on the verge of victory, the Gefkarri would sweep in and take it all away.

Clever. Traitorous bullshit, but absolutely devious. Only, that didn't quite work either. Why not let the Delvadr play their final card?

Except they couldn't. Cadian Galas, the insane marine mech pilot, had stopped them with the prior race's Arcfire weapon. The Gefkarri had nothing to do with that.

Rutker searched the ceiling for a long minute, trying to think through the details of how that whole thing went down. He was there, after all. Well, at least he watched the Arcfire rake the sky, incinerating dropships, carriers, anything over a couple of hundred meters off the surface of the planet and out as far as middle orbit.

And then, he'd been the first on the scene, sorting out who had done what to whom. She'd conveyed the whole thing to him after he figured out it was she who was driving the Delvadr Elite mech and not one of the pompous alien dandies.

He regretted ever learning Delvic. What an inane bunch of buffoons. How demoralizing to find out that your own race was on the brink of extinction due to what was essentially a race of rich idiots.

So Galas wiped out the Delvadr, except for the ones that got through early at least. Before that, she had managed to take out a pack of Deathhounds, *another* feat he couldn't quite get his brain around. And there was something about an overlord or a necromancer? Again, some kind of dimensional thing. He wondered if that *thing* had anything to do with the creatures D'avry kept mentioning. Dimensional shifting monsters.

Maybe he wasn't completely insane after all.

Rutker pushed himself back to the nearest wall and hung his head low. Running solo again. He was used to it, but now he was a prisoner of war and he had no way of letting Katherynn know he was even alive. He pulled what little hair he had in frustration and slammed his fists into the floor.

Rutker let his anger burn hot. This was his tool. He let the anger build into a blazing inferno and then he just let that fuel everything he did, every thought he had until he'd laid waste to every obstacle in his way.

Righteous fury. That was what had seen him through two decades of battle. That was what had gotten him through this last little walkabout on the pirate mercenary-infested planet below. That was the weapon that was going to get him through this trial now. He would see Katherynn and his sons again, and Maker have mercy on anyone who stood in his way.

CHAPTER 7

THE HANGOVER

Rutker woke alone. His neck and shoulder ached. His hip was asleep. But he'd slept. He actually slept. That was something.

He stretched, hesitantly, feeling out every kink. He tried to bend at the waist to limber up a little, but the pressure in his gut was exceedingly uncomfortable. He pushed on his sides and they felt tender but hard. He'd neglected his physical health. Evacuating his bowels had just not been in the cards over the last few days.

Constipation was just a nuisance until it wasn't. There wasn't access to facilities in the cell. He didn't know what his captor's long-term plan was, but judging by the accommodations, there wasn't one.

Maybe it was an attempt to humiliate and demoralize him. That flicker of anger burned a little brighter. He reminded himself he was a prisoner on an alien vessel orbiting around an unknown planet. Waking up to hopelessness was not how he did things. He would assess the situation, catalog his assets, and formulate a plan.

Rutker stared across the floor of his cell and all thoughts of planning disappeared with a lump of vines slouched against the far wall.

He snapped to attention.

"D'avry!"

Rutker was up and running before he knew it, skidding to a stop next to the pile of twisted vines and roots.

Within was the pale and haggard body of the young mage.

He slapped his face repeatedly. Little slaps. mostly.

"D'avry... D'avry... Wake up, kiddo!" He was so excited to have him back that he only barely recognized that he was ecstatic to see him alive.

Thick eyelids fluttered and finally, one crust-covered eye peeled apart. Rutker realized that there was a vague tattoo of eyeliner he'd never realized was there. That was ... unusual.

"D'avry. Were you always wearing makeup?"

"Whuh?" he replied groggily.

"Eye makeup. Did you always have that? I never noticed it before."

"Oh... Um, yeah. That's a marked thing. The priesthood. Long time ago."

"Kid. You're like what, twenty-three, twenty-four? You're not much older than my boys."

"Mmm... yeah, something like that."

"What do you mean? You don't know your own age?"

"Last few years ... kind of a blur. Been pretty much on my own since the whole thing back in T'Serkus. You know, with Goslyn."

"The princess you were going to marry?"

Another eye peeled open, and he blinked them both sluggishly. D'avry's eyes were bloodshot. If he didn't know better, he'd have assumed he was just severely hungover.

D'avry tried to lick his lips with a dry tongue and when it stuck, he just pursed them and nodded instead.

"What happened to you? Do you remember anything?"

D'avry went to move and stopped against the vines. He looked down in confusion, but then slowly the vines untangled themselves from around him until he was sitting flat on the floor with his back propped up against the wall.

Rutker had unconsciously backed away and now looked at the mage with that scrutinizing stare again.

"Was that the ship that just did that, or was that you?"

"Uh, I think that was me," D'avry replied looking mildly confused again.

The Hangover

Rutker folded his arms and looked down at the mage. "Care to explain?"

"Um…" He searched the air for answers, digging through murky memories Rutker assumed. He liked the kid despite the way he came off when they'd first met, all cloak and dagger and mystical nonsense. Not much had changed, but now they at least had some shared experience and he felt like he was getting to know his motivations and character a little more.

"…I think that the part of me that knows how to manipulate magic, on an unconscious level, maybe, just figured it out on its own. I've always picked things up quickly, but … didn't really know you could do that with different kinds of magic. It's not exactly like that on E'rth. All our systems are much more structured. Not sure why that is." He tilted his head, considering this new fact.

"While you were sleeping, you figured that out?" Rutker asked incredulously.

"Well, it appears that way. Doesn't it? My, you're grumpy this morning. Even for you," D'avry said as he stretched and rubbed his face.

"Do you remember anything of what happened to you when that psycho tree woman attacked you?"

"You mean Seda? Oh, she's really not that bad, I don't think."

"So, when the Gefkarri aspect choked you out and dragged you down into her little dungeon, that wasn't all that bad, you think?" Rutker mocked.

"Well, I don't think it was really like that exactly. I mean, yeah, she's a little … aggressive, but I don't think she actually means harm. Well, let me take that back. The Gefkarri as a whole is a callous being. And she's part of that, but there's more nuance to it, I think."

D'avry was beginning to perk up a little as he chewed on the conundrum of their captivity and the nature of their unintentional host.

"How so?" Rutker asked, moving to a place against the wall where he could interrogate the mage more comfortably. He leaned against it, started to fold his arms, thought better of it, and slid his hands into his pockets instead. He imagined it would look less threatening this way. His wife had hinted that he came off as intimidating when talking with his boys. That maybe they'd open up a little more if he was a little less intense. This was a good opportunity to practice.

D'avry visibly relaxed.

"Well, when she said she was a seedling, that's a partial truth. I think the greater tree just sprouts new trees and those saplings shoot roots down into whatever soil is there, rather than growing up out of it. Seedlings are whole new entities. Like the Pentarch is itself an entity. Do you know how many millennia ago it had to have been born in anticipation of responding to this event?"

Rutker shook his head. D'avry shook his head too, but more in wonderment.

"Yeah, me neither. But it was a long time ago. That means that the Gefkarri has some sort of prescience. Farsight. And I mean *far*.

"And another thing. It takes its magic with it. That's," he searched the ceiling again, "I don't know what that is. It's something else though.

"I'm bound to place. When we left E'rth, I lost contact with the arcanum, the ethereal strata or medium. That is until we boarded this ship. Then I instantly felt something new. Now, I think I would recognize and possibly be able to manipulate a new source of magic if I found it. That's why the Gefkarri is so interested in me. And, by extension, us," he said, motioning between them.

He looked up and away, nodding as thoughts seemed to coalesce in his head. "Yeah, that makes a lot of sense."

Suddenly, his eyes shot wide.

"Rutker, are we moving?"

Rutker was surprised by the question, but even more so by the fact that he already knew the answer. He'd known it for a while and it just hadn't registered.

"Oh, shit. Yeah, we're definitely moving. Katherynn... The boys..." Now he started to panic.

"Are fine," a new voice interrupted.

Rutker and D'avry shared a tired acknowledgment between them before turning to find a new aspect. Similar, but not the same. This one's eyes were a pale amber, and she wore a tight-fitting robe of ivory which was almost an identical shade to Seda's complexion, though the skin of this aspect was darker by a few shades. Where Seda's coloring was ash, this one's coloring was a deep rosy-brown like cedar.

The Hangover

"Who are you? Where's Seda?" D'avry asked.

"Where are you taking us? What's happened to my family?" Rutker demanded.

The new aspect appraised them cooly, her amber eyes glowing ever so slightly brighter before cooling again.

"I am Theal," she said, her lips curling into the faintest sneer. Her disdain, or maybe worse, repulsion, was more than evident without a more visible display.

Rutker stepped forward and Theal's eyes grew bright with warning. He paused.

"Where is my family? Are they still on Gell—" He stopped himself. "Are they still on E'rth? The planet we've been orbiting? Are they okay?" His hands balled into fists as he spoke, blood rising in his face. He forced himself to cool down.

Theal considered him and then, after a long delay, said, "Katherynn and your sons, Mads and Macq, and Colonel Dexx, along with the rest of the remaining crew of the *Xandraitha's Hope*, are all well and being taken care of."

He took an involuntary step back, in light of this new information. But he still had questions. "What does that mean? Taken care of?"

"That means that they are here. Guests of the Gefkarri Pentarch."

"I want to see them. Now."

Theal looked at him again. Her demeanor was resolute. Unyielding. It was clear she wouldn't give away anything she didn't intend to. She was as immovable as the tree of which she was part.

"That won't be possible," she said, beginning to turn her attention to D'avry when Rutker started forward. Vines exploded from the ground and pushed him across the cell to the wall. He slammed hard and then was held fast as he struggled to catch the breath that had been knocked out of him. He roared in frustration, but Theal paid him no attention.

"Let's take a walk, shall we?" she asked, but it didn't sound like a question.

Then the wall of the cell retreated and beyond was a space, miles across in every direction. The perimeter of it was a great sphere of honeycombed crystalline material, revealing the vast blackness of space beyond streaked through with long, brilliant lines of multi-colored light. The space was so large that there was a visible haze of atmosphere.

Rutker had seen moons that could fit inside it. In fact, he was certain most of the EDC's remaining interstellar fleet could fit within those walls. Hundreds of ships the size of the *Xandraitha's Hope*, at least.

At the center of the space, a verdant canopy shimmered with rolling waves of amber and crimson and then barren branches, only to be replaced with new growth as the cycle started again. Interspersed among the undulating color waves were speckled groves of steadfast evergreens and muscular strands of ironwood. It was like nothing Rutker had ever seen before. A dull roar like a distant wind carried the cries of birds and other animals. Here before them was exactly what had been described—the tree that was the root of worlds. Suddenly, he could believe it.

And, somehow, it was contained within a ship.

Rutker had seen some things. But this was nothing like anything he'd ever even imagined.

A boom and then a deep moan caused flocks of birds to take flight and the waves of seasonal color fanned out from a single point at its center.

Theal's eyes brightened in apparent surprise. She looked at the other two and then the railing of the catwalk and the floor itself grew outward, stretching toward the massive forest that took up their entire field of view. The trio stood in place as the material of the ship under their feet grew outward and down toward the super-entity known as the Gefkarri Pentarch.

Rutker swallowed back bile, not from the unnatural sensation of movement but from the sheer scale of it. It was beyond anything he could think to compare it to. The size of the ship that contained it, too, was absolutely stupefying. But beyond that, the only thing he could think about was, what on Epriot did it want with them?

D'avry had not told Rutker that the Gefkarri aspect, Seda, had infiltrated his mind.

He didn't know how to tell him that without turning the man against him. He was already skeptical as it was. To let him know that he had possibly been compromised by their captor, an alien super entity that bordered on deity, no, wait, by nearly all working definitions, *was* a deity. At least a minor one.

Regardless, now was not the time to have that conversation. And besides, he didn't even know how he felt about it. He didn't feel good about it. It was a gross overreach of personal space, rights, whatever. But, there was a part of him that was, somehow ... honored?

No, that wasn't quite right. He hadn't had time to deconstruct the experience, he just knew that, well, he just knew things now that he hadn't known before. And he was certain that the Gefkarri knew everything there was to know about him, including his friends and what they were trying to accomplish with the artifacts.

He'd have to think deeply about what that meant later. The enemy of mankind knew about his little plan to thwart it... Scary stuff. But, again, something for some later pondering. Right now, D'avry needed to sort out what he'd just learned.

It was still fragmented and incomplete, but he was certain that Seda, while an aspect of the greater being, was also an individual. At least kind of. As much of an individual as one could be while still part of one massive collective mind. So whatever the collective knew, Seda may not know, but she *could*. The true and oldest part of the tree of the world knew many, *many* things. Too much for an individual to know.

Also, it thought very deep thoughts. And the things it knew and the thoughts it had, it had known and thought a very, very long time ago.

Seda, by comparison, at the approximate age of 5,427 solar years old, knew very little. And yet, by comparison to D'avry's own knowledge base, she too could be a demigod in her own right. The power of this creature was, well, they just had absolutely no hope of defeating it. But that was now a non-issue, as D'avry had learned of the Gefkarri's true plan with the sabotage of the Epriot-Delvadr Peace Treaty. To take over Epriot Prime as the front lines on a battlefield against an interdimensional blight known as the Void.

All done. Mission accomplished. Now what...

Sometimes you get the answer you need and realize you have to go back to the question. D'avry had wanted to know who their enemy was. Well, it turned out that it was the Gefkarri, but in a way, the Gefkarri were allies against something else entirely.

D'avry had been wrong about the nightmare creatures that were hunting Deven. They were not the ones who had enslaved humanity on E'rth and managed the rise and fall of its civilizations—for purposes he still had not yet ascertained, by the way—but they were an existential threat to it. And, apparently, to the galaxy as a whole.

D'avry had only just learned what a galaxy *was*. He was very excited to go back and tell his professors at Academie. If he lived that long.

Right now, what he knew was that they were traveling very fast, away from the planet he called home. And from his friends. And from Deven. That hit him in the gut. Somehow, that affected him in a way that the others didn't. How was that? He'd only just met her.

And now he was going to break a very big promise—his vow to return and bring her back from the time of the airships and mutant mages and to solve the riddle of the gray town.

That was one little morsel that had eluded him in his download with the great tree god. He wondered why. Then he slipped back into his thoughts about the wounded warrior girl from what was technically his future, even though he himself was technically from the future as well.

His brain hurt, and his heart was hollow. He thought about their last moments together at the top of the mountain after the aftermath of the meteor strike and ensuing battle.

His only hope was that the work that he did here, with the Gefkarri, would be enough to ensure humanity's freedom. He understood that those were the stakes. Not why or how exactly. But he hoped that understanding would come. It had to.

The verdant mass of the Gefkarri grew and grew before them until it was all they could see. Flocks of white crested birds glided just above the treetops, while the howls of some kind of primate echoed through the canopy back and forth over miles of surface. The smell of it, carried on a warm breeze was healthy and vibrant, and yet there was something subtle, something … foul.

Then, when they were roughly a quarter of a mile away, the catwalk stopped. Thick strands of twisted root extended from the main sphere to the ceramo-metal bulkheads of the ship. He flashed back to what it had looked like as they made their final approach toward the ship. He had used his waning spellcraft in those final moments to do so.

There was a large flat fore section and then a reflective sphere that projected from the middle which was then connected to a rear section that was thicker and slightly taller. He thought it looked like a brick resting on its narrow side with an orb somehow melded into its midsection. Like that, but sleek and absolutely massive. All the cities of T'Serkus and all the other nations could fit inside it.

D'avry rubbed grit from his eyes. He was feeling better than he had when Rutker had woken him. Still a bit jittery. He was sure he was different somehow. His hand drifted up to the outline of the lantern door in his chest. He didn't have to remove his long jacket and shirt to know that within it the artifacts were moving again—but backward. That probably was an important bit of information. But like so many other things, he had no idea what it meant.

"You never answered my question," Rutker stated, now twenty minutes later, having finally regrouped somewhat after the awe of their surroundings had subsided.

Theal ignored him, rapt attention on the whole of the Gefkarri Pentarch itself.

"From up here..." she said, mildly shaking her head.

Rutker reluctantly turned back to the Tree of Worlds. D'avry was mildly surprised to see that even the aspect wasn't immune to awe at the sheer magnitude of it all.

The boom echoed again only now they could feel it in their bodies. It was all they could hear and then the low groan, like eons of prayers being lifted all at once.

"Yeah, well, I still want to see my family," he added.

"Soon enough," Theal replied.

"When?"

"When we get there."

"Where's there?

"The Epriot System. We'll be there within the hour," she replied turning only slightly, her eyes still locked on the display playing out before them.

D'avry and Rutker snapped to her, mouths open. The hint of a smile turned the corner of her mouth.

The shimmer of seasons swept past them, yellow, orange, crimson, barren gray, and then green again. The groaning, too, rolled in waves.

Theal's amber eyes bloomed and then faded. She turned to D'avry, "It's time for your lessons."

"What lessons?" Rutker demanded.

Theal ignored him.

"You will lead and unify the armies. The great tree shall be your source. And, perhaps the planet will yield its bounty. But, we are concerned it has been tainted. It is so close to the Void. How could it not?"

"Wha—" D'avry tried to ask.

"With you as a conduit of power for the Gefkarri, we shall unify the efforts of our allies and—"

"I'm sorry, what allies exactly?" Rutker interrupted again.

Theal's eyes cooled as she turned to address him,

"Why, the Delvadr of course," her hand came up to ward off the follow-up question, "and the Chareth-Ul."

"The who? The chair..."

"The Chareth-Ul. You may know their Deathhounds," she said, a wry smile turning the corner of her mouth.

Rutker sucked in air, his hands going to his head in dumbfounded exasperation.

"We would NEVER be allies with the Delvadr. OR the Chareth-whatever ... the Deathhounds?!?" he spat out, "What gives you the right!?!"

A boom roared through the space, shaking the catwalk they stood on and rattling their lungs within them. After which even Rutker dared not utter a word. And then after a suitably reverent time,

"Let us make haste," Theal offered as the scaffold retreated back to the band of catwalks that ringed the equator of the massive forest.

"I can walk you know," Rutker informed her, the veins in his forehead threatening to pop out.

Theal, per usual, ignored him, preferring instead to keep him fast in the clutch of vines and roots. She moved him along with her and D'avry as they continued, not back to the cell, but instead to a destination she didn't bother to disclose.

The ship, long, sleek, gray like everything seemed to be in this time, stood, dwarfed by the space around it. D'avry could barely make out the roof, just the lights that pierced the darkness above. The hangar, he'd heard it called, was large enough to have been a parade ground for an army five times the size of that he'd seen assembled before the vaulted spires of W'Therbad, the rulers' palace where he'd first met Goslyn, then crown-princess of his homeland of T'Serkus. That place and time seemed so far away now. Impossibly far, and by any human measure, it was.

He'd felt so far removed when the Astrig Ka'a had first taken him. But now? He couldn't even get his mind around the distances that separated them.

"You think of her often."

"Yes," D'avry replied, knowing exactly whom Seda was referring to.

The two stood looking at the *Xandraitha's Hope*. Rutker had been allowed to enter it on the condition that he'd follow the instructions of the Gefkarri down to the minutest detail.

The man, to his credit, didn't immediately agree. But, upon reflection on their current circumstances, the fact that an inter-dimensional adversary was even now entering the field of battle and that the Delvadr were already engaged (and faring poorly they'd been told), he reluctantly agreed that any help was better than watching his planet be invaded by yet another far-superior force. Threatening the already fragile remnant of humanity. He'd been even more encouraged by the knowledge that Katherynn, his wife and apparently a shrewd diplomat in her own right, had assumed command of the ship and Colonel Dexx was resting in the brig. The boys, Mads and Macq, were heading up security in the absence of the marine contingent who'd met an untimely end at the beginning of the whole debacle. Rutker seemed pleased that at least things were coming around somewhat.

"What happened to you?" D'avry asked.

"What do you mean?"

"Why did Theal come to escort us to the Gefkarri? Surely much honor must be associated with duties of that nature."

Seda said nothing.

"I am here now. Isn't that enough?" A lone tendril snaked from her hand to touch the back of D'avry's. He pulled his hand back, massaging the spot where a tiny trickle of blood appeared. He shot a wary look in her direction.

"Your tricks won't work on me anymore."

"You profess as much." She pouted, but a sly smile crept onto her lips. "Now, join me. The battlefield, eons in the making, awaits and we must be as one."

D'avry breathed out a sigh, shaking his head. He closed his eyes, and the world exploded into color. Before him, a virtual battlefield projected from the very mind of the Gefkarri into his own. Though he didn't remember much of it, this was similar to what had happened when the Gefkarri had first connected to him telepathically. This is what had happened when he'd been taken from the cell. And what he'd not told Rutker once they were reunited. He wouldn't have been able to deny his incredulity. Truth be told, he wasn't even sure he could *be* trusted.

In his mind, he stood upon an outcropping of rock, high above folds of jungle and river that looked like any on E'rth. In the distance, smoky smudges hung in the air above a burnished edge of light where the great forest was afire. Beyond, slits of darkness peppered the skies above and creatures of darkness squeezed through, their spindly arms extending like cancerous webs.

He shivered as he recognized them. Below, the ground bubbled with waves upon waves of darkened figures moving forward in fits and spurts, rolling across the terrain like a veil of inky sky.

To his right Seda appeared, one palm upright like a knife blade before her heart. The other held similarly but opposite before her forehead. Her eyes were closed. He could feel her presence lean into him, drawing him into the connection. When he let his mind go, threads of pale brilliance crisscrossed the air for miles and miles before them in every direction. Then he saw that some of these threads terminated where the two of them stood, and others connected to elements on the field of battle.

Now he saw giant mechs, metal creatures like Rutker's own, but many times that size. They bounded across the terrain from the north. Farther beyond that was another robotic beast but of a size unfathomable. An island on three legs. Large enough to hold E'rthen cities within it.

It belched corruption and spewed coal smoke and sulfur into the air. He realized that the other mechs, massive in their own right but minuscule beside it, also dripped with corruption.

His skin crawled as he touched the threads connecting these metallic beasts with his mind. Bile rose in the back of his throat and he felt Seda take control of the interface. His sense of her mood grew tense, transactional. A marked shift from how she was with him.

But this was what the Gefkarri were here to do. To connect the various elements of the defense against the Void. They were the masterminds. He reached out again, swallowed down the bitter sick, and supported her effort. The lines of light grew subtly in intensity, and he was able to see, or feel rather, even more. Beyond the filth of this northern element, there were others on the field.

He focused on these now and felt a foreign mind behind them. Flat, impassive, callous, and self-absorbed. This was the consciousness of the Delvadr. The invaders. They weren't a hive mind like the Gefkarri, but they were of one mind in that there was very little distinction from one to another. Humans, he realized, were vastly independent in nature by comparison.

And then he sensed some of this with the corrupted ones, the Deathhounds.

"It is because some of them *are* human," Seda answered this unasked question.

"Those are the Deathhounds, then. The possessed. They traded their souls for power and for continued existence."

"Sad. But yes. Something like that."

"There are so many."

"The Chareth-Ul have been preparing for this battle for a very long time."

"I see."

"I doubt you do. You cannot fathom the desperation. You have carried out your mission alone and yet, you have never felt the depth of that kind of desperation. That's why I picked you."

"You what? You picked me? What does that mean?"

Seda didn't respond right away.

"Have you ever wondered about your magic, the Astrig Ka'a?"

"Of course. What it is. What its purpose is."

"Yes. But have you ever wondered how it anticipates your needs? How it seems to be guiding you?"

"Yes. I have wondered that."

The battle beyond had seemed to pause momentarily but now resumed. He could feel Seda manipulating the lines of power, shifting the flow of magic, not touching it but facilitating it so that more could move where it was needed. Where this happened, the battle surged.

Black figures clashed with corrupted mechs. The air shimmered and then was filled with sleek, armored forms that blistered with streaking missiles and piercing light.

"You do realize that is not how magic works."

In D'avry's mind, he turned to look at her. The wind welling up from the field below tousled the long mahogany locks of her hair so that it waved in a subtle way like the vines she often commanded.

"What are you saying?"

She moved his attention back to the field of battle. He felt himself reach out and guide one of the lines of magic to a black and silver mech that had just been swatted from the air by one of the blackout beasts. It crashed to the ground, rolled, and as it came up, D'avry's ephemeral line connected to it and it was as if he was in the battle.

He felt the movements of Void hordes and of the beast and the mech's plasma blades sprang to life, whipping viciously as the robotic form maneuvered through the landscape, fighting and running and then severing chitinous arms before bursting into the air and away to safety.

D'avry snapped out of the point of view of the mech and back into his virtual self.

Seda stared at him, eyes bright, wary almost.

"D'avry we're here to influence the battle. To facilitate movement at a strategic level. The Gefkarri can act in such a way that connects the disparate elements of the combined forces; the Delvadr, the Chareth-Ul, and our own units that we will bring to bear once we can enter orbit."

The Hangover

D'avry wanted to dig into a couple of things, but it was all happening too fast. What did she mean by 'once we can enter orbit'? And why was she telling him about the network effect of the hive mind being extended to include those of its allies? He'd understood this purpose when they'd first taken him against his will and brought him into their collective consciousness. That was a whole other mess he needed to unpack, but here were other problems he needed to understand. What was she getting at about the Astrig Ka'a and why had she not mentioned the Epriots in all of this? It was their planet, after all.

"Seda. What's humanity's role in this battle? Why are they not mentioned with the allies?"

The aspect focused her attention back on the field. There was a pause and then he felt her presence overlaid upon his own as if he were about to play an instrument and she was positioned around him, guiding his hands and arms.

"We must focus on the task before us. So much is at stake."

"Seda. Humans can be possessed by the Chareth-Ul. And I am able to manipulate the lines of magic, here on Epriot Prime even—"

"It is a simulation. We don't know that for sure."

"Still, you, the Gefkarri, are creating the simulation and the greater mind has deemed it salient to pursue it as such. What I'm asking is, if humans are Paenarcanum, able to use any magic, is that why the Chareth-Ul can turn them into Deathhounds? And if so, what *exactly* is humanity's role in this battle?"

The world simulation came to an end, and the two stood staring at each other with the racket of equipment moving around the hangar in the background.

Seda's hair was back in place in a long plait draped over her shoulder. Her eyes were dim now, barely more than that milky jade he'd seen the day before. She lifted her chin.

"We shall see what role humanity will play. There is much that remains a mystery. Only when we set foot on the battlefield will we understand the rules of the game."

That was new. To this point, the Gefkarri had known everything. Or at least projected as much. D'avry didn't like it. There was something that Seda wasn't telling him. And it was big. World-shattering big. And then there was the question of what she was hinting at about the Astrig Ka'a. She seemed to imply that in the same way that the two of them had manipulated the elements on the field of battle, the Astrig Ka'a was doing the same with him. But what did she say? That magic didn't work that way? It's passive. It exists. It doesn't move or manipulate people any more than gravity or the wind. Only other people did that. Was she implying that he was being manipulated by the magic? Or more importantly, by someone or something behind it?

CHAPTER 8
HOPE NOT LOST

Katherynn dropped her tablet when she saw him. She covered the short distance in an instant and was crushing him in shaking arms, sobbing. Rutker had never seen her like this. But he understood it. His cheeks were hot and wet. He couldn't hold her close or hard enough,

"Oh, babe ... my sweetheart, my Katherynn," he bubbled out, shaking his head and burying it in her shoulder-length hair. He sucked in a huge breath and it caught. He saw his boys. He motioned for them and they broke across the space, slamming into them. Rutker lost balance and the four of them crumpled to their knees, still locked in each other's arms.

"Dad! You old goat. I knew you were alive!" Macq breathed out.

"We knew it. We knew there was no way. Dexx! I'm going to ring the living—"

"That's enough. That's enough for now." Rutker laughed. "For now. It's about this. Us. I'm so glad to see you're all okay."

The other three nodded and pressed harder.

"I knew it wasn't true," Katherynn hissed in his ear, shuddering. Her breath was hot and he felt that warmth all the way to his soul.

"Oh Maker, I missed you all," he managed. "Thank you. Thank you, Maker..."

"You can thank the Gefkarri Pentarch," Theal offered unhelpfully in her smooth, even tone. Apparently, her ability to materialize anywhere extended even here, aboard the Epriot diplomatic vessel, the *Xandraitha's Hope*.

It was Rutker's turn to ignore her, however.

"Who is that?" Katherynn whispered in his ear.

"Don't worry about it. A problem we're going to find a solution for," he whispered back before the four of them stood to face the newcomer.

"We'll talk soon," he assured them, taking a moment to stare into each one of their faces. "I'm so proud of you guys. And you," he said, staring last into the hazel eyes of the woman who'd stood by his side for nearly three decades—bearing and raising his children, burying friends and family, enduring wave after wave of a relentless invasionary army. He wiped her cheek one last time and turned to face this new oppressor—Theal, the aspect of the so-called neutral Gefkarri.

She stood there looking the part, coldly aloof.

"Are you done?" she asked in a clipped tone, smiling deprecatingly.

"For now," Rutker responded and then stepped forward, "What's the meaning of this? You want something or you wouldn't be showing me to my family. Is there something I must agree to?"

Theal's eyebrow arched the tiniest bit, and she smiled again.

"Your acquiescence is meaningless to us, but reuniting you with your family does suit our purposes. As I've explained, we're returning you to your homeworld. However, something has been simmering for some time. Even before humanity called Epriot their home. Or Epriot, for that matter. This system, you see, much like others throughout the galaxy, sits dangerously close to an alternate galaxy in an alternate universe."

"Wait, how does that work?" Katherynn asked. "Are you suggesting that we're touching another dimension?"

"No. It would be painfully obvious if you were. As it stands, the two universes overlap, but with zero contact. Don't ask me to explain it to you. This part of this galaxy is simply just close. Close enough for the Void, powerful interdimensional travelers, to cross the breach."

"Has this always been like this? If so, why haven't they breached into our world before?"

"Good questions. I like this one," she said in Rutker's direction, showing for the first time any semblance of personality. He smiled in agreement, but it was a look that still held an element of threat in it. Theal continued as if she didn't notice it, "The universe is expanding. The galaxies move within it. So too, the larger structure binding the many expressions of reality."

"Expressions of reality?" Mads asked, looking at his parents and then back to the Gefkarri.

"These are nuances," she said, turning in his direction, her eyes flaring slightly as if seeing the young man for the first time.

"Now we get to the good part," Rutker deadpanned.

Theal nodded and continued, "We've entered Epriot Prime's Far Orbit but must not venture any farther."

"Because of the Arcfire," he concluded.

She nodded again.

"And it's byproduct."

Rutker cocked his head at this.

"The mid-orbital band, if you haven't seen it." She waved her hand and a large display shimmered into view, showing a dust belt of darkly glittering refuse surrounding much of the tan, white, green, and blue-streaked planet beyond.

Nods of understanding were slow but ubiquitous. In the intervening weeks since the final assault had been decimated by Captain Galas and the resurrected Arcfire, the carnage that hadn't fallen into the gravity well, or spun off into space had settled into a thick metallic haze, effectively squelching communications and creating a huge safety hazard for any vessel, but especially for one the size of the Pentarch flagship.

"It would take too long to maneuver the *Tahlah* into a position for comms and besides, a substantial cleanup effort will be required.

"This ship, your *Xandraitha's Hope*, will disembark and continue through the mid-orbital band to establish comms with your supreme command and have the Arcfire disabled."

"Why would we do that?" It was Macq this time that interjected.

"Because the Void are here. Now. And it will take a combined army. The army of the Gefkarri along with two others you know, the Deathhounds, or Chareth-Ul, and the Delvadr."

"The what???" Mads and Macq cried out simultaneously. Katherynn's hand shot up to her mouth as her face turned shades darker.

"You expect us to join forces with those genocidal sonsofb—" she began.

Rutker reached for her, and she shook him off, stepping forcefully toward the aspect. Rutker reached out again, successfully this time, and pulled her back even as Theal's eyes bloomed with indignation.

"Babe."

She whipped her attention back to him.

"Babe. What she's saying is true. I haven't been able to tell you everything that went on back there on E'rth ... or Gellen ... back there. The Void that the Gefkarri is talking about, they're there too. Or they will be at least. That is, if you trust that lunatic magician, D'avry."

"Who? And how did you even run into someone on Gellen III? Was he one of the pirates?"

"D'avry? No. He's, well, I met him in the caves. Kind of a long story, but he's partly how I got here, in this mess. Which at least that turned out somewhat okay," he said, looking at the three of them. He let out a deep sigh as the realization of that settled in. He had his family back. Now they had a new adversary. And their old ones were so scared by it that they were willing to join forces.

He turned back to Theal.

"Let me get this right. You want us to take this ship closer to the planet so they can see that it's us and maybe not add your flagship to the blanket of orbital carnage? You really think they'll go for that?"

"If they've met the Void? Yes, they definitely will."

"Have you not been able to get in contact at all with EDC Command?"

"We have, with little luck. Those who we have been able to reach have had little knowledge of the Arcfire or who may be operating it."

"What do you mean, 'operating it'?"

"We sent an envoy when we arrived."

Rutker's brows shot up at that. "And that didn't go well. And you want us to go out there?!?"

"Why wouldn't you have had one of us hail EDC Command? Why don't we just do that now?" Katherynn asked.

"It didn't seem necessary at first. We'd hoped to communicate with your command to negotiate terms of occupation, but even while we did so, the Arcfire—"

"I'm sorry, did you say occupation?" Katherynn demanded.

"Of course."

"We are the diplomatic entourage. Any negotiations should have happened through us."

"Katherynn, you must understand the position that you are in now. Your diplomatic ship has been seized by the Gefkarri Pentarch. There is no truce between the Delvadr and the Epriots because the needs of the galaxy supersede such a trivial arrangement. We will occupy your planet and facilitate the unified forces defending it against an external threat, the likes of which no one in this galaxy has ever seen. Your permission is entirely irrelevant."

"But you need our help to open the front door," Rutker replied.

Theal was silent.

"And if we don't, we'll die under the boots of an interdimensional army that neither the Delvadr nor the Deathhounds or even the great and mighty Gefkarri can deal with on their own. Is that right?"

"The Gefkarri is already fighting this battle on many fronts. But that is a fair assessment."

"When do we leave?"

"In less than an hour."

"What's the holdup?"

"We're waiting on your companion."

Rutker breathed out a sigh, "That sounds about right."

D'avry boarded the *Xandraitha's Hope* and was escorted through several long white corridors, brightly lit with a continuous blue runner carpet and image after image of people in strange garb upon the walls. These were clearly of royalty or military of rank and it struck him, how even with such an amazingly technological society, humans still worked so hard to appear important.

A couple minutes of walking and one very uncomfortable elevator ride later, he was ushered onto the bridge. D'avry was introduced to Katherynn, poised and proper, with an understated confidence. And then Mads, the older and more soldierly version, and Macq, who was thinner and had the air of an academic, or considering Rutker's family, a tactician.

Theal and Seda regarded each other cooly, D'avry noticed. If he wasn't mistaken, it seemed like there was a rivalry between them. An odd thing for manifestations of what was supposedly one mind.

He'd met that mind or at least a small fraction of it. It seemed very much unified in that experience, though he had little recollection of the entire encounter. He'd have to ask Seda about it later.

Once he'd reached the bridge, the vessel lifted off almost immediately. He saw this through the windows that he was certain must just be viewscreens. He equated this to how he viewed things through the small drone he'd taken from Rutker in the caves. He wondered if Rutker knew he still had it and if he'd care. Rutker, as much as he was tied to the machine in a way, seemed to have no desire to go back to it.

It was D'avry's understanding that the man was actually a pilot of airships much like this one, but smaller and faster. The man was a warrior, no matter what his weapon.

D'avry had been informed of their mission and how they were going to approach the planet in the hopes of communicating with whoever was blowing space-going vessels out of the sky. To him, that seemed like a terribly bad idea. Like waving your naked arse at a wall of archers and then stepping closer in case they couldn't quite count every pimple. He was told that the communications from the ship would be more effective closer in. This was because, currently, there was a massive band of destroyed vessels encircling the planet. This due to the exact weapon they were trying to avoid.

He chewed his lip nervously and observed the people around him. They all seemed to be taking it in stride, though he noticed a vein on Rutker's temple that had a tendency to protrude when he was stressed. Or angry. Now that he thought about it, there were precious few moments in the span of their relationship when he hadn't noticed that vein in his temple.

D'avry took the moment of downtime to put his thoughts in order. He closed his eyes and assumed an 'entering' breathing pattern. Immediately, a calm and buoyant sensation infused his body, which was odd. He didn't open his eyes, but he was certain that he was levitating. D'avry continued to calm his thoughts and felt the surfaces of the interior space of the bridge in his mind. He felt them as certainly as if he'd done so with his very own hands. He drifted back toward a row of seats that lined a wall and anchored himself in that space.

In his mind's eye, he could see everyone, could feel everyone, and he could feel that greater presence. Butterflies tumbled in his stomach as he touched it briefly. A shudder spread out from that point of contact, and then a connection blossomed. There was something unidentifiable there, something old and something new.

Through his greater awareness, he saw Theal, the other aspect, engaged in conversation with Rutker and Katherynn. Mads was staring at him with a surprised and concerned expression. The other one, Macq, was nowhere to be seen. But Seda, while she appeared to be following the conversation between the others, was fully focused on him. He didn't know how he knew it, but it was a certainty.

D'avry tugged at the connection to the greater consciousness and found information, ideas, and directives all flowing to and from and through him. But he also found that it flowed away from him as well. A sudden pang of fear seized him and the connection clenched, but not entirely. He realized that there was most likely much more to be gained from this exchange than he could possibly give, so he continued. He also realized that during his initial induction, he most certainly gave up all he knew already. He had no recollection of that interaction, but he was certain of it.

As he opened his mind, he saw the battle unfold on the planet's surface. Saw season after season of warfare and watched the tide of it ebb and flow. He saw himself, guiding massive armies of mechanized monstrosities against a tide of blacked-out bodies. He saw their thousand-armed beasts, and there were other, even darker things waiting at the portals. His blood ran cold and then, for a fleeting second, he saw a glimpse of something that shook him to his core.

A Chareth-Ul, Deathhound mech, lay dissected upon a ridge of stone. The human body of its soulbound pilot lay meters away, bleeding out in a scouring wind, but beyond that lay two more bodies. Human ones. They were not dressed as pilots and he could tell they were not soulbound. They were mages, of a sort. All three were casualties of the mech's destruction.

The connection shut down, and he gasped as his meditative state was ripped apart. He dropped abruptly from the air to the leather-like lounge and his eyes fixed on Seda, even as everyone else on the bridge turned his direction to see what the disruption was about.

D'avry scratched his shoulder-length blond hair and smoothed it back, blinking and trying to reclaim that last image, to lock it into his memory. He knew it was important. He knew that it was the key to everything. He just didn't know what it meant.

Katherynn regarded him inquisitively and then walked across the red carpeted floor to where he was at. It was similar to that of the corridors that lined the ship, but here it was red with burgundy trim and the leather furnishings were all a deep, dark brown. She was a woman of average height, but there was a simple beauty to her. And in some way, a hard elegance, like highland royalty, D'avry thought. Rutker had told him that there may be less than 250,000 Epriots left after the forty-year siege. That number staggered him, but it was a fraction of what once was.

These were the remnants who'd survived. Rutker and Katherynn were two of their leaders. Given the honor of negotiating a truce with invading forces. D'avry filed this away as she drew near and sat next to him in the lounge. He knew Rutker fairly well at this point. Considered him an ally but was under no delusions that he would simply do as D'avry demanded. D'avry had pushed that envelope with the man and knew that he resented it but that he saw at least some of the truth behind the situation.

When D'avry had told him that Dexx was the saboteur and that the diplomatic packages were empty, he'd not believed him. But then, D'avry'd been proved right. It's partly why he'd agreed to go on the recon mission to the Gefkarri ship.

He knew Rutker trusted him, but only just. This new, formidable person in the mix could change that dynamic. And the two were married, so he assumed they were in agreement, though he knew that wasn't always a certainty. And they were back on their home turf. Allegiances could certainly be difficult to judge.

And, to make matters worse, the Astrig Ka'a wasn't here to guide him. No bailouts. No clever insights. Even his friends might not be his friends.

He thought this last and Seda sprang to mind. She was a wild card as well. Clearly, her allegiance lay with the hive mind, but ... he sensed something else there. Some little niggling doubt. He wanted to put much more thought into it, to get his mind around all of what had transpired and ultimately to how he was going to get back to E'rth, but he was concerned that too much focus, too much emotion would draw unwanted interest from the Gefkarri mind. He knew that it was possible to put himself, and present—and future—humanity at risk by doing so.

"Are you okay?" Katherynn asked. Despite his interrupting what was a serious matter of ships and orbital debris and planetary defense systems, she didn't seem perturbed with him. Rutker's wife exuded calm and caring. And intelligence. And D'avry understood that it could just as easily be a trap. All the while, he could feel Seda's attention like a heavy blanket on his psyche.

"Yes, thank you," D'avry replied, trying to brush off the last several years of dry camping and hustling for survival and skip back to the part of himself that had been an academic and a member of the Royal Society of Architects. And even his own pedigree as an underlord... as much as *that* ever gained him. He took a breath and smiled.

"I'm just working through the mechanics of this new magic and," he paused to form the right words, "it's considerably more ... involved than any previous I've encountered."

"Really? In what way? We don't actually have magic on Epriot Prime. Or any of the worlds we once occupied here in this system. I think it's fascinating that it's even a real thing."

D'avry had never considered that there were people that didn't know about any kind of magic at all. He'd assumed that Rutker was just used to something different from what D'avry had demonstrated. To be fair, D'avry had never heard of anything like what he did with the Astrig Ka'a.

"The flow of magic is different, with the Gefkarri," he told her. "It feels less and somehow more ... tangible. And ... it has a character to it that is very different. It's a form of nature magic, something we'd call Sylvan in my time-place."

"*That* raises so many questions, but let me focus on the original one. So not only is magic a real thing but there are different *kinds* of magic then?"

"Oh, yes. Not many, but, well, I guess there are quite a few. We have different kinds of practitioners of that magic, priests use it, but then there are wizards and sorcerers and necromancers," he cringed as if suddenly smelling something foul, "...and they employ different styles, but I'm the only one that I know of that uses the Astrig Ka'a."

"Astrig Ka'a? What's that?"

"Well, it's ... different. It's, well, it *was* more of a luck-based thing. It would just pop up and do whatever it wanted."

"*It* wanted? What do you mean by that?"

"Well, most magic is a type of energetic force and its practitioners use different means to manipulate it. Their ability to do so is based on the technology of spell weaving, potion craft, alchemy ... things like this. It can all be influenced by magical objects or objects made to be magical. Does that make sense?" He asked.

Katherynn squinted and nodded slowly as if indicating that maybe it didn't, but she was getting a general idea and he should continue.

"So, the Astrig Ka'a, though ... it's a force and would just take me to random places to meet with different people or do bizarre things. Right before this latest adventure, it dropped me outside an outpost and compelled me to drink and wager until I got run out of town. Then I stepped through a wall and I was a caribou in a river before turning back into my human form, where I nearly drowned and froze to death before I fell into a party of warriors trying to save a librarian from an undead orc warlord."

Katherynn was nodding but not in a way that meant she believed a word he said. Her eyes darted to Rutker, who just shrugged.

"An undead, like un-dead, like not living, but somehow ... animated?"

"Yes. By magic! A necromancer or necromantrix, I guess? She and the warlord were conspiring to usher in a new age where orcs ruled and humanity was their slave, but they tried to do it by capitalizing on a prophesied cosmic event—a red star fallen from the sky. Only instead of getting the army they desired, a new entity entered through a rift in space created by the fallen star. A dark army. The Void, I'm told."

"So, what the Gefkarri is saying is true?"

"Oh, yes. The Gefkarri never lies. Except by omission." He nodded to Seda and Theal, who deigned to ignore the poke.

"I see," said Katherynn, glancing back to Rutker and then returning her attention to D'avry before a shadow of a thought crossed her face, "D'avry, you said the Astrig Ka'a compels you to do things. Wouldn't that imply intelligence, a plan?" He nodded, not liking where this line of reasoning was going.

"Then who is it that controls the Astrig Ka'a? Is it like a god or something, like our Maker?"

"That's a great question. I don't know the answer. As I've said, I'm the only practitioner of its magic that I've ever heard of, and I've researched a lot. I've been chewing on this question for a while, but it's only been recently that I've operated under my own volition. Just since the lantern door, that I could, in a way, control outcomes rather than just being subjected to them. But still, it seems like the Astrig Ka'a intervenes. I don't know what it wants, but I think it has to do with—" he glanced covertly in Seda and Theal's direction. "Well, I think it's to do with the greater good of humanity. Since it's a human-centric magical construct," he finished lamely.

Katherynn nodded thoughtfully.

"Well, it doesn't matter much now though, since your magic is localized, right? That's what Rutker tells me and I've gleaned from our ... new allies."

"That's true. Now I'm a practitioner of the Gefkarri magical system and soon, who knows, maybe there is magic on Epriot Prime?"

As he said that last, he felt both Seda and Theal's attention fully on him. Their eyes were glowing with renewed intensity.

Suddenly, one of the viewscreens flashed, and a subtle rumble ran through the ship.

"What was that?" he asked, standing up but not quite sure for what purpose. Just general preparedness, he guessed. Before anyone could respond, he felt Seda and Theal's minds engulf his own and somehow the extents of the vessel. There had been contact with a foreign body and a glitter of debris sprayed away from the point of contact, along with a tiny bit of mist. Beyond, he could see the surface of the planet, half of it in darkness, the other half partially concealed in clouds, with tan and green and blue streaks peeking from the cracks. He was dumbstruck by the solitary beauty. A whole planet. The whole of the world that these people came from was below him. And upon the surface of it were the blood-thirsty Delvadr. And the loathed Chareth-Ul. And the unstoppable Void.

And here he was, connected to yet another wildcard entity, and between them all, like children playing on a busy street, were the humans. His race seemed so small and insignificant before such might. And yet, he knew that somehow humankind was the key. A universal key that could be used by anyone because of their ability to channel any kind of magic. Paenarcanum.

D'avry's mind flashed back to the bodies discarded by the destroyed mech. Were they using their magic to aid the mech? It was a Deathhound, so the pilot was a human who'd been coerced sometime in the past. Given long life in return for enslaving themselves to a machine of war. But the other two, that was a new twist.

Another flash of light entered the view, but this was from the planet's surface.

"Stop the ship!" he cried, "Reverse! Pull back!"

"Do it," Katherynn called out to the pilot, and the ship shuddered.

D'avry expected all of them to go flying, but then he remembered that there was some technology in effect that dampened the motion for the occupants. Rutker had explained that to a small degree. It sounded like magic to him, but they could call it what they liked.

"What's our status? Was it the Arcfire?"

"Yes, Ma'am. But we appear to be just at the outer limits of its effective range. Hence the density of the debris at this distance."

"Okay, can you hail EDC Central Command? Or anyone?"

"Afraid not, ma'am. We've had a call out on auto for the last half hour. It's still a garbled mess. It could be the other forces operating on the surface, scrambling comms. I wouldn't put it past the Delvadr, not trusting the temporary cease-fire."

"It could be a number of things. Or a combination," Rutker offered. "Do we know if there's a size limitation to what the

Arcfire can lock onto? I recall that some of the Elite mechs still breached orbit while other ships were being destroyed. Maybe smaller craft can make it down."

"What are you thinking?" Katherynn asked, a wary look in her eye.

"I'm thinking a HALO operation could work."

"What's that?" D'avry asked, certain that he wasn't going to like the answer.

CHAPTER 9

THE DEFILER

Epriot Prime, Preta Compact, Monther Accord

Galas's eyes fluttered open. Barely discernible through her dusty visor, she saw a shadow falling toward her out of the sky. It *looked* like a shadow. And it was about to land on her. For a shadow, it had really big claws and oddly glowing eyes.

With her head pointed downhill, it was relatively easy for her to pull her feet toward her chest and max out her repulsors just as the shadow crashed down on top of her.

Two things happened; the shadow creature rebounded back up into the air with a shriek, and Galas shot down the hillside of rock and rubble on her back.

It was a bumpy ride. And her head felt every bump. And so did the rest of her.

Within the relentless jostling, she felt a cool rush of chemicals course through her body. It might have been a pleasant sensation if she didn't feel like a hand grenade thrown in a blender.

"Welcome back," Raph offered cheerily.

"Good to be back," she gritted out through impact after impact until she finally skidded to a halt by rotating 180 degrees and sliding up onto unsteady legs.

Above her, the hillside crackled with shadowy figures as the Savages closed in. Farther up, a black cloud rolled over the ridge. But it wasn't a cloud. It was the other two regiments that had

The Defiler

just entered the battlefield through the dimensional rift created by the blackout beast.

"Maybe want to rethink that answer?" Raph asked.

Galas's mouth moved but nothing came out. Her focus drifted past the neon haze of SortieNet data to settle on the severed end of one of her grappling lines. Beyond that, the closest contingent was drawing in. She retracted the line, withdrew a replacement tool head from a storage compartment, and started running. She didn't know where to, just away. She needed time to think.

The Targe IV was a fast suit. On the fly, she tuned it to boost speed while she evaluated the BattleSpace model. It was pretty simple. Wide valley before her. Hordes of Void creatures and a dimensional rift containing possibly endless numbers more behind her.

Death seemed inevitable. But dying wasn't an option. High Command needed to know what was going on here on the southern continent. And Seraf was out there still, somewhere, with no idea that she had a mother. And, even more than that, one who loved her with every fiber of her being. She needed to know that.

And also, dying was bullshit.

Galas screamed across the terrain now that it had flattened out. She could keep this up for a little while. Five minutes maybe. Faster by far at a flat-out sprint than she could do on her own, but still, it was a *sprint*. She was going to gas out and from what she'd seen thus far, the Void pack could keep this up much longer.

That reminded her about the unknown element on the battlefield. She needed eyes on that massive issue before she could clear the area.

She fitted the tool head to the cleanly severed end of her grappling line as she ran.

"Raph, send two of the drones out to get eyes on what that new element is on the battlefield back there."

"Done. Do you have a plan for surviving long enough to actually tell someone about it?"

"Working on that."

"ETA 30 seconds on those drones."

"Great." She leaped a ravine, then a sandy wash, and then bounded up a low scrubby hillside. Ahead of her was 40 kilometers of the same. She was getting winded. She wouldn't make half that distance even if she slowed to a more moderate pace. Dread started to settle in. Then a new voice cut through the audio circuits but it was garbled,

"...Galas ... on way ... taking ... damage..."

"Jinnbo! You're alive! Are you okay?"

"Sorry ... can't ... hear well. You're saying ... good?" Jinnbo asked in his husky voice. That was *maybe* a good sign. She found this usually was indicative of his aggressive alter-ego. As compared to the simpering puddle of goo from earlier, anyway.

"No. Are *you* good?" she tried to restate as clearly as possible.

"Can't hear ... taking damage ... heading ... away."

His voice disappeared into static.

"No! Jinnbo! Don't go. I need you here!" She snapped a screenshot of what she was looking at in the BSM—her at the front and a fanned-out horde of enemy cursors behind her—and forwarded it to him. She hoped the image would make it through intact when the audio couldn't.

A similar image returned. At first she thought that the message just bounced back but closer inspection showed Jinnbo, in the Delvadr elite mech was also fleeing a horde of Void creatures, but, good news, he was angling her way. She angled slightly toward him.

Then the drone footage from the battlefield came online.

"What. The. Actual ... f—"

"Galas. It's a Deathhound. I think," Raph told her as the red cursor in the expanded Battlespace Model showing the original battlefield turned blue.

Galas did a double take. The two live feeds filled her dashboard. Both zoomed way out to encompass the behemoth before them. A city on legs, spewing clouds of black smoke, pouring rivers of black and orange filth from yawning, cavernous conduits.

It was a mech alright, but one to dwarf even the lunar mechs she'd piloted during the Delvadr second wave. By far. Multiples of multiples. This one mech could carry hundreds of traditional 5 to 40-ton Deathhounds.

And then, as if on cue, dozens of the smaller mechs streamed out of hangar bays scattered along its sides, falling a kilometer to the ground on sinewy threads that must have been cables as thick as Galas's waist.

The whole thing lurched in agonizingly slow motion, lifted a four-pronged foot, and then nearly thirty seconds later collapsed back down onto it. The ground buckled and shuddered with visible ripples emanating outward.

That's what the booming had been. The deep, resonant, far-distant boom.

Galas's mouth fell open as she struggled to absorb what she was seeing.

"The Deathhounds. They've had this all along?" she asked, unbelieving.

"No, the *Chareth-Ul* have had this all along. The Deathhounds are just what we call the possessed human-driven small and medium-sized hunter-killers."

"Where did you learn that?" Galas asked, panting now from the exertion of her flight and still reeling from the shock of this new revelation.

"I've been piecing together data from the Sanctum at Daxn where you defeated Sun-Thurr."

"*We*," she panted out, "*We* defeated."

"You did the fighting."

"Yeah, but you helped figure out … how he was using … his dimensional shifting ability. Wait, wait just a second?," she said as a realization began to resolve in her mind, "What's going on here? Is Epriot Prime the battleground for an *interdimensional* war? After all … we've gone through? With these preening alien bastards?!?" She snarled. She was going to have to slow down soon.

Raph tuned the O2 mix, administered electrolytes and without permission, goosed her levels of adrenalin.

"Oh! Oh, geez. Take it easy with that," she scolded, but the effects were immediate, "At least give me a warning."

"Noted. The old forgiveness versus permission thing."

"Yeah, spare me," she said but her mind was already back on the big issue. Not the hordes chasing after her issue, or the hordes attacking and chasing after her co-pilot who was driving her mech issue, but the Epriot Prime being ground zero for an interdimensional war issue. This after she just saved the bloody place.

She'd worked so hard to save her people. To save the planet and now it was going to get stomped into oblivion by armies that

Exile of the Pan Arcanum

were somehow even more terrifying than the one she so narrowly routed only two weeks prior.

The Delvadr were no slouches when it came to warfare and there were hundreds of billions of them and they had some of the best tech the Galaxy had to offer, but what was playing out in the Battlespace Model was absolutely gut-wrenching. For a second, she thought she might be sick. She knew Raph was monitoring her biometrics and rushed to head him off at the pass, "No, I'm not actually going to be sick. I just feel that way."

Silence. It meant that he was, in fact, about to administer anti-nausea medication but didn't want to have to justify that action and set a precedent.

A chime echoed through the audio circuits. Galas was still trying to get her mind around the situation. And despite Raph's efforts, she was slowing down. All of this may end up moot. She couldn't outrun the horde behind her.

Jinnbo crackled through, "Captain Galas?"

"Captain Major!" she yelled back ecstatically. Absolutely thrilled to hear his voice, "Field Colonel, actually."

"Oh really? That's great, I hadn't heard." He responded. He had heard, he'd just been in one of his deep melancholies.

A racket rang through the audio and she realized he was, as he'd stated before, under attack. Also, he and the mech were close enough for the power armor's limited comms to pick up.

A shriek echoed through Jinnbo's feed. Galas's blood ran cold.

"Gotta go," Jinnbo shouted before the feed went dead.

"Jinnbo. Jinnbo!" She was certain that was the last time she would hear his voice. That shriek was the same sound that she'd heard when she'd kicked the void creature off of her up on the hillside. What chance did Jinnbo have against one of those? Especially in the close quarters inside a mech.

She carved hard to the right to cut short the distance between herself and her imperiled copilot.

"Galas. Do you think this may be the time to consider making a very difficult decision?" Raph asked. His tone was meek, but firm. Almost apologetic.

She assumed he meant the kind of difficult decision that involved letting one's co-pilot fend for himself and likely die so that at least *someone* could get away and provide critical intel to

EDC High Command. He was an AI after all. And he had a legitimate concern, but …

"No. It is never going to be the time for that." She'd lost too much already.

The chime happened again inside the SortieNet.

"What *is* that, anyway?"

There was a pause, "It may be something requiring your attention at another time."

"Something for another time? I don't understand. It sounds like what you're saying is stay focused and don't die, then we can talk." Galas scanned the BSM but didn't see anything new. She didn't like to be told what was and was not important by her AI. Regardless if he was right most of the time.

"I can't see what's new here. Why can't I see it?"

"It's because the newcomer isn't on the battlefield, Ma'am. It's in the sky," Raph provided in his usual, casual academic tone. "But really, I think it can wait."

She desperately scanned the data from the SortieNet. There was nothing in the sky. But then she saw what he was talking about on the long long-range array. The intrastellar map. There was a large blip next to Epriot Prime. Something the size of a small moon was parked in far orbit.

"Raph. Someone just parked a moon outside our planet. How is that *not* relevant?"

"It's not a moon. It's a Thune build, like the Delvadr use but nothing that matches our files. I've never seen anything like it. Of course, there's a lot of interference due to the band of debris hanging around up there."

It was true. The sky was so thick with wreckage from the failed invasionary armada that the sun's light was dimmer than usual and occasionally large chunks of debris would present themselves as partial eclipses. Two weeks after the carnage, and flaming chunks of debris were still falling from the sky—and would be for months to come.

She checked the BSM and the feeds again. She was converging on the path of her mech and the hordes behind each were converging on each other when suddenly a massive blast washed a concussive wave across the plains and with a huge wall of dust along with it.

Galas flew off her feet, flipping through the air before hitting the ground and rolling to a halt. Suddenly the sky was dark. The flood lights on either side of her helmet lit up but did nothing to illuminate what was above her. Her eyes darted to find some point of reference and slowly found the edges of the structure. Far to the sides gray sky peeked around the edges of something that bore more resemblance to a city than anything else. Her mind flashed back to a shuttle approach to one of the massive EDC interstellar carriers. It was like that. Only this had legs.

Waterfalls of filth crashed to the valley floor from above. And, then hundreds of thin filaments shot out from the sides and belly of the structure. And on them, what seemed to be tiny little spiders began to descend. Only, it was clear that they were not tiny at all but rather, quite large. Mech-sized in fact.

This was what she'd seen in the video feeds earlier. This was the Chareth-Ul mother ship, or rather, mother mech. Somehow referring to it as a mother of anything defiled the word. And descending upon her from above were hundreds of Deathhounds. More than had ever been seen in one place. Until earlier today at least. She was not excited about this discovery. She was the opposite of that.

Her concern about the hordes chasing her was legitimate. But right now, all she could think about was Jinnbo in their mech. Fighting a mech in a power suit, she knew from experience, was a losing game. Fighting hundreds? She hoped beyond hope he'd found some way to stay alive and keep her mech intact.

Jinnbo's sensitive ears detected a disturbance. A howl that sounded like it came from a wounded animal filled the interior of the heisted mech he was finally getting to pilot. He was doing an excellent job too, stomping across the plains like a gestating Fnurlik heifer.

Somehow Captain Galas had fallen out the back but she could take care of herself. She was a god-like warrior queen, slaying hordes with a saucy glare and dual-wielding plasma blades. And rockets. And in some cases, rocks attached to ropes.

He split his consciousness between the multiple demands of driving the mech, evaluating the SortieNet's battlespace model, and using his echolocation abilities to detect the whereabouts of the creature that had hacked its way inside and was, he was sure, stalking him in order to end his life. He, Jinnbo, of the semi-royal line of Fnurlik herders. Ghastly behavior.

His ability to use a gland in his throat to generate an ultrasonic sequence of chirps that then resonated within a gel-filled cavity in his head was all new. Post-evil-twin rite of passage new. As such, he wasn't very good at it. Still, using this ability, a large figure that roughly resembled the creatures now swarming the countryside seemed to be darkening his doorway.

Jinnbo thought commands through the SortieNet hardware in his head and Raphael the AI took over piloting the mech. He did this while he unclipped and rolled out of his co-pilot's seat. The seat blew up in a cloud of stuffing as the nightmarish being burst forward and slashed multiple times where Jinnbo had just been.

Only now, he was out the door and down the hall.

The creature shrieked again. This time with more rage. Jinnbo darted down the hatch into the OPS module as he tried to formulate his plan for not getting similarly eviscerated. He chirped, but it turned out that he couldn't quite do echolocation around corners. But he was sure he'd get a second chance soon enough.

Then sparks and a great rending noise erupted from the far corner of the space as a new creature squeezed through the opening. It stalked through the space, at first on all fours and then standing upright as it seemed to sniff the air. Its red eyes squinted, but then the creature blipped up the ladder and through the hatch.

Jinnbo let his stealth slip back to his comfortable default of natural pigmentation and his jungle print shirt uniform. It was tiresome camouflaging to a moving environment, and now he needed to move.

He could have squeezed out the hole just created by the Void creature and escaped to freedom. He may still, but for now, he could not have the creatures destroying the mech. If anyone was going to do it. It'd be himself. Jinnbo Nraljherder, Third (and favorite) Nephew to the Crown Matriarch.

He maneuvered a paw through a series of movements within a virtual interface and a storage cell slid up from the floor. On it were grenades. He grabbed two and headed for the hatch. He chirped and found that with a reflective wall and ceiling above him, he could kind of "see" down the hall. Two creatures were there. He carefully set an armed grenade at his feet and chucked the other on, banking it off the wall and listening to it as it rolled down the corridor toward the creatures.

Of course, they blinked away as soon as they recognized what it was. Of course, they blinked in the direction of where the grenade had come from, which was down the hatch. And, of course, Jinnbo was through the hole in the exterior of the mech and clinging to the outside when the actually armed grenade went off.

A double-burst of bright white light punched through the hole.

"What did you do?!?" Raphael asked, and then continued, "Where are you, anyway?"

"I... I..." but Jinnbo couldn't finish the sentence. Killing those creatures was just so ... sad. His insides churned with palpable anguish. And he wailed it out, "What have I done? They were so..."

"Deadly? Remorseless? Evil?"

"Pure! And beautiful..." he whimpered, "They were pure and beautiful, like big, black puppies that just wanted to play... and I KILLED THEM."

"Just hang on, Jinnbo. I've located you, I think. We'll get Galas to help us out. Would you like that?"

Jinnbo couldn't bring himself to respond. He just held on to the outside of the alien mech and wallowed in the shame at what he'd done.

And then an explosion, louder than anything he'd ever heard before, shook the earth and threw dirt and dust hundreds of feet into the air.

It took a moment, but when the air cleared, there before him was a mech like nothing he'd ever seen before. And it all still meant nothing in the face of the horror he'd committed.

CHAPTER 10
PELL-MELL AND BERZERK

Her mech *was* intact. But she wasn't sure for how long. And she was gassed from the long sprint. She doubted it would matter. The wave of black closing in on her from behind, to her right, and ahead was impossible to count. She was an optimist by nature, but ... this was bleak.

She scanned the field ahead. On the other side of a foot that was larger than her whole village of Kozst—and taller than any building in it by multiples—was her mech. And it was racing toward her.

"Atta boy, Jinnbo!"

Raphael, however, highlighted a small dot below the mech's command-and-control module mounted in the middle of its broad chest. Just below that was the offending speck. She zoomed in and was pretty certain she was looking at nothing.

"What are you highlighting? It just looks like a smudge of carbon next to a gash in the armor."

"Check your thermals."

She made the switch and there, plain as day, was a Jinnbo-shaped hotspot.

"No," she exclaimed in the way that people do when they can't believe what they're seeing because, frankly, she couldn't believe it.

She'd left him in charge of the mech. And now, well, *it* was still operating, but he was not on the inside where he belonged.

Technically, she acknowledged that he was close enough to pilot the mech with the SortieNet hardware and Raphael's hacks but... she zoomed in... his body language gave the impression that, in addition to clinging to the outside of the mech for dear life, he was in a not-good place emotionally. The hang of his head, the slouch of his shoulders ... he was at the low swing of the emotional roller coaster,

"Oh, Jinnbo... now?!?"

Deathhounds touched down. Void creatures launched into the attack.

Pretty much all hell broke loose as the behemoth mech overhead shifted its weight and started to lift that one gargantuan foot off the ground. Galas dug deep and sped forward to get to it. She hoped going over it would be faster than going around, but one of the larger mechs, a Chacma-class, landed in front of her. It was built out for riot control with a chain blade on one hand and a concussion shield on the other.

Probably the right call, she thought as she slid between its legs, zippering its underside with laser and plasma fire before it could shield up. A pack of the wolf-like Savages hit it from the side while the pilot tried to regroup from the unconventional attack, but it was hopeless.

The pilot ripped loose with everything he had, swinging the chain blade and shield wildly, rockets, and laser cannons firing in every direction. Galas was able to slip through in the chaos, but then another Void creature blinked into her path. Her plasma blades were out within a fraction of a second of the collision. She punched through the supernova blast, feeling a weird tingling in her chest as she did. But then it was over and she saw her narrow window of opportunity shrink to nothing as the foot rose out of reach.

She leaped anyway, hoping to make up the distance with repulsors, but a Void creature caught her foot, knocking her sideways and pulling her down into the deep, dark impression.

Under, it is. She lanced out with her plasma cannon at the creature while launching a grappling line at the bottom of the foot that was quickly rising away. A dangerous game, playing around under the feet of giants. The creature below her burst into a blinding ball of light. She felt that tingle again. She wasn't sure what that sensation was, but she hoped it didn't have any lasting effects. Not likely, of course.

The ground dropped away fast, even as the wave of hordes flooded into the colossal imprint in the earth beneath her. *That was lucky*, she thought, but then that feeling quickly began to fade as she rose higher and higher into the air. Where was she going to go before the foot came down again?

At that moment, that's exactly what started to happen. Instead of swinging up toward the foot, it was coming down at her with increasing speed. She flipped upside down and initiated her repulsors in the reverse mode, which caused them to act like magnets.

She stuck the jarring, inverted landing and watched in barely suppressed terror as the ground rushed up to meet her.

"Ahem," Raphael interrupted while highlighting the mech still racing across the ground in her direction. It had collected more bad guys. Jinnbo was still clinging to the space below the command module and clearly unable to help.

"The global network is still down, due to all the trash in near orbit, but I've established line-of-sight laser comms with the hijacked mech," Raph was saying, but Galas had already taken over.

Her SortieNet dashboard was split between feeds from her suit and from the mech. Both launched into the air. Her, coming down off the bottom of the massive mech's foot, and the hijacked mech blasting at an upward angle with massive amounts of lift. Galas had forgotten just how reliant the Delvadr Elite mechs were on powered flight when they weren't skulking around with their stealthing on.

The ground was a carpet of Deathhounds and Void creatures locked in mortal combat. Rockets exploded on the ground and in the air around them. Galas's mech flew into view below her and she lashed out with her grappling line just as she shunted the mech's shields. Tricky business.

They were going to be sitting ducks until she could clear the Void creatures and get inside. That was, unless the city-sized boot chasing them down to the ground didn't get there first.

Galas's grappling line caught. She swung underneath and stuck her repulsors. A Void creature blinked into view from the edge, silhouetted by a setting sun that had finally dipped below the cloud cover. It leaped straight at her, but she'd already blasted off and was swinging away as she blistered the creature with plasma. Meanwhile, she corrected the mech's flight to avoid errant laser fire from below, which assisted her swing back to the topside—technically it's back and arguably the worst place to be hanging out on an unshielded mech due to its reactor pack.

She filed that away as another of the creatures blinked into view. Galas split her virtual dashboard between armor ops, mech piloting control, and the shrinking window of daylight between the Chareth-Ul mech's colossal footsole and the ground rushing up to meet it. Her stomach clenched. The gap was despairingly small.

She ran forward, placed her line, and swung precisely down to the front. Just below the command module, passing two more Void creatures along the way. Galas adjusted the mech's flight, angling for the narrowing gap of daylight.

She switched to thermals and saw Jinnbo's form just as she clanged down around him.

"Hold on buddy," she said as she shot another line to her right and cinched down as hard as she dared without crushing him.

Then she cranked the repulsors to full, and the mech catapulted forward. The Void creatures, who'd blinked forward to catch her, tumbled uselessly off the speeding mech, unable to find purchase when it wasn't where they'd left it. Daylight between the foot and the horde of creatures covering the ground diminished to nearly nothing as they cleared the edge.

A massive boom and burst of light exploded behind them as Galas struggled to pull the mech up out of its shallow, exceptionally low-altitude dive. Mechs and creatures sped by beneath and to the sides of them. They flew through flames and shrapnel. Galas shunted the mech's repulsors back to 100 percent while boosting shields, and they tore through exploding Void creatures like a meteor. Then the shielding skipped off the terrain. A blinding display of arcing purple-white plasma played out only meters behind her as she clung to the mech, protecting her co-pilot with her power armor-clad body.

The mech bounced off the terrain once more and then into the air just as a Deathhound loomed into view before them. Filth and sulfur smoke belched from stacks on its back as it brought its chain guns up to bear.

Galas went to use one of the mech's grappling lines to anchor to the ground and spin her end for end, but she'd forgotten that Delvadr mechs don't carry those, so instead she lanced out her plasma blade, driving it into the ground which accomplished nearly the same thing. Albeit with less grace and a hell of a lot of flying rock and arcing plasma.

Her mech flipped end for end. The Deathhound opened fire and then she slammed her repulsors to full once more.

The other mech took the combined force of her repulsors and her momentum, full to the chest, launching into the air and exploding from reactor failure along the way. That explosion cleared the straggling Savages in the area. Galas's mech hit the ground and Galas and Jinnbo both lost their grip, falling ten full meters to the churned-up earth below.

Luckily, Galas was in her power armor and could take a fall. Jinnbo, well, he was a monkey-fox-bat thing and so simply glided to the ground without incident.

"You came back for me..." they both said, which would have been sweet except for the Deathhounds and Void creatures collapsing on them from all sides.

They shared a quick glance of concern before bolting in separate directions. Jinnbo back up into the breach in the mech's hull and Galas around the backside to the cargo entrance since she wouldn't fit through the hole in the mech's torso.

"Raph, hold 'em off!" Galas cried as she slipped into the open hatch and hunted for a place to strap in, deciding just to hold on to rigging in the main corridor rather than dismount from the suit again.

Laser, plasma, projectile, and rocket fire erupted from all around the mech as text floated across the inside of her corneal implants,

[Raph: On it.]

"Jinnbo, you locked in?"

Another message, this one a video simply of him nodding his head while fighting back tears.

I can't wait until this hormone thing is over with, she thought as the mech leaped off the ground and initiated flight mode once more.

The mech was rocked by concussions from missiles and rockets exploding against her shields, but they managed to put some distance without getting tangled up. She watched as the city-sized mech bloomed from just a foot to a leg and then to the entirety of it in its full glory before slowly, over an inordinate amount of time, it diminished to a distant silhouette, occasionally lit up from below by the ongoing battle.

A ding chimed in the SortieNet.

She barely registered the noise, but it didn't sink in as to what it was. She was just too exhausted. But then it did it again.

"Raph? Make it stop. Wait. What is that again?"

"It's the moon-sized alien craft parked in far orbit."

"Frag. Forgot about that."

"Are we headed to EDC High Command?"

She fought with her better instincts.

"No. Kind of. We'll hail some jarheads and let them know what's going on down here. Meanwhile, we've got a date with the Arcfire. I don't care if it's the Saints of Galapides V on a holy mission of galactic charity. They can join the dust cloud if they think they're coming down here."

Two hours later, the sun was dipping behind coastal mountains in a dazzling display of pink and amber that defied the planet-shattering revelations from earlier. The dark, non-reflective belly of a marine heavy transport—affectionately referred to as a Pond-Bumble—swooped into view. It blew a wall of dust into the air, thrashing a stand of spindly m'neccam trees before hovering over the left shoulder pauldron of the Hail Mary. That's what Galas had decided to name her hijacked mech on account of the absolutely, mind-numbing implausibility of completion of the Arcfire mission. Not to mention that little soiree with the Void and the Chareth-Ul defiler earlier.

So, the name seemed fitting. Galas, over her lifetime, had not seen much use for religion. But there seemed to be no end of evil, so it just stood to reason that there must be something pretty damned good hiding somewhere out there in the universe to balance it all out.

She decided she'd go easy on the Saints of Galapides V if it was them up there, but she was pretty certain it wasn't. And Raph wasn't placing odds. So there was that.

Another transport was off in the distance, humming over the hills just west of them.

It would take both to carry her to the other side of the Preta Compact—an archipelago of chunky islands that amounted to a continent of their own and the site of most of the Delvadr remnant's activities thus far. An area now holding the dubious honor as the site of first contact with The Void and the first incursion by the Chareth-Ul's massive, city-sized Defiler mechs. Galas had named it a Defiler partly because of its obscene size—it held hordes of Deathhound mechs and masses of bug-like Makrit psych-bullies and psych-hoppers amassed on its plaza-sized decks.

But the name Defiler stuck when she saw, perched atop its vast surface, three large temple structures, dark-robed figures with antler horns and arms outstretched as if conducting a demonic orchestra had stood there. They looked nearly identical to Sun-Thurr, the dimension-shifting necromancer she'd slain beneath the mountain, in the Sanctum at Braex.

Galas tapped her fingers impatiently. She'd been trying to meditate away the growing knot in her stomach that never seemed to go away. Time was running out. With each passing minute, the strange new Thune-built megacarrier drew closer to Epriot Prime's inner orbit.

She huffed out, blowing a strand of auburn hair out of the way just to have it fall back into her face. Galas reached behind her where her cap was sitting and slid it onto her head. She realized she hadn't expected it to be there. She'd gotten so used to her dead ex-boyfriend's malevolent shenanigans that she almost missed them now that he was gone.

She lived a strange life. She could admit that. Her eyes focused on the growing image of the second transport as it blocked out her view of the diminishing sunset.

It'd taken an hour of flight time to hit the exfil site, twenty minutes to establish communication, and nearly thirty minutes just to convince the closest marine command post, an isolated island that most everyone had forgotten about, that she was who she said she was.

Most assumed she'd died months if not years ago. To say that the Epriot forces that remained at this point in the war were scattered and ill-informed was putting it mildly. Some estimates said that there were less than a quarter million humans left. Anywhere. And those were not conservative numbers.

Very few were not actively engaged in the fighting, that was for certain. That meant that there were grandmas and grandpas driving mechs, flying transports, hell, leading infantry. After forty-three years of staging what amounted to a fighting retreat across the solar system, humanity was a breath away from extinction. And the few members left were hard as nails and more than a few were bent beyond recognition and very difficult to negotiate with. Of course, it didn't help her argument that she was driving an enemy mech.

First, they'd argued that they didn't have the resources. Then they'd argued that she couldn't possibly be *the* Cadian Galas because she was dead or lost in some uncharted jungle or other, killed by Deathhounds no less. Lastly, they argued that they just had no way of interfacing with the alien hardware she'd stolen.

She called bullshit on all of it. The fact that she was hailing them from a Delvadr Elite pretty much answered the first two questions. Only *The* Cadian Galas could have heisted an Elite and only an Elite could have gotten her this far. And the last question? Well, after all that, she wasn't about to let some low-level jarhead tell her they couldn't give her a lift because they couldn't figure out how to use their grappling lines. Even if that jarhead pilot was old enough to be her grandma.

What she didn't tell them was that she was ready and willing to shove her own grappling lines right up their collective asses to get the job done. But by that point, she didn't have to.

The other Pond-Bumble hovered up beside the first, dropped two mag plates on heavy cables, and within seconds they were peeling out, Hail Mary's boots skimming the fiery orange-pink foliage of towering tumenum trees as they cleared the edge of the rise.

Marines complained a lot, but in the end they would always get the job done.

The trio swung west, toward the luminous glow of the Horseneck Nebula as it rose above the horizon and grew in brilliance with the sun behind them just beginning to dip over the horizon. She settled in for the rest of the journey, just as trees gave way to golden dunes, streaked with long shadows, which in time succumbed to crystalline turquoise seas diminishing into a deep violet and then finally to full black with splinters of starlight cast by the nebula.

She could have flown Hail Mary herself and not waited, but by the time she hit the shores near Nadas Barrn her power cells would have been expended, and she would have had to stop to sleep and run her rocket fab over max to refill her stocks. There was no way she was going back into that jungle with only a partial armory. Also, she wanted the EDC to have a direct download of everything the SortieNet had recorded for analysis purposes. Humanity couldn't afford to let their tattered global comms network garble that hard-fought data.

Plus this way, she was fresh and ready and could figure out exactly who she was about to blow out of the sky with the Arcfire before she did it. That was the one thing about the prior race's planetary defense system. You couldn't just leave it on autopilot. Someone had to man the trigger even if that man was a woman.

CHAPTER 11
THE DEBRIS FIELD

Epriot Prime, Middle Orbit, *Xandraitha's Hope*

"So you're saying that outside of this craft, it's dark, there is no air, and it's so cold the fluids in my body will freeze, even while I—what was it... depressurize? *And* it's hundreds of miles to the planet's surface. So far, in fact, that we'll need to strap rocket engines to our bodies to hurtle us very fast toward the planet and then to slow us down enough that we don't burn up in the atmosphere or make a very small but personal-sized crater on the surface? And you thought *my* plan was stupid?!?"

"This is not an *atypical* mission. We do this sort of thing all the time," Rutker argued.

"Do you???" D'avry asked, his voice cracking, running his hand nervously through his long blond hair.

"When have you done this sort of thing before?" Katherynn asked.

"Well, EDC Marines do this ... frequently. I've been trained on it, just never had to do it personally. However, I did have to ditch at near orbit in one of my last engagements. It went ... as well as could be expected anyway."

"You never told me that," Katherynn said, eyeing him and then casting her gaze toward Mads and Macq, who quickly looked away. She smiled curtly.

Rutker grimaced. "It was classified," he grumbled, not looking at her.

"I'm sorry, I'm still stuck on this armor suit and rocket thing. Aren't we in a debris field? Doesn't that mean something?" D'avry asked, trying not to let the desperation he was feeling creep into his voice.

"Yeah, that'll be the tricky part," Rutker conceded.

"You say that like it's the *only* tricky part. It sounds like it's *all* tricky parts." D'avry's mouth was dry. His peripheral vision was beginning to shrink, and he felt a faint tingling in his extremities.

Seda stepped in. "Do not worry, Mage D'avry. Our link will help you maintain composure and focus."

"Actually," Theal interrupted, "I think it's best if you stay on the human ship and act as a node for our link to the Pentarch. Since your connection to this human is stronger and more likely to overcome the distances involved."

Seda's eyes flared almost imperceptibly and then cooled.

Theal continued, "I will perform this HALO drop, assisting the humans, and then conduct the negotiations with their Central Command before establishing the link with the Chareth-Ul and Delvadr remnant."

Seda smiled. "Of course, Aspect Theal. That is ... the most prudent course of action. I will ensure the link between the Pentarch and yourself via the human mage is stalwart." Her attention shifted to D'avry and seemed almost apologetic. D'avry was struggling to understand the dynamics between this pair. He was also unnerved by the fact that he was infinitely more comfortable around Seda, with her disquieting interest in him and terrifying temper than he was around Theal.

Rutker stepped forward. "Just why do you need D'avry for any of this? Don't you have your own self-contained magic or whatever?"

"Yes, they do," D'avry jumped in, not liking the way that everyone was talking about him like he wasn't in the room, "But because this is a different planet, which supposedly has its own ethereal field," he said, looking to Theal and Seda to be sure he'd gotten the term right. "It helps to have me along since humans are Pan Arcanum, or universal in terms of magical energy and environments. That means that in addition to being able to utilize the native environment's magical field, I will be better able to facilitate the link with the Chareth-Ul and the Delvadr as well.

"The Gefkarri Pentarch's collective mind has the processing capacity and scalability to manage all aspects of the battle, but I can help to bolster that communication."

A thought occurred to him, and he turned to the two aspects. "Is that why the Epriots aren't mentioned as a separate fighting contingent on their own? Do you intend to train others of us to perform the same role that you intend for me? I mean, that would make sense—"

Theal stepped forward abruptly. "The role that humankind will play in this engagement remains to be seen."

"What do you mean you haven't determined what role we'll play? Epriots are fighters. We've held off the Delvadr with their numbers and superior weaponry for decades." Macq retorted. Mads's arms fell to his sides and away from his body as if he were ready to start the fighting right then.

"Your kind were on the brink of extinction until you stumbled upon a prior race's technology, which saved you by only the barest of margins. And, in the end, was only a reprieve before the real threat arose," replied Theal. "The Gefkarri will determine how this battle plays out. Do not think this is the only theater." Her hands spread wide. "We are the Pentarch. Just one of many aspects of the greater being."

Then her hands branched out to create clusters scattered throughout the space of the bridge. "All are engaged in campaigns against the incursion across the breadth of the galaxy. The Septarch is already lost." One of the clusters shriveled and retreated back. "And that, for lack of a unifying force."

She looked at D'avry. "Certainly, humankind will play a role. But wasting that resource as cannon fodder may not serve the greater good." She turned her gaze to Mads and then to Macq and then to the rest of the men and women assembled on the bridge. "I will be the one to determine that. That is why we must make haste to the surface before the Void rolls over the scattered armies assembled before it and makes the question moot."

Theal then turned to Rutker. "Capt. Major, please lead the way to our suits and to the airlock so we may disembark immediately," she said, motioning with an open palm toward the back of the ship.

Rutker's lips pressed into a thin line. He turned to Macq. "Go get Col. Dexx. We're going to need him to spell out to EDC command how the Gefkarri intend to engage the Void with the help of the Delvadr ... and the Epriots," he said pointedly, looking at Theal. "This was his plan all along anyway."

"Wait a second." Katherynn grabbed his arm. "You're not leaving me here are you?"

"Yes, that's exactly what I'm doing. You don't have experience for this kind of jump and if things go wrong, you'll need to work with the Gefkarri to manage a solution that doesn't involve blowing our home planet to pieces. They haven't brought that up, but it's the only option left if they can't get down to the surface because of the Arcfire," he looked at Theal once more and then at Seda before focusing again on Katherynn. He grabbed her arms in his. "Mads will stay here with you and the rest of the crew." Mads seemed about to object, but a look from his father quelled his fire. He drew himself up and nodded.

Then Rutker leaned in to kiss his wife and D'avry heard him whisper, "I suggest you get to know Seda real well. She's the only one around here with a conscience. Maybe. Besides, I don't trust anyone else to negotiate with the Collective. Just you."

Katherynn nodded, lips pursed. Clearly not happy with this turn of events but accepted his evaluation.

D'avry, on the other hand, was shocked that she seemed just as ready to jump out of a perfectly good spaceship as Rutker was. The whole lot of them were completely mad.

Macq exited to round up the traitorous colonel. Rutker, D'avry, and Theal headed toward the main corridor that would take them to the armory—or what was left of the armory after the sabotage attempt that caused the *Xandraitha's Hope* to crash land on E'rth in the first place. D'avry eyed the char marks and hastily repaired surfaces. He tried to dispel the feeling that they were a portent of what the future had in store for them.

Though she was in another part of the ship, D'avry could feel Seda's focus on him as he stood on the edge of the platform looking at the broad, cloud-streaked surface of a planet that took up almost his entire field of view. Turquoise oceans, pink sand deserts, vibrant orange forests peeked from behind those clouds. And surrounding it all was the inky blackness of space. It punctuated just how foreign this entire experience was. Flexibility had always been a strong suit, but everyone had their limits. He was miles beyond his.

D'avry's breath rattled loudly in his ears through speakers that amplified his voice and allowed him to communicate with the others—Rutker, Macq, and Dexx at least. He could communicate with Theal at will telepathically. And he always had Seda in the back of his head now. Her wry smile and apparent amusement at everything that caused him discomfort also caused him discomfort.

Her being in his head was an egregious invasion of privacy, but he couldn't undo it. He just had to be very careful with his thoughts. The voice inside his head that usually stayed inside his head was now on permanent broadcast to the whole of the collective that was the Gefkarri Pentarch. Which was beyond embarrassing. He just had to be mindful of how prominent those thoughts became. He realized now that some were like whispers and others were as good as shouting.

He'd never realized how randomly offensive his own thoughts were until they were being listened to by an alien super-entity. Oh well. They asked for it. But it was a drain on him, mentally, having to constantly adjust the volume of his thoughts.

Rutker tapped him on the shoulder and he jolted, feeling like he was going to fall all the way to the surface of the planet. His eyes shot wide. "What're you doing?!? You nearly gave me a heart attack."

"Breathe D'avry. Slow and steady. And don't lock your legs. You'll constrict the blood flow and pass out. And then when you do wake up, you might be choking on your own vomit." He smiled and gave a thumbs-up.

D'avry looked away. "Thanks for the pep talk," he mumbled. When he didn't hear a response, he looked back at Rutker quizzically.

The man shook his head. "I don't know how you understand my language. I always assumed it was your magic, but it doesn't seem to help you understand hand gestures. This means 'good' or 'okay'." He did the sign again, and D'avry nodded.

He then turned it over. "This means bad. Got it?"

D'avry gave him a thumbs up and Rutker smiled. It would have been disarming if it wasn't so foreign to their interaction thus far, the smile that was. It made D'avry somehow even more nervous.

"Now remember, I have your suit linked to my own. It's going to mimic my movements but delayed and about a thousand meters back. You do not need to manually adjust anything, you just need to jump when I tell you to jump and enjoy the ride. Good?"

D'avry did the thumbs thing again.

"Good." Rutker smiled. It appeared genuine, which was the unnerving part. He really seemed to be enjoying himself.

"What if something goes wrong?" D'avry asked, trying to keep his eye from twitching while he said it.

"It won't. I'm going to guide us through the debris field. We'll slow down as we approach the atmosphere. We'll freefall for about ten minutes and then I'll kick in our rockets again. Actually, they're spool repulsors, but I didn't figure you'd know what that meant."

"It's okay. I don't technically understand what rockets are either," he said, smiling, though he could tell Rutker didn't quite buy it. Instead, the Captain Major flashed the thumbs up and turned away toward Macq and the Gefkarri aspect, Theal.

Dexx apparently already knew the drill. The look on his face didn't encourage optimism. D'avry didn't like the look of him to begin with. His face was angular in a blocky way; hard and calculating. The face of a man who could sacrifice 43 of his own men and call it collateral damage.

D'avry could sense Theal's trepidation and there was a tiny part of him that he allowed to enjoy it. At least he wasn't the only one that was scared out of their mind. He had the sense that Theal simply exported unwanted emotion to be absorbed by the collective. He wondered how she did that. It was a cool trick.

He felt Seda laughing at his discomfort and he ignored her. *Don't worry, you're not out of this yet*, he thought.

He found that he still just knew things, even though he wasn't in contact with the Astrig Ka'a anymore. There was some sort of latent magical ability, either intrinsic to himself or to humankind. He wasn't sure which. It could be that he simply absorbed magical power like a leach and could use small amounts of it on a discretionary basis. The whole thing was fascinating that way. If he ever lived to tell about it, he would be the discoverer of a whole new branch of magical research. It could also be that the universe itself had an underlying layer of an ethereal nature. Could the planets and celestial bodies be just a focus of it? The same way that the artifacts he was hunting for seemed to focus aspects of the Astrig Ka'a. There it was again, that word. Aspects.

There was so much to learn. He found that he was looking forward to setting foot on this new planet and exploring the ethereal powers there. To have his real powers back... He quickly suppressed the thought, not wanting to give too much away. But to have his powers back and not be chained to either Theal or Seda in order to tap into it? He couldn't wait.

Then maybe he could figure out a way to get back to E'rth. Of course, there was this nagging issue of humanity still being stuck on Epriot Prime to be used as a pawn in some massive interdimensional battle.

Used—that was the operative term. He thought of his own predicament, chained at least figuratively, to his Gefkarri handlers. Used or used up? That was the question, and he didn't like the answer that seemed the most likely.

His stomach twisted in knots. That was exactly why Theal was less than forthright about humanity's role in the battle. They *were* going to be used. War-slaves, he believed, was the term. He barely registered movement off to his left until he heard the word, "Jump!"

D'avry froze in place. He knew he was supposed to go but couldn't make his feet move. Then his repulsors fired automatically. His stomach contorted again as he screamed through the acceleration until he had to breathe to scream again.

"D'avry! Do I have to mute you?" Rutker's voice came over the comms.

He blinked and breathed and watched helplessly as the glowing disk of the planet stabilized in his forward view, and the deepest black engulfed everything in the periphery.

Instead of his own breathing, he felt the vibration and heard a low roar, not dissimilar to the sound of a large waterfall he couldn't see. He breathed in and closed his eyes, trying to meditate his way through the terror.

It started to work. A little. Then something jostled him out of his shallow, meditative state. Then a few more somethings pinged off his armor suit.

"Guys ... er, people? Team? I don't know what to call this squad? Are we a squad?" His voice was rising with each question.

Maybe Rutker had muted him after all.

Katherynn's voice came over comms. It was a bit garbled but still strong.

"Xander One, this is Xander Base."

"Xander Base, this is Xander One Actual," Rutker replied.

"Rutker, we have a problem."

CHAPTER 12

THE ARCFIRE

Epriot Prime, Preta Compact, Braex
(Capital City of Antiquity)

The Temple promontory at Braex jutted out of a vine-choked mountainside like a boar tusk. Before it, large swaths of jungle had been burned away. Charred stone structures of peculiar design basked in the warm yellow rays of Epriot Sol's radiation for the first time in millennia.

Galas banked the newly-dubbed Hail Mary toward the temple plaza carved out of the mountain a thousand meters above the river below. A wispy white plume cascaded from the temple structure itself, toward the valley floor.

She remembered having to climb the falls at Xiocic, Braex's sister city to the south. The first half she'd done in Betsy, her old mech. The second half, in just her power armor. She also remembered falling down that waterfall after a too-close rocket detonation temporarily crippled the suit.

Here, at Braex, she'd fought for her life, first against her co-opted mech, and then within it. Oddly, the fight was against the combined threat of the Deathhound Overseer Naar who—in addition to being soulbound to the Chareth-Ul—had been possessed by her psychotic poltergeist ex-boyfriend. In life, Drakas had always been a little jealous, but homicidal? Apparently, death does something to a person.

Not even Galas could rationalize away that toxic aspect of their relationship.

The somewhat less-than-pristine Hail Mary dropped gracefully to the stone-cobbled plaza grounds while she continued her scan of the area. Everything *seemed* in place. Just like she left it only now there were no fiery streaks of inbound dropships or spacecraft wreckage scarring the sky.

Off in the far distance, there was something going on though. She hoped it wasn't another one of those dimensional rifts, but there was smoke and the occasional flash of light. She'd have to investigate it later. Right now, she had an unwanted visitor in outer orbit and they needed to know that Epriot Prime was a no-fly zone.

"Jinnbo, I'm going to EVA. You feel up to running the show?"

"YYYESH!" came a deep and deeply disturbing voice, although anything could be considered an improvement upon his mental state from earlier.

"Jinnbo? You good, little buddy?" she asked, realizing he was probably in the build-up stage of one of his rage-out moments. This by-product of having to vanquish one's evil twin as part of a rite of passage was apparently a very, very well-guarded secret.

"Jinnbo?"

All she could hear after that was quiet sobbing. "Okay, good talk. You're in charge now. Gotta go blow some shit up," she said.

And then, aside to Raphael internally, she whispered, "You're in charge, okay?"

"Of course. And I'm also coming with you," Raph responded.

"Huh? Oh, yeah."

"We're a team."

"Yeah. Still seems somewhat ... weird though ... having two personas in two different places."

"If I can split my processing between Hail Mary and your power armor—"

"Marguerite," she interrupted.

"Um ... Marguerite? Then why shouldn't I assist both you and our illustrious co-pilot?"

"When you put it that way..."

"Galas?" came a simpering voice through the main channel.

"Yes, Jinnbo?"

"Why is my face leaking?"

"Jinnbo, you have to remember, you're an alien species that I'm not entirely familiar with and which does not exist in my SortieNet records. When you say your face is leaking, I have to assume that you mean that your face is actually leaking."

"Uh-huh."

"Do you mean, 'Why are you crying?'"

"Uh-huh." He sniffled, hocked up something phlegmy, and swallowed. Galas's stomach folded on itself, but she bulldozed through.

"Well, it's because you're going through a cascade-crash of hormonally induced emotions due to having killed the evil twin that you spawned when you ate all of those hallucinogenic acid frogs and went catatonic," she provided in her most matronly tone, though to be fair, her patience was running exceedingly thin.

There was silence for a moment and then, "I miss him," Jinnbo glubbed.

"I know, Jimmy. I know," she said. Though, how he could possibly miss a psychopathic version of himself who had tried to kill him *and* Galas—that part was important—she did not know.

"Gotta go now, Jimboy. You're in charge," she said, slipping back into the open shell of her power suit, Marguerite, and feeling the gel pads conforming to her body before the chest plates hinged close and sealed her up.

And then aside to Raphael, she said, "You're really in charge."

"I know," Raphael said as her visor slid down and sealed as well.

Galas exited the mech through the rear access hatch that was located, embarrassingly, on Hail Mary's backside below her repulsor pack. Which in Galas's mind made her look like she was exiting the mech's rectum and then dribbling down her leg.

Raphael stifled a laugh. The flyer one drone provided an excellent feed which he had redirected to Galas's HUD so she could see the whole thing.

"Nice. Real nice."

"You look like a human poop," sniggered Jinnbo, who apparently had been studying human physiology and was feeling back to himself for the moment.

She ignored him, dropped to the ground, and jogged across the plaza to the temple where the Arcfire control center was housed.

The structure, made entirely from native rock, was precisely crafted but devoid of any markings. Galas knew that this was because the prior race made heavy use of holographics and there was a radiation signature that the city's AI used to propagate its network. Except here. They kept the temples separate. Which she was thankful for since the Braex AI had gone mad in the interim time since the Priors had left.

Where they went, nobody knew. Why they didn't properly shut down the city AI, suggested that they intended to come back or left in a hurry. What that meant was that while there were still some usable systems, such as transport to the southern city of Xiocic, and the northern city of Daxn, Braex was mostly unreliable.

Sadly, deep inside the mountain, where the city of Braex extended as a fortress, was the Sanctum. A repository of knowledge and a place of some religious value although, Galas had no idea what for.

The last time she was there, she was too busy killing hordes of psych hoppers and Makrit acolytes, or psych bullies as she called them. Oh, and also the so-called demon-god Sun-Thurr, which she understood now, was not a demon-god—whatever that was—but more of an interdimensional conman. He did have substantial powers and appeared in the Braex histories, so in a way, he was a bit god-like. Maybe a demigod. Hard to say.

"Raph, have you tried to hail the enemy vessel?"

"*Alleged* enemy. And yes, I have. Hail Mary's comms aren't up to the task and the global network, as you know, is compromised, so ... no luck."

"They *are* the enemy because they are not us and they are here. We're all that's left after a 40-year extermination campaign that's ravaged our system, so yeah, anyone here on a ship *that* size is either here to steal what's left or take over. Try hailing them again."

"Of course. The issue with comms appears to be two-fold. First, there is a prodigious amount of debris in the atmosphere, of which you know. Since you pretty much made all of it by grinding the Delvadr invasionary force into a thin paste with the Arcfire."

"I like your artistic flare with that description. Carry on."

"The second issue with comms appears to be more local in nature."

"I don't like the sound of that. It's not the Braex AI, is it? Or more of those blasted Mantid Zeta looters? Tell me it's the MZ's. I want a piece of those guys sooo bad."

"It's hard to say, but something local is jamming us. I've had to switch to a high-power packetized protocol just to maintain sync with Jinnbo in the Hail Mary only 150-meters away."

"Oh. What do you think that means? Company?"

"Yes."

"Okay. Keep your sensors peeled."

"That doesn't make sense, but then neither does the colloquialism you're bastardizing. I will, however, maintain a vigilant watch over a broad spectrum of sensory data."

"Too many words, Raphael."

"Peeled. Keeping my sensors," he flashed a video image of Galas rolling her eyes dramatically, "peeled."

She couldn't help but chuckle.

Galas walked down a stone corridor that emptied into a wide open space with a high domed ceiling. She took in a deep breath of canned power armor air and walked to the center, where a small dais sat devoid of any decoration or anything. Then she unlocked a storage compartment in Marguerite's leg and produced a hefty stone with markings on it in the form of a bent line with three sets of concentric, broken circles—one at either end and one in the middle. This was a representation of the three cities of Antiquity. She sat the stone in a minor depression in the middle of the dais and the whole room sprang to life with light and movement as the Arcfire control room readied itself for the business of destruction.

From the floor, stone rose into the shape of a reclining lounge. Galas plopped down and unsealed and folded her gauntlets back. An array of light coalesced into an augmented reality interface before her as the ceiling melted away to form a panorama of the Epriot sky.

The air was alive with buzzing and humming that slowly wove in and out of harmony with one another. She'd seen and heard—and felt—all of this before, but it was still hard not to be overwhelmed by the display of prior race tech, dead for thousands of years, and come back to life.

"Okay."

She swallowed and scanned the hazy band of obscuring stars and planets beyond. The moons of Skleetrix and Cyclopedae were visible high in the sky, despite the fact that it was daytime outside. She realized that the display was adjusted to show what lay in the upper atmosphere and within the various orbital bands without showing the atmospheric interference of light. She hadn't put much thought into it last time. She was much too focused on just destroying every last object in the sky.

Galas adjusted focus. Rotating the image so that it panned through, not just the sky above Braex but the whole of Epriot Prime's atmosphere. She had no idea how the whole thing worked, but then that was kind of the point of hijacking another race's technology. If you could have done it yourself, you would have.

The humming rose and then subsided as if readying itself for some industrial-strength anarchy. She was ready too.

She spun through the various views and came back to the anomaly resting just outside the debris field in Epriot Prime's orbit. It was not in geosync above EDC High Command—located in what was left of New Varhus, the most recent replacement capital city. That's what she would have expected for an entity wishing to negotiate with the Epriots. This massive craft, another Thune-built monstrosity, was positioned directly overhead. Here. Over Braex. She tried to let that sink in.

That meant that they knew about the Arcfire. Which meant that they were most likely more of the Delvadr scum that she had exterminated several weeks back.

"Some people never learn," she sighed and then realized that the Arcfire guidance systems would not lock on to the craft. She panicked a little before realizing that it was because it was out of range. Just beyond the debris field. She breathed a sigh of relief.

"Okay. Maybe they *do* learn, but that still doesn't make them smart." That's when she saw that there was another craft in orbit. A smaller one and it was much closer in.

She zoomed in on the holographic display spread across the domed ceiling. It was a shuttlecraft, and it was drawing near to Epriot's inner orbit. She clucked disappointingly and, without hesitation, lashed out with the Arcfire. A thin filament of plasma flitted up into the atmosphere, combined with similar filaments from the north and south temples. The combined stream arced up into the sky. Where the shuttle used to be. Now only a few shimmering particles remained.

"That should send the proper message. Now let's wait and see what they do." She settled back into the chair and tried to put her hands behind her head, but in the Targe IV armor, it didn't quite achieve the degree of comfort she was looking for. Instead, she just folded her hands in her lap, twiddled her thumbs, and whistled the first song that came to mind. It was from her childhood on the Hillal, her father's mech. The band's name was something to do with a self-inflicted lobotomy. She closed her eyes and headbanged softly while impersonating the sounds of thrashing percussion and chunky, distorted power chords.

An hour later, an itch on Galas's nose was keeping her from dozing off. She scratched at it and decided that she would finally have to do something about her bladder too. As much as the suit could handle it and would simply filter and process the fluid, she still couldn't justify messing herself for the sake of convenience. She'd only do it if she absolutely had to. Of course, she was manning the planet's sole defense against interstellar aggressors, so ... there was that.

"Do you really think Marguerite would appreciate that?" Raph asked.

"Don't you have something better to do than monitor my physiological needs?" Galas growled, midstream.

"Actually, that is one of my primary functions."

He refrained from saying that *someone* had to wipe her ass for her, but she knew he was thinking it.

"How's Jinnbo doing? He hasn't tried to kill himself yet, has he?"

"No. He's actually displaying an unusual amount of self-restraint. He is crying again though."

"Poor fella. Just keep him on lock. He'll probably rage out any moment."

"Of course. Um, Galas, are you seeing this?"

On the dome of the ceiling, a tiny spot of light was nearing the debris field. It looked like an errant star.

"What the..."

She zoomed in using the holographics of the Arcfire's augmented reality interface. The small dot expanded into a standard-sized transport of familiar design.

"It appears to be one of ours," Raphael finished for her. Galas was certain that he didn't approve of her copious use of vulgarities.

"Who could it be? It's not a Delvadr vessel, but it does look ... kinda like..." She trailed off as her memory tried to fill in the gaps. In her defense, she could barely count on one hand how many concussions she'd received in the last 56 hours alone.

"If I'm not mistaken, it's our own diplomatic vessel. The *Xandraitha's Hope*."

"How can you see that?" She shook her head and searched the air, thinking about all the possibilities. "Well, shit. We don't know it's our people. It could be a Trojan horse. We know a thing or two about those."

It had been a Trojan drone that had disabled her own power armor when she had come head-to-head with Demon Betsy, the co-opted version of her own mech. The ploy had been initiated by Jinnbo's evil twin in an attempt to destroy all that her co-pilot held dear. It had also been a Trojan drone that they used to shut down the Delvadr elite mech that Galas, Jinnbo, and Raphael had heisted and was now their very own Hail Mary. So, she was justifiably cautious about such things.

She flicked out an untargeted whisp of Arcfire plasma just to get their attention, whoever they were. The ship reversed course quickly and pulled back to a safe distance in middle orbit. The SortieNet provided status on the ship's location in orbit. At roughly 400 km altitude. It could stay in its current position for a year or more with little to no orbital maintenance. It was a good call. If it were Delvadr, they'd probably just go back to the ship and wait for backup before proceeding with orbital bombardment. So this was a good sign.

Another twenty minutes went by uneventfully and then a couple of cursor dots lit up near the Epriot ship. One more, and then a fifth. They were tiny.

"Are those ... jumpers?"

"It would appear so."

"Through that debris field? Ballsy. I'll give them that. Have you tried to hail them again?"

"Still no luck. I've sent the same high-power, digitized packets and all I get back is garbled chunks. We really should—"

"We really should what?"

"Oh no. Company..."

"What? Where?"

A large boom shook the walls and echoed through the complex, followed quickly by several more.

"What was that? Who's out there, Raphael? I thought you were keeping your sensors peeled!"

"It's an Elite."

"Shit. I guess that explains the comms issue?"

"That would appear to be the case."

"Can you and Jinnbo handle this? I've still got these jumpers to deal with."

"Perhaps the jumpers are a lower priority right now? It'll be twenty-five minutes at least before they're atmospheric. That's if they make it through the debris field."

"Fair enough. Can you patch Jinnbo through?"

"No. The stone and the jamming have caused me to unsync and allow full-autonomous operation to the better-suited Hail Mary AI."

"What does that mean, Raphael 2.0 is in charge?"

"Essentially."

"How do I get in this fight?"

"You'll need to be outside the temple, at least. Of course, that would be incredibly stupid."

"Right," Galas affirmed as she jumped up and sealed her gauntlets and visor before running for the door. "Let's get to work."

Galas stepped out into the bright light of the sun, only it wasn't sunlight. It was Hail Mary taking a full barrage of rockets to the chest. Galas dove for cover as explosions drove the machine backward.

"Jinnbo! Move! What are you doing?!?"

"I don't want to live anymore! It hurts too much," he cried.

"Raph! Gimme control!" she snarled.

Suddenly, she saw what Jinnbo was seeing. Hail Mary leaped back, blasting its repulsors, and then a swath of plasma fire scourged the hillside south of the plaza grounds where she'd seen a grayed-out cursor disappear a fraction of a second before.

She, too, initiated active stealthing. Hail Mary's icon grayed out but remained centered in the rotating 3D battlespace model.

She boosted the mech back and to the left, near where the northern edge of the plaza fell away into a tumble of trees that ended a thousand meters below in a lazy bend of the river.

Then she deployed flyers and stealthed as well, and the whole BSM resolved into ultra-high definition. Galas scrolled through a handful of imaging filters, looking for anything that might give away her or the enemy mech's positions.

She almost forgot that she was actually outside the mech, lying in an undignified heap near the entrance to the temple where she'd landed after that first explosion.

With the other mech stealthed out, it could be standing a few meters away and she wouldn't be able to tell. Delvadr tech was that good. Not that it was their idea. They just had deep pockets and liked to fight. That wasn't quite true. Most of them didn't care to fight if they could help it. But they did love to win. And deep pockets helped.

A disturbance in the air above her signified a repulsor field. It was about thirty-five meters up and dropping. Then there was a soft thud from ahead of her.

Shit. Now she knew where the enemy was, but firing on him was completely out of the question.

She wanted to know why Raphael 2.0 didn't take control of Hail Mary's defensive capabilities when they were attacked but she didn't dare try to communicate with the mech again with the enemy so close.

She thought the question to Marguerite's Raphael, and he whispered back, "Jinnbo must have found the manual override. Delvadr units have those as a failsafe in order to disengage their AI. Their machinery is top-of-the-line, but their AI leaves something to be desired. I never realized I needed to disengage that feature on Hail Mary. This is my fault, Galas."

"This is no one's fault. Jinnbo is just going through some heavy shit right now and I left him in charge. No, wait, I left *you* in charge, but he was still in the mech and we all know that if there's a way to screw something up, Jinnbo will find it. It's a gift, really. And now that gift has been supercharged with teenage angst."

That thought made her think of her daughter, Seraf. *Wrong time*, she told herself. *Now, is not the time.* But her chest constricted just the same. She had to find her after all of this. Even if Seraf wanted nothing to do with her. Galas just needed to know she was okay.

A heavy grinding noise told her the enemy mech was shifting its stance, getting ready to move. She had to do something quick. Then her audio circuits picked up a whoosh of air. She looked up and was stunned to see an access hatch open in mid-air and a Delvadr pilot or engineer poke its head out.

The alien crewmember peered around, its black eyes and gray-blue skin the only things physically distinguishing it from a petite-sized human.

From experience, she knew there'd be a crew of three or four. In an Elite, one of them would be royalty. Though there were so many members, Galas doubted that there was anyone, not a member of the royal family in some capacity.

She was shocked that she wasn't discovered. To be fair, she was still lying on her side in the shadow of one of the flying buttresses that stood on either side of the temple entrance.

She realized she was holding her breath, but dared not move regardless. The crewmember's head popped back inside. She heard voices and then the Delvadr reappeared and dropped the 15 meters to the plaza stone, assisted by grav-tech of some sort.

Galas watched him look around and then dart inside the temple. Not good. But the hatch was open still. The Delvadr crewman couldn't do much. The ships were out of range. Comms were being actively jammed. He could take the stone key but, then what would he do? Go back to his mech?

She rolled a strand of demo cord across the entrance and attached a prox trigger.

"Raph. How long would it take you to take over the AI if I got you inside?"

"A minute. Maybe more if you want me to do it without notifying the crew."

"Good. One more thing: Where's the override?"

"Engineering. If this is the same class mech as Hail Mary."

"Perfect," she said before leaping and boosting up the 15-meter gap to land just inside the open access hatch.

"Dammit. This isn't the same class mech."

She said this while staring at a dozen Delvadr marines preparing to deploy.

That's when Hail Mary materialized and launched a salvo of missiles, and fired all of its laser and plasma Cannons.

"Dammit, Jinnbo!"

"YYYESSHHH!!!"

The mech shuddered under the barrage. Galas flipped a concussion grenade in the midst of the marines as one of her flyers zipped in and attached itself to a control panel and she fell backward through the access hole.

The world tumbled end over end and Galas ripped her grappling line in the direction of what she hoped was the mech's underside. It connected and suddenly she was whipped out in front, where an explosion slapped her back the other way, right at the entrance.

She got her bearings just in time to see the first Delvadr crew member step through the opening with the stone key in hand.

"Nooooo..."

The demo cord blew, ripping the crewman apart and flipping the stone key in the air. Galas released the grappling anchor, flinging herself toward the temple where she caught the artifact, bathed her suit in Delvadr chunks, and then slammed into the corridor wall, upside down.

She watched Jinnbo unleash an unholy amount of armaments at the Elite mech from both her current position as well as through Hail Mary's SortieNet link. This was a lot to parse, even for her highly tuned pilot's mind. What she could make out was the Elite's active stealthing faded as it stepped back, bumping into the temple—which she felt through the floor where her helmet was currently resting—and then beginning to teeter backward where it would completely crush the Arcfire temple, humanities hope, and Galas along with it.

"Jinnbo, no!"

In a last-ditch effort, she re-seized control of Hail Mary, shot the mech's grappling line, and restrained the enemy Elite's fall. Hail Mary skidded forward but then caught traction, furrowing huge rows of cobbles in the process.

"Got it!" Raph cried.

"Wait, what?" Galas asked, confused, since she'd just seized the enemy mech herself.

"Got it. I'm in. I have control of the Elite," Raphael clarified.

"Oh, good," she replied while focusing on holding that same mech from falling into the temple while simultaneously keeping Jinnbo from hacking Hail Mary's control suite.

"No. No. No. Nooo," Jinnbo roared, slamming on every panel in the cockpit module.

Galas was lamenting having to repair all those surfaces when three Delvadr marines in battered armor suits dropped from above. They spotted her just inside the entrance and charged forward.

Galas rolled to the side as plasma bolts peppered the wall. She was sprinting down the corridor even as she launched a solitary rocket from Hail Mary's nacelles. The explosion eviscerated the pursuing marines and shot her like a cannon into yet another wall.

Jinnbo reacquired control of Hail Mary as everything went black.

CHAPTER 13
ORBITAL DECAY

Epriot Prime, Middle Orbit, Somewhere over the Preta Compact

As they drew nearer the planet, a swath of dust and debris materialized ahead of them. Suddenly, D'avry's suit shuddered and the pull of the repulsor engines dragged on him like a sea anchor. How long had he been daydreaming? He realized they must be going very fast and getting close enough that they needed to slow down before burning up in the atmosphere, as Rutker had explained to him. D'avry's pulse raced as his feet swung around in front of him. Below, he could see that shimmering gray haze becoming more pronounced.

"What kind of problem Xander Base?" Rutker asked

D'avry was listening to the unfolding drama while trying to decipher the myriad glowing lines and text on his visor's virtual dashboard, whatever that was.

He was doing this to calm himself down, but it wasn't working. He felt Theal's influence crowding his mind, trying to force him to be calm, but that had the opposite effect. It was akin to someone trying to coax a person to sleep by putting a pillow over their face.

But then the lines and text on his screen started scrambling in an even less calming way. He strained to ascertain what the issue was when a highlighted dot appeared below him. It was flashing orange and then it began flashing red just before his armor twisted and something zipped into view and slammed into his repulsor pack.

D'avry watched the glitter of ceramo-metal shrapnel disappear up and away just as his armor began to spin in a wide, flat arc. He tumbled and then it began whipping him wildly the other way as he spun out of control. Still falling toward the planet, of course. Better to be a small crater than to go spinning off into the void, he thought dismally while squinting his eyes closed and trying to force himself into a meditative state.

"I am peace. I am light. I am peace. I am light. I am peace! I am light," he yelled louder and louder, hoping that somehow he could just bum-rush his way into inner bliss.

Something grabbed him. His eyes sprang open, and he was staring into Theal's glowing almond-shaped orbs. Her visor was pressed to his, and he felt his suit stabilize even as she forcefully crashed into his consciousness.

And then another jolt rattled him as someone else latched on.

"Hang on, kid. I'm going to manually release your pack," Rutker said over the comms.

"You're going to what?!? Don't I *need* that?"

"Errggg," Rutker grunted as he wrenched on the release mechanism.

Then there was nothing but silence.

Everything faded, and D'avry was fully engulfed in the dream state induced by Theal.

D'avry saw Deven, but he couldn't talk to her. They were in the place known as the Gray Town, on a balcony overlooking rooftops that stretched away into the mists below. They were higher up than they'd ever been before. And below, on the rooftops, were hundreds of the Void creatures.

Deven slipped back into the shadows, her own raven hair disappearing into the darkness, causing her pale skin and faded red lipstick to stand out in contrast. She still had warpaint on her cheeks from the battle with the blackout beast on top of the mountain in D'avry's time-place. Her red lipstick was faded, but she was still breathtaking.

D'avry breathed in a shuddering breath and reached out even as she turned away, used her borrowed magic to blink away to the door, and then quickly out. He'd forgotten about the newfound power that the magic ring he'd given her provided. He'd have to run to catch up.

He dashed for the door and caught a glimpse of her as she bounded up to a walkway a level above. D'avry took flight in the raven form he used to conjure accidentally. Now he was familiar with this form and winged confidently up into the air.

There were more of the creatures. He watched Deven pick her line, expertly avoiding their scrutinizing gaze. They sniffed the air in her passing, but only for a moment before returning to scanning the structures. And waiting, D'avry realized. But for what?

He flapped higher still. Deven was covering ground more effectively as the creatures' numbers began to dwindle.

The structures changed the farther up the hillside they went, he noticed. Where below they had been mere shanties, here they were growing to be warehouses and things of a decidedly more industrial nature. Still, the place was empty. It was like a ghost town, but one that was abandoned even by the spirits.

D'avry caught movement below. Deven saw it too. She looked as though she was going to follow but then he saw her look up at the sky. His heart leaped when he thought she would see him, but then she just turned and followed whatever it was that she'd seen a moment before.

Then he was ripped out of the Gray Town dream and into something else.

He saw a planet that looked like E'rth as he'd seen it from the dropship on his trip with Rutker to meet the Gefkarri. Only this planet had a band around it, a faint gossamer strand. But then he noticed something of a structure to it, like a lattice-work surrounding it.

The vision was only there for an instant when he felt himself slipping out of the dream. He jerked himself back. He saw two moons: one was blue and gray, the other was white and the white one looked like it had been destroyed, or was being destroyed? He couldn't make sense of it.

And then he saw a field of battle. It was the same place he'd seen in the simulation with Seda. There before him was the destroyed mech with the dying pilot and the two human mages.

In that moment, he was reminded of the mutant mages on the Eleven Sevens. He thought of the way that those mute simpletons were fully given over to aiding the ship through magic. They had no sense of identity. Their only joy was their connection to the system.

What D'avry sensed now with this Deathhound and the magic of the Chareth-Ul was somehow darker even than that. There was no joy. There was only the barest diminishing of pain. He shuddered and was yanked back once and for all.

By the Astrig Ka'a, what have I gotten myself into? he thought quietly to himself. *And can I get myself out?*

Now he was looking at a different planet and watching its clouds glide past him as he fell toward its surface. He remembered that he didn't have a repulsor pack anymore and panicked a little.

Little crater, here I come.

"No. We've got you," Theal informed him telepathically.

He looked to his right and saw that she had her arm looped around his. Rutker held him similarly on his left. His own arms were interlocked in front of him and the power suit had locked all the joints in place so he couldn't slip out if he grew too fatigued.

"Okay. I guess you do."

"What's that kid? You back with us?" Rutker asked, sounding relieved even though he was clearly focused on sticking the landing at the Arcfire temple.

"Yeah. Yeah, I'm back."

"Good. Quick status report. Dexx is gone. He split when you had your little repulsor issue. Macq went after him. So now it's just us three. Oh, and we're dropping into a hot LZ."

"What's an El Zee? That sounds bad the way you say it."

Theal jumped into the conversation. "There's a battle going on at the Arcfire temple. Though it appears to be drawing to a conclusion."

D'avry looked down. Way far below, he could see the tops of what looked like two huge statues on opposite sides of a courtyard. Then a streak of fire shot from one of them and exploded against a stone building.

"Doesn't look concluded to me."

"Oh, believe me, there was a lot more than that before. Hope the good guys won. If it's Galas down there, then there's a pretty good chance," Rutker replied.

The repulsors bucked hard again as Rutker worked to slow their descent even more. Probably to let things simmer down before they landed in the middle of it.

"Is Macq going to be okay?" D'avry asked as he tried not to focus on the activity below.

"Macq? Yeah, the kid should be fine. He may not catch the Colonel, but he can take care of himself. He's like an encyclopedia of military techniques and tactics. Doesn't have the brawn of his brother, but he's as sharp as they come."

"Oh, okay. Good," he responded, but something like an itch in the back of his mind kept pulling his attention from the conversation and the situation at hand. He thought it could be Theal, or maybe Seda messing with him, but it didn't feel right.

He looked off to his left past Rutker's helmet and he could see smoke and fire way out in the distance. He could feel the same sensations from when he'd done the battle simulation with Seda back on the Gefkarri flagship.

D'avry reached out with his magical senses and could feel tangibly, the Chareth-Ul interdimensional magic, though faintly. He couldn't feel the Delvadr, but they were different, anyway. He'd have to use Epriot Prime's native ethereal fields to do that, and that's when that niggling itch made sense.

He couldn't feel anything.

That wasn't right. He could feel *something*, but it wasn't an actual force. He closed his eyes and let his senses wander. This part was getting more familiar to him as he'd been exposed to his world's magic and then the chaotic magic of the Astrig Ka'a and then the Gefkarri's particular brand of arcana, but still, he was coming up blank. And then something happened. Something undefined. An ephemeral wave. Just a glimpse of ... nothing.

He felt the suits jostle again. They were drawing within a few hundred feet of the temple. A surge of panic ran through him. He had to know what it was he was sensing. And then he felt it again, but intensely this time. It was nothing, but it was a *tangible* nothing. That didn't make sense.

He focused as intensely as he knew how and what he saw was like a well of darkness, and it had its own kind of gravity. The planet was pulling him down, but this darkness... It was pulling him in, like, into the mountain.

Theal's grip intensified. She must have felt some kind of sympathetic response to this inner tug-o-war. And then the blackness itself reached out and plucked him from reality.

Rutker and Theal decelerated suddenly without the young mage clutched between them.

He should have been shocked that the kid had disappeared, but by now, it was a pretty regular occurrence.

Theal, on the other hand, he could tell by her body language, was fuming. He tried not to smile so broadly that it was obvious through his face shield.

They glided slowly to the ground as far as possible from the open area between the Delvadr Elite mechs. It gave Rutker an uncomfortable feeling, being so close to these monstrosities. Even in the Long Rifle, he'd have felt vastly outgunned.

He noticed that one of the mechs had a grappling line attached to the other. And that the second one was leaning precariously over the temple structure.

Even more reason to touchdown well away from the pair.

He tried comms again and was relieved to hear someone's voice, even if it wasn't Field Colonel Galas.

"Hello, Captain Major Novak. It's wonderful to see you again."

"R—Raphael? Is that you? Where's Field Col. Galas?"

"I'm here," came a groggy voice just as he saw someone in power armor exiting the temple building. Despite being stone, there were still little bits of refuse on fire from the previous rocket blast.

"You're late to the barbecue," she added as she strode unsteadily across the courtyard where she'd spotted him and his companion.

"Yeah, looks like. What's the story with these beasties?" He motioned in the direction of the two mechs. "Trying to build your own squadron to go with that promotion?"

She laughed. He could see her wince through her visor.

"Raph, can you conduct a deep scan and then use the flyers from both mechs to set a perimeter? I don't want to be surprised again," Galas said, through comms.

"What about meeeee???" came a pathetic voice.

"Jinnbo! So glad you're back. Feeling stable or not-so-much?" Galas said, in a manner that was decidedly more maternal than Rutker would have expected from the storied warrior.

"I don't want to die, if that's what you mean."

Rutker gave her a side-eye.

She shook her head and shifted her hand side to side with the palm down, as if to say, 'Don't worry. It's all under control.'

Somehow, he doubted that.

"Who's yer friend?" she asked while staring at Theal, a note of steel in her voice he hadn't heard before. Except when she was talking about hunting down the remaining Delvadr, he corrected himself.

"Forgive me. This is Aspect Theal. She's an ambassador of the Gefkarri Pentarch."

"Hmm. Whaddya want, Miss Aspect?"

"Theal will do. And you can start by disabling your planetary defensive weapons so that we can deploy our troops and save your species from annihilation."

"Fat chance."

Theal's eyes began to glow.

Galas stepped forward. "Don't even think about it, bitch. Unless you think you can go through me and my two companions." She thumbed over her shoulder toward the two mechs.

They turned to face the trio. Shoulder nacelles slid open to expose rows of rockets ready to fire.

Theal's eyes cooled. "I see. Perhaps you'll allow the *Xandraitha's Hope* to enter Epriot Prime's atmosphere so that it can transport us to EDC High Command where we can negotiate with someone with a rank worthy of the task?"

"Yeah, that's not happening either."

"Col. Galas. My wife and son are on that vessel," Rutker informed her.

"Rutker. I'm a fan of your work. Really, I am. But no. Nothing is getting through the atmosphere without EDC approval. I will call a transport and they will fly you across the Straights of Eldomitik, all the way to New Varhus, where you can plead your case. I don't care what they decide, one way or the other. What I *do* care about is making sure that this weapon continues to protect our skies until orders come down from on high to do otherwise."

Rutker bit his tongue and nodded his understanding. "Of course, Field Colonel. You know about the Void then?"

"That's what you're calling them? Weird. That's the same thing we came up with."

"They have another name—"

"Can it. Really, not interested," Galas interrupted and turned her attention back to Rutker.

He stepped forward. "And you heard that the Deathhounds are here as well?"

"Have you seen those things?" Galas asked.

"No."

"They're fragging ungodly huge. I mean ... no joke. They look like they can transport several *hundred* Deathhounds. And thousands of Makrit."

"Makrit?" he asked. "What are those?"

"Well, the little ones we call psych hoppers. They're like half-centipede, half-kangaroo and they jump and fly a little and the worst part is that they use a stun attack. You can't get close to them, or they'll knock you out and make you shit yourself. Not fun."

Rutker gave her that skeptical look again, but it cracked into a grin. "Sounds like you know from experience."

"Damn close enough. Then there are the acolytes. They're bigger, tough as hell, and they use some pretty exotic weaponry. The ones I ran into had grenades that punch a hole in reality. Sucked a two-meter sphere straight out of here and put it somewhere else. This huge fish monster thing was half in, half out, and then it was half a body." She motioned with a hand slicing across her waist.

"Good to know," Rutker said with a grimace. "Theal here says that they're our new allies. The Gefkarri is like a hive mind. They're going to unite all these forces against the Void with some kind of multi-army supernet. They believe it's the only way to defeat them."

Galas shrugged. "Again. Tell it to the lofty ones. I don't plan on working side by side with any of those knuckleheads, but you can go ahead."

"It's for the good of the galaxy. If we fail here—"

Theal started in, but Galas was already walking away and calling in a transport now that comms were no longer being jammed.

Theal turned to Rutker. "She's fun," she said, deadpan.

Rutker chuckled. *Gefkarri have jokes. Who knew?*

He hailed the *Xandraitha's Hope* and spoke to Katherynn about the current state of things. Updated her about the situation with D'avry and Dexx and then reluctantly about Macq.

He could hear her suck in a deep breath and let it out. "He's alright. He'll be alright."

"I know he will," Rutker agreed. "He's a smart kid, and he's well-trained."

"Yeah. I know. I'll let Mads know. He's down in engineering, chatting up that ensign with the dark eyes."

"Really? That doesn't sound like him."

"I know. I think he's worried about you two with this drop. And a little bit irritated he didn't get to go."

"Yeah. I'd be too. But Mads is more of a soldier. And down here, I need a tactician."

"I know. I just can't tell him that."

"Yeah. Well ... he'll get his chance to do his part. We're a long way from over. Make sure he keeps his head in the game."

She chuckled. She was laughing at him, and he knew why. When he'd been that age, he was doing everything he could to get her attention and had run into more than a few scrapes with his superiors in the process.

He smiled, "Okay. I know you've got things handled up there."

"Damn straight. Now handle things down there, so I don't have to come down and do it for you."

"Aye-aye, Ambassador."

"Aye-aye, Capt. Major."

A Pond Bumble rolled up and touched down on the temple plaza. Between the bumble and the two mechs, there was precious little space. Rutker jogged over to where Galas was just dropping down from the mech closest to the Arcfire temple.

"Field Colonel—"

She interrupted him with a wave. "Don't stand on formality with me, Rutker. In a battle of attrition, the cockroach wins. They only gave me a promotion cuz they were too shocked that I was still alive to do anything else. Whaddya need?"

Rutker pulled up short, momentarily at a loss for what to say. It didn't make things any easier, considering what he'd come over to tell her to begin with.

"Today?"

"Well ... the matter is..." he scratched his head and winced.

"You're killin' me. Is it about the tree lady and her big, bad family?"

"Kind of. Not really. I told you about my son and Colonel Dexx and that we're missing another member of our crew."

"Yeah."

"Well, that member's name is D'avry, and I'd be doing him a disservice by not telling you to keep an eye out for him."

"Rutker. What are we talking about here? What exactly was this crewmember's role?"

"Well, that's the problem. He's not a member of my crew. Or that of the *Xandraitha's Hope*. He's from E'rth. Gellen III according to our charts, but those are all screwed up because of all the crap that went down with the peace talks."

"He's from another planet? Not from this system."

"Right."

"So, what species are we talking about?"

"He's human."

"Human. How's that possible? We abandoned all interstellar flight decades ago."

"Yeah, well, that's not all—and you're going to love this one—he's from the future."

"I'm sorry, did you just—"

"Yes. I did. And there's more. He's some sort of magician or something. Like a sorcerer."

"Did you hit your head on the way down, Captain Major?"

"Yeah, I know. However, he provided information that was impossible to have known regarding the contents of the diplomatic packages. And," Rutker shook his head, not believing he was saying this, "he can teleport, or something like that. I've watched him walk into walls, and that's how he slipped away right before we landed."

"He sounds very much like someone I know. Well, someone I killed rather," she said, tilting her head side to side as if it were a simple parsing of words, knowing and killing.

"Well, this guy is legit. He's what the Gefkarri are so interested in. Somehow, he adjusted to be able to use *their* magic. That's impossible, according to them. There are no other races that can intermix magic like that. Except for humans, apparently. And he's the first to do it."

Galas's eyes squinted as she seemed to be catching up with real stakes at play.

"So, where did he go?"

"We don't know," Theal provided as she walked up to the two.

Galas ignored her.

"We don't know." Rutker echoed Theal's statement from before. "But there was some weird mumbling in our comms just before he disappeared from out of Aspect Theal's and my arms. His repulsor pack got hit. Theal and I locked arms with him to slow down his descent and right when we got into visible range of the temple, he disappeared. Not invisible. Gone. Like poof."

Galas looked at him and then at the Gefkarri and back at Rutker.

"I could feel his thoughts," Theal provided. "Feel him being pulled away. He said something about a blackness, but his thoughts were fixated on an idea, something like *null-magic*? I'm unaware of what that could be and my link back to Aspect Seda and the Pentarch is diminished without D'avry's presence."

"Well, ain't that a bitch," she said, emphasizing the word as she glared at the Gefkarri ambassador. "So, what do you want me to do about it?"

"Just keep an eye out, in case he pops up. He does that. And … I wouldn't want you to shoot him … much."

She nodded slowly. "Okay, so if a human *sorcerer* from another planet's *future* pops up, *don't* shoot him? I'll see what I can do. Now if that'll be all?"

Rutker nodded, his lips pressed into a thin line of mild chagrin. "Something like that."

"Okay. Good talk. You guys take care now. And Rutker? I hope you find your son. I really do." She was about to walk away, but stopped and turned back. The expression on her face and her demeanor had softened. "Rutker ... look. Maybe you can keep an eye out for me too. A girl named Seraf. She'd be a couple of years younger than Macq. Probably looks a bit like me."

"Probably?" He scoffed and then, when she stiffened, realized he was wading into dangerous waters. A lot of people had known loss. Not everyone knew if their relatives were alive. And if it'd been a number of years, maybe not even what they looked like anymore. "Don't worry, Galas. If she's anything like you, she'll stand out in a crowd."

Galas nodded. Looked down and then back up. "Thank you," she whispered. She swallowed and turned away abruptly. "Now get off my hilltop before I put a Targe IV-sized boot up you and your twig's backside! I've got work to do." Galas waved them off and while the mechs positioned themselves to defend the temple promontory, and she disappeared inside the opening to the temple itself.

"Did you hear that, Raph?" Galas asked.

"I did."

"What do you make of it?"

"About the Gefkarri Pentarch? Sounds plausible. Seems unlikely they'd be here under any other pretense."

"Yeah. What about a magician? You ever heard of such a thing?"

"There's a lot of strange stuff in the universe. From a scientific standpoint, ruling something out because there's no precedent for it is the epitome of not-very-scientific. So why not humans with magic?"

"Guess you're right. What do you think happened to him?"

"I didn't bring it up, though maybe I should have, at least to you, but some of the Sanctum records mentioned a null *field*. A vortex of sorts, but I didn't see the relevance during the time of the Arcfire mission and assumed maybe it was some kind of mythology. Not all of the records we received from Sun-Thurr were complete or untampered with."

"Why does that not surprise me?"

"Because he was just as shady as he was powerful?"

"Yeah. That's exactly why. What should we do?"

"You're asking me?"

"Nah. I just wanted to be inclusive. I'm heading back to the Sanctum. You're in charge. Protect the temple. Keep Jinnbo from killing himself."

"Temple? Check. Jinnbo? I make no promises."

Galas smirked as she jogged toward the portal at the far end of the courtyard.

"All these Raphaels are going to be confusing. What's the new mech gonna be called?"

"Rosie?"

"Rosie? *That's* your suggestion?"

"It's better than Gladys."

"Actually, I kinda like Gladys."

"How about Seraf?"

There was silence.

"Nevermind. Stupid idea," Raphael amended.

"No. I like it. Seraf, Hail Mary. You two hold down the fort."

"Aye-aye," came the decidedly masculine responses from the two mech AI's formerly known as Raphael.

"Go ahead and modify your voice patterns to match your new designations.

"Yes, Ma'am," came Hail Mary's response. Fittingly feminine.

"Aye-Aye," came Seraf's, still militant but slightly higher alto.

Sniff. "Aye-aye," sniffle, came Jinnbo's belated response.

"Hang in there, buddy. This can't last forever," Galas encouraged.

[Galas: Can it?] she thought to text, asking for Raphael's reassurance.

[Raph: Dunno. I hope not] floated across the SortieNet display on her corneal implants and on her visor's HUD.

She modified the data output to just run through her implants while she wondered about the state of things with poor Jinnbo. Then she pulled operational metrics for Hail Mary and Seraf and one for her beleaguered co-pilot as well. She dragged them with a thought to one side of her dashboard so she could stay up-to-date with them while she and Raphael were in the mountain.

"Raph, will we be able to maintain contact with the team once we're at the Sanctum?"

"No, Ma'am. I could maybe find a way to use the Braex network, but with the AI so scrambled, we're lucky just to get the portal to work. "

"Okay, well, hopefully the girls will keep him safe."

"They will do their utmost."

Galas squeezed past encroaching vegetation and then into the narrow tunnel beyond. Chaotic holos burst into the air and sprayed across the ceiling, walls, and floor, which made it look like some kind of deranged dance party.

"Ugh ... not this again."

"If you ever wondered what the inside of an insane AI's mind looked like, this is it."

"I may be sick."

"Poor Marguerite. I barely got her cleaned up from the last time."

Galas chuckled weakly as she neared the portal chamber and stepped inside. It was the same thing, flashing, twisting lights in a hallucinogenic rainbow hurricane.

"It's here too. This is worse than before."

"It does appear so."

"What does that mean?"

"I don't know. I guess we'll find out."

"You're a lot of help. I hope our mage doesn't have a weak stomach," she said as she stumbled to the center of the room and fumbled with the console's VR interface. Thankfully, it was still set for the Sanctum from the last time she came through. She reversed the path of travel and stepped into the inner circle. There was only a momentary pause before she felt the twist and fold of manipulated physics.

CHAPTER 14
SOME RANDOM DRONE

Epriot Prime, Braex, The Sanctum Complex

Galas's world re-congealed. That was the best word for it. After feeling an intense sensation of falling in every direction at once, her reality re-solidified, causing her to feel frothy like a freshly poured protein shaken. Which, technically speaking, wasn't too far from reality.

The low-ceilinged portal chamber, with its descending concentric circles leading to the portal dais, was a chaotic vomit of multi-colored holographics, just like the one at the temple plaza. *We need to do something about this AI problem.*

She realized she felt bad for it. If it could go insane, didn't that mean it could feel pain? Wasn't that the mind's response to overwhelming emotional trauma?

She strode more purposefully than she felt out of the chamber and straight to the large double doors that would exit to a vast subterranean lakeshore. The Sanctum building was at the far end of the underground ridgeline that diminished into a little peninsula and then a couple of small islands.

As she recalled, there would be broken carapaces and dried goo by the truckload between here and there.

She pushed on the door and it didn't budge. She pushed again with similarly unspectacular results. Galas pinned the repulsors and put her shoulder into it. The door blew off the hinges and wedged itself into a pile of desiccating psych hopper bodies taller than she was.

She was glad she was breathing recycled air. The surviving psych hopper hordes must have beaten themselves to death trying to get in after she'd fought her way through them and managed to get the doors closed. Who knew that maybe they weren't immune to their own psychic attack? That was something she'd never considered before.

Bummer.

Galas pushed through and climbed over the pale gray shells until she was on solid rock again. That was a detail she'd forgotten. They were shiny black when they were alive and trying to kill you. This gray color was … offputting. But still, the trail of carnage that littered the ridgeline was impressive. Even by her standards.

"Damn." She let out a low whistle.

"You were in the zone."

"I'll say. I thought my arms would fall off from swinging those half-assed flails for so long," she agreed, referring to the chunks of rubble she'd anchored her grappling lines to. When that rock had broken away intact, it was ultimately what caught Sun-Thurr off-guard as he'd materialized for his final attack. And it was that same oversized set of chain maces that had dispatched so many psych hoppers, keeping them at a safe distance and doing to their insides what plasma and laser fire could not do to their hardened shells.

Looking over the carnage washed in the harsh illumination of her floodlights was supremely eerie. It was also a foolhardy thing to do if there were any that'd survived the massacre. Or if there was some other nightmare she'd yet to encounter down here in the depths of the Prior's mountain keep.

With a thought, she quenched her helmet-mounted floodlights and switched to an IR/Thermal filter. It was a composite image she'd crafted that she found quite useful. Not only did it help with outlines and depth of field, it highlighted things that could blend in with the surroundings but still gave off a heat signature. Even a residual one.

That last part was key. A minor splash of multicolor light revealing thermal residue could betray where someone or something had been just moments or even minutes before.

Nothing stood out now. The place was dead. Literally. Still…

Galas walked at a leisurely pace down the raised cobblestone road, trying to imagine what this place would look like in the light. Maybe the Priors saw in a spectrum that humans didn't?

Something buzzed past. It wasn't a hopper. More like a hummingbird. A big hummingbird.

"Raph? Any idea what that was?"

"It was a really fast little drone."

"Did ya see where it went?"

"Seemed to be heading toward the Sanctum proper."

"Who would have a drone down here?"

"Beats me."

She picked up the pace to a crouching sort of jog. She held off on deploying her plasma blades, since the crackling purple-white light would definitely give her away. It was a certainty that whoever was using that drone had a night vision filter working, but no sense in making it easy on them by lighting up the whole esplanade.

D'avry's head was killing him. Probably because he was pinned against a wall upside down. He didn't know what it was at first, but his power armor gel couches were occasionally massaging his muscles to keep the blood from pooling in his head. He was thankful, but they couldn't squeeze the blood from his skull back up into his body. He wasn't sure how long he could hang upside down without dying. Obviously, he'd never tried it. He imagined his head just popping like a ripe tomato. That didn't calm his nerves.

Neither did the seven-foot-tall woman with large, gold and silver-dipped antlers protruding from her skull. It was a nice rack. He wouldn't tell her as much. She didn't seem to have much of a sense of humor.

When he'd materialized here—wherever *here* was—she had been standing in the middle of the room, arms raised, incanting something in a foreign tongue. That was particularly odd since he had an ongoing spell of enlightenment that facilitated speech with anyone and everyone he'd come across, even someones from other planets and solar systems, such as Rutker, the Epriot-born mech pilot, or the Gefkarri aspects. But this woman's speech remained a mystery.

Another peculiarity, and one that he found deeply disturbing, was that when she closed her gold-irised eyes, they appeared to be stitched up with thick black sinew, and a new, dimly glowing crimson eye opened up in the middle of her forehead.

When she saw him appear, she seemed surprised and, with a flick of her wrist, he'd been slammed into the wall, ten feet up and fully upside down. She'd asked him something, but he'd been unable to understand it, which seemed to infuriate her.

She asked again and when he didn't respond, she'd used magic to retract his helmet's visor, and then she'd pressed a gold and silver-tipped antler point into the fleshy corner of his eye and demanded one more time.

He'd sputtered out something unintelligible even to himself, but she seemed satisfied and turned away to work on whatever it was she'd been doing before he'd so rudely interrupted her.

That's when he remembered Rutker's drone. He wasn't sure he could manipulate it now, without the power of the Astrig Ka'a.

And at first, he couldn't. Then he started to explore his senses for arcane energy. The chamber they were in was deafening with something that was not magic but was like a hurricane force of something ... other. It was like ... *opposite* magic, if that made any sense at all. Maybe it did. He was new to this *other-planet* magic system ... thing.

He needed to find a journal so he could jot, all of these findings down. *Okay, no more distractions,* he chided himself.

D'avry could only think of this local, reversed Epriot magic like a lodestone. Pushed one way toward another stone and it would join with it. Flipped over, it would repel that same stone all day long. This room felt like that inverted stone. He would have called it a *null*-magic, but it didn't cancel anything. It repelled it. And it did so, vehemently.

This place, he was left to conclude, was a nexus of opposite magic. He'd never heard of such a thing.

D'avry tried with his senses to reach for this new kind of field, but it slipped away and around his grasp. He tried for twenty minutes and the only thing he had to show for it was an even greater pounding in his head. It felt like it wanted to split open and, if he were being honest, he was feeling more and more inclined to let it do so. The throbbing in his temples was grinding him down.

With nothing else he could do, he watched the woman. She spewed an unending stream of arcana in a sometimes guttural, sometimes dry, reedy tone. Sometimes she spread her hands wide to the floor below, sometimes she shook her fists to emphasize a point. It was the most frightening thing he could think of until he remembered the submerged chamber near where he first met Rutker. That was the absolutely most terrifying place he'd ever been until he realized that it was magic that had generated that fear. It was a spell, much like what was used on the drums of the orc warlord when the storm had broken, and flights of flaming arrows rained on his companions like hailstones.

D'avry had to admit, it'd been an eventful few weeks. He'd made friends, lost them, found them again, lost them again, made more friends, lost those, met a girl, lost her, found her, lost her again, saw her in a dream reality ... so on and so forth.

In all of that, he'd made a lot of enemies. But they just did not seem to go away. The Void walkers, for instance. They were here on this planet. In an entirely different corner of the cosmos! But then, so was he. This drama was playing out in different places and times and even dimensions. But what was the unifying theme? What was the genesis?

The Gefkarri. The answer came to him like a sledgehammer to the head. A sledgehammer to join the other sledgehammer that was already ringing his cranium like a temple gong.

The Gefkarri was—or were—at the beginning, he still wasn't quite sure how to refer to them/it. But they were here. How did that affect humanity? He understood that they were going to use the humans here on Epriot Prime. Use them like magical augmentations for their armies, just like the mutants on the flying airship the Eleven Sevens, but in a way that was somehow even more sinister. But he just couldn't quite figure out how E'rth played into all of this. Or what it was that the Astrig Ka'a was trying to get him to do.

It was clearly driving him to gather artifacts and people around him. But for what purpose? Then there was the Void. It seemed clear that they threatened the Gefkarri in some way. Enough that the Gefkarri came here to fight them.

He couldn't make the pieces work together.

Then there was the Gray Town, that space between spaces. It was tied to E'rth, yet somehow, was not *on* E'rth. What he'd seen there this last time was ... beyond words. Machine didn't quite cut it. It was too vast. And then there was the lattice-work, like an ephemeral net strangling the planet.

A thought began to germinate in his mind, but he wasn't quite ready to run with it. And then something caught his eye.

A trick of the light drew his attention to something at the woman's hip. A talisman. Her hand brushed it and then she reached upward again, chanting that foreign, primal invocation.

He didn't know what she was doing, but was sure he wouldn't like it. His attention went back to the talisman. He reached out with his magical sense, so still, so silent, and caressed the barest edge of that talisman and something happened.

He felt a flow. Real, powerful, arcana. It wasn't anything he'd touched before, but it was familiar. Chareth-Ul magic. This talisman, this device, was pulling from another source. It was quite obvious now. This was a tiny, stable little rift.

The woman was deep into her incantation. Her body shuddered under the force of her words. It seemed as though the room's light was somehow being sucked out of it.

He stole a little more of the magic and directed it through the drone in his pocket inside the suit. It perked up. Wiggled its way up his body to where his neck met the gel of the power armor. He twisted and contorted until the orange-sized object finally squeezed through and flitted away along a curving row of columns.

He directed it high and along the edges until it came to a staircase that spiraled along the extent of the deep, cylinder-shaped chamber.

D'avry used a tiny amount of magic to see what the drone saw. It raced along the stairs, volume upon volume of books and tomes lined the walls. Down in the center of the chamber was the woman, and he saw himself pinned to the wall behind her until the drone circled away before coming back into view, another level higher with himself and the Chareth-Ul priestess, another level down.

Galas entered the Sanctum. Of her own free will this time. *Thankfully*, she thought to herself. Last time she'd been compelled to enter by Sun-Thurr in some strange and deeply violating way. He'd done something to her when they'd first met and he'd somehow magically downloaded almost all the missing professor's research into her SortieNet files. How he'd pulled that off was still a mystery.

The whole interaction made her skin crawl. She'd been around some weirdos before, but Sun-Thurr was on another level. Several levels. And in her expert opinion, those levels were down and smelled of sulfur.

The drone flashed by again and this time she chased after it until she came across a crumpled mass in the middle of the Sanctum floor.

"Speak of the devil," she spat.

After swatting him through the air with her handmade chain mace weapons, she'd finished the job with one well-placed repulsor augmented boot. The result was not pretty. Little dried bits of Sun-Thurr's head and upper torso were fanned out across the floor. Even though it was dry now, she still had to gulp down the bile that was trying to work its way up. Sans adrenalin, she found her stomach getting increasingly queasy over things like this.

The out-of-place drone buzzed its way back up and hovered above the body of the not-so-demon-god-after-all, Sun-Thurr. It dropped down near a satchel attached to Sun-Thurr's broad leather belt. The bile threatened to come back up as she wondered what animal that skin had been taken from. All the fauna she'd seen from Sun-Thurr's world had hard chitinous armor. She forced the question from her mind even as Raphael introduced a minor sedative into her bloodstream via the suit's micro-dosing system. She felt a cool wave wash through her and knock down the jitters a bit. She simultaneously loved and hated having an onboard nanny. But sometimes it was a good thing. Like right now, when she was considering losing her lunch rather than sorting out what this drone was doing or where the missing mage might have gone.

All of a sudden she could think clearly again. This drone was being directed to get her attention and to lead her here. There was clearly an inquisitive mind behind it, otherwise it wouldn't be taking an interest in the corpse of a Chareth-Ul priest, and especially at an article of that corpse's clothing.

She reached down and paused. Bad memories rightly informed her body's fear circuitry to move with caution. She looked at the drone again and it rotated its sensor array down to 'look' at the satchel on Sun-Thurr's belt the way a dog would look at a morsel that it wanted its owner to give it. She shook her head and sighed before reaching down to grab it.

Nothing happened. It was just a pouch. She pulled it off, and the drone slid in close, pointed its sensors down at the pouch in her hand, and then back at her face. She looked down at the pouch. It did too. She looked back at the drone. She could swear it was getting irritated.

"You want this?"

It bobbed up and down in an over-exaggerated manner.

She chuckled again to herself. Now she was taking orders from a drone. Which, now she could see, was an EDC make. A way older model too. There weren't a lot of older model anythings in the EDC corp since most everything in service was in a perpetual state of getting blown up and replaced with new.

With a few exceptions, she thought, until she remembered watching Betsy, her old mech, tumble several hundred meters to the bottom of a waterfall. But then, Betsy didn't quite die there either. After Galas had abandoned her, she'd been co-opted by the Deathhounds and then destroyed in a reactor explosion instigated by a Trojan drone that had been disarmed and then re-armed to self-destruct. Marguerite here was the only piece of original equipment she had left. Except for Raph, that was.

Galas took a knee and then unlocked her gauntlets so she could fasten the pouch to the drone. There were fastening strips and other supplies in a storage compartment under an armor plate on Marguerite's upper thigh. She hesitated to pick up the pouch with her bare hands, poked it quickly with a trim fingernail and when nothing happened, grabbed it and the drone. But when she touched the drone, her world twisted upside down and she was staring at the backside of Sun-Thurr again. Only his antlers were gold and silver and his voice was all wrong.

She tried to look closer, but a headache came on so suddenly it felt like it was splitting her skull in half. She let go of the drone when she'd finally gathered the presence of mind to do so.

"What the f—"

"Galas. Are you okay?" Raphael asked. "Your vitals spiked and your brain activity scrambled into completely unrecognizable patterns. It was like someone—"

"Else's brain was in my head? Yeah. It was just like that."

"Care to explain?" Raph asked.

She remembered something about the image she was seeing. She had been staring out of a power suit and there was a whole lot of darkness. But not darkness like an absence of light. Darkness, like all the shadows gathering in one spot. It looked like bad magic. Knowing what Sun-Thurr was capable of, she worried that this new person was trying to open a rift right here in the Sanctum. To do what? Or to bring what through? She had no idea. But having a portal for the Chareth-Ul right under Braex, where the Arcfire resided, was absolutely never going to happen while she was alive.

She wrapped the fastening strip around the pouch and then attached it delicately to the floating orb, careful to avoid touching it again.

"Raph. Do you think you can tap this feed?"

"Well, considering that the drone is not currently broadcasting to another source, I don't see why not."

It wasn't broadcasting. How was that? Magic? That sounded stupid even inside her own head. But was there another way? Had she been seeing what Rutker's magical buddy had been seeing? What was his name, Davery? Dafferty? Oh, well. Didn't matter.

Within seconds of the request, an image of herself kneeling on the Sanctum floor, staring back at herself, popped up on her HUD. Raph had successfully hacked the drone.

"I look like shit. Why didn't you tell me I look like shit?"

"I seem to remember a very explicit 'No Nannybot' rule being imposed early on in our relationship."

"Fair enough. Still, friends tell each other stuff like that," she replied. Then to the drone, while extending her hand in a broad sweep, she said, "Lead the way."

CHAPTER 15
WAHR-ZEN

A wave of shadow bloomed from the center of the room, black tendrils of smoke billowing across the floor. The Chareth-Ul priestess turned back toward D'avry, a self-satisfied smile on her face.

"Now. Where were we?"

D'avry swallowed hard, which was hard to do upside down. All of a sudden, he could understand her. Was it because of the magic he'd stolen?

"Oh, you understand me now. How interesting you are. What a sweet ... little ... bauble," she purred in her low, rasping voice. "I am Wahr-Zen. Battle Priestess of the Kuhl-Rahdar."

D'avry smiled anemically.

"This won't do at all. Let's have a proper look at you," she said as she slowly scribed a circle with one long, black-taloned finger.

D'avry's power armor grated against the stone wall as it rotated on an axis where his head was the center. He breathed out in relief as the blood drained from his face and he felt it flow into his extremities. The priestess Wahr-Zen was even more terrifying when viewed right-side-up.

She stepped closer. Even though his feet were still dangling nearly a foot above the floor, they were eye to eye. She stepped closer yet again so that there was only a foot or so between them. Her scent imposed itself upon him. It was a weird amalgamation of old wood, spice, and alchemical fire. There was an undertone of soot from a coal fire and yet some sort of musk. He had no idea why his senses were processing this specific information at this exact moment. He found that magic had a way of manifesting itself in very peculiar ways.

She leveled her gaze on him, her gold and black-flecked irises, mesmerizing and dangerous in that they further blended the distinction between person and creature. Then she closed them, purposefully, most likely to emphasize the emotional impact of black sinew diving into the flesh of her eyelids and cinching tight.

He tried unsuccessfully to suppress a shudder, and a smirk crept onto her thin, cruel lips as the eye in the middle of her forehead sprang open, bathing him in a deep, crimson glow.

He couldn't take his eyes off it. Felt like he was falling or like his soul was being poured into it. He wasn't quite sure how, but in a knee-jerk response, he severed the connection. Her eyes shot open in surprise and outrage.

"How did you do that?" she demanded, her hand balling into a fist as pressure increased on his body from all sides. He couldn't breathe. Unconsciously, his gaze shot down to the pouch at her waist as he tried to draw some tiny amount of power from it to fight back.

"Ooh, clever boy," she said, turning away and plucking the pouch from its resting place. D'avry's connection to it ceased entirely. Somehow, she had shut him out.

The priestess spun back around, the fine chains adorning her antlers whooshing through the air. She held the pouch clutched to her chest. That devious smile was back.

"What are you? Where are you from?" she demanded. Then another thought occurred to her. "And how did you know to come here, to this place?" She pointed slowly down at the floor.

"I didn't," he stuttered out. "I was pulled."

"Pulled? How?" Her eyes grew wide with interest.

"I don't know," he confessed. "I was trying to sense the ethereal field on this planet, but there wasn't any. Not exactly anyway."

"Not exactly ... what do you mean?" Her eyes narrowed again as she scrutinized him, sizing him up. Possibly trying to understand whether this puny human presented a threat in some way or just how much usable information could be extracted from him before his body couldn't take anymore. From her expression and her posture, D'avry's guess was she wasn't quite sure, but she was willing to find out.

He didn't want to say anymore but couldn't help himself. It was like the words were being pulled right out of him.

"There is no magic. But there is an *anti*-magic. Or maybe just another side to it. I really don't understand it."

"Blasphemy. I like it..." She tapped a talon on her thin gray lips. "What is your name, puny mage?"

"Avaricae D'avry. Underlord. Once-brother. Practitioner of the Astrig Ka'a."

Again, the words poured out, and he was helpless to stop them.

"Astrig ... Ka'a?" she asked, clearly intrigued by this last bit of information.

"It is a magic. Where I'm from, anyway. But, a new kind of magic."

"A *new* magic? There is no new magic. There is only old magic, rediscovered."

The look on her face seemed to go from interest to something bordering on hunger. The essence of this woman was death, wilderness, sexuality, and, somehow, more death. Suddenly, he felt like he didn't understand it the way he thought he did. Death, that was.

It was more ... nuanced than he'd ever imagined. He'd always been certain that death was black and white. On or off. You were alive, or you were dead. No in-between, but everything about this woman—that's what he guessed she was—was the in-between. Not-quite-dead. Not exactly alive either. *Other* was the only way to explain it.

There I go, getting distracted at the worst possible time again...

"Show me," she said and his power suit peeled open on its hinges and he was extracted from it. He drifted out while his jacket and tunic peeled open and were ripped down to his waist to reveal the gold and crystal lantern door in his chest.

The power suit flew to the side with a wave of her hand as she strode forward. D'avry was pushed backward through the air until his body was pressed up against the coarse, and exceedingly cold, stone wall again.

"Hmm. What little secrets do you keep in here? I expected to see your heart, but I see you do not have one. But you're human, are you not? And you're not from this planet?"

D'avry felt compelled to answer each question, but as he went to do so she kept asking more and more as if she already knew the answers.

"Again. What are you doing here?"

"I'm here to defeat the Gefkarri. To stop them from using the humans on Epriot Prime as slaves to feed their war machine."

She laughed coarsely. The glowing crimson eye closed as the sinew of her sutures retreated and she opened her normal, gold-flecked eyes once more.

"Fat chance of that, little human mage, Avaricae D'avry of the Astrig Ka'a," she turned, the jeweled chains on her antlers swiping his face before she started away.

"As much as they feign neutrality, the Gefkarri are nothing if not a war machine. And if they have their sights on something, it will take an awfully big lever to lift that terrible gaze." She reached out into the swirling sphere of shadow suspended in the space before her and drew out a tiny little dribble of inky arcane energy before turning her palm over and watching it slip back into the roiling mass before her.

"An awfully big lever, indeed," she said, clapping her hands together as if dusting them off of any residue. "Now, as much as I'd like to keep you around as my own little pet, I'm afraid you will just get in the way of my rather intricate machinations. And besides, the girls get so petty around fresh meat." She looked at him hungrily, but then her eyes narrowed to slits.

"Ooh. Two for the price of one." The priestess's hand shot up and tugged at something invisible in the air and a person in an armor suit came tumbling from the spiral stairway several stories above. They slammed abruptly to a halt, hovering face down, just above the swirling black mass of arcane energy in the center of the room.

"And who is this? An accomplice?" The armor suit's visor slid open to reveal a pretty face. An auburn lock of hair slipped forward. "A lover? Business *and* pleasure." She clucked disapprovingly. "D'avry ... simply scandalous."

"Well, my dear, your timing is impeccable," she said to the woman in the power suit. "I was about to send your boyfriend here through the portal to make sure it works before calling my own minions. I can't have them dying while on the job. The payout for martyrdom is nothing short of extortion, let me assure you." Her face soured, and then brightened.

"You recognize me, don't you? This isn't your first experience with the Chareth-Ul? Let me guess, the Deathhounds? Yet if that were the case, you'd be dead or one of us by now. And we haven't yet been united with our human counterparts for the battle to come. They still have much training. Many rites of initiation ahead of them before they can be of any real use. Trust me, I've seen it with my own eye." Wahr-Zen emphasized that last.

D'avry couldn't see her face, but by the look on the woman soldier's face and the pale crimson glow bathing it, he could tell that the Chareth-Ul priestess had opened her third eye.

Bad things happened when she did that. He could feel the power coursing through the talisman and being consumed by the priestess.

The woman soldier, whom he could only assume to be Colonel Cadian Galas, inched downward toward the swirling mass of shadow. It was obvious she couldn't move. The priestess had her immobilized much the same way that she had him.

He needed to shift the balance of power. He'd been guiding the drone back to this location all while he and the priestess had been having their... conversation wasn't quite the right word for it. Interrogation was more like it.

He'd been forced to stop with the drone when she'd removed him from his suit and pinned him there. He still didn't have a way to utilize the anti-magic native to this world, but he could sense the other talisman through his connection with the drone. A connection he was thankful was somehow still in place, as weak as his own magic was without a source to pull from.

But now, there was a little hope. He couldn't use the talisman through his link to the drone, but he could bring the drone close enough to use it that way. If he could guide it down to himself without the priestess noticing, at least.

The drone she'd been following just stopped. Galas peered over the edge of the stairs that circled the perimeter of what was essentially a seven or eight-story tall library carved into the stone below the Sanctum. It was a good size, roughly ten or twelve meters across, and there were no railings on the stone steps. The floor was still a good twenty meters down from here. She was thankful that the crazed AI holographics that were prevalent above did not extend down to this area.

Still, what she saw was absolutely bizarre. In the middle of the room was a large sphere of black. It looked like a ball of space, only there was some sort of movement, swirling like eddy currents within it. Next to it was a Chareth-UI, like the necromancer Sun-Thurr. This one, however, had gold and silver antlers that were adorned with fine chains and jewelry. Okay, that wasn't weird.

Behind her, pinned to the wall, was the man she assumed to be Rutker's missing magician. Great! She found him. Mission accomplished. Oh yeah, and try not to shoot him.

He was a good-looking kid, from what she could tell at this distance. Blond, thin, and lightly muscled—not like a soldier, more like someone used to spending a lot of time outdoors. He was in his twenties, most likely. And he had some sort of augmentation built into his chest. Seemed like an odd thing to do but, to each their own.

There was a flash of movement from the Chareth-UI as she reached up and before Galas could react, she was falling. She tried to fire her grappling line but couldn't. The floor raced up to meet her; she thought she was going to fall right into that sphere of blackest shadow but then jerked to a halt less than a meter away.

She caught her breath. She was looking at the Chareth-UI now and could see she was a woman or at least feminine in a harsh, demonic sort of way. Galas glanced quickly at the young mage. He seemed relieved to see that she hadn't been sucked into the swirling ball of black directly below her. That made two of them.

"And who is this? An accomplice?" the feminine version of Sun-Thurr asked.

Galas's visor slid open without a command. Her bangs drooped down in her face.

"A lover? Business and pleasure," the woman teased. "D'avry ... scandalous."

The woman said something about a boyfriend and a contract but Galas was too focused on the fact that she had worked so hard and barely got the edge on Sun-Thurr, and now, here this woman was, equally, if not more powerful and just as twisted.

"You recognize me, don't you? This isn't your first experience with the Chareth-Ul? Let me guess, Deathhounds? Yet if that were the case, you'd be dead or one of us by now. And we haven't yet been united with our human counterparts for the battle to come. They still have much initiation ahead of them before they can be of any real use. Trust me, I've seen it with my own eye."

Galas's pulse raced. They were going to use the Epriots as slaves. After all that fighting to save the planet from the Delvadr, now they were just going to be handed over by that double-crossing Gefkarri hive mind. She used to *like* trees.

Then the woman Chareth-Ul closed her eyes. Black sinew sowed them shut and a new, blazing red eye opened up between her eyes. Galas's breath caught in her chest. *Well, it's been a good run anyway. I just hope I don't turn into as much of an asshole as Drakas when I die.*

Her only regret, besides dying at the hands of a Sun-Thurr wannabe and not being able to save the planet once more, was that she wouldn't be able to see Seraf one last time. *Sorry, kiddo.*

She sent a thought-to-text message to the drone.

[Galas: Raph. Deliver the package.]

She then smiled at the woman-monster before her.

CHAPTER 16
HELL ON EPRIOT

D'avry didn't end up having to do a thing. The drone shot down from above and landed right in the palm of his restrained hand.

He reached through his arcane senses and drew power through the talisman within the pouch attached to it. He was unfamiliar with the magic and with the artifact, so the inrush of ethereal force came crashing through like a rogue wave.

Wahr-Zen sensed it and spun around, her eye blazing like a brilliant red sun. Through the power, D'avry drew up darkness around him and prepared to launch it at her when he saw that the Chareth-Ul priestess had dropped Col. Galas. She fell into the mass of swirling shadows, but then a grappling line shot out and snared the priestess by her antlers and yanked her back. She disappeared into the morass and they were both gone before it imploded on itself and disappeared entirely.

It was over in less than a few seconds. The room was suddenly brighter, and in the aftermath, it was disturbingly quiet. D'avry had dropped to the floor and didn't even realize it. He stepped forward, shocked. He could hear the dull rush of blood in his ears. Felt his chest pounding.

His boots scuffing on the stone floor sounded like the loudest thing he'd ever heard. They were both gone. It was Farn all over again. How could he have avoided that? Was Galas still alive? What about the Chareth-Ul priestess? Would she be back?

Defeat settled like a millstone in D'avry's heart.

"D'avry, I presume?" a somber voice split the silence from somewhere nearby. He turned to look, but there was no one there. Then the drone tugged at his hand. He detached the talisman pouch and tied it to his belt, the same way that Sun-Thurr and the priestess Wahr-Zen had. The drone drifted up to eye level, and the voice issued from it.

"Is she gone for good?" it asked in a voice that sounded far too wounded to be coming from a small flying machine.

"I don't know. I think she's in the realm of the Chareth-Ul. If they made it through. The woman seemed concerned about the viability of the portal. I think that's what that was." Something informed him that was indeed the case. It was a certainty that flowed from this new arcana attached to the talisman. The magic itself wasn't speaking to him but seemed to power some inherent cognitive ability he had. A knowing. He was used to this with the Astrig Ka'a, but there was another element to it with the Astrig Ka'a.

"So then it's *possible* that she's alive?"

"Yes. It's possible," he replied, though it seemed like an unfounded hope.

"Can you get her back?"

"I don't know. Maybe. It's going to take me a little bit to understand the rules of this new Chareth-Ul arcana. It's powerful. And desperate, in a way. I don't like it. It feels dirty, no, corrupted. It's broken. And then there is the anti-magic that's part of this place. This world," he motioned around him, "This room is a nexus for it. That's something meaningful, but I don't know quite why. The priestess seemed very interested in it. Either that or the Arcfire, I'm not sure exactly. Maybe both. Who are you, by the way?" D'avry asked.

"I'm Raphael. Galas's AI. At least a limited version of it, bound by the limited resources of the drone," and after a moment, "... and I'm also a wingman."

That statement was sobering. "I'm very sorry. She was a brave warrior."

"You don't know the half of it," Raphael agreed.

"I'm sure I don't." D'avry massaged his pounding temples. "So, what now?"

"Galas's mission was to protect the Arcfire. The elite mechs, Hail Mary and Seraf are on that. AI versions of myself are operating them, which violate more conventions than even I can count as far as the EDC is concerned. But then Colonel Galas's co-pilot, Jinnbo, is onboard the Hail Mary. Though he's not the most reliable commanding officer right now.

"Beyond that, we have the large alien vessel in outer orbit and the *Xandraitha's Hope* in middle orbit. Galas swore to keep them there until the EDC weighed in," the AI, Raphael continued.

"Then there's the Chareth-Ul and Delvadr contingents waging war against the Void, with new portals popping up all over the planet.

"And lastly, there's this new information about the Chareth-Ul and Gefkarri training humans to be magical power supplies or conduits of some sort, in order to supercharge their mechanized forces, though, to be honest, I haven't the foggiest idea how that would work. Or how they could get them to go along with it. But, it doesn't sound good for Epriot Prime. The humans that are left, that is.

"You know there used to be twenty-eight *billion* of your kind spread across this solar system? A quarter of them perished on Guisse IV alone. Now there may be no more than 250,000."

D'avry's jaw dropped. His mind struggled to grasp the numbers of lost souls the AI was telling him, "I can't even begin to comprehend those numbers. Just the survivors alone, 250,000. There may be that many people in the two capital cities on E'rth's main continent. In my time, at least."

"In your *time*? We should speak more of that later."

There was silence for a moment.

"There's one more thing that you're missing."

"What's that?" Raphael asked.

"We need to get every last one of the survivors off this planet and away to E'rth. That's the only way to save them from a life—and maybe an afterlife—of slavery. And, it's what has to happen for humanity's beginnings on E'rth. Otherwise, I'll never be born and grow up to end up here in the first place. I think, anyway," D'avry added that last bit because he wasn't sure. He hadn't asked to teleport from place to place and he certainly hadn't asked to travel back and forth through time. He certainly hadn't been prepared in any way to deal with the possible repercussions of changing things in the past. He realized that may or may not be exactly what he was doing right now.

"So, you're not only from another planet where humankind exists, but you really are from some point in the future? Is that possible? I mean, of course it is, theoretically. I just didn't know anyone was actually doing it."

"It's the Astrig Ka'a."

"Magic."

"Yeah. It kind of tells me what to do and where to go."

"You're saying that your magic does that? It has a will of its own?"

"Why does everyone keep asking that? No. It doesn't."

"Then who is in charge of this Astrig Ka'a?"

"I'd love to find out," D'avry said and then remembered that terrifying subterranean cavern where he'd first met Rutker and thought maybe he didn't. Want to find out, that was.

It's just magic, he told himself. *It's just a spell of terror.*

Didn't matter. Terror was terror and enough of it could still kill you. Or at least that's what he'd been told in Academie.

"D'avry, we need to stay focused," Raphael said, "You're saying that we need to evacuate every remaining person from this planet to a new planet you call E'rth? Your home planet."

"Yes. Or they will be subjugated and sentenced to war at the hands of the Gefkarri and Chareth-Ul. Or maybe just the Chareth-Ul if that priestess Wahr-Zen gets her way. I think she was trying to co-opt the Arcfire and maybe this anti-magic nexus for herself in order to keep the Gefkarri out. Just a hypothesis. But, I think the Chareth-Ul want Epriot Prime for themselves and I honestly don't care. What I do care about is keeping either of their hands off of our people," D'avry provided, while inspecting the area where the priestess had summoned the portal.

"Well, the Arcfire is keeping the Gefkarri at bay, at least for the time being. But even as we speak, Rutker and the Gefkarri Aspect Theal are headed to New Varhus to speak with EDC High Command. And the traitor, Colonel Dexx may already be there. And who knows what deal he's going to try to arrange."

"That's if Macq didn't find him first," D'avry provided.

"Sure. That's another facet of this whole convoluted situation. But we can't count on it. And as much as I want to go after Galas, in light of this new information about these training camps, I think humanity's only hope is for us to go to New Varhus ASAFP."

"What does that mean? Assafp."

"Now. It means now. In Galas-speak."

It didn't feel good to leave, but D'avry had to agree. The greater mission, the one Galas sacrificed her life for, was to save humanity. He'd figure out a way to find her and bring her back if he could.

Raphael continued, "Now, let's figure out the fastest way to New Varhus. I think we need to get topside, disseminate the plan to the team, and call in another transport. If there's one to be had. Though, in reality, Jinnbo will have to do it since he's the ranking member of the crew with Galas gone. I'm just an AI and you're, well, you're not even from this planet."

D'avry sensed the energy of the room one more time just to let the impression of it settle in. He might need to come back here. Then he reached out with his magical sense through the talisman once more. The black sphere was an echo in the middle of the room. Not there, but also not, not there either. It could be re-opened. He just didn't think it was smart to try it just yet.

There was a lot of power in this connection to the Chareth-Ul realm. He'd seen their machinery in his simulation with Seda, the Gefkarri aspect, and his personal tutor in their form of magic. He'd felt it off in the distance even as he'd sensed this nexus of anti-magic within the mountain.

There was so much here to learn and to understand, and he had no time to do it. He reached through the talisman again and drew some of that dark power into himself. He sensed the relics in his chest flutter. The black flaming arrow stuck through Gemballelven Farn's tome seemed to resonate with the influx of arcane energy. That made him nervous. He drew on the power a little more and felt it writhe and twist in his ethereal grip. It felt like a living thing. And, in that moment, he had an uncomfortable revelation. That sensation was very much like the Astrig Ka'a.

He stretched his neck from side to side as he wrestled with this new thought. It'd have to wait. If he ever got back to E'rth, he would find his answers. There was still another mystery to unravel there. What was with all the artifacts and what were he and the others actually fighting against? What was it that the Astrig Ka'a was preparing him for? His mind flashed on the latticework he'd seen in his vision—the net around the planet. Was that it? What did it mean though, and what did it do?

"D'avry. We need to go," Raphael vocalized through the drone. Of course, he wasn't speaking through it as if he were someplace else. D'avry's understanding about computers was limited, but it didn't seem possible that this small drone had the computing power necessary to house the massive mind that was an AI. At one point Rutker had tried to explain that computers could be both centralized and decentralized and that they housed billions of books worth of information inside of crystals. Maybe this was a remote device or maybe it was a part of the whole that was the AI known as Raphael. He wasn't sure, but he'd have to stow those questions for later. He just liked understanding the nature of his allies when he could. And of late, that had been more and more of a luxury he couldn't afford.

Drawing a little of the power, he transformed into the raven and flapped a couple of times before settling to the ground.

The drone rotated and paused a moment, "Unprecedented. Nice trick," it said before speeding up into the far reaches of the lower Sanctum. D'avry sprang into the air behind it.

Galas awoke from an unintentional nap for ... she honestly had no idea how many times she'd been knocked out in the last couple of days. Four? Five, maybe? The nanomachines must be working their tiny little asses off to re-establish the myriad neural connections that had been savagely ripped apart in all that chaos.

She stared across a dark stone floor. It was damp. The walls were darkly glistening. More stone by the look of it. She tried to push herself off the floor, but her head fought back and she choked down bile.

Not again ... not again ... not throwing up in my suit ... not throwing up in my suit. She continued the mantra in her head, hoping to talk her body out of following through on its promise. She laid her head back down on the floor and stared across the room absently.

Where was she? She'd been screwing around again. That was how these things always happened. Picking fights with the wrong people. Or groups of people. Or aliens. Or groups of aliens. The idea of antlers came to mind and suddenly her blood ran cold.

Just then, movement from across the darkened room drew her attention. A figure sitting in the enveloping shadows was *almost* impossible to make out. Until a glowing red eye slid open, bathing that person, or thing, in a diffuse light.

"Ah, I see you're up. Good..." the Chareth-Ul priestess crooned in her dry, husky voice, and stood up to her full height, antlers nearly brushing the ceiling of what Galas now realized was a cave structure of some sort. "Let's have a chat," she said, enunciating each syllable with precision.

Suddenly Galas flew from the floor and was pinned to the ceiling, face first. Her armor ground across the stone, causing little sparks in the foreign material that crackled and hissed in the darkness. "Well, you've really done it this time, haven't you?"

"Done what?" Galas choked out, feeling the pressure of being forced into the ceiling on her body as much as on the armor itself. She could barely breathe.

"Well. I didn't realize it when we first met, but you're a marked one. Tell me, how did you escape the Deathhounds? It's their job, upon pain—insatiable, unrelenting suffering—to bring you into the fold."

"Where are we?"

"Pfft. Little matter. We'll get to that. I'd say you forfeited your right to ask the questions when you dragged a battle priestess through her own portal. The gall! You really have a set on you. Must have been why you were chosen to begin with."

"But I thought the Deathhounds just chased a bounty," Galas gasped out, her curiosity getting the better of her despite her discomfort and desperate need to find a way to escape.

"True, but that's just half of the story. Only the ones worth taking would ever have a bounty on them. A convenience. Nothing more. The real purpose was always to fill our ranks with the worst, most fearsome, most loathsome. The elite of the depraved. Congratulations, my dear, you're a real wicked bitch."

The magical hold on Galas rolled her over, so she was facing down toward the floor.

"I did some thinking while you were taking your little nap. Puny humans. So fragile, but then capable of creating mechanized armor and plasma weapons, and even more importantly, capable of integrating with our own magic." She clucked, shaking her head in mock disbelief. "What a treasured gift."

She walked slowly across the floor of the cave room. Galas could see intricate scrollwork covering every square centimeter of the floor.

"Admiring the decorations? You've stepped into my playpen now. Oh, the exquisite anguish you'll experience here," she said, closing her eyes as if the idea were of supreme delight, which Galas had no doubt was true. Her stomach twisted and her throat tightened. She *really* needed to find a way out. "You see, when you pulled me back into my own portal, well, that's a bad thing. A terrible thing, in fact. Certain annihilation for most, but lucky for you, I'm not most. I'm Wahr-Zen, battle priestess of the Kuhl-Radhar, commander of the Temple City Mech, Ul-Tenaacht. The devoted one.

"I've served lifetimes within my art and, given how ruthless and treacherous my sisters can be, never go anywhere without a backup plan.

"Of course, you might have been better off just becoming some tiny bit of flotsam in the vast expanse of the materium, but there are greater things in store for you. I'll see to that.

"Now," she said, putting a taloned finger to her char-black lips, "Let's get you into something more ... suitable."

Galas desperately tried to send a thought to text, but that's when she realized the SortieNet, and even worse, Raphael, wasn't there. The suit was dead. And Galas ... was alone.

Her suit sprang open along its seams. She tumbled forward into the open air. Galas carried the movement into a somersault, landing heavily on her feet, and continued the roll forward on the ground. She cut the distance to the priestess and launched forward, her shoulder connecting with the woman's stomach, which knocked the wind out of her and sent them both to the floor.

The woman hit with a grunt. Galas rolled to the side, but as she moved to her feet to run, a talon swiped across her calf and Achilles tendon. The pain lanced up her leg, and she screamed out as she limped as fast as she could toward the only exit she could see, a faint light in the far corner of the room.

Laughter echoed from the chamber as Galas made her way down a tall, narrow corridor. It followed her as she mounted a set of spiral stairs with unequal-sized steps. The scrollwork flowed along the walls and spilled onto the floor as she came to a great vestibule with columns and doors along one side and more columns surrounding openings to the outside along the other.

Beyond the openings was nothing but a pale crimson sky. Her eyes fixed on the doorway at the far end of the room and she sprinted, but the pain in her leg reminded her of the injury. She looked down hastily to assess the damage, but she wasn't bleeding like she should have been. Instead, the long ragged gash was dark black, with spider-like veins branching out from it. Her stomach clenched. *What did that bitch do to me?* It had to be some kind of poison. Her pulse raced, and she started for the far door, but the pain was intense. Not normal pain, but a throbbing, energy-sucking, hopeless sort of pain.

She pushed forward, the laughter still echoing from the corridor behind her. She stumbled, hitting her face on the floor. Galas pushed herself back up. The pain built. It had to be poison.

She kept moving forward—even if it was slowly—it was all she could do. She fixed her eyes on the far door. After long seconds of fighting her way forward as if through a flood, she realized the doorways to her right were filled with figures. Darkly glistening carapaces greeted her. Psych hoppers. Her blood ran cold again as fear and the memory of their psychic stun attack gripped her insides.

She kept pushing on. She was only halfway through when she saw them. Standing tall, in contrast to the hunched hoppers, were two of the acolytes; the formidable Makrit she called bullies. They too had no faces, just blackened dome-like carapaces greeted her.

One of them reached into its hip pouch, which she knew held a weapon like none she'd ever seen before the Arcfire mission. A grenade that bent space.

She stopped in her tracks. Without her suit and in her current state, she had no chance at all against them. Her eyes darted to the opening out onto a cliff. She looked down at her leg, with its growing black tendrils of spidery veins emanating out. The pain was almost unbearable. So intense she couldn't catch her breath.

Without a thought, she lunged toward the opening. She heard fluttering wings behind her. The hoppers were in pursuit. She only had seconds. If that.

And then she was there, pushing past the columns. Beyond and below her, amidst a broad valley riddled with magma-filled rivers and surrounded by volcanic peaks, was an immense field of battle, captured like an insect in amber by some sort of bubble of what Galas could only imagine was arcane energy.

Surrounding it, spaced every so often, decaying and dilapidated mechs. But mechs that were homes to cities. Some were still standing. Some lay partially crumpled, with one leg broken and the other intact. Yet others were in complete disarray. The bubble stretched out to partially envelop these broken mechs. Beyond them, arcane energy flowed into the bubble from temple-like structures hastily scratched into the hard, basaltic rock of the valley floor.

Galas stopped in her tracks. Inside the vague blue haze of the bubble, the battle raged but in excruciatingly slow motion. Barely discernable movement. It was the Deathhounds fighting there. And their adversary? The Void.

She heard the flutter of wings pause just meters behind her. The rustle of fabric farther to her right, beyond that.

And then a familiar voice came from just behind. The skin crawled on the back of Galas's neck.

"So, now you see."

CHAPTER 17
THE INITIATE

Chareth-Ul Reality Zero, Enclave at Ak-Umbrech

The wound in Galas's leg felt like it was on fire and burning its way up. With every pulse, she wanted to crumple to the ground, curl up into a tiny ball, and cry it all away. That was not like her at all.

Desperation and despair gnawed at her mind. But the sight before her, the battle between the Void and the Chareth-Ul in a landscape that looked like hell itself, held her transfixed. Her great fear was that this was an image of the fate that awaited her home world of Epriot Prime.

That's when she realized the true hopelessness of her situation. She was, according to her understanding of things, in an entirely different dimension. There was no way back. Except through one of *their* portals. And how was she going to accomplish that, surrounded by hoppers and bullies and—worse by far—the battle priestess Wahr-Zen?

The pain in her leg bloomed anew, and she wilted, nearly toppling forward. Wahr-Zen came up from behind. She spun her around and, with a taloned finger beneath Galas's chin, lifted her off the ground. She must have used her telekinetic ability to assist because the pressure under Galas's jaw was excruciating, but not enough to lift her bodily. That would have pierced the flesh under her jaw as easily as a fishhook.

Galas's feet dangled uselessly as she slipped out past the opening to hang helplessly in free air above the cliff. The updraft was hot and carried the stench of rotting eggs. She realized there must have been some kind of invisible barrier at the opening and she had just passed through it.

Wahr-Zen stepped to the edge, and the wind jostled the jewelry in her silver and gold dipped antlers. Her eyes, flecked with gold and black, opened wide as she held Galas effortlessly at arm's length. She turned her this way and that.

"You don't really look like much, do you? I'm sure you're fair for your kind, but, for a warrior, you're just a waif of a thing. You must be truly cunning. I saw the carnage. All the Makrit minions. The bodies of the acolytes broken, nearly beyond recognition."

"Sun-Thurr did that," Galas squeaked around clenched teeth, doing her best not to move her jaw and risk another of the poisoned gashes, especially so close to her brain.

"Yes. I saw him too. What a depraved buffoon. To think, he had the oyster of Epriot Prime in his hands all this time and squandered it. Waiting until the battle had nearly reached its zenith and Chareth-Ul hovered at the brink so he could present himself as the savior, seizing power for himself.

"Well, he may have doomed two races to annihilation." She looked at Galas again and her eyes narrowed. "Or maybe not. You vanquished him, and the acolytes, and hordes of their minions. You, without any magic, in spite of being Pan Arcanum?"

"Sorry, I don't speak crazy bitch. Maybe you can rephrase that?"

"Oh, poor dear, I think you do speak 'crazy bitch'," she said, smiling a luxurious smile. "I think you're fluent, in fact. I mean, look at you. I peel you out of your power armor and you're at me like a wounded animal. I think it's who you are. Desperate. Feral. And I think that's why you are marked. And it's why you will become one of us."

Galas tensed. That's what this was about? What did they possibly expect to get out of that? Her own government could barely put up with her endless depths of bullshit. Hell, she could barely stand it herself.

"I see inside you," Wahr-Zen drew close, the black sinew sowing her eyes shut and the crimson eye bloomed to life in the middle of her brow. A visceral chill ran the length of Galas's body from head to toe. The infection in her leg grew warm. It reached through her like a sickness, pulsing up her thigh, warming her groin, gripping her stomach. And then branching upward and outward to fold itself around her heart, pulsing as it crept up her neck, throbbing as her face flushed with the pressure and intensity of it.

Sweat beaded over every inch of her body. It dripped from her hairline into her eyes, stinging them, filling them until she couldn't tell the difference between them and the warm tears streaming down her cheeks. The pain was so intense that she couldn't control her body. Snot ran from her nose into her mouth as she sobbed and choked, voicelessly. Who knew what else she'd lost control of?

The memories from her life crashed through her mind in a torrent of loss and joy, anguish and pride, anger and loathing, hope, and hope dashed to pieces. She saw the look on her mother's face when the *Righteous Fury* was attacked and fell from the sky to destroy their home and half the archipelago with it. She saw the pride in her father's face as she manned the Hillal for the first time and the look of fatherly anguish as he recorded his final message to her before his mission to rescue the downed freighter that ultimately cost him his life. She saw the first lung-clearing cry of her daughter Seraf the day she was born. And the looks of joy on her surrogate parents, Matko and Sonnra's faces as they looked upon her for the first time.

She saw Drakas' bumbling uncertainty when he came to thank her for saving his crew after they'd taken too much damage during the lunar assault on Skleetrix. His look of betrayal and anger when the Delvadr sappers attacked their base in the Spires before he chased them out, ultimately dying at their hands once he was singled out, alone and under-gunned.

She saw Betsy tumbling to the base of the waterfall at Xiocic after Galas had sacrificed her for the best interests of the mission to save humanity. A valiant, but in the end, fruitless sacrifice as the Delvadr, Chareth-Ul and Gefkarri had chosen Epriot Prime as the site of their ultimate battle against the Void.

Through bleary eyes, Galas saw Wahr-Zen's face as she drank in her memories, feeding on her emotions like a ravenous parasite. The look of ecstatic satisfaction on her face made Galas's stomach churn, and she cut it off. Shutting her emotions down to gray stillness. No hate. No happiness. Just inner nothingness.

The priestess's eye diminished and her normal gold and black-flecked eyes opened. The smile on her face was smug and knowing, and Galas felt ultimately exposed. Humiliated like being torn from a lover's embrace and cast naked and alone before a crowd of millions.

The only thing Galas was left with, after all of that, was shame—instead of joy and delight at hearing her daughter might possibly be alive. She felt shame. Shame for having lost her. Shame for not having the strength to never have brought her into this world. This horrible life of living under the constant threat of annihilation. Shame at not having the will to go find her at the earliest opportunity.

The Delvadr weren't going anywhere after they'd been cut off from what was left of their armada. She should have gone to her then, but there were so many excuses. The worst of which, the most honest, was that she was no kind of mother. She wasn't *worthy* of being in her life.

To find her, it wasn't about Seraf; it was about Galas. It had always been about Galas. It was about a sad, lonely little girl in a middle-aged woman's body who buried her brokenness under tons of ceramo-metal armor and rockets and, better than that, the bloodied bodies of her enemies. She felt a cold chill come over her as the heat of the poison washed away.

Wahr-Zen was nearly face-to-face with her. She could see the faint age lines around her eyes and mouth, even though her ashen skin was stretched tight as a drum. She could see the weariness in those eyes, hiding under zealous fanaticism. And beneath the wickedness and hunger, there was a desperation that Galas realized looked very familiar. She cringed internally, but Wahr-Zen's smile grew wider and more devious.

"I see ... everything."

Galas swallowed. She felt the woman's talon pierce the skin beneath her jaw. Around the pain an awareness dawned. Of a thrumming, a great hum like that of a hive or maybe a massive...

Bee.

Wahr-Zen grabbed her by the back of the neck and turned her to face the valley again. From around the rock that Galas could now see served as the base for a great castle-like structure, a massive black creature hovered into view. It was like a huge, black wasp with four wings but instead of legs it had long chitinous tendrils and instead of a tapered thorax it had a long tail that ended in wicked-looking spikes that crackled with blue-white energy. She thought it would give even Hail Mary a run for her money.

The creature's face, similar to the Makrit bullies and hoppers behind her, was blank, black, and smooth. Upon its back was a scaffold with a covered awning and two ornately crafted chairs.

"Come. Let me show you around your new home. For the time being, anyway. Until we take over Epriot Prime and shut the dimensional gateway for good."

"New home? Take over Epriot Prime? Not on my life."

Wahr-Zen chuckled like a knowing mother whose toddler had just defiantly claimed she would not be going to bed, ever.

"My dear. It is not *your* life to give. It is *mine*. And until I demand that you lay it down for my sake, you will do exactly as you are told when you're told to do it."

The creatures hovered close, and a walkway folded down from the side of the structure to provide a path. Wahr-Zen glided forward along the gangway. The second Galas's feet hit the floor, she bolted for the side, launching herself into the air only to be yanked short. She dropped, but swung into the slope of the creatures' carapace, hanging from her neck.

Her hands went to her throat as she struggled to breathe; her own weight choking her against a thick metallic clasp.

She kicked and tried to scream, clawing at her bonds until her body was too weak, and the breath wouldn't come and darkness crept in all around her.

Galas woke again.

"Frag," she croaked as she tried to roll over and thought better of it.

This was like a bad dream. Each time she woke up, it was worse than the time before. Then she realized that type of dream was called a nightmare. Her eyes dropped to her body, which was clad in a tough but supple cloth, like a kind of silk. It was crimson and embroidered with fine gold and silver scrollwork.

She swore the lines seemed to pulse with light as she shifted in her seat, which she now realized was one of the ones she'd seen attached to the carriage strapped to the wasp creature. A wasp with a decidedly Chareth-Ul kind of twist. It had to be a genetic experiment. The loud thrum of its wings came into her awareness and she wondered how she'd missed it when she first woke up.

A gust caught her hair, and strands of it fell into her eyes. She tried to brush them away but realized her hands were bound by chains to a clasp around her waist, similar to what she'd had around her neck earlier. Taking personal inventory, she realized her throat was raw, her right leg still felt as though it were on fire and her head might actually be killing her. She hoped it would.

Her focus moved from her internal drama to the great one unfolding before her. Not only was she perched atop a horrible genetic anomaly, but she was surrounded by overcast skies illuminated by what was clearly a red dwarf sun. And below her was a Vulcan hell to beat anything she could have dreamed of. Magma flows, jutting obsidian and basalt structures, dilapidated mechs, and … oh yeah, a massive glowing time bubble surrounding an interdimensional battlefield. That.

Wahr-Zen was standing at the edge of the platform, her hands clasping a railing, that, like everything with these people, looked to be clad in religious pageantry. Ornate scrollwork on glossy black, maybe wood? Galas couldn't tell. Possibly some nasty bug excretion formed into wood shapes. Whatever. She needed to ditch this place. Like now.

"Ahh, sleeping beauty. Come." Wahr-Zen waved her hand and Galas flew to her feet and started gliding toward her. "Join me."

"Bite me."

Wahr-Zen looked at her hungrily, as if considering that very thing before changing her mind, "Tempting, but no. We breed for our sacrifices. I don't think you'd pass our purity standards. Virgins only, dear." She smiled and turned away to face the battlefield locked in stasis before them.

"We used to be like that. Pure."

Galas choked on that and Wahr-Zen shot her a look from the corner of her eye,

"This was once a lush wilderness. Forest and lakes, tributaries and languid seas. We flourished as a species until resources grew scarce. We fought, I suppose, like all species do. Some of our kind studied genetics, and we found ourselves in a race to destruction as each side created greater and greater beasts with which to destroy the other.

"Eons passed, and the decline of indigenous species spelled the slow and inevitable demise of our ecological system. Warfare wrecked the atmosphere. The planet turned black and turbulent. We were forced to pursue other venues as our home planet hurtled out of balance and into a cycle of environmental disaster that we could not survive.

"We bred creatures that could and that only accelerated the system collapse. In turn, we renewed our exploration, but no suitable planets within our ability to reach existed. But our mages invented a way. They learned to travel the dimensions, and we sent out emissaries and explorers but with shockingly pathetic results. One would think that the universe is teeming with life. And it is, in pockets. And those pockets, it turns out, are densely packed and jealously protected.

"We made some incursions, but none were as effective as the Deathhounds. The turning of the Epriots into soulbound warriors in mechanized armor."

"You stole our people."

"We saved your people. They were going to die anyway," replied Wahr-Zen, nonplussed.

"At your hands."

"Semantics."

Galas tried to fold her arms and turn away, but the cuffs wouldn't allow her the luxury of righteous indignation. So she just looked the other way instead.

"Our explorations did accomplish something. We drew the attention of another race of creatures. The Void. They were slowly taking over one of the dimensions our sorcerers had visited. We wrote it off and returned here. They followed."

"The battle before you is the result. We had no way to defeat them. We didn't have the resources or the time to build up a suitable army. So we stole the resources. The Deathhounds. And we made the time." She gestured at the great bubble that filled the entirety of the space before them.

Galas turned. "You *made* time?"

Wahr-Zen smiled. "Traded really. You see, time is slowed inside the bubble, effectively halting or at least greatly slowing down the advance of the Void against us. This can only last so long. There was never a version of this story where we won. There are too many of them. An entire galaxy beyond our dimension. But, in the slowing of time on one side of the bubble, there's the acceleration of time on the other."

Galas stared again at the aged and crumbling mech cities surrounding it. That was what she'd seen without recognizing it. They were crumbling into oblivion and being rebuilt before her very eyes. Now that they were up close, she could see it.

Her mouth dropped open. She worked saliva back into her mouth to speak. "Your people. They're caught in a temporal vortex. What are *you* doing *here*?"

"I and a retinue of others left our loved ones in search of yet other worlds. Sun-Thurr was among our number. Only he held out on us. Didn't tell us about the bounty of your world, just provided a barely adequate number of recruits to stave off our queries about progress and possibilities. We were all quite busy with our own endeavors. Trying to save one's species is an all-consuming quest, as you well know." She nodded in Galas's direction and Galas despised the fact that she knew so much of what she held so dear.

"So fighting this battle will eventually end in defeat and you plan on taking over Epriot Prime and locking the door behind you. But the Void are already there. How will that work in the long run?"

"Astute observation. The dimensional alignments, much like the cosmos, are in constant movement. The alignment with your time-place is only momentary. Like a solar eclipse. When it's done, it's done. There are still thousands of years to go. Many thousands of years, but that's a fighting chance. We've held the Void off here for as long. But the direction of the battle is obvious and, like you said, they are already on Epriot Prime. And elsewhere."

"Elsewhere. In our galaxy?" Galas's attention was fully on the battle priestess now.

The Initiate

"Mm... indeed." Wahr-Zen nodded slightly in her direction, her attention still on the frozen battle before her. "The Gefkarri fight on many fronts. But we don't need their help on this new battlefield. We have ... other means of ensuring victory."

"Oh yeah? What are those?"

"In due time, my apprentice. In due time."

Gala's heart stopped at those words. She remembered the feeling as the infection in her leg had taken over her entire body before she'd tried to jump to her doom. She felt it now. The pain echoed in her body.

Her skin crawled as she imagined the corruption in every cell of her being. She closed her eyes. The warm wind buffeted her skin and tousled her hair. Sinew grew from the skin around her eyes and pulled them shut as a burning, like a coal ember on her skin, grew between her brows and suddenly, the world sprang open before her in glowing, milky, multispectral splendor. Lines of flux bent outward from the battlefield before her. Gossamer strands radiused inward toward the temples, combined into great interwoven threads and those threads weaved together with yet others to form vast cables of arcane energy that flowed into the temporal bubble that quivered and wobbled before her like some massive jello mold made of the stuff of the materium itself.

Galas's mouth opened, and it was like a million-strong choir surrounded her, screaming in unison. She clutched her head and tried to stop it, but the screaming grew and grew and grew until she couldn't take any more and succumbed to the torrent surrounding her.

The spectral light collapsed into darkness and then she was there on the floor of the platform, staring at her own hands, gray in pallor. Nails black like talons.

CHAPTER 18

THE REMNANT

Epriot Prime, Articles Corwin (Northern Continent), Merrat Valley outside of New Varhus

Rutker wasn't pleased at the turn of events.

As the marine "pond bumble" crested the last huge slab of aquamarine and white-striated sandstone dunes, the Merrat valley spread out before them. Hazy bands of morning fog languished upon a maze of lakes and tributaries that made up the valley south and west of the legendary Spires. Ordinarily, this was a stunning sight with the early morning rays shining like molten gold across waters bounded by shadowed foliage, but this morning, all this was rivaled by a city-sized mech that squatted at the far end, belching smoke and defiling the natural beauty of the valley with interdimensional sludge and the sacrilege of its very presence.

The Chareth-Ul mech wasn't alone. Rutker, from his perch behind the pilot and copilot, forearm braced against a slanting support member, squinted into the sun.

"How many are there?"

"Hundreds, sir."

"An exact figure, Capt. Warbrand?"

"352. No, 355. It keeps going up, sir. Something is interfering with our scans."

"That's a lot of Deathhounds. I didn't know there were so many. Or that they had anything like that," the co-pilot, Lt. Tillery, said.

"No one did," said Rutker.

"The Gefkarri did," Theal provided unhelpfully.

They were both still in their power armor, making quarters cramped behind the two pilots. Earlier, they'd stored the repulsor packs in the back of the craft, but it was tight just the same.

Rutker was inclined to ignore her again, something he found he wanted to do most times, but this changed everything. He might need her now. He had no idea how to deal with the Chareth-Ul. All he'd ever known of them was that as a mech pilot, you didn't want to draw the attention of the Deathhounds. If you did, you either ended up dead ... or one of them. Or maybe it was both. No one knew.

"Reduce airspeed and take us wide to the south. I don't want to get notic—"

A squeal of static interrupted him and then a cold, raspy voice came over comms.

"Transport shuttle M5447 you will land at Airfield Camp Zun-Karlduum, highlighted in your navigation display. You will land and surrender your craft. Go directly and know that prayers to your gods will be met with silence, for your planet is now a grand temple of the Chareth-Ul. Any attempt to deviate or stall will result in your craft being expunged and your bodies resurrected into the soulbound armies of the Deathhounds."

Suddenly the craft jolted a few degrees to the north, and the pilot wobbled the control stick to no effect. He turned to Rutker. "I've got nothing. They just took over," he said in stunned amazement.

"Can you override the autopilot?"

"No," Theal commanded. "You'll only get us killed. Patch me through."

The pilot looked at her and then to Rutker, who nodded affirmation. "Worth a try," he grumbled.

The comms squealed again.

"Chareth-Ul Defiler, this is Aspect Theal Alumen of the Gefkarri Pentarch. I am here to facilitate the integration of the armies of the Chareth-Ul and Delvadr, and to determine the disposition of the human remnant. I must speak to your ranking Battle Priestess at once about these matters."

Static played over the output speakers.

"Chareth-Ul Defiler, again, this is Aspect—"

She was interrupted by a burst of static and then...

"Great Aspect Alumen," a new voice broke in, the words dripping with false deference. "You will be greeted at Camp Zun-Karlduum upon your arrival."

"I wish to speak to the Battle Priestess in charge immediately," Theal countered. "Redirect us to a shuttle bay on the Defiler so I may speak to her in person."

"That ... will not be possible."

Theal's eyes blazed, "I demand—"

"You will *demand* nothing. Your ship is stuck in outer orbit and you have no authority on our planet."

And then the comms went dead, the only noise was that of the engines as the shuttle dropped in altitude and headed for a large field surrounded by a cityscape crawling with five to ten-ton Deathhound mechs—Aardwolf and Shrikes outfitted for close-quarters work or crowd control, from what Rutker could tell.

Within minutes, they were drawing closer to the ground and already the ominous hulk of the Chareth-Ul Defiler towered hundreds of meters above them. Fantails of spillage tumbled from a half-dozen holes on its sides and belly while yellow-tinged clouds billowed from stacks and from what looked like temple ziggurats on its massive deck. The prevailing winds carried the foul air skyward and east, slowly dissipating out amongst the towering Turnedring rock spires in the distance. The presence of the spires gave Rutker a modicum of hope. Maybe there was a resistance to be mounted there. There would be no such action here in the former Epriot capitol.

"*Their* planet. Well, that went well," said Rutker, eyebrows knit, jaw clenched, referring to the failed negotiation a few minutes prior.

It was Theal's turn to ignore him as she quietly fumed.

Rutker took one last look at the shelled-out city as they dropped down below the rooftops of the taller buildings and skimmed over lower ones before the transport shot out over a field of grass. Stretching along the far extents of the parade grounds was a tent city like nothing he'd ever seen before. Multicolored and filled with tents and stackable units of every shape and size. It stretched at least three kilometers long and was half again as wide.

They must have rounded up every last remaining New Varhus resident and had them housed here at the mech parade grounds. He looked around at the husks of building after empty building surrounding the fields. There were more than enough residence towers still standing within a kilometer to house five or six times the number of people that had to be gathered in tents and stacks. And yet, the Chareth-Ul had them here, in the damp winter cold.

Part of the re-education, he realized. That's what this was. The entire population of humanity that remained after a 40-year campaign of genocide by the Delvadr, and they were made prisoners of war by another race of zealots—cattle to be used or slaughtered. *By Maker, I've only been gone two weeks!*

His head and shoulders dragged toward the ground, like on a long 2G departure in a Phalanx, only this was accompanied by a great hollowness in his gut. He thought about Macq and where he might be. And Dexx, though he could really care less about the traitor. Then his mind drifted to Katherynn and Mads, and he was suddenly relieved that he had left them safely in orbit aboard the *Xandraitha's Hope*. Maybe they would find a way out of this.

What were his options? Stay and fight? Fat chance. He'd have to be delusional to think there was a scenario that involved humanity holding Epriot Prime after this. This real estate just turned toxic. And, if D'avry's existence was any indicator, E'rth was a readily available resource. He'd been there himself, breathed the air, felt the dirt beneath his feet. He could maybe overlook that ominous presence he'd stumbled on in the cave network beneath the flats. To be honest, between the demonic Chareth-Ul and the ravenous Void, he'd take those creepy caverns any day of the week.

Now he just had to figure out how to destroy a Chareth-Ul Defiler and several hundred Deathhounds so he could relocate a quarter-million refugees out of the solar system when it was questionable if they had any ships left for the task. They certainly didn't have a carrier, which was what they needed. Though who knew what the Gefkarri ship was capable of? It was like nothing he'd ever seen before, custom-built to transport a magical, sentient forest the size of a small moon. Musings.

His stomach somehow felt even more hollow. He hoped D'avry's situation was better than his, but then he was just as certain that the meddlesome mage would find a way to make matters worse. That was one thing the kid was good at.

Rutker straightened under the load and braced for the landing. The commandeered shuttle drifted over a damp, gray wetland, passed comms arrays, and slowed to a halt before a squad of five Deathhounds standing on the tarmac of the landing area.

The view from the temple plaza of the jungle beyond, minus the burned-up parts, was breathtaking. There was a thickly humid breeze. The thrum of insects filled the air, and over all of it, hung the pall of impending doom.

D'avry paced the temple plaza with a hand on his chin, tapping his lip with a finger, deep in thought. He shook his head and leaned heavily on the foot of the Hail Mary. Or Seraf, he wasn't sure. They were equally menacing and looked nearly identical.

He spoke into the empty space before him inhabited by a solitary drone hovering a few feet away,

"Raphael, if you can't hail anyone from the EDC, then we only have one choice. Flying to New Varhus in one of your mechs will leave the Arcfire woefully under-protected, which we can't do knowing that the Chareth-Ul want it for their own purposes and the Gefkarri want it disabled so they can come down and occupy the planet.

"The only way that we're going to get to EDC High Command in time to do any good is if we allow the *Xandraitha's Hope* to enter the atmosphere, pick us up and take us there."

"You're certain you can't use the Chareth-Ul portal tech?" Raphael asked through the drone's external speakers, which were weak and tinny.

"Good thought, but as much as I try, I just can't seem to make anything stable. Power's not the problem, it's about guiding or containing that power. Watch,"

D'avry lifted his hands, and they were immediately engulfed in shadow. A dark, metallic wind swirled within and then shot out in streams of lightless vortex that spiraled together up into the air and snuffed out with a loud clap.

"I like it! Do it again," came a gleeful voice over the drone's speaker.

D'avry shot a questioning look at the drone. "How many people do you have in there?"

"That was Jinnbo. I patched him through so he could be a part of the conversation, but I'm afraid his condition is deteriorating rather than getting better."

"Do it again!" Jinnbo shrieked manically in a deeper voice than before.

D'avry was concerned. "He doesn't sound quite right. Can I see him?"

"I don't see why not," said Raphael. "Jinnbo. Would you like to come out and say hi to our new friend D'avry?"

"Oh, yes. Very much," came Jinnbo's voice, sounding all of a sudden rational to D'avry's ears.

A hatch opened at the rear of the mech that Raphael had referred to as Hail Mary and then a large bat-like creature slipped out, glided in a wide spiral, and then settled to the ground in front of them with a quick leathery flutter. The creature, which D'avry assumed was Jinnbo, stood nearly four feet tall, had a face like a fox and his body was something between that of a monkey and a bat. As D'avry watched, his upper torso, covered in scales and fine fur, shimmered into the likeness of a button-up tunic with silhouette images of what appeared to be tropical plant leaves and flowers on it.

The creature smiled a toothy smile. "Howdy. I am Jinnbo. The commanding officer of this mech unit and pilot of the Hail Mary. And I'd very much like to see your magic show. Pleeeease?"

D'avry looked at the alien creature, somewhat surprised and still trying to make sense of the multiple personalities he'd heard come out of it. He didn't know if all members of its species were as schizophrenic or if this one was just broken.

Raphael tried to help. "Jinnbo has recently completed a very intense rite of passage, which has caused a substantial rush of hormonal responses that his body is still struggling to normalize. So if he seems a little ... excitable, well, that's just how things are for the time being."

Jinnbo arched his eyebrows twice in the universal sign of mischief and then settled back into his unsettling grin.

"I see," said D'avry, while not entirely sure that he did. "It's a pleasure to meet you, Commander Jinnbo." D'avry offered his hand and purple tongue shot out, slurped at the front and back of it, and then returned to its owner, who looked at him quizzically. "Sorry. I thought you had snacks. Do you mean for me to grasp your hand in the manner of a human greeting?" Jinnbo asked, smiling and then extending a delicate furred paw with talons, thankfully retracted.

D'avry smiled and grasped Jinnbo's hand. The moment he did, images, noises, ideas, and feelings exploded into his mind with such intensity, he stumbled back, eyes wide. He rubbed face and then covered his mouth before dropping it to speak.

"Is *that* what's going on inside your head ... all of the time?" D'avry asked, the place where his heart should be, hurting at the thought.

"You could see that?" Jinnbo asked sheepishly while tracing the outline of a cobblestone with a toe talon. His expressive eyes were full of shame and uncertainty. And fear.

"Just then I did. Is it like that all the time or just since this 'rite of passage' you underwent?"

"Only recently. Why? Is that bad?"

"No," D'avry assured him, shaking his head, sounding much more certain than he actually was. "I just don't know how you manage it. That's all. It's ... a lot."

"It's only manageable sometimes. When I'm angry, it goes away. That feels nice. But then, I'm not a nice person when I'm angry like that," he said, sullenly, staring down at the fresh line of soil he'd extracted from between the cobbles and an ant colony that had been disturbed in the process. He looked at them greedily for a moment and then seemed to think better of it.

"Can I see again?" D'avry asked, extending his hand once more.

Jinnbo looked at him, one eyebrow raised, and then reached out hesitantly. It happened exactly as before, only this time D'avry was almost ready for it. The images and the sounds and feelings burst through his mind.

He drew a bit of the Chareth-Ul power around him and felt the chaos of the flood begin to calm. Slowly, a clamoring of voices began to separate into individual ones. After several moments, D'avry began to weed them out and separate them. The rush was still intense, but soon he was able to formulate a picture of some of what was going on and he let go.

He looked at Jinnbo again, realizing a tiny bit of what may be going on with him.

"Jinnbo. In your culture, how big a role does religion play?"

"Not very. We don't much care for superstition."

"Oh," D'avry replied, a little surprised by that. "Well, then what about your ancestors? Do they play a very big role?"

Jinnbo perked up and then settled into a perplexed sort of head-tilting gesture. "Yes and no." He searched the air for the right words, getting distracted by an insect, which he slurped from the air and then returned to the train of thought almost seamlessly. "We honor our ancestors. But we do not deify them. We never speak to them or ask for advice like some cultures do, if that's what you mean."

"Why not?"

At first, Jinnbo seemed mildly offended by this question, but then seemed to search his memory again. "Well, I guess because that's just foolishness. They never talk back."

"Huh. Give me your hand again."

Jinnbo reached out reluctantly and D'avry grabbed with both of his. He pulled on the Chareth-Ul magic again and concentrated on one of the voices within the multitude, a soft but resolved voice.

An image of vast spreading branches came into his mind. One branch, large enough for five men to walk abreast, led away at a gentle slope. He followed it out to a confluence of several other boughs. It formed a gathering place of sorts that overlooked a spreading valley. Large, winged creatures with two long tails spiraled upon thermals in the hazy distance.

D'avry's attention was drawn to a presence to his right. The wizened face of an elder member of Jinnbo's race looked up at him. The eyes were milky but keen and the scales of its skin portrayed a thick, golden medallion upon its sagging chest. The rest of him was clothed in the suggestion of tawny brown robes with fine red trim.

D'avry turned to the elder and bowed deeply.

The creature looked at D'avry's empty hands.

"No snacks?"

D'avry was mortified. He was in a shared mental experience. Of course, he hadn't brought any snacks.

The creature, seeing his expression, laughed and grabbed his hands.

"Thank you for bringing this child back to us."

D'avry looked and Jinnbo was there next to him, sitting in the Lotus position, eyes closed. When he looked back at the elder, he saw that he was surrounded by many others. They lined the bowery, the great branch, and as D'avry slowly spun around, he saw that every bough within the massive tree was crowded with elders and many who were younger. He realized that these were Jinnbo's ancestors. This was the torrent of noise and voices and ideas and feelings of anguish, torment, and frustration.

D'avry looked again at Jinnbo. He was crying. Weeping, actually, but somehow it seemed like they were tears of happiness.

The wizened elder reached out and touched D'avry on the chest. His eyes burst open, and he was no longer in the elder tree. He cast about to get his bearings again and found that he was back at the temple plaza.

"Are you okay?" Raphael asked from the drone.

"Uh, yeah. I think so," D'avry replied, a bit shaken. And then he looked down to see Jinnbo sitting cross-legged, just as he'd seen him in the dream state.

"Is he okay?" Raph asked.

"Um, I think he's going to be. He might need a year or two of quiet reflection though. I think his ancestors have a lot to tell him."

"Do you break everything you touch?"

"Yeah. That's pretty much what I do," D'avry conceded.

"Can you stop it, please? We need to pool our resources and start solving some of these problems instead of making new ones. Now I don't have an officer who can request transport from EDC."

"Why can't you do that?"

"I'm just a mech AI, designed to streamline the operational side of a battle machine. Not a commissioned officer. I can send a distress beacon, but that's a local alert and there are protocols and, well, this is pretty much the most isolated location on the planet outside of the poles. And the EDC was in shambles to begin with, so..."

"So we need to call up Ambassador Katherynn Novak on the *Xandraitha's Hope* and request that they transport us to New Varhus. It's our only option." D'avry responded, trying to maintain focus while part of him was still readjusting back to this present reality. He realized he spent an inordinate amount of his time doing exactly that.

"There's a somewhat gargantuan problem with that. Once we let the *Xandraitha's Hope* through the Arcfire's defensive envelope, the Gefkarri capital ship may decide they should try it too."

"But they can't because of the Arcfire and if they do, problem solved. Right?"

"Actually, that's not entirely true. The only person that we have available to operate the Arcfire is, well, he's drooling."

D'avry looked and Raphael was right. Jinnbo was drooling. He wondered if he did that too when he meditated.

Raphael picked up where he left off. "Additionally, and even more important, is the fact that when Galas fell through the portal, she took the artifact with her. That artifact is the key to the Arcfire.

"I replayed the video feed. After the battle with the Delvadr ambushers in the mech now known as the Seraf, she reclaimed the artifact. But with everything that happened. She either didn't remember to put it back or was afraid Jinnbo might go maniacal again and do something ... irreversible. No worry of that anymore," Raphael said and rotated the drone so that its most prominent sensor array pointed at Jinnbo and then back again.

D'avry took that moment to jump in. "It's a good thing that he's not a harm to himself or others though. I think anyway. Besides, this could be an evolutionary shift for his species. A new age of enlightenment. I just reintroduced him to his ancestors. Imagine, all that knowledge ... guidance, and wisdom ... gone to waste and then brought back again," D'avry replied, shifting from feeling defensive to feeling not a bit envious.

"Really? That's what you were doing? Anyway, I'm sure the Cycarians are very appreciative. But still, the state of things with the Arcfire leaves the planet unprotected. If the Gefkarri figure that out by trying to send another shuttle or something like that, then that's that. They're here for good, no matter what the EDC says."

"Okay, so that's one problem. The other problem is that they may not need a shuttle to figure that out. They might just read my mind."

"Explain," Raphael said tersely.

"During my short time with the Gefkarri, they infiltrated my mind. That's maybe a little dramatic. How about they invited me into their collective without my permission?"

"Pause. Let me get this straight. You were *invited* into the mind of the Gefkarri collective?"

"Yeah. Or I crashed it. One or the other, but the result is the same."

"So, they know what you're thinking and you know what they're thinking? Like a telepathic link directly to the collective conscience of our enemy? But it goes both ways. So you're a spy, really. You can't be trusted to keep a secret and you may even act against the best interests of your own species..."

"That might be overstating things a bit."

"It might? How so?"

"Well, so I haven't had enough time to sort everything out. They definitely did crack my head open and take a good look around, but then they handed it back. The sense that I got was that there was more there—and less—than they bargained for.

"That's when they assigned a couple of handlers to me. Aspects Theal and Seda. Well, I think Theal is more of the political attaché, and Seda was meant to be my mentor with their version of the magic, but then, like I was saying, I think they were surprised that there wasn't really all that much to teach. I kind of just hit the ground running."

"Okay, that's all truly fascinating. I mean, really, it is pretty stunning from a scientific standpoint, but we've still got a situation on our hands. The Gefkarri want to occupy the planet and they want to use humanity to help them do it. And humanity might not live long enough to see what victory looks like in this situation. Or equally as bad, the Gefkarri, Chareth-Ul, and Delvadr could all fail, in which case, humanity again loses everything. Oh yeah, and you might be a traitor without even knowing it."

"I think I'd know it. And by the way, I'm doing things to mitigate that possibility."

"Oh yeah? Like what?"

"Stuff. Magic stuff."

"Consider me mollified."

"For a computer, you're awfully sarcastic."

"I've been working with Galas for nearly the last fourteen years. And, my adaptive programming isn't really all that discriminating."

D'avry nodded, not sure what to add to that. Other than having a quick flash of connection when she'd touched the drone while it was under his control, he didn't really know her very well. There wasn't enough time. And he was being tortured by an interdimensional witch. One thought did percolate through that burst of connection though. Galas was hyper-focused on the task at hand, but there was something. A fleeting regret, a longing…

"What is Seraf?"

"It's the mech. It's what we named the mech that we took from the Delvader that followed us here when I downloaded a version of my programming into its processing core."

"No. What does it mean?"

"That's rather personal."

"I read it from Galas's mind. It was the only thing outside of her mission—and her teammates—that meant anything to her. What, or who, is Seraf?"

"That's Col. Galas's daughter. She thought she'd lost her in the second wave of the invasion. She only found out a few months back that she might still be alive. She'd vowed to find her after the remaining Delvadr threat was eliminated. Given the state of things on the planet … maybe it's best that Galas … I don't know. That doesn't make any sense, but I just wouldn't want for her to go through that again. She's the strongest person I've ever met, but that would break her."

D'avry nodded again.

"Well, I guess all we can do is try to save as many people as we can."

"Yes. The more that we work this through, the more there seems to be only one viable answer," Raphael responded.

"Which is?"

"We need to retreat. Flee. Evacuate. Whatever you want to call it."

"Well, being that my reality depends entirely on mankind establishing itself on E'rth, I have to agree with you. Now, how do we do it?"

"We need ships. Which we don't have. The *Xandraitha's Hope* is one of a handful of vessels the EDC has left," Raphael provided.

"How many people can fit on that ship? I didn't see the whole thing very well but, I'd guess maybe a couple hundred?"

"The standard crew is twenty-eight, but it's capable of transporting up to two hundred fifty-five with no modifications. Now, it may be possible to make modifications to the cargo hold and to engineering and operations. But, we're talking about a trip that took Rutker and company nearly a week? Say we could boost capacity by 500 percent. With a round trip of fourteen days, it would take nine months to evacuate the entire population with that one ship. And that's if we could modify the life support systems to accommodate that many people."

D'avry's stomach sank. Raph continued, "Even if we scrounged up a dozen similar vessels, it'd still take several weeks of continuous operation. We'll be lucky to get a couple of days. And if your mental barriers aren't as robust as you think they are, maybe hours."

At that point, D'avry was only half listening. Something was itching in the back of his head. He recognized it as the psychic link with Theal. She was upset and he could feel it. How? He had no idea. Even now, he was only vaguely aware of Seda. They had a stronger connection, but even that was ... tenuous with her out there in middle orbit and Epriot Prime not having a viable ethereal field.

What's going on? he wondered.

D'avry pulled a small amount of power from the talisman at his hip and felt a chill in his chest and in his hands. *Here it comes*, he thought, the physical effect he'd been expecting for a while now. Magic always had a catch. He'd been wary of playing fast and loose with a magic that he could tell at first touch was twisted beyond recognition. The priestess was indication enough, but now he was feeling the real magic sink its hooks in his flesh.

He reached out again and willed himself to be resolute. Theal's presence came through so strongly he could swear she was standing next to him. He didn't crack an eyelid. He just trusted his intuition. Somehow, she was very close to the Chareth-Ul. And she was terrified. That sent a shock through D'avry's system.

"...so then, we'll need to access the Spires directly," Raphael was saying.

"Raph. No time. Something's gone very wrong. We need to get to New Varhus immediately. I'm instructing Seda to come get us. Please tell Katherynn the same, but try not to broadcast it. I'm taking precautions so that only Seda and not the Gefkarri corporate will hear me."

"What's the matter?"

"I said, no time."

D'avry massaged his temples as he closed his eyes and tuned Raphael out completely.

In a heartbeat, his consciousness was one with Seda's own.

"Aw, you missed me."

"No time for games, Seda. Theal is in trouble and you need to keep this between us. Can you do that?"

Her demeanor changed dramatically, growing tense ... furtive. "Do you know what you're asking?"

"I have an idea." There was a meaningful pause. If he were being honest, he'd admit that he did not have an idea.

He'd wondered about her strange affinity toward him and wondered about her absence early on in their mentorship. He was fairly certain that she had been punished for some dereliction of duty. Theal had been brought in to oversee things from that point on. He didn't understand how or why, but he could tell there was some sort of connection between Seda and himself.

He was worried that he was testing that bond right now. But there was nothing that could be done about that. He was even more worried when he realized how long she was taking to make this decision.

Helping Theal on the surface should not go against any commands of the corporate body, but it was possible that she understood much more of what was behind D'avry's request. In fact, he was certain of it.

His blood ran cold. He may have just betrayed everything and everyone he'd ever known in one brash moment of arrogance. Thinking he could fool a hyper-intelligent being that was tapped directly into his own brain. *What an idiot.*

"I'll do it."

"Wait, what?" he exclaimed out loud.

"We can't let any harm come to the ambassador to the esteemed Chareth-Ul and Delvadr forces, can we?" she asked and he could hear the deception loud and clear. She was conveying that message back to the greater collective.

"You will allow the *Xandraitha's Hope, only,* to enter Epriot Prime's atmosphere?" she asked.

"Only for forty-eight hours. Long enough to recover the ambassador and establish lines of communication with the Epriot government," he told her and felt that communication pass on to the greater being.

Maybe, just maybe, all was not lost.

CHAPTER 19

INTAKE

Epriot Prime, Articles Corwin, New Varhus Detention Center (Camp Zun-Karlduum)

There were more effective ways to remove human hair, but few were as humiliatingly personal as being held down and gone over the top to literal bottom with a set of motorized clippers. Rutker had a high tolerance for discomfort. And even humiliation. Both were temporary. He was, however, relieved to leave the temporary intake facility with all the parts he went in with.

The Chareth-Ul's minions, large centipede-faced creatures with four thin but surprisingly strong arms, had taken his power armor and left him with a set of confoundingly complicated robes, leggings, and arm wraps. He looked like he'd mugged a monk. Everyone around was wearing the exact same outfit. And haircut. He'd caught his reflection in a window and wasn't even sure if he was looking at himself or someone else.

Separated from the others, he scuffed through puddled water on the parade ground tarmac as he was herded toward the trainee encampment. He had no idea if they were released before or after him, but assumed they were all sent to different sections of the encampment to amplify the feeling of being helpless and alone.

Humiliate. Isolate. Demoralize. The re-education had already begun. Next was to apply a constant, low-grade level of discomfort. Not enough to cause a revolt, but just enough to wear down the detainees and make them compliant. That's what all this tent business was about.

Supposedly there were empty bunks already stocked with personal necessities, he just had to find one. Rutker had other things in mind first. He glanced back over his shoulder at the intake facility, a converted office space facing the parade ground proper. Five Deathhounds guarded the office complex. Four others were being retrofitted in a motor pool building farther on. And their shuttle? It had lifted off of its own accord within seconds of their stepping foot on the tarmac. No luck using that to escape when the time came.

Rutker wondered what happened to the Gefkarri ambassador, Theal. After he'd been separated from the other two pilots, she had been ushered, with little respect or regard for her position, into another room in the facility. If he were being honest, it gave him no small amount of enjoyment to watch, but it certainly didn't improve their situation.

But this was no time to relish difficulties heaped on an adversary. Especially when that adversary seemed more or less to share a common enemy with oneself. Theal seemed resourceful enough, and as much as the Chareth-Ul blustered, Rutker just couldn't imagine Delvadr blowing off the help against the Void that the Gefkarri represented.

But then, he didn't know the Chareth-Ul at all. His only exposure to them was through the Deathhounds, which, if that was any indication, maybe he needed to reconsider his next steps.

Rutker shivered and rubbed his newly shorn head as an early winter breeze rose up. To make matters worse, the robes he was given did little to fend off the chill. Another carefully crafted inconvenience. He tensed his muscles to build a little heat and shifted his focus to the issues at hand.

He'd assumed the radio contact from the Chareth-Ul and subsequent mistreatment had been mostly bluster and posturing, so they were in a better position to negotiate now that the Gefkarri were in orbit. But maybe that wasn't the case. Maybe they were *that* confident that they could defeat the Void and had every intention of doing it without the Gefkarri's help.

If that were the case, then Theal was in real trouble. Rutker honestly couldn't care less. The way she and the Gefkarri as a whole spoke about using humanity made him so angry he could barely think straight. As it stood, he needed to consider that Theal would not be a help to the human cause and he would need to rally his people before they got sent off to the front lines to be used by the Chareth-Ul. It was clear that humanity could in no way coexist with any of these alien races. There would be no negotiation. It was rebellion or death.

His people's only hope was to get off-planet and E'rth was the only option.

How to get there? He really had no idea. He hoped that D'avry had some sort of trick up his sleeve. He had to be honest, as much as the kid mucked things up, he also had quite an arsenal when it came to magic. When things got down to it, he usually found a way to overcome.

Rutker decided it was time to start praying for D'avry's success. He realized he hadn't thought about him much at all since he disappeared on the descent to the planet's surface. Maybe that was an oversight? He'd had his hands full just getting Field Colonel Galas up to speed and getting this far along in the mission. Becoming a POW wasn't part of the original plan but, all good plans needed to adapt to reality. This was one hell of an adaptation.

Rutker sidestepped a cluster of people who appeared to be waiting in line for a meal. The looks on their faces were sullen. They didn't have the fire in their eyes he expected of his countrymen. Maybe it was too much for the psyche; fighting and finally winning against a relentless enemy, just to have them replaced by someone or something even worse?

That feeling of betrayal and desperation definitely resonated. Maybe he was no different from the people he saw here. He'd just been thrust into the fight in a different way. They'd been sent here to rot with crummy food and meager conditions, whereas he'd been thrust back into the fight by sabotage and deception. His reintroduction to the fight had been one of extremely poor odds. But these people? Having a mech the size of a city just show up like this one had. It must have seemed utterly hopeless from the start.

His thoughts turned back to the kid, the mage, D'avry. He thought of him as a kid. He was just a few years older than Mads and Macq. That still qualified in his mind. He was pretty sure he didn't even like him all that much, but maybe he was starting to grow on him.

Now though, it was becoming clear that Rutker might need his help. Humanity wasn't getting out of this one without the two of them working together. Besides, if he really was from the future like he claimed, he needed the Epriots to establish a colony on E'rth. Rutker hadn't put much thought into it before. He'd always just assumed it would be a small contingent that did that, but now? It seemed as though fate was driving them to a mass exodus as the only option.

He paused in the middle of the path and took a moment to look around. The city surrounding the parade grounds was a shelled-out husk, dismal in the gray light of an overcast sky. Before him, tents stretched as far as he could see amongst the low, rolling hills. Farther on to either side, near the perimeters of the field, were a few scattered trees, but not many. Nowhere to run. Nowhere to hide.

Somehow he was going to get upward of 250,000—the whole of the human remnant if there were even that many left—out of the detention center. The fact that all of humanity could now reside in a small portion of the planet's capital hit Rutker harder than he was ready for.

He'd had his head down during the war. It was all about living one more day. And then, when it was over, it was almost too amazing to be true—saved by some mythical weapon from antiquity. And then they were on the peace treaty mission, and then that had been waylaid. He met D'avry and was convinced to get to the bottom of it by infiltrating the alien ship … and on, and on, and on.

One thing just led to another, and he'd had next to zero time to sort it all out. Then there was his family. He still had them at least. Well, actually, that thought led to another snag. Macq. Where had he ended up? Here? He was confident in Macq's abilities and intelligence. Having him run off to chase the traitorous Colonel Dexx while they were mid-descent had been a foolish thing, but there was merit to it.

Macq, after all, had dealt with Dexx the whole time Rutker had been running around on E'rth and knew that he wouldn't miss out on a chance to promote his own agenda and leave anyone and everyone else holding the bag.

Letting Dexx get to EDC High Command before they did would have been a huge problem. Rutker couldn't blame Macq for going after the traitor. But it made things infinitely more complicated. He couldn't do what he needed to do and look for his son.

He was certain that if Macq wasn't here already, he'd be showing up any time. But before that, Rutker needed a plan. How to get 250,000 people off the planet?

The most obvious answer was on interstellar craft. But the Epriots didn't have anything like that left. There were some medium transports like the *Xandraitha's Hope* still in service. If there were any here in the city, they were either destroyed or locked down somewhere. He'd need to find them.

Then there was the Spires. The bases hidden within those rocky towers held whatever was left. Mechs, fighters, transports. He imagined an exodus like nothing ever seen in human history. But the mechs and fighters couldn't make the journey to E'rth. Unless there was a way to use a portal like the Void or the Chareth-Ul did. He had no idea how that worked. Theal and the Gefkarri didn't use that technology either, so even if he knew where the ambassador was, she wouldn't be a help on that front either.

That was a strikeout. The only ship big enough to hold all the refugees was scattered across the bottom of the ocean hundreds of kilometers to the north. New Varhus had been lucky in that it had not been in the path of the *Righteous Fury* when it had been attacked at the start of the second wave of the Delvadr invasion. He understood that Colonel Galas's own hometown had been destroyed by that crash as the space-going supercarrier came apart under gravity it was never meant to withstand.

Rutker was getting lost in his thoughts. At this point, he'd been wandering the dismal camp at the south end of the mech parade grounds, looking for familiar faces. There weren't any. New Varhus was largely made up of civilian contractors, so while there were very few people who hadn't seen military action in some capacity, these weren't the folks he'd typically consorted with. And sadly, those he did consort with were always the first to go.

Rutker continued to scan the scattered crowds of refugees. His time was running short. In the morning, the priests would pull everyone out into the fields for training. He'd need to find a place to sleep before then. He'd hoped he'd see someone he knew who could help orient him to what was going on and who was heading up the revolt he'd assumed had to be already in progress. The faces he'd seen so far gave him no comfort that that was the case.

He came up to a yellow and green stacker that would house twenty or more people; As good a place as any to get started. He poked his head inside, but was immediately greeted by the sound of wailing children. He turned around without saying a word. Some kind of ad hoc daycare. Probably not the best place to instigate a rebellion.

Farther ahead was a small quad area with clusters of people gathered around the periphery. In the middle was a group that appeared to be doing some kind of dance or meditation. Weird.

As he drew closer, he saw that the exhibit was led by two Epriots who were dressed differently than the others. Their robes were similar to his own—and everyone else's—but theirs were black and red.

He picked out one of the clusters that was watching the others and slid up beside them. The look on their faces was more like what he'd expected to see everywhere, brooding and irritable.

"What's all this about?"

One of the people in the group, a man in his late fifties judging by the wrinkles on his face and hands, looked at him. He looked him up and down and raised an eyebrow. "New guy, huh?"

"Yeah. Just this morning."

"Sorry to hear that. Not one of the lucky ones to scamper up to the Spires, then?"

"There's folks up there still?" Rutker asked, his heart skipping a beat, though he'd known it was likely some of the remnant were up there.

"So I hear, anyway. But not for long. Deathhounds are mounting up to go flush 'em out. Gonna be a fight, but, the numbers are no good," he said, looking around to encompass the whole of the occupation and the hundreds of Deathhounds within the city, plus those coming and going from the city-sized Defiler mech looming over everything.

Rutker followed his gaze. The thing blotted out the sky. Toxic sludge poured from orifices scattered over the entirety of its block-like form while carbony smoke blew easterly toward the distant spires in question. He realized that's probably what was adding that bitter, sulfuric scent to the air. It was a constant compliment to the fugue of stale humanity covering the muddy camp.

"Anyone able to warn them?"

"Hah! Who's gonna do that? Look around you," the man replied bitterly.

Rutker nodded and let out a small sigh. "So, you never answered about this group here. What are they up to?"

"Same thing you'll be doing tomorrow. The ones leading them were military intelligence types that had been researching the Deathhound phenomenon. Now that we've been taken over by them, they're helping the priests get all of us laymen up to speed."

"Military intelligence? Sounds about right," he said, shaking his head in disgust.

"I see we hold them in about the same regard. I'm Churl Agaus, but most folks know me as Gygr."

"Marine then?"

"Oo-rah," he said under his breath, casting furtive glances left and right to be sure he wasn't drawing undue attention.

"I'm Novak. First name's Rutker."

"Well, ho-ly shit. We got a bona fide celebrity in our midst." The man laughed, rapping the arm of the man next to him, who also had the build of an old grunt. The second guy had a decidedly unpleasant face. The look in his eyes, though, more than his features, unnerved Rutker.

"What happened to that peace treaty you were s'posed to be working out?" The first man growled, finishing with a well-worn sneer.

"Yeah. Double-cross."

"No shit. You're telling me one of our own's responsible for this shit show?"

"There's a whole lot more to it, but yeah, one of our own."

"Lemme guess... Dexx."

Rutker was taken aback. Both by how much the man knew and how obvious the answer was to him.

"Yeah. Seen him? He's probably around here unless he hasn't made it back yet. I lost him on the HALO jump back to the planet's surface. Arcfire wouldn't let us through. My son went after him."

"Damn, Captain. You *have* been busy. Maybe I was a bit brash in my initial assessment. Considering our present situation, you can forgive my cynicism." He nodded in the direction of his companion. "This here's Monster Mind."

The man beside him smiled through a set of teeth that looked about as rough as the rest of him.

"Monster Mind? Gygr? Nice to meet you two." Rutker shook both their hands and returned to watching the group in the quad as they performed slow-motion hand movements and body positioning while chanting strange guttural intonations.

"That really supposed to do anything?" Rutker asked, mildly disturbed by the display. He didn't know if he was more bothered by the fact that magical mumbo jumbo looked so out of place here or that it was his fellow compatriots who were taking part in it. He settled on the latter.

"Apparently, humans are *gifted* in the arcane, but we never knew it," Gygr replied.

"That's what they're saying?"

"Supposedly, it's why we can become Deathhounds in the first place. It's what allows the Charcoal-heads to bind our souls to the machinery. Makes sense. I sold my soul to the Corps years ago."

Rutker chuckled darkly but wasn't sure that Gygr was actually joking. His partner just grunted acknowledgment.

"Charcoal heads, huh? The Chareth-Ul? So I'm doubting you guys are just going along with all of this? Taking part while humanity collectively sells its soul to the enemy in order to fight a whole new one we never knew anything about?"

"You see us over there with them?" Monster Mind asked, talking for the first time. His voice was surprisingly mellow, almost pleasant. It betrayed an intelligence that went well unnoticed just on appearances.

Rutker looked at him as if for the first time, and nodded. "Good. Cuz I have another idea."

Rutker laid out his thoughts on how to utilize the underground transit lines to get out of the city and up to the Spires, where they could warn the others and round up as many transports as they could get their hands on. They would save as many as they could. That's all they could do, and it had to be enough. Somehow he'd have to figure out a way to find Macq in all of that chaos as well as contact Katherynn and Mads in the *Xandraitha's Hope*.

Getting past the Gefkarri flagship was the last hurdle. One problem at a time, though. For now, they had to figure out how to break out of the detention center and get down into the transit tunnels and then somehow do it before the Deathhounds got there. But, there was a reason the Spires were humanity's fallback position. Being Kilometers-tall rocky columns, they were inherently difficult to approach except by air, and the Chareth-Ul seemed to be a very ground warfare-based culture.

CHAPTER 20

HOPE RE-IGNITED

Epriot Prime, Somewhere over the Straights of Eldomitik, *Xandraitha's Hope*

D'avry hated to admit it, but he was happy that Seda was here now. The amplifying effect of her magic was welcome, and it acted as a counterbalance to the twisted arcane energy that flowed through the Chareth-Ul talisman.

He sat in his new favorite spot, levitating above the leather couch off to the side of the bridge. Katherynn was in her usual place beside the captain, talking through logistics and strategy over a transparent spatial positioning table that currently was showing a map with a lot of ocean on it. Mads was always by her side, acting as a helper, but D'avry was certain that he saw it more as a security measure after the double-cross by Colonel Dexx back on E'rth.

Seda cast a casual eye over the proceedings of the humans, but consciously, her focus was always squarely on D'avry.

He couldn't quite figure out what that was about. At times, she seemed even more interested in him than in the interests of her own kind, which seemed impossible considering she was a member of a massive collective consciousness. He would have to ask her about it at some point. He was getting more confident that she would answer honestly.

In the beginning, he had been terrified of her. Partly because of her power, partly because of the foreignness of it all—the technology, the new species of intelligent beings—but also because of her overly intense interest and desire to toy with him. It seemed to amuse her to no end to taunt him. Now that it was a known constant, he could work with and around that attention.

At this exact moment, he was drawing on her magical aura. The greater Gefkarri mind was a far-distant echo. Off-planet and without a relay in between, it was nothing more than a presence, like vague sunlight through a thin layer of high clouds. It was there but barely felt.

Theal, on the other hand, came through like a coronation trumpet—piercing and bright. She was in extreme pain. Seda was surprisingly ambivalent about this. They were supposed to be two members of the same mind, but they couldn't be more different and had always had something of a competition between the two. A power struggle of sorts. D'avry couldn't spare any more time for that quandary. Right now, it was all about what it meant.

Why is Theal in pain? She is the ambassador to the Chareth-Ul and Delvadr and is supposed to be coordinating the link between those two societies with the Gefkarri hive mind.

This clearly was not taking place. There was fear, anger, and outrage all playing over the telepathic link. The closer they got to New Varhus, the more intensely he felt her suffering and the more excruciatingly detailed it became.

None of this made much sense from an arcane perspective. Magic could be localized but the ethereal field was ubiquitous. It was everywhere all at once. Or at least, that was usually the case.

Here on Epriot Prime, it appeared to have been permanently shunted by the alien race that lived here before humanity—reversed so that it was inaccessible. For what reason he couldn't fathom.

Right now it was beyond his ability to comprehend, so he just had to accept it. So what he was left with was riding the inherent magical field provided by Seda and reaching out to the field generated by Theal. That and what he could pull from the plane of the Chareth-Ul.

What was truly baffling was that he felt Theal as much through the connection the three of them shared as he did through the talisman.

That he could not figure out. Still more bizarre, he felt Colonel Galas out there somewhere as well. With what he saw happen—her dragging the priestess Wahr-Zen back through the dimensional vortex—he just couldn't see how he would be able to sense her at all. He was pulling arcane energy from their world through the talisman, but he didn't have the same link to Col. Galas that he did to Theal. He and the mech pilot had only briefly connected when she had touched the drone he was controlling while he was being tortured by Wahr-Zen. It was intense but brief, not even on the same level as what he was experiencing now with her sidelined co-pilot, Commander Jinnbo.

D'avry was torn between great sadness and great relief at having introduced the Cycarian to his ancestors. It took him out of the current fight and left humanity's backdoor open to the Gefkarri, but what his species had gained through that connection could be invaluable to them. Barring, of course, that Jinnbo survived to return to his planet.

There was always a caveat.

The current one for D'avry was that as they drew closer to their destination, he drew greater information *from* Theal, but it was uncertain whether he could get *enough* information to help her. And also to keep them out of harm's way when they did arrive.

Time was not on their side. The irony that he frequently traveled *through* time and had done so to get to this specific point *in* time was not lost on him.

Seda's attention was fixed upon him again. He was an amusement to her. A shiny bauble, like Wahr-Zen had said. What was it with these women? They were all completely insane. The only one he'd met who was perhaps not completely mad was Deven. And he'd sent her to another time on a planet far, far away from here.

That thought was truly depressing.

He'd expected to be able to see her in his dreams again, or maybe to communicate through the gray town, but since he'd left E'rth, that connection was completely severed. He even missed the connection to the Astrig Ka'a, as frightening as it was most of the time.

Though now that he spent more time with the Gefkarri magic, he wasn't sure that there weren't similarities. Another quandary to sort out at a later date. There was quite a number of those. He felt like his mind was being pulled in a thousand different directions.

"We're an hour out," Katherynn informed them all.

He *really* needed to focus.

D'avry closed his eyes, slowed his breathing, and drew even more from Seda's aura. He sensed a moment of concern before she gave over and let him take as much as he needed. Then he pulled on the talisman. He was finding that the Gefkarri magic acted almost like a crucible for the raw flow of power that was the Chareth-Ul arcana.

Then he turned his focus to Theal. An image ripped through the open space between D'avry and the others, casting the whole bridge in ethereal blue-white light.

There were murmurs of astonishment from the others, but D'avry couldn't be bothered. He was seeing through the image in the air between them. It was a view through Theal's eyes and it turned his blood to ice.

There, in the middle of a large room made of dark stone or metal, was a form he recognized. He wasn't sure if it was Wahr-Zen, but from this angle, it sure looked like her.

"What's Theal doing in the Chareth-Ul dimension?" D'avry asked out loud as he realized what he'd done; that he was in effect broadcasting the telepathic link they shared, but in a way that was magnitudes greater than anything he'd done before, or even knew was possible. The Chareth-Ul power was unpredictable, to say the least.

Seda didn't answer at first as she took in what was going on before her. Before them all. She stepped forward hesitantly,

"D'avry, she may not be. They're most likely on one of the Defiler temple mechs. Probably here on this planet."

"How can you tell?" he asked, almost absentmindedly, as he examined the viewing portal hanging in mid-air in the middle of the bridge.

"That woman is a battle priestess. Their temples are physically located on those massive mechs. In their realm, they don't have terrestrial cities. They have defilers, or what they call temple cities. So to your point, they *could* be on the Chareth-Ul plane. But it's just as likely that they are somewhere *here* on *this* planet.

"And, being that I don't have the benefit of the Chareth-Ul talisman you have, yet can sense Theal's emotions so intensely, I'd say the latter is the most likely."

That twisted D'avry's assumption on its head, but he couldn't argue. It was entirely possible, just not what he was expecting.

Katherynn stepped away from the planning table, slowly approaching the vision. The glowing light around the edges reflected in her eyes as she drew closer,

"Okay, let's assume you're correct. It still doesn't tell us why they're treating her this way? Don't they *want* help from the Gefkarri Pentarch?"

"Something has obviously changed. We knew of the trouble on their planet, knew the Void were there in force and that the Chareth-Ul were actively engaged in defending against them. We just didn't realize how bad it had gotten. Judging by the number of Defiler mechs showing up here on Epriot Prime, it's possible that they're in the midst of retreat. Maybe not yet full-scale, but ... there's no way they could provide this much firepower and maintain their defenses for long.

"Maybe they think the human remnant is enough of a boost to their forces to hold them off? Maybe they intend to use the power of the Arcfire to turn the Void back," Katherynn suggested.

Seda's eyes glowed green and then cooled. "There's wisdom in your words, Ambassador Novak. Their interest in humanity is clear. But if they wanted the Arcfire, why not just take it?"

"Yeah, well, I may have had something to do with keeping them from getting it," D'avry added sheepishly. "Actually, Colonel Galas did most of the work. She sacrificed herself and broke the portal by pulling Wahr-Zen back through it. I had assumed it was a portal to her own dimension or realm or whatever. I didn't realize it could just be a dimensional tunnel from one place on the planet to another."

"Right place at the right time. You really are quite extraordinary, Avaricae D'avry, sorcerer of the All-Magic. Fate seems to have plans for you."

D'avry was uncomfortable with that idea. He didn't want some *other* invisible force directing his path. He had too many as it was.

The image between them blazed brighter, drawing his attention back to it.

The priestess, who looked like Wahr-Zen, turned to face Theal and stared at her oddly. It seemed as though she was looking through Theal's eyes. In the blink, she shot forward so that her face filled the portal and suddenly D'avry was certain she was staring right back at them.

"She can't see us, can she?" Katherynn asked in a whisper, stepping away from the portal.

He barely heard her. Suddenly, D'avry felt as though he was being pulled into the portal. The force was undeniable, and it took everything he had to resist. The battle priestess's hand came up and began to twist into a ball, and D'avry pulled back with all his might.

Seda pushed arcane power to him and screamed out, D'avry slammed the link shut.

He hadn't realized it, but both he and Seda had been pressed up against the ceiling in those few short seconds. When the link shut, they fell to the deck.

D'avry blinked away spots of light and pushed up onto wobbly arms.

"Are you alright?" came Katherynn's shaken voice.

He looked up and saw Mads as white as a sheet. "What happened?"

What did happen? Suddenly D'avry thought of Seda. And belatedly of Theal.

He tried to reach out, but that link came back frighteningly empty. He looked around and spotted Seda still lying on the floor face first. D'avry crawled over to her and reached out.

"Don't. Touch," came her muffled response.

D'avry hesitated. "I don't... I don't understand."

"You don't want to feel this. I'm blocking you so you can focus. Leave her to me," she said. Her voice was tight. He couldn't read her thoughts through the link, but he could easily read the anguish in her voice. There was so much he didn't understand or could even guess at. But he did know that Theal was gone. Burned out. Wahr-Zen, or whoever that was, had somehow reached through her trying to get to them.

D'avry couldn't imagine what that must have felt like, to have your own mind used as some kind of portal. Then he remembered his first experience with the Gefkarri. Maybe that was why they were so surprised by him. They'd never expected him to survive their interrogation. They had been attempting to take his knowledge and instead, they had unwittingly taken him into their own collective consciousness.

Now things were beginning to make sense. Now he understood why humans hadn't been involved in their plans at first, but were being brought into those plans. It was because the Gefkarri hadn't realized that humans could be integrated into or even facilitate the link between the various races. The prior race's null-magic effectively hid humanity's gift.

Katherynn asked again, "D'avry, are you okay?" He felt the warmth of her hand on his shoulder. This was a good human being. He was happy that Rutker had someone like her beside him. He deserved that. He was also thankful that she had not gotten hurt by his careless use of magic he didn't understand. Rutker would never have forgiven him. He wouldn't have either.

D'avry nodded dumbly. He wanted to reach out to Seda in the same way. To console her for the sense of loss that she was experiencing, but at the same time, he never wanted to look at her again. In the beginning, she had intended to kill him. Or at least expected that the search for information within his mind would do that. That explained why she was so hot and cold too. And even now, to a degree, her fascination.

Then something that had been bothering him clicked in his mind. He turned back to Katherynn and the others. "We have to stop. We can't go to New Varhus."

He couldn't know for certain that's where Wahr-Zen's Defiler was, but he recognized that the closer they got to their destination, the stronger the link to Theal had been. And when he saw that Theal was in the presence of the priestess ... something didn't quite fit. If that was Wahr-Zen, then where was Colonel Galas? Was this where the portal led, or was this another battle priestess that looked like Wahr-Zen? He was pretty certain it was her. How many could there be? That was a terrifying question. And were they all as powerful? Another good and terrifying question.

He was working himself into a panic.

Think, D'avry.

Theal had gone to New Varhus to negotiate with the EDC but had run into the Chareth-Ul instead. It was obvious now that they had taken over and had no intention of working with the Gefkarri, let alone allowing them on the planet. Unless it was under their terms, that was. The fact that the priestess had just killed the Gefkarri ambassador was a pretty strong signal of what they thought of partnering with Seda's people.

"We need to stop. Re-group," he continued.

"We have to find Rutker and Macq. We have to save humanity from those demonic psychopaths." Katherynn asked, pointing to where the image had been.

"That's true. But we can't go up against one of those Defilers in just this." He motioned around them, indicating the diplomatic transport ship. "And I can't go up against a single battle priestess. Let alone two or three or however many they have on one of those things. Not yet. Maybe not ever."

D'avry rolled back onto his butt and rubbed his face. Days' growth of stubble was turning into a thin, scraggly blond beard. He realized not only was he tired, but he was frozen to his core. The Chareth-Ul magic again. He shivered and pulled his long jacket close.

"Your lips are blue. How is that possible it's environmentally controlled in here?" asked Mads, still looking at him as if he were an apparition.

"It's the magic. The Chareth-Ul magic is wild and twisted and powerful … and all magic takes its toll."

"Yeah, well, you might want to watch that. You look like shit."

"Thanks."

"No problem."

"I hate to be a downer, but now what?" asked Raphael as the drone slipped out of D'avry's pocket and hovered up to head height.

"You've been in there the whole time?" Katherynn asked.

"I'm a mech AI at heart. My purpose is to facilitate integration with mech ops, but also to keep my pilot alive. Being that Galas has a version of me on board her power armor, I'm doing that job even now … I hope. D'avry on the other hand, seems to be well beyond his depth in all of this, and yet, in many ways, we seem to need him.

"Since I can't monitor every aspect of his anatomy like I could in a suit or a mech, I'm using the limited resources I have available to me. This drone body has limited capability, but I'm able to glean quite a lot through proximity. Plus, the confluence of magic and technology is a real mind-bender."

"That's what you were up to?" D'avry asked.

"Yes. We should share notes about your experience. I would be very interested to know what was going on about eight-and-a-half minutes ago. Right before the vision opened up in the middle of the bridge."

"Uh, yeah. That'd be okay. Maybe later."

"I will remind you."

"Okay, so 'Now what?' I think is what you asked. Well, *now* is when we figure out how we're going to get the entire human population of this planet all the way to E'rth."

"Wait, what?" Mads asked. "We're going to run?"

"Yeah, what he said," Katherynn tagged on. The rest of the crew went on about their business, but it was obvious they were all raptly following the conversation as events played out.

"The *only* option is escape. We're surrounded by four different alien races. All of which want us dead or to use us as magical cannon fodder. And all are vastly greater in number and more powerful to boot."

"Cannon fodder?"

"Um, as a commodity. It's a military term from a time, somewhere between yours and mine actually. Did your people never use explosive-propelled projectiles?"

"Well, sure, way back. I think I get your meaning though. Humans in this environment are a weapon to be thrown at the enemy," Mads provided.

"Yes, but much worse than that," said Seda, rising slowly to her feet. Her face was gaunt and her coloring was pale. "The Gefkarri wish to use your ability to interface with any magic as a conduit. To aid the link between the allied races for a more unified assault on the Void."

"To act as puppet masters, you mean," Katherynn scoffed.

"Call it what you like. But the Chareth-Ul, who you know as Deathhounds. Their intentions are..."

"They bind the souls of their victims to the machines they operate. Their wages are temporary relief from constant suffering. I've read the classified material," Katherynn provided.

This was news to D'avry. He didn't even know that was possible.

Katherynn wasn't going to be convinced that the Gefkarri were the good guys here. "You're trying to justify your actions as something less than slavery, just because you believe that the Chareth-Ul will somehow be a worse kind of slave master. You may be right. But slavery is still slavery."

"And extinction is forever," Seda replied.

There was silence for several long moments after that.

D'avry stepped in. "As I was saying before, we need to fall back to E'rth. Let the Chareth-Ul and Gefkarri and Delvadr duke it out with the Void on their own."

"So, how do we do that?" Katherynn asked, but her steely gaze never left Seda.

Raphael answered, "We need to find as many transports as we can get ahold of. The Spires may be our best bet, but we'll have to fly dangerously close to the Defiler to get there."

"I imagine that Wahr-Zen knows we're coming now." D'avry provided.

"The battle priestess? The woman we just saw, whom you believe still has Colonel Galas?" Katherynn asked.

"Yes. I don't know what she's capable of, but she's very confident and very cruel. I feel fairly certain that Colonel Galas is alive, but I can't imagine what she's going through. And yet, I don't know what we can do for her," D'avry responded.

"Galas can fend for herself. There's a resilience to her, unlike any human I've ever met. She'll find a way. Besides, I'm there to help her," Raphael responded. It sounded a little like pride coming from the drone's speaker, "But the one thing that we absolutely must do if we can, is to save her daughter, Seraf. It was the last thing on her mind when she thought that she was sacrificing herself to take out the priestess and her vortex," he added.

Katherynn folded her arms and alternated her focus between the mage and the drone. "So you two are suggesting that we just gather up a quarter-million people and ship them off to the same planet that this ship crashed on a few days back? That backwater rock? No offense," she added in D'avry's direction.

"None taken. It's the only home I know. And, as far as I can tell, being a backwater is one of its greatest advantages."

Katherynn nodded. "I guess I can't argue with that. Back to this plan, though. Beyond finding ours and Col. Galas's loved ones, how do you intend to get all of those people out of here? The last ship we had capable of carrying that many people crashed into the ocean in millions of pieces nearly a quarter century ago. I don't even know who we'd use to pilot it if it were possible to put it back together. Which it isn't. The idea is completely ludicrous."

"So there *is* a ship that can do it?" D'avry asked, suddenly intrigued. He'd been stuck on a problem while everyone else was talking. If humanity could help the Gefkarri and the Chareth-Ul, what would it take for them to help themselves?

CHAPTER 21
THE RESISTANCE

New Varhus Detention Center (Camp Zun-Karlduum)

Rutker and his two new friends... maybe *friends* was a strong word, cohorts perhaps. Rutker and his two new *cohorts,* Gygr and the enigmatic Monster Mind—whose real name was Gus he'd learned—were navigating through the camp's southernmost extents with several similar-sized groups spread out behind and to the sides. They followed, but not too close and not in the same aisles. There were fifteen in all. Gygr had promised more if they could find them by the time they reached the rally point.

It was before dawn, so there weren't a lot of people out and about yet and they had to try very hard to go unnoticed. The fact that humanity had been reduced to the few surviving fighters through a decades-long campaign of genocide meant that anyone who saw them knew something was up. He just hoped that they wished them success in whatever it was they thought they were up to.

The military intelligence types they'd seen the day before, guiding the others through training exercises to better prepare the masses for pairing with their Chareth-Ul oppressors, concerned him though. It meant that some of their number had been turned or were just so deluded by the prospect of power that they were willing to go along with anything.

What concerned him more was that there was still no sign of Macq or Dexx. In fact, there had been no new prisoners through the intake facilities since he'd arrived a day and a half prior. Rutker had to prepare himself for the real possibility that the two had been lost, either in the descent or upon landing, or there were a myriad of equally horrifying options. They could have run into trouble on their journey over land, or run into Deathhounds, or even worse, the Void.

He couldn't bring himself to dwell on it. He had to keep that tiny flame of hope alive. Macq was strong. And smart. And capable. And a better man than Rutker could ever hope to be.

Rutker's big strength was simply that he was a fighter. A doer. He chose to pursue the right thing. Or at least whatever was 'most' right when it came to warfare. Macq had an ethic that went beyond just the needs of survival. He and Mads both had gotten that from their mother.

He's alive out there somewhere. He has to be.

They were nearing their destination when a man dressed in black robes stepped out from the entryway of a tent. He and Rutker locked eyes and Rutker could read the dawning of comprehension within them. There was no time to think. He whipped a perfect left hook to the jaw with the open palm of his hand. The man's head snapped sideways, and he crumpled. Not a power punch, but a precise one. No broken bones in his hand and the man? Well...

Rutker weaved his arm through the other man's as he was falling and Monster Mind slid in behind him and did the same. They barely broke stride as they pulled the unconscious man into their ranks and just kept on heading forward.

Rutker had no idea what they were going to do with him, but he thought at least the man's robes could come in handy. And maybe they could get some useful information out of him.

The group drew near the edge of the camp, and now was going to be the difficult part. They needed to belly crawl 1000 meters to the motor pool. This was where mechs were serviced or fitted for activities on the parade field. This was the only entrance to the lower transit tunnels that he knew of on this end of the city. There were connectors that went to the capital buildings and definitely to the airfield on the city's northern outskirts, but that was about it. They weren't widely known about as they weren't for mass transit, just military brass and the inevitable political activities where the interests of the two sectors co-mingled.

However, this crawl was going to be a problem unless they managed to do it before the sun was up. Otherwise, fifteen white figures crawling through the grass would stand out to anyone aboard the Defiler who happened to look down.

Who knew what means of surveillance they might be using to keep track of the prisoners? He did know that they had Deathhounds stationed around the perimeter. Maybe that was deterrent enough. It certainly should be. Even en masse, the remaining humans could do little against such a force.

Rutker leaned the body of the MI traitor against an outcropping of rocks and slapped his face to wake him up.

"Hey, buddy. Wake up. Hey. Buddy…"

"How hard did you hit him?" Gygr asked.

"I don't know, not very—"

The man who'd been feigning sleep leaped forward and grabbed Rutker by the throat. He was strong and rightfully feared for his life. Rutker staggered back, grabbed his wrists, and kicked the man over him as he fell to his back. They both landed in the mud and scrambled to their feet in a low crouch. The man dove forward, feigning a tackle, but came up with an uppercut elbow instead. Rutker's vision split into shards of white as his head snapped back. Dazed, he dropped low under a blow that would have shuttered him and drove forward into the man's stomach. The two toppled to the ground, and the man stopped fighting.

Rutker sat back, wary, ready to pounce, but the man didn't move and he saw why. He'd body slammed him to the ground, atop a shallow mound of exposed rock. This wasn't like the practice mat where he'd learned his defensive techniques. This was the real world and in the real world, this sort of shit happened. He was just lucky that fate broke in his direction.

"Well, so much for information," Gygr observed.

Monster Mind grunted in agreement. Rutker just sat on his knees in the mud, sucking in air. That MI guy was no slouch. He really rang his bell with that elbow. Well, now at least he was awake. Rutker's tongue found a small shard and traced its origins to a chip in one of his front teeth. Great. After crawling through the muck, he not only looked and smelled like a transient, but now he had the smile to match.

The only silver lining in all of this was that the man was close to his size and weight. He started to undress him and swap out his own white robes for the man's black ones. He hoped that he wouldn't need them. If it came down to bluffing their way through, they were as good as dead.

The slog through the grass took way too long. They reached the tarmac at the far end and were forced to sprint, one at a time to the closest hanger, all while sunlight was beginning to pierce through the jagged teeth of the Spires, kilometers off in the distance. The good news was that all of those white robes were a dingy gray and brown now. Gygr had made sure every one of them rolled around in the muck to cover up any bright spots. Wouldn't do anything against IR, but there was only so much they could do.

Once they were all gathered at the hangar, Rutker peered around the corner of a large, mech-sized door. Nobody was worried about security apparently. He was hoping that it was empty, but instead, he saw four Deathhound mechs all lined up beneath a mobile gantry. They were partway through being fitted with a backpack of sorts, only these were for some purpose he'd never seen before. Alien tech, he guessed until he saw the closest one and there was someone inside of it.

"What in Skleetrix is that?" asked Gygr. He'd stepped up behind Rutker and was looking at the same thing.

"No fragging idea. Is that how they're using us to 'pair' with the Deathhounds? We're riding shotgun into battle? There's no protection whatsoever. We're right next to the reactor. On the 'outside' of the mech," Rutker finished in breathless exasperation.

"What do you think it does?" Gygr asked.

"I don't know. They don't use the same power source. That's what all the toxic sludge is from, but I don't know how it works."

"They pull from the Chareth-Ul home world. There's some sort of power there and the soul binding allows it to be channeled into the machine," came a voice from farther back. Rutker, Gygr, and Monster Mind turned as one to see a tall man with the shadow of a beard that was blaze orange. Rutker remembered seeing him the night before, but they hadn't been introduced.

"How do you know all this?"

"I pay attention. The MIs talk all sorts of stuff if you act interested."

"What else have you learned?"

"Just that there's a limit to the flow. I think that by adding more of us to the machines, the Deathhounds may be able to boost their speed and firepower. That's what I gather, anyway. To be honest, I never expected to find out," the red-bearded man provided.

"The Gefkarri thought that we would help them control the battlefield like some kind of magical SortieNet, but for all the races. Maybe the Chareth-Ul found that it boosted their machinery, and they didn't need the Gefkarri telling them what to do? That might explain why they seized the Gefkarri aspect. They certainly didn't appear to be interested in negotiation," Rutker surmised.

"We're short on time. Sun's up," Gygr observed, his delivery low and seemingly unruffled.

"You're right. See that two-story building across the way? That's where we're headed."

"Alright. Monster, take three others and secure the building. I don't want all fifteen of us stranded out in the middle of the quad. We'll work in closer and take up positions, ready to go when you give the signal."

"Got it. Red and you two. On me," said Monster Mind before he started sprinting across the tarmac in a low crouch. The other three followed in similar fashion.

Commotion from the other side of the hangar warned them of something coming. And then heavy rounds began tearing up the ground near the running men. They scattered, Monster Mind breaking away left and then back to the right. The gunfire followed him and one of the men got cut down. The other two were heading for an ancillary building when the machine gun fire stopped and Rutker heard the familiar thud and whoosh of repulsors.

A shadow stretched across the open space before a Deathhound mech boomed to the ground and started firing again. It was a five-ton Chacma. Not a big mech by any stretch but more than enough to cut down the lot of them.

"Now!" Gygr yelled. "Get to the next hangar before the other four join the fight."

Just as Rutker started sprinting for the next hangar, he saw Red and the other man lunge for the shelter right before it exploded from rocket fire.

This was going badly. Rutker looked for Monster Mind, but he was out of sight. Probably on the far side of the transit building now. The Chacma driver figured this as well and leaped between the buildings to where he assumed the man would be, spewing heavy machine gun rounds the entire way.

Rutker just reached the next building when he heard stirring within the first hangar.

"Dammit. We're screwed."

"You four. Find us some weapons. Next building over looks like operations. It may have an armory," Gygr said and then pointed at three others. "You three, go find out if either Red or the other guy made it, and then break for the transit building when you can. Ruck and everyone else, we break for the transit building once Monster Mind gives the signal."

"I don't see him. Do you think he's even alive."

"Don't worry about Monster. He doesn't look too bright, but it's an act. Dude's a fraggin' genius."

Just then, the Chacma rounded the corner, its chain guns spinning in anticipation of a target. It appeared to be looking for him still. Rutker froze. They were completely exposed but at an oblique angle to the mech's line of sight. He was suddenly thankful for the MI man's black robes. The mech continued around the corner of the transit building and that's when the driver saw the other men who'd headed off to check on Red and his teammate. The mech burst forward and on its back was Monster Mind, hanging off of one of the empty backpack units.

There was no one inside, thankfully. Monster Mind waved the team over. He'd found a way or made a way inside the building.

Rutker bolted, not looking to see if the others followed him or not. There was a tiny window of opportunity and he was taking it. Sometimes, in the heat of things, the oddest things pop into your mind. Right now he was realizing how cold his head was, now that he had no hair at all. Even the skin where his eyebrows had been was uncomfortable as he ran.

He was thankful for the tiny distraction from the fear and the feeling of breathlessness from the sprint. He still had a hundred meters to go when gunfire zippered past him to his left. On instinct, he broke right. He sprinted as fast as he could as a trail of rounds ripped across his path and he skidded to a stop before running the other way.

As he turned, he saw chaos. There were a few bodies, dirty white robes splashed red. Elsewhere, there was unidentifiable carnage scattered across the tarmac. A few of the men were still running, each in a different direction, which was probably the only reason why he was still alive. He broke directly for the transit building, hoping the chaos would shield him from being targeted next. Again, his black robes were helping him as plentiful targets in bright white drew the pilot's attention. He felt for the others.

Then he realized the gunfire was coming from the other hangar. He didn't know where Gygr was or who was left. He just ran until he was around the corner, away from the action, and he saw what Monster had done. A corner of the building was blown apart and there was access directly to the stairwell.

He didn't stop to think or to look for the others. Someone had to make it to the Spires to warn the others. Just as he was tucking inside, he saw the Defiler mech on the other side of the sprawling parade grounds. It was beginning to shift its weight to move. He knew where to.

That's how they were going to deal with the resistance at the Spires. That thing was so tall and massive, it could fit between only a few of the Spires, but it would be the perfect base of operations to clear out each enclave, one by one.

He knew from experience that the heaviest defenses were at the base of the Spires. With the Defiler, they could infiltrate a hundred stories above that. Also, with its contingent of small mechs, they could breach maintenance and transport tunnels, while the medium-sized mechs attacked the hangars.

He had to get there before it did. Otherwise, they'd be lucky to have enough survivors to fill *one* transport.

He hoped Katherynn had enough sense to punch out early enough when all hell broke loose. He had to get a message to her. She needed to go now, while there was still a chance and before the Gefkarri suspected resistance.

Rutker took the stairs three and four at a time. Not thinking about it, just going as fast as his body would take him. He hit the bottom floor three levels down. He didn't hear anyone following him which was bad. He didn't know if there would be any roadblocks to getting out of town, but then he didn't know if the transit system even worked.

The lights came on as he triggered proximity sensors. He hustled down a corridor and the clearance area with its turnstile scanners appeared. He hoped the systems were still up. They had to have been running on reserve power for at least a week without any maintenance.

He slapped a palm on a scanner and it chimed its acceptance. "Thank Maker!"

Rutker pressed through the turnstile and saw a waiting hover bus. The lights came on as it lifted off the ground. *Let's just hope there's someone left to warn.*

CHAPTER 22
BREAKING IN

Macq and Col. Dexx watched as the Deathhound guarding the perimeter turned and started firing at someone on the other side of the hangars. What a stroke of luck. The two darted looks either way and started sprinting for the closest building, careful to stay well behind the Deathhound mech—something made easier once it leaped forward after its quarry.

They wanted to be gone before the other mechs turned to engage. Or perhaps they wouldn't since they were quite clearly guarding the perimeter from attack from without more than they were from any attempts to escape. That was odd to Macq. It seemed pretty clear that almost all the remaining Epriots were located here. This and the Spires were the two fallback positions, and this was the Capital, after all.

He and Dexx pressed in close to the wall of a small utility shack. It was probably a control house for perimeter lights and security for the parade grounds. They had these scattered every so often. Dexx peered around the corner before motioning for him to follow. Macq did so, his mind still reeling at the fact that they were now working together when, initially, he had every intention of killing the man and had no qualms about doing it. Maybe that was false bravado. After all, he'd never killed anyone before. Still, he'd been more than ready when he'd seen Dexx drifting toward the fringes of the pack after the mage had been struck by debris during the HALO drop.

Macq was going to jettison the man's repulsor pack and let him fall all the way to the surface of the planet that he'd betrayed. There was a poetic justice in that. But as they angled for New Varhus, which Macq had anticipated was the man's plan, he couldn't catch up and then when he did, there was a whole new problem to grapple with—a mech the size of a small city looming over the Epriot capital. It was clear that the Chareth-Ul thought the planet was theirs and that the Gefkarri were never going to breach the planet's atmosphere.

Mads was bigger and tougher, but Macq had always been good at math and strategy. Even though his innermost desire was to see Dexx suffer for being a backstabbing piece of ox tripe, preferably from arm's length, he also recognized that it was humanity versus everyone else in this scenario, and at least they had that one thing in common.

In the end, logic won out. It made the most sense to work together. Plus, there was a time when his father had admired Dexx, at least as a soldier. Lastly, there were probably very few people who would have been better at looking at the issue before them and putting together a plan of action.

Right now, they needed to get inside the perimeter and talk to the detainees. It was clear any chance at negotiations was over. Now it was about resistance and, knowing the Epriots, there was already something brewing.

Macq sprinted forward in his power armor. They had discussed leaving their suits behind in order to blend in but decided it would be better to stash them somewhere inside the parade field perimeter so they had access when they needed them. Right now, he was glad he had armor. Minimal weapons, of course, but it was something anyway.

Another mech joined the fray from the hangar, and Dexx veered toward the backside of the building it emerged from. He was trying to keep them out of the conflict, which Macq could respect. He caught a glimpse of a handful of men in what looked like gray robes running around and getting absolutely slaughtered out on the tarmac. He was at a loss to imagine what they could be thinking running out there like that. They must have a reason, but damn, that was some bad luck.

He caught up with Dexx at the last hangar.

"Should we try to see what's going on? I mean, this might be the resistance we're looking for?"

"Nah. There's nothing over here but mech bays. Maybe a small armory. Not unless someone was trying to get into the transit tunnels and make their way up to the Spires. But that would be way more organized than anything I expect to find here. All the smart ones are already holed up and dug in. We're just here to spread the word to be ready and then move on ourselves."

"What about Dad and the others? Could they be here already?"

"It's possible, but not likely. With trouble on the descent and then trouble on the ground when they got there? They might be showing up today if they were even able to get a transport. And if they're smart, they'll circumvent New Varhus entirely and just make their way to the Spires."

"Huh," Macq acknowledged, not really sure what to say.

A fresh peel of machine gun fire paused briefly and then Macq heard a whoosh of rockets before an explosion lit up the space between buildings.

"Are you sure we shouldn't help? Those guys are getting shredded."

"You're a smart kid. What do you think we can do about it? These suits are not battle units. Do you think throwing rocks at a bunch of Deathhounds will do anything but get us killed? We need to use this distraction to get across the fields. Now, let's go."

With that, Dexx rounded the corner and sprinted for another one of those utility shacks. Macq hustled behind him.

Just beyond the shack, they found an area with low bushes and reeds and stashed their suits. Something unexpected though, was a dead body dressed in muddy white robes.

"Looks like those guys came right through here. Wonder who this was?" Macq asked.

"I'm guessing he wasn't down with the plan. Notice anything weird about this guy?"

"You mean beyond the fact that he's really bald? I mean, even his eyebrows..."

"Well, there's that. From what I saw of the battle at the hangar, we may have to match that style to blend in. We may also have to dress the part. This guy is more your size. Why don't you take those robes, slip in there and find me a similar get up."

Macq squinted at Dexx. He was right. His build was shorter and stockier for sure. Macq didn't like the idea of letting him out of his sight but then, where was he going to go?

Macq was out of his armor and swapping out his clothes when the huge mech standing at the edge of the city started moving.

"What do you think they're doing with that?"

"I'd say they've pretty well got New Varhus locked down and now they're off to deal with the contingent holed up in the Spires."

"Why would they bother? And why are they bothering to round up all the humans here? Are they going to make Deathhounds out of all of us? Can they even do that?"

"Good question. You're smart like your old man. The Gefkarri seemed to think that we were going to be useful in the war against the Void. Maybe the Deathhounds believe the same thing. If so, that's a tactical advantage, since that means they need to try to minimize casualties. That's a good thing."

Macq looked at Dexx one more time. He could have stayed in his armor and had the tactical advantage over Macq, but he didn't. He couldn't quite figure out the man's angle. If he was as bad as he assumed he was, he would have killed Macq at the first opportunity. And he was crafty enough to do it. Then again, he'd sacrificed an entire squad of his own men when he'd sabotaged the armory on the *Xandraitha's Hope*.

Macq realized he was staring.

"Got something to say, kid?"

"Nah. It's nothing."

The man just nodded before continuing,

"I would have assumed they'd just try to demolish the Spires with heavy ordnance, but now, I'm thinking that they'll try to roust everyone out. No way they'd get in on the lower levels without heavy casualties, but if they take that thing in there? They could breach the spires much higher up. No one would be expecting it. The remnant of the EDC High Command holed up there, thinking they're safe ... haven't got a chance."

"We have to warn them," Macq implored.

"How? Think kid. Going to the Spires was the right thing to do before. But now? Now is going to be our only chance to rally a resistance here. It may still be ridiculous odds, but at least now it's possible."

"What then? Say we break out of here?"

"That's where I'm hoping your mom and dad will come in. Maybe they'll convince Galas to let the Gefkarri planet-side. That'll swing things a little bit in our favor. If not, I'm hoping that they'll at least be able to get the *Xandraitha's Hope* down here to pick us up. I'll keep an eye out for either of those two things while you're grabbing gear in camp. Now, hurry up before people come looking for this guy and find me standing over his half-naked and fully dead body."

Macq didn't agree, purely on principle. But it was clear that they were running out of time in a hurry. He fixed Dexx with a hard stare as if that would pin him to the ground where he stood, which sounded like the safest thing to do, but instead, he turned and got to business, making his way toward camp. The faster he got this done, the better.

The sun was fully up now, and it appeared that most people were assembling out on the fields for some sort of training. He thought it looked like some sort of monastic exercise session. Maybe it was true that they were training humans to use some kind of foreign magic. He shook his head. Life had been hard enough before when they were just fighting the Delvadr.

He let out a huff of pent-up anxiety and frustration. Now they were as good as conquered. Their capital city was occupied and all of humanity—what little was left—was being forced into some bizarre cult.

Up ahead, he saw men in black and red robes going from tent to tent. Probably making sure that everyone was out on the training fields. He'd have to be quick. He slipped into the first tent with an open door and bumped into a girl in her late teens. She had her hood up, but he'd caught a glimpse of a dark strand of hair before she slipped it back. That made her not like the others. He could tell she knew he'd seen it. She bolted for the door and he caught her arm.

"Wait. I'm not going to hurt you."

She yanked her arm back and broke his grip by bashing his forearm down hard on her knee and made for the door, but he caught her hood from behind and her feet flew out from under her. She landed flat on her back, losing her breath in the process.

Macq drug her back into the tent.

"I don't know who you are, but the men in the black and red robes are coming. You and I have to hide."

She wheezed and blinked toward a low cot resting on a rattan rug.

He looked at her questioningly.

She pointed and this time he realized she was motioning toward the trunk that rested vertically next to it.

"Move the trunk," she squeaked out.

He crossed the cramped space and followed her suggestion. Underneath was a rattan rug which he rolled out of the way to reveal a small opening.

"In there?" He whispered. She was barely going to fit. He didn't think he could.

She crawled over on hands and knees and slipped in head first. From inside, he heard her say, "Slide the trunk back in place when you drop down. You'll want to face the door. Tunnel only goes one way."

He heard voices outside, just one tent over.

"Dammit," he cursed under his breath and then slid feet first into the hole. His feet barely touched the ground when his chest got stuck. He was cutting it really close. Macq exhaled as much as he could, and he felt the girl pulling him down. He just managed to get the trunk in place as he heard someone enter the tent.

It was dark in the hole. He could feel the girl was right in front of him. When a dim light bloomed between them, he saw her hand holding the handle of a knife. He couldn't see the blade, but he felt it press against the side of his Adam's apple.

His eyes locked with hers. They weren't the eyes of an innocent young girl. They were hard. There was no question whether she would use the blade if he gave her a reason to.

He could hear her breathing and he could hear the man rummaging around above.

"No one in here. Sure you saw someone?" the man called to someone else outside.

"Yeah, pretty sure. Didn't look like he was bald either, but I only saw him for a second."

"We're gonna have to do another clean sweep. Maybe move all the tents a sector at a time."

"No need. The other Defiler shows up in two days. The battle priestess has enough mechs fitted out that everyone left gets paired up. Whoever's not ready ... well, it's on them. We gave them every chance to do the training."

"How can there be that many Deathhounds on one of those things? After the last group shipped out, there are still over a hundred thousand people here. Even two to one that'd be—"

"Try three or four to one..." the muffled reply trailed off.

The man had exited the tent and both of the men's voices were becoming difficult to hear. Macq strained to make it out. He shifted, and the girl pressed the knife harder.

"Okay, okay." He whispered and settled back, "I told you I'm not here to hurt you."

Her tight-lipped smile suggested she didn't believe him. She pressed the knife point in until he was sure he must be bleeding.

"Look at my hair. I'm not from here. Me and another guy broke in while something was going down over at the hangars. We're here to mobilize a resistance. Obviously, that's in your *personal* interest, don't you think?" he said pointedly, looking at the strand of hair that'd slipped back down into her face.

She didn't budge. He could tell she was doing the math on whether or not to just kill him and take her chances.

His hand flashed out, slamming the knife against the wall as he thrust his head forward, catching her on the brow. A lot of the force of that blow was absorbed by the hem of her hood, but it made the statement that needed to be made.

He deftly removed the blade as she staggered back, landing on her butt just a couple feet away.

"Okay, you wanna try this again?" He asked while slipping the blade into the drawstring of his robes.

She massaged her forehead, staring murder back at him from the floor. The small flashlight she had been holding was lying on the tunnel floor between them.

"I said, do you want to try this again? Otherwise, we can do it the hard way."

"What're you after?"

"I told you. I want to get in touch with whoever is leading the resistance against the Deathhounds."

"Well, there isn't one."

"What do you mean, there isn't one? This is Epriot Prime. We're the last of the humans left. There's no way that we're all just lining up to be war slaves for the Deathhounds."

"I'm telling you. No one's fighting it. 'Cept a handful of jarheads and some crazy pilot that just showed up yesterday. That was probably that scuffle you heard earlier."

"Wait ... what pilot?"

"Some famous dude. He was the one they sent to do that treaty and stuff," she offered that thin smile again, "Apparently that didn't work out too well, otherwise we wouldn't be in this mess."

"Capt. Maj. Novak? Was that the pilot?"

"Dunno. Why's it matter?"

"That's my dad. He wasn't supposed to get here this quickly. That means those poor bastards getting torn to pieces this morning were with him."

Macq's legs buckled, and he sat down hard on the tunnel floor. His hands went to his face. *I just let him die. He was right there in front of me and I just let it happen. He must have been heading for the spires through the transit tunnels like Dexx suggested. But what if he made it into the tunnels and was headed to the Spires? Did he know that the Deathhounds were coming?* It was too hard to tell. He racked his brain trying to remember if the Defiler had moved after the firefight was over or during. He couldn't remember.

"That's a real geffer. Sorry to hear that. Now get outta my hole and forget you ever saw the place."

"You're a real piece of work, you know that?" Macq said, stung by her callousness. She looked at him, nonplussed, and shrugged. He thought it looked like she was trying a little too hard.

"What'll you do if they come clear everyone out?"

"I'll get by. Seems to be what I'm good at."

"What's your name?"

"Wella ... or Seraf, depending on who you ask."

"Why's that?"

"Grew up in a boarder. They named me after the town they found me in. But then some folks came round and said they wanted to adopt me. The guy was s'posed to be my real dad. Sperm-donor or something. My mom is s'posed to be that mech lady. But, apparently, she's been a bit tied up. So, it seems we both know important people that still aren't around to help. Now, you gonna leave or what?"

"Wow. That'd be something."

"What, having Galas for a mom? Real hoot."

"I was supposed to meet her a couple of days ago—Colonel Galas, that is. But we got diverted on the drop."

"Balls. What drop?"

"The drop from *Xandraitha's Hope*. Your mom was back at the Arcfire temple—the thing that wiped out the Delvadr, in case you hadn't heard. Anyway, she wouldn't let us breach orbit, which was really kind of a pain in the backside, but I totally respect her for standing her ground. It was the right thing to do. Anyway, we were having trouble with comms, so a handful of us had to go down live and in person. But the only thing small enough to avoid the Arcfire weapon was power armor, so we had to jump.

"The problem with that was, halfway down Colonel Dexx, the traitor and saboteur, decided to bug out. I followed him here. When we saw the Defiler mech, Col. Dexx and I realized we needed to work together rather than kill each other. Which, to be honest ... jury's still out, but for the meantime, it's an uneasy truce."

"What're you, like, fifteen? And you're chasing some hotshot bad guy across the starry heavens and breaking into an internment camp surrounded by Deathhounds? Some story, dude."

"Yeah, you're right. I wouldn't believe me either. But, it doesn't really matter, I guess. Everyone here that's left is gonna get turned over to the Deathhounds for battle—whatever that means—and my dad is either dead or halfway to the spires by now and may or may not know that a Defiler will be showing up within a couple of hours. Dammit! This situation sucks. I don't know what to do. Haven't had to do this kind of thing on my own before..."

"Well ... um, what'd you say our name was?"

"Macq."

"Mack Novak?"

"Macquil."

"Mackwill? Yeah, I'd stick with Mack. Anyway, Mack Novak, it sounds like this place is a lost cause. You don't know if your dad is dead, so maybe try to find out. Or if he is alive, maybe you can catch him on his way to the Spires," Seraf offered, "And sorry for being kind of shitty about your dad. It was rude. No excuse for that."

"Yeah. Sure, I get it," he said. He was staring at the ground, trying to get all the puzzle pieces to fit together in his head. "If I go hunting around and don't find anything, it doesn't tell me if he's dead or alive. If he's alive, he'll be showing up at the Spires for one hell of a siege. I don't think they want a lot of casualties because they want to use us for battle, so he might actually fare okay.

"If he's dead already, there's nothing I can do at that point. I want to know. Especially since there's a good chance that my mother will be showing up here, in which case she needs to be warned that there's another defiler on the way. I guess I should go poke around over there and see what I can see. Especially if it's like you said and everyone is just going along with the Deathhounds." He looked up at her, shaking his head. "Which sounds absolutely insane, by the way."

"Tell me about it."

"Seraf, do you have any other robes handy? For someone shorter and stockier than me?"

"No, but we should be able to scrape some up with everyone out in the training fields and now that the first patrol has passed us."

"There will be more?"

"Oh yeah. Every couple hours."

"Alright. Should probably get a move on then," replied Macq, and then after thinking for a second, "Hey, do you want to come with me and Dexx? There's a good chance I can get you hooked up with your mom. If we make it out of all this alive, that is."

"Nah. She would have come for me if that's what she wanted. Good luck, Macquil. Sorry for trying to stab you in the throat."

"No problem. Sorry for knocking the wind out of you and head-butting you in the face. Quite a goose egg you got there."

She touched her eyebrow gingerly and winced, "Yeah. Nice. Here, let's get you out the other way. We'll pop up in Guss's place. He's stocky enough and keeps his robes ... kinda sanitary. Plus, I wanna check on him."

It took several minutes to negotiate the narrow tunnels, but when they did get to Guss's place it looked like it'd been ransacked.

"Wow. This is not like the old guy. Jarhead, ya know. Looks like he and the others left in a hurry."

Macq pulled himself out of the hole in the ground and looked around for himself. "Do you think he got nabbed by the black robes or…"

"Or do I think he was fool enough to get in a tussle with a couple of mechs with your old man? Yeah. I do actually."

"You think he was with my dad this morning?"

"Yeah. That makes a lot of sense. He wanted nothing to do with all this magical nonsense."

"Well, I don't know if it's *all* nonsense. The Deathhounds are real and they use some kind of interdimensional mumbo jumbo. Also, that HALO drop that I did was with a guy named D'avry from another planet. A *human* from another solar system that thinks he's from the future."

"Ha. Well, he'll fit right in with these numbskulls from military intelligence."

"No. I don't know about all of it, but that guy is legitimate. He can levitate and speak to the Gefkarri telepathically. Way out there stuff," Macq said, shaking his head in amazement.

"Okay. That sounds real nice, but what does that matter now? Guss is gone and your dad is too."

"Well, D'avry was with my dad. Maybe there's a way that they made it through."

"I wouldn't hold out hope but right now, there's a defiler on its way to the Spires and another one on its way here. I don't plan on sticking around," she said.

"We really should stick together, Seraf. Let's grab a set of robes for Dexx and get back with him to figure out if he's gotten in touch with the *Xandraitha's Hope* or seen anything else."

"This is the bad guy from the peace treaty? You don't trust him. Why should I?"

"Well, you shouldn't. But right now, he wants to not get caught as badly as we do. And he's got military clearance that may still be able to be leveraged. Maybe there's an armory over at the hangar complex. Maybe we can use the transit tunnels to get clear of the parade fields. I don't know, but I think we should regroup and figure it out from there. Plus, I told him I'd be back, so that's what I'm going to do."

"Yeah, well, good luck hotshot," she said with a casual salute. "I think I'm better off on my own."

She headed for the door, got nearly outside, spun around and nearly bowled Macq over as she grabbed his wrist and pulled him toward the back of the tent.

"Never mind. Going with you guys."

"Black robes?"

"Yup," she said while lifting the back wall of the tent and scurrying under.

He shook his head and followed as quickly and quietly as he could.

"That's the second time today you said you saw something and there's no one there. You need to lay off that homemade shit you're cooking up, Pascal."

"I swear I saw someone. And there's nothing wrong with my homebrew. You just got a weak stomach."

Macq heard the men bickering as he led Seraf off through the tents and out toward the edge of camp.

CHAPTER 23
SPIRES AND THE RIGHTEOUS FURY

Macq and Seraf made it back to the rally point where he had last seen Colonel Dexx, but there was nothing there but the body.

"Oh, hey ... I should've probably mentioned this."

"What the frag, Novak?!?" Seraf shot off the side of the trail and bent over, breathing through the urge to throw up. "Seriously? You killed some dude and took his robes??? What kind of ... sicko..." She burped. "Gimme a second here."

"Yeah. No problem."

She came up for air. "What kind of sicko kills a dude and steals his robes? You gotta real problem Macq."

"No, this wasn't us. We found him here. But, yeah, we took his clothes. You good?"

Seraf was still a little green. He moved to pat her on the back but thought better of it when she glared back at him. "I think the resistance had a problem. Maybe he was a traitor or I don't know ... maybe he was one of the black robes."

She shot a glance in the direction of the corpse and stared back out over the field. "Uh ... maybe. Everyone looks the same around here but, yeah, he kind of reminds me of one of those guys. I usually tried to avoid them." She shook out her shoulders and hands and then drew herself up straight, but still avoided looking at the bald, dead guy on the side of the trail. "So where's your notorious friend? This Colonel Dexx."

"Um ... that's a great question. And, to be honest, I don't like the answers that are popping up in my head. Something never felt right about him working alone on all of this. Now I'm even more convinced that he might be trying to get in contact with someone."

"Here?"

"I don't know. I guess."

"Does that seem right? I mean, this is a detention camp. Don't saboteurs and double-crossers usually find a way to stay out of situations like this? I mean, that's the point, right? Self-preservation."

"Yeah, you have a point. But, it seems like a lot of things didn't go according to plan. Not with the Chareth-Ul taking over the planet, rounding up every last one of us. And now they're on their way to the Spires."

"So, I'm no expert at military coups and political intrigue, but I'd say none of that really matters. If you want to save your dad, if he's still alive—sorry—and if you want to stop the Deathhounds from taking over, then we're short on time."

"Yeah. Seems that way." Macq worked his way around a large rock. "But at least my power armor is still stashed away safely. Ooh and look, so is Dexx's. That's odd. You ever use power armor before? It might be the safest way to get out of here."

"No. I grew up in a boarder. You think they just train up all the orphans on the latest mil-tech?"

"Well, I don't know... maybe?" He shrugged.

"Nope. They don't."

"Well, it's pretty easy. I can walk you through it. I think we need to make our way out of here and covering a lot of ground really fast may be the best way to go, rather than slinking around and getting shot up by Deathhounds."

"Sounds dicey. Not gonna lie, I kinda like it." Her face brightened with the first genuine smile he'd seen. Just then, a boom shook the ground. Seconds later, they watched as a concussive wave tossed a large number of tents into the air and blew past them, knocking them off their feet.

"What was tha—"

Seraf started, but then her gaze came to rest on the Defiler mech that had just appeared at the edge of the parade grounds, near where the other, larger one had been. This one was only about half the size of the first, but it differed in the fact that it was largely on fire and covered in creeping black shapes that looked like ants from this distance.

"So much for two days before the next one shows up. Oh, no. Those are Void." Macq turned to Seraf. "Get that armor on now."

"How?"

Macq laid Dexx's suit out flat for her. "Twist the helmet. With the suit empty, the chest entry will pop open, and then you can slip right in. The suit will do the rest. Then put the helmet back on and lock it into place. Watch."

He showed her how. All the while, explosions echoed from above. Deathhound mechs and other creatures fell or jumped from the massive machine. Some of the creatures fell and glided on glistening black wings, others just plummeted to their doom. He had no idea what the flyers were but didn't want to stick around to find out.

"Are you good? We should hit that transit tube. Get out of sight and on our way to the Spires. If there's a shuttle, maybe we can get there before the big Defiler does."

"Are you crazy? We need to get out of here," Seraf demanded.

"There's no place that's going to be safe from the Void, except maybe the Spires. In the meantime, there're Void creatures here," pointing at the flying creatures descending from the Defiler en masse, "and I don't know what those other things are, but I doubt they're friendly. Just follow me. I'll try to hail the *Xandraitha's Hope* on the way."

With that, Seraf stood up on uncertain legs. "Oh this is really weird. It's like walking on bouncy balls while wearing an oven."

"You'll get used to it. Just keep moving. We gotta run."

She took a few steps, almost fell over a couple of times, and then started to look a little less shaky. Every stride was an improvement. Thirty seconds later, they were jogging along at a decent clip, two to three times what they could have done on their own.

Thankfully, the Deathhound mechs had pulled back from their positions at the perimeter and were now busy engaging with the Void creatures that had attacked the new Defiler. As such, Macq and Seraf had a clear shot right to the buildings within the hangar complex. The transit building stood alone. Luckily, as something of a military nerd, Macq knew what to look for.

He ran up to the front door and smashed it in. For some reason, he expected to see people inside, but it was just an empty lobby, the kind you expected to see in a military ancillary building. The far corner was a stairwell, and beyond that, a corner of the building was missing entirely.

"Well, at least that explains why the door was still locked. I'm beginning to wonder whether or not this is what Dexx was up to. He seemed to be more interested in the Spires than anything else. He probably just sent me off on a wild goose chase hoping I'd get caught."

Movement in the fields beyond the building turned out to be a handful of the flying creatures from before. Macq zoomed in using the suit's HUD. The creatures looked like an amalgamation of centipede and kangaroo and they formed up into a vee pattern upon hitting the ground.

Looks like they hunt in packs. A shiver ran down his spine. "We should go."

He sprinted to a wall adjacent to the stairs for cover, darted a quick glance toward the creatures, and then slipped down the stairs. Seraf just went down on her chest and crawled to the stairs, sliding down to the first landing head first.

"That's one way to do it, I guess."

"If it works, don't fight it," she replied as she got up and brushed her suit off. "This thing's *fun.*"

"Yeah, well, don't get too excited. It's not a full combat version."

She shrugged. "One step at a time."

Two levels down, they found the security checkpoint.

"Shoot. I doubt I have enough clearance to get through here."

He opened up his gauntlet and placed his palm on the reader, which flashed green.

"Wow. That's lucky. They must have opened everything up when the Deathhounds arrived. Maybe they were trying to get everyone out?"

"I dunno, but it's not going to matter if there aren't any shuttles," she said, pointing ahead of them.

Macq looked across the compact underground utility yard and Seraf was right. All the bays were empty. He ran over to a column-mounted call station and hit the first location on the map in the Spire compound—Alpha Tep. A pleasant chime responded, and the location turned green.

"Oh, maybe there's a shuttle being summoned. I'm not really sure how this transit system works. My studies were mostly on mechs, fighters, the old interstellar craft ... that kinda stuff."

Seraf didn't respond. He glanced her direction and from what he could see of her face through her visor she didn't seem interested. In fact, she looked worried.

"What is it?"

She brought an abrupt finger up to her helmet in a hushing motion. From above, he heard a scraping noise. His imagination ran wild but barely needed to. The most likely horror was the creatures they'd just seen. They'd probably seen them dash for the stairs and came to investigate. Or maybe they were just hiding from the Void. It didn't really matter which.

He pulled her around the column and out of the line of sight from the stairway. Macq enhanced visibility in his display until he caught a reflective surface that provided him a visual of the stairwell. That image plus the auditory sensors gave the SortieNet enough to work with to build a light version of a 3D BattleSpace model. He didn't have all the fancy neural mods, so he had to use eye focus and finger movements to navigate the system. He flicked the image over to Seraf's HUD as well.

The two of them watched silently as one of the black centipede-shaped heads of the flying predators materialized in the SortieNet display. A red dot materialized in the battlespace model and then another followed. Macq had seen three of them, but he guessed that maybe the other one was up top keeping watch.

The creatures slipped out of view of the reflective surface he'd been using to track them, but the red dots were still clearly visible in the BSM. At first, they were sticking close together, which made it easy to keep the column between him and Seraf and the bug creatures, but then noise off in the corner of the room caused one of them to head in that direction.

Macq couldn't see what was going on, but then, all of a sudden, the whole space lit up with a staccato burst of light and the sound of automatic gunfire. He watched as the two red dots converged on the far corner of the room. One of the bugs screeched horribly and there were shouts. Three new dots sprang up but in blue.

They were all in the corner of the room and a utility closet he'd not seen at first.

Gunfire again played across the room as the other bug burst from the stairway and raced for the area with all the noise. There was another screech and then all went silent.

"Do you think that was your dad?" came Seraf's whispered question through the power armor's audio link.

"I don't know. I didn't hear his voice in all that racket. But I can't be sure. Those bugs sure take a lot of damage though."

Macq noticed that the blue dots in the BSM had all gone to an alternating blue and gray, indicating that the SortieNet was uncertain as to the unit's status. The red dot continued to move around the area and then turned its attention to the rest of the transit shuttle bay. That wasn't a good sign.

Seraf and Macq continued to keep the column in between the creature and themselves and to do so as quietly as they could. It was a good-sized area, big enough to fit seven or eight transit shuttles queueing for the tunnels, so the echo wasn't great but it could have been worse.

The creature was beginning to veer in their direction, but then noise from above seemed to catch its attention. It started bounding in the direction of the stairwell and disappeared from view.

Macq broke immediately for the corner where the fighting had taken place but did so as quietly as he could.

"Stay where you are for now, Seraf. I'm going to check and see if I recognize anyone and grab weapons if I can. If those creatures come back, you need to take the shuttle and warn my dad if he's there, or at least warn someone at the Spires. I figure we've only got about an hour before that thing shows up."

"I told you I wasn't sure if I was on board with your plan. So don't get caught and I won't have to decide whether or not it'll weigh on my conscience if I bail out."

"Fair enough," he replied as he turned back to scan the area.

As he drew closer to an overturned counter, he saw one of the unconscious men. His breath caught in his chest for a long moment as he struggled to recognize the man's face. *Nobody I know, I don't think.*

However, the SortieNet did recognzie him. With the close-up visual, it was able to positively determine that the man was dead and that his name was Giddr "Poizn Asp" Marth. He was a Marine Corporal. Macq grabbed the assault rifle that was lying next to him, his sidearm, and energy charges.

"Sorry, Giddr. You understand," he said, closing the man's eyes before continuing on.

He checked the rifle's charge, deemed it adequate, and let it settle into the magnetized open holster that angled across his torso. At least his quasi-mil-spec armor came with that feature. He could function hands-free now and still have his rifle at the ready.

Next, he checked the area off to the left of the counter that had been out of sight when they'd entered the depot initially.

He had to step over one of the bugs to do it. It was oozing from projectile holes in its abdomen. There were no wounds but multiple ricochet marks on its chitinous top side. Macq filed this information away. It was the same with the other body as well.

As he drew farther back into the utility closet, he found the other two humans. These, the SortieNet did not recognize. Neither did Macq, thankfully. One thing that he thought was strange was that the SortieNet instantly recognized that the first man was dead, but not so with these two.

Macq crossed over to the closest man. There was blood running down from both nostrils, but other than that, he looked unharmed. Then his eyes shot open, and he started screaming,

"Ahhhh. Ahhhh, I can't move! I can't move!"

"Whoa, buddy. Relax. Calm down," Macq said through the armor's external speaker, but the guy kept yelling. He heard noise from above and had to make a split decision. He darted for the column where Seraf was waiting and just made it before two more red dots popped up in the BattleSpace and headed for the screaming man. "Dammit, dammit, dammit," he cursed and moved to go after the man, but Seraf grabbed his arm. Her eyes through the suit's visor said everything: 'You can't jeopardize *your* life when so many others are depending on you.' At least that's what he chose to read.

The man yelled out more desperately and then was cut short.

Macq closed his eyes, trying in vain to squash the flood of emotions that washed over him.

Seraf patted his shoulder. "You couldn't do anything for him. You saw what two of those creatures did against the three of them. One of them was a marine. It was smart for you to run when you did."

Macq understood it wasn't meant as an insult, but it stung. He *had* run. And left an injured man to die.

Just then a ding interrupted the silence, meant to notify passengers of the approach of one of the shuttles.

"Dammit. Bad timing," he said over their private channel.

Lights emerged way down in the tunnel and the two creatures raced past them, half-hopping and half-gliding on buzzing wings.

Seraf looked at Macq with wide eyes. "You don't think they're going to—"

They heard dual impacts and watched the shuttle lights continue closer until the whole thing came into view as it entered the lit area. There were no large bug bodies squashed on the front of it, but then the bugs were nowhere to be seen either. The shuttle glided to the end of the path and settled down.

They waited a moment longer, just to be safe, and then sprinted for the shuttle. Once aboard, there were no controls or way to tell it to go like there would be in an elevator.

Macq was about to say something when a voice came over the shuttle's audio circuit, "Please prepare for departure. Stow personal bags and take a seat or handle. The shuttle will depart in eighty seconds.

"Oh, okay. Any sign of those bugs?" he asked.

"Nah. You know we're barely going to get to the first Spire in time. We're probably just going to die within minutes of getting there."

"No, my dad is warning them. I'm sure he's made it. It's going to be alright."

"And what about your mom? Did you get in touch with her?"

"No. Couldn't get through the jamming. As soon as that new mech showed up, comms were trashed again."

"You think she's going to get caught up in all this mess?"

"I hope not. Before, the big Defiler might have had things locked down, but this one has its hands full."

As if to emphasize the point, a massive boom shook the ground above and below.

"Oh. That didn't sound good. I hope some of the people up there are making it out," Seraf said, but Macq didn't give them very good odds at all. Not with the bugs and the Deathhounds and the Void creatures. It was complete chaos up there. He felt bile building at the back of his throat when he thought about it and had to swallow to settle it back down. There was nothing that could be done, except save as many as they could at the Spires.

Something popped up on the BSM. It wasn't a red dot. It was gold, which meant it was something other than the bugs and humans that had been cataloged so far. That only left one choice. It had to be one of the Void creatures.

It appeared near the stairwell. And then, in a split second, it was halfway across the boarding platform.

Macq grabbed Seraf's arm and pulled her slowly down so that they weren't visible to the creature while they were below the shuttle's windows. Then the voice issued from the audio again.

"Prepare for departure in ten seconds," it said.

The gold dot blipped closer. The shuttle began to lift off the ground and the Void creature charged forward. Macq jumped up and opened fire on full auto, spraying projectiles wildly at a blacked-out nightmare. It looked like a shadow in the shape of a humanoid wolf and its eyes glowed with an inner fire. He concentrated fire at its chest as the shuttle began to pick up speed. The creature leaped closer and some of the projectiles must have connected because it stumbled and rolled and then burst forward again, landing on the back of the shuttle.

Macq's rifle stopped firing. He looked down and the display read zero. So did the HUD in his power armor. *Stupid,* he cursed at himself as he pawed his hip for the charge canister and ejected the old one, but Seraf yanked him back and he lost the can. The creature swiped through the air where he was just a fraction of a second before. It stared down at them. Seraf scampered backward down the aisle and the creature blipped away, landing right in front of her. She froze. The creature drew back a clawed hand and was just descending on her when Macq slammed the clip home and fired.

The creature burst into a brilliant ball of white light just before its claws reached her. They both sighed in relief, but then a shriek echoed from the tunnel behind them.

The back windscreen was completely blown out, and a buffeting wind whipped through the interior with increasing fervor. Macq spun and saw another of the Void creatures burst forward with one last leap. He fired away, but the creature dodged right and left before landing on the back of the shuttle. Macq kept firing until the gun ran out again, but the sound of gunfire kept coming. He turned to find Seraf firing the sidearm he'd retrieved from the fallen marine with both hands. The creature exploded in a ball of light, but Seraf kept firing and firing until the pistol just clicked repeatedly with each pull of the trigger.

Macq walked over to her. She was still pulling the trigger. He put his hand on top of the barrel and pushed it down. "I think you got it."

She nodded absently, biting her lip nervously as she stared out the back of the shuttle into the darkness before letting out a big huff.

"I think you got it," he repeated. "We're safe now. Good job, Seraf. You did really, really good."

She nodded again and swallowed before plopping down on a seat next to where she'd been standing.

He dropped into a seat next to her, sucked in a deep breath. His heart was bursting with adrenalin. He looked back at the tunnel too, and reloaded before lowering his own weapon down. He was still waiting for something to burst from out of the darkness.

"Are they gone?"

"I think so. But I don't want to turn my back on that window."

"It's too dark to see anything back there."

"Yeah. I know."

"Let's just move up to the front and rest. We'll keep our eyes on the window while we rest."

"Good idea."

"Macq ... thank you."

"For what? You saved my life back there too."

"Before that. You protected me from the bugs. And then from whatever that thing was. And for getting me out of the camp. You were right. If I'd stayed..."

He nodded dumbly. "Yeah, well. You saved me from getting caught with the black robes, so…"

"Well, you *are* delivering me to almost certain doom, so maybe we're not quite even…"

He laughed, letting out some of the nervous tension. "Fair enough."

CHAPTER 24

THE GATHERING OF FIVE

Epriot Prime, Articles Corwin, *Xandraitha's Hope*

"That section could be big enough. But I still don't see how this can possibly help."

"You're probably right. I don't either, but at least we know there's a possibility," D'avry said, staring at the mapping table and the highlighted chunks of sunken spaceship littered across it. They'd veered slightly north on their way to New Varhus and were now hovering over the wreckage about 5000 meters off the surface.

"Again, *what* possibility?" Katherynn asked.

"If I tell you, you're going to say that I'm crazy."

"That may be so, D'avry, but you're going to tell me anyway because we're out of time and out of options."

D'avry looked at the woman and then looked a second time. "You're very forceful, you know that? Anyway, how about I show you instead? Hold my hand."

"I'm sorry, what?" asked Mads as he stepped between the two.

"Mads, it's okay. Let's see where this is going," replied his mother. She reached out her hand and grasped D'avry's own.

"You too, Mads. And Seda. Maybe not the Captain, no offense sir, but you have a job to do. Is there anyone else available to join us?"

"What is this, some kind of seance?" the captain asked.

"Seance? No. We don't need to talk to any ghosts right now. Though I'm sure there are plenty down there," D'avry said, cocking his head in confusion as he responded to the man.

"Ambassador Novak, you can't possibly be serious, entertaining this ... man's bizarre notions?" asked the man.

"Please, Captain Camlin, is there anyone else on staff that can be spared?"

He looked preoccupied for a moment, but then D'avry realized he was using his augment to converse with someone else on the ship.

"Ensign Presche will join you. Her people have a long history of interest in things of an esoteric nature. Ordinarily, I wouldn't humor such a request or such a preoccupation in one of my officers, but given the demands of the situation..."

"And the fact that humankind may well depend on it," D'avry muttered under his breath. Seda's eyes flared blue, but she said nothing. She didn't need to. He could feel her amusement.

It made him angry.

You were going to kill me when I first boarded your ship, he thought over their shared connection.

True. Not intentionally, but we knew it was likely.

He didn't have a response to such brazen honesty, he was seething.

But then you not only survived, but you seized the connection, forcing yourself into the collective. We didn't know what to do with that. Some wanted to punish you by death for such an offense, but then something within the collective, very old and very rarely expressed, responded. It wanted you connected. That's when I was ... assigned to you. As your mentor.

"Assigned" wasn't right. D'avry was more than certain she was holding something back. He would get his answer later. He was still mad, but this new information had him curious.

The door to the bridge whooshed open and a woman with short brown hair in her late twenties entered the room. She was generally attractive, with soft features that contrasted with intense, dark eyes. Ensign Presche was wearing tradesman coveralls over her officer's uniform, so D'avry assumed she was from engineering.

"Ensign Presche. I think I have something you'll find ... enlightening."

She observed the circle of people around the map table holding hands.

"Will we be speaking to your mother, or perhaps your grandmum, Captain Camlin?"

He shot her a dark look but didn't scold her for her insolence.

Without a further word, she stepped up and joined the circle. Her eyes went from one person to the next and then settled on D'avry. She nodded as if confirming a suspicion.

"Five. Okay, everyone. You don't really need to do anything except be present."

"What happened to the Gefkarri aspect Theal isn't going to happen to us, is it?" Mads asked, clearly not pleased by the turn of events.

"Probably not. We're not attempting anything like that, just doing a little exploring."

And with that, D'avry reached out psychically to the other four. He was already connected to Seda, so that was a given. The other three were hesitant, so he reached out tenuously at first, but it wasn't really like they had a choice at this point. They'd entered the circle and with Seda's power behind him, the avenues of opportunity began to present themselves.

D'avry waited until each connection was stable, comfortable even. Then he took the consciousness of everyone within the circle into himself. He felt their presence. He felt their hearts beating, their lungs expanding and collapsing as they breathed. He felt the blood pumping through their veins and then he felt Seda even more as she stood beside him. Her energy flowed warmly through him, through everyone. It was like a fragrant breeze on a summer's day, but within it were notes of harmony and discord.

D'avry recognized this as the people within the circle. He maneuvered through their collective presence until he came to the one he knew must be Mads. He reached out and felt his fear, and the anger that was the result of that fear.

"Calm your minds. If you cannot, you're free to leave the circle," he said aloud. But to Mads, he said quietly, in his mind, *You may leave the circle, but the best way to protect your mother is to stay by her side. It's your choice.*

D'avry felt the inner turmoil tense and then ease. The discordance within the flowing energy evaporated. The song grew louder and more full.

He focused now on the lantern door in his chest and the artifacts within it and felt them begin to turn in response to the magic. They spun faster and faster. He felt the flutter of power around him harmonizing with the artifacts. The power of the magic spell he was weaving doubled and then doubled again. He wondered if this was their purpose all along, the artifacts. Something like this anyway.

D'avry felt his hair tousled by a physical breeze and recognized that within the bridge, the air was stirring. *That's good. That's very good.*

He focused again on the energy provided by Seda and amplified by the people around him, and then he took them all down. Out of the ship, into the air, down into the waters, deep below the surface until it grew dark and close.

And then he willed it to be light and the depths of the ocean bloomed into aquamarine and a large dark shape loomed into view from below. He felt stirring within the song but held steady, guiding the collective entity toward their objective.

Breathe, he thought to them, and some of the trepidation dissipated.

He drew them closer to the object. It was itself like a city, but where the Defiler mechs were squat and rectangular, this was wide and tall, and much, much longer.

The *Righteous Fury* lay on the ocean floor, stretching out for many miles before and behind them. He sensed the many lost souls and his heart ached with that loss. The panic and distress, the near-hour-long wait as the ship disintegrated in the atmosphere and finally crashed into the ocean, barely missing most of the island continent and the capital city with millions of refugees surrounding it.

The feeling coming from the others was that of wonder and sadness and nostalgia all mixed together. And there was mourning too. Some had known people lost, either to the crumbling ship or on it.

D'avry pressed on and sought a section of the wreckage that was strong enough still to be raised. A sudden note of alarm echoed through the body and he realized their shock at what he was intending to do. At the impossibility of it, but then also in a way that it felt somehow sacrilegious or disrespectful to the souls they, in some intangible way, felt all around them.

He weighed their worries and reminded them that this was an attempt to save many more. To save the people that the *Righteous Fury* had been employed to defend. They were going to give that magnificent ship one more chance to do just that.

He felt their hesitation dwindle and then the magic swelled again, surprising even him. D'avry was making it up as he went along here. He'd only intended on gauging how much the others could amplify his own powers, but then the experiment took on a life of its own. He'd decided to go directly to the source of his interest. The great ship. And as the magic grew and harmonized and doubled on itself, he'd learned that it was possible to raise a section. But now he knew that they were at the end of their ability, as great as that was. He needed more people or ... he needed a boost.

Slowly, D'avry reached out to the ship and began to apply pressure. He felt Seda's focus on him intensify as she began to understand what he was going to attempt to do. She knew that they weren't yet strong enough. She knew what he would have to do to increase their power. He felt her hesitation, but then she loosed herself to him, baring every bit, and he took everything she had.

The wind on the bridge was whipping now like a maelstrom. They were somehow there on the bridge and thousands of feet below the ocean. And somehow, still somewhere beyond that, in a place that only existed within the spell that D'avry was weaving.

When D'avry reached into the power of the Chareth-Ul talisman at his side, a shockwave ripped through the *Xandraitha's Hope* and through the waters. He heard voices yelling and screaming but in a chorus of power. Everyone around him in the circle raised their cries, not in anguish but as some small outlet of the power that was rushing through them. It was an autonomic response. The voices boomed through the waters and the great ship began to lift off the floor of the ocean, displacing millions upon millions of gallons of water.

As it rose, it grew lighter. Minutes passed, the voices never ceased, the wind never ceased, and the coldness within him never relented.

Half an hour later, the *Righteous Fury* crested the surface of the waters and basked in the sun for the first time in nearly twenty-five years. A part of it anyway. Water poured from its scored and crusted surface in horsetail plumes of white as waves crashed against its sides.

All five of the members of the circle lay on the floor of the bridge, panting breathlessly, drenched in sweat but shivering, eyes rolling wildly as they re-engaged with the reality they'd left over thirty minutes prior.

"What... did we ...?" Katherynn tried to formulate.

"Yes," D'avry responded between breaths, his blond hair plastered to his head. "Yes, we did," he said, beaming and chattering at the same time.

Captain Camlin stood off to one side. His eyes were wide and wary. "Are you alright, Ambassador?" he asked in a clipped tone.

"Yes," Katherynn gasped out. "Yes, I am."

"We feared the worst, but none of us could separate you. We were unable to break the circle in any way. So, we had no choice but to wait it out."

"It's good that you didn't. You might have killed us all, Captain. In the future, be sure not to tamper with things you do not understand," scolded D'avry, but he couldn't yet put much vigor behind it. Then he realized he hadn't heard from Seda yet.

He looked for her and found she was still. But not unconscious. He could see the glistening trail of a tear that had run down her too-perfect face.

"Seda, what's the matter?"

She just shook her head and refused to look at him. He didn't know what to make of it. He was sure it was not a small thing. Another thing for later, he assumed. Still, this was a moment of victory on so many levels. They did the impossible by raising even a small portion of that ship. It showed him that humans did have the capacity to amplify magic when it was not their own. They had in this moment just done that with Gefkarri magic and the magic channeled from the Chareth-Ul realm.

It meant that maybe they had a chance. If they couldn't fight, then maybe, just maybe, they could manage to escape.

"Okay, mage. Now what?" asked Ensign Presche, her face glowing with excitement and exhaustion all at once.

"Yeah. Raising a portion of the ship big enough to carry every human left on the planet is neat and all, but getting it to fly? How do you think you're going to do that?" Mads asked.

"One miracle at a time. One massive miracle at a time..." D'avry replied, flopping an arm over to pat him on the chest.

The Captain cleared his throat. "Well, while you were desecrating the resting site of the single-largest loss of life in Epriot military history, our scanners detected that the Chareth-Ul Defiler that had been stationed just outside New Varhus, has left."

"Now is our chance to get over there."

"Then we should take it," Katherynn responded. "I imagine that the wreckage of the raised ship isn't going anywhere. I mean, I sensed that while we were all connected. That the bulkheads are whole..." she said, shaking her head in awe and fascination.

"Yes. I believe that is true. I have to admit that I don't quite understand how we did what we did, but somehow, the water inside was expelled or converted. The bulkheads that are intact are firm and the *Righteous Fury* will float for the time being."

"What we need now are more people. A *lot* more people. All of them," D'avry finished.

"Okay then. Let's get to New Varhus and find our people," Katherynn responded while pushing herself off the floor to resume her post at the mapping table. "Captain, can we get comms established with the refugee camp?"

"We're trying even now, but there is yet to be a response. We'll keep the query on loop. Hopefully, someone will find some equipment and respond back and tell us what's going on down there."

"Okay, we'll just have to go and find out for ourselves. Take us. As fast as this bucket will go."

CHAPTER 25

BETRAYED

The Spires, Base at Alpha Tep

"I take it things didn't go well with the peace treaty," stated Head of Houses, Sloss Reddum from under bushy white brows and just over old-style wire-rimmed spectacles.

Rutker had reached Alpha Tepp without incident. Managed to make contact with the soldiers stationed there without getting shot. He even managed to get an immediate meeting with the EDC heads and military higher-ups gathered there. The ones that were left anyway. All in under an hour.

"No. They did not," replied Rutker. "We were waylaid by pirates and mercenaries on a backwater planet called Gellen III or E'rth according to the indigenous peoples. It was due to the efforts of a saboteur. That saboteur was Colonel Ardent James Dexx, a member, as you know, of our envoy. He was working with not just the Delvadr, but the Gefkarri Pentarch who was supposed to preside over the treaty talks as an impartial moderator. That moderator that now sits in far-orbit in a specially designed Thune mega-carrier."

"We ... had our suspicions."

"Did you?"

The Head of Houses sat up in his seat. "I don't know what you think you're implying, soldier, but—"

"I'm implying that there's no way in hell that Dexx did this on his own and that he has co-conspirators on this council and within the heads of the EDC, but none of that matters because right now we have an interdimensional threat tearing our planet apart, which makes our former enemies, the Delvadr look like a bunch of mid-grade woodscouts."

Reddum made to retort but Rutker wasn't done. "*And*, despite the best efforts of the Gefkarri hovering just off our planet, the Chareth-Ul, whom you might know as the creators of the Deathhounds, are heading *here*. Now.

"Not only have they demonstrated that they do not wish to work with the Gefkarri, who are locked in orbit because Field Colonel Galas has had the good sense to keep them there with the Arcfire, but they have decided they want the planet for themselves and are willing to fight the interdimensional beings known as the Void, tooth and nail to keep it. What's even more pressing is the fact that the human remnant on this planet plays a critical role in their plan to do that—a role, by the way, that doesn't end well for us. Lastly, I will tell you that one of those carrier-sized Chareth-Ul temple mechs is on its way here now and should arrive in less than two hours if I estimate correctly."

"A Defiler. On its way here? You could've led with that Captain-Major."

"With all due respect, Head of Houses Reddum, I needed to know what I was dealing with. Now that we all know that there will be no deal-making once the Chareth-Ul arrive, I suggest we go about girding our defenses for an enemy that will be ignoring the ground levels entirely and boring directly into our defenses midway up."

One of the generals, P'odn Rutker thought, stood up, and walked to the side of the chamber where he started barking orders in hushed tones to a subordinate. Two others, another general and a Grand Marshall, did similarly.

With every branch acting autonomously, Rutker's hopes for this defense were plummeting rapidly.

"Captain Major, what of your wife and sons? I understand that they were with you on the voyage," Reddum had the decency to ask.

"Well sir, Katherynn and Mads are still on the *Xandraitha's Hope* in mid-orbit, waiting for authorization to enter the atmosphere. Macq accompanied me and a few others on the HALO jump to the surface to meet with you all, but he was lost when

Dexx tried to escape. I hope for the best, but fear the worst as I haven't heard from him in the last 36 hours."

Reddum blew air out his white-stubbled cheeks at that. "I'm sorry to hear that, Capt. Major. However, my understanding is that we picked up a transport that matches the specs of the Hope entering the atmosphere earlier today. They appeared to be heading for the antiquity city of Braex, where we understand the Arcfire to be located. So, either Colonel Galas has had a change of heart or possibly lost the Arcfire to the Chareth-Ul or some other entity, maybe even the Delvadr themselves, if there are any left. Impossible to say with comms the way they are."

Rutker's heart dropped when he heard that Katherynn and Mads were planet-side. He'd taken solace in at least that one tiny fact, that they weren't trapped on this planet and might be able to rendezvous with the refugees once he'd organized an exodus. Now he knew that was growing less and less likely by the minute. At least the Defiler mech was no longer at New Varhus. But the bottom line was that now all of his family was scattered to the winds in the middle of a five-sided war.

A thousand emotions battled for dominance, but he kept his soldier's façade in place.

"Head Reddum, there's more. We need to defend here long enough to get everyone to any available transports and mobilize for a full-scale retreat. That planet, Gellen III, is our only hope. It's habitable and there are indicators that humans have colonized it before. I have brought back one of the ... inhabitants of that planet and he is readily assisting me in this effort."

"You want to what? Abandon our home planet and retreat to another one? An interdimensional battle is on our soil soldier. We must do our part to stem the tide of that blight. We will not be going anywhere. In fact," Head of Houses Reddum stood up and addressed the room in general, "take this man somewhere to get showered and fed, he's had one hell of a journey and deserves a couple of minutes rest before ... well, before we greet the Chareth-Ul threat."

Two armed soldiers slid up to either side of Rutker. He let out a long, quiet sigh. This had been the unrecognized fear haunting his mind. This was what he had known all along must be. Dexx wasn't working alone, and the resistance was no resistance at all.

Just a peaceful transition of power to an alien force. Once New Varhus was under occupation, then the Spires would be ceded without a fight.

It made sense, which was the problem. It made sense, but it was still wrong. Rutker had just not been able to accept that reality until it was staring him in the face.

He realized that he'd needed that. It was just too easy to consider it his usual skepticism. How could humanity possibly go willingly into indentured servitude to an alien oppressor? Especially after all these years of fighting tooth and nail against the Delvadr...

Rutker snapped a crisp salute, shook his head, and turned without prodding from the guards. He knew where to go. The confinement facility for Alpha Tep was three levels down. One level below the West Hangar Bays.

The three strode down a wide main corridor floored in grating, dotted with bright industrial overheads, but everything else was hewn red rock. There was a part of him that felt good to be back. The smells were familiar, not unlike a space vessel but with an earthier undertone. He couldn't believe it was over like that.

After risking life and limb on an alien planet, breaking into and then being imprisoned on an alien ship, HALO jumping to the planet's surface, being imprisoned again by a whole other alien race, and after all that, failing at the finish line by being imprisoned by his own people.

He'd had his balls shaved for crying out loud!

And then he realized that his worst fear had materialized—everything now lay in the hands of the kid. The energy seeped out of his muscles.

On the bright side, how could D'avry screw this up any worse than it already was?

Rutker was allowing himself a rare indulgence, to wallow in misery, when he caught sight of a familiar face.

Striding up the corridor was Colonel Dexx. He looked genuinely happy to see Rutker, or at least to see him flanked by guards.

"Capt. Major Novak, I trust they're treating you well," he said as he passed by, most likely heading for that very same chamber.

"Where's Macq?" Rutker growled, struggling to keep from choking the life out of him.

"Huh ... I dunno. Haven't seen him," Dexx replied, feigning ignorance.

Rutker could tell he was just trying to get a rise out of him, which meant he wasn't responsible for any real harm that had come to him. If he had been, he'd have led with that and let Rutker dig his own grave by attacking him in front of armed guards.

"Frag off, Dexx," Rutker spat.

Charges of insubordination were the least of his problems. The colonel chuckled as he walked away.

One of the soldiers cleared his throat and Rutker got the hint. He resumed his journey to the detention area. Then he saw another face he recognized, a certain marine with a face that looked like it'd been used to stop a transport.

Monster Mind's eyes betrayed surprise but then dropped back to studying the grating as he walked along. Rutker thought he saw the barest nod as the man passed.

One level down, he caught a reflection of someone following them. Two corners later, when they'd entered an empty corridor, Rutker skipped forward as he heard rushed footsteps closing in from behind. Two beats later, and the guards were unconscious. Monster Mind was gathering their gear and handing some of it over to Rutker.

"I'm really glad I ran into you back there."

"Mmhmm. I bet. I take it the bigwigs weren't too keen on picking a fight with a temple mech?"

"No. They were not keen on it. In fact, it's pretty clear that this has all been worked out. When they switched sides from the Gefkarri to the Chareth-Ul, who's to say?"

"Probably around the time the Defiler showed up in New Varhus," Monster provided.

"Yeah, maybe so."

"So, what are we going to do?"

"We're going to go find a ship and get the hell out of here. Anyone that wants to go with us can come along. To be honest, we need everyone we can get since, in my humble opinion, we're essentially starting over as a species. I'm sure with all the people here, there must be some dissenters.

"Oh yeah. I passed several floors where it's clear they're keeping the refugees confined to those levels. Making it look like it's for their own good, but it's obvious to anyone with an eye for that sort of thing that they're just as much internment camps as what we left in New Varhus."

"Bastards. Okay, you go down and rally anyone you can." And then he remembered something. "Did anyone else make it out of the hangars with you that can help? Gygr?"

"Yeah. A couple." The man's visage hardened. "Not Gygr though. I think a few more were still back there, but I don't know if they hopped a shuttle or just bugged out."

"That's too bad. Sorry for your loss, Gunny. We'll honor him with how we live or how we die. But let's focus on the former. You get the people. I'll get the ride. We've got less than an hour. Once I secure the ship, I'll come help you open up the way to the West Hangar. Just one level down from here."

The two worked out a few more details and then Rutker headed for the stairs to the next level down. Even if there wasn't a big enough ship in the West Hangar, it was big enough to hold *a* ship and he'd be able to search the rolls from there. His thoughts drifted to his family. He prayed that he could find them. And D'avry, he realized, shaking his bald head. *I must be losing my mind, but I really hope the kid is doing okay.*

CHAPTER 26
CHANGE OF PLANS

Somewhere West of the Spires

The shuttle rattled and Macq jolted from the daze he hadn't realized he was in. To be fair, it'd been one adrenalin pulsing adventure to the next since jumping out of a perfectly good spaceship and rocketing for Epriot Prime's surface.

He'd stuck tight to the colonel even though the more experienced man did everything he could to lose him, even pulling a high-g, last-minute course change to land on the far side of a lake.

It almost worked, but Macq was lighter and more maneuverable. As they drew closer to their destination, their in-suit sensors told them everything they needed to know. Lots of bad guys from both sides in just about every direction.

It'd taken them all of about five minutes to come to a reasonable accommodation in regard to killing each other. In short, it could wait. Humanity had to survive in order for proper justice to be served, and Dexx was willing to let that play out. He was confident that history would side with his pragmatism. Macq had no such delusions but could agree that the likelihood of either of them making it across the territory on their own was next to zero. They were better off working together.

He blinked away the fuzzy-headed thoughts and realized the Seraf was staring at him. All of a sudden he was self-conscious.

"What?"

"You know you twitch when you sleep?"

"I wasn't sleeping. Who could sleep after that?" he said, motioning toward the blown out window at the far end of the shuttle.

"Apparently you. Anyway, it's kind of cute. Like a puppy."

Macq fumed but couldn't think of anything clever to say. Seraf just smiled happily, enjoying his discomfort. And then a boom shook the shuttle again, only this time the interior and exterior lights flickered.

"Whoa, what do you think's going on—"

She was cut off when the lights went completely out and the shuttle started to grind to a halt. A deafening boom rattled through the tunnel and the shuttle jumped, tilted all the way onto its side, and ground to a halt with sparks filling the whole of the tunnel.

Macq grabbed Seraf and pulled her toward him and a support rail he was holding onto for dear life. The shuttle came to a stop, and they went flying. Everything was dark and quiet when the sparks ceased. They were smashed up against the front wall of the shuttle, but they were okay. All he could hear was his own breathing and the sound of his heart pounding in his ears.

"What ... the..."

"Are you alright? Seraf? Are you okay?"

"Ugh, yeah. I guess. What just happened?" She asked as she tried to stand but found the wall that was underneath her had little flat area to stand on.

"Dunno. Didn't feel like an earthquake. Felt like a bomb went off."

And then a loud groaning greeted them as the tunnel ahead shook and rumbled before daylight struck through the dust and grit ahead.

They were both speechless as they struggled to make heads or tails of what just happened. Macq was the first to move. He pressed forward, kicked out the front window of the shuttle and jogged ahead to the caved-in area that had just been exposed. He got there in time to just catch a glimpse of the bottom of a huge structure as it lifted away into the sky.

He was without words. Again. What he was looking at was the bottom tread of the defiler. Or at least that's what it had to be. What else *could* it be?

Seraf moved up beside him. "Why'd you leave me back there? It's creepy as hell."

"I think that was the foot of the Defiler mech we were trying to beat to the Spires. Twenty seconds faster and..."

"Splat. Damn, I guess when it's your time to go, it's your time to go. Luckily, it wasn't ours." She patted his shoulder. "Okay, what now, hot rod?"

"Well ... we're not going anywhere in the shuttle. I guess we could keep to the tunnels, but we could just get stepped on again, or not and the tunnel could still collapse. Same difference. I'd say try to catch up with the defiler and hitch a ride. We wouldn't get there early but, I don't know, maybe we could come up with something."

He looked up at the fifteen meters of earth and ravaged construction materials. Maybe hitching a ride on that thing's foot wasn't such a good idea.

Just then something garbled came over his suit's sensors, "... Distress... forced landing... Varhus..."

He couldn't make it out, but it didn't sound good, and he didn't know who could be sending a signal. Well, he did, but right then he was praying to Maker that it wasn't who he thought it was if they were being forced down in New Varhus.

"Did you hear that? Sounds like a mayday. Someone's going down in a ship," Seraf said.

"Yeah. Here, wait..." he tuned the signal and applied filters, stuff he'd learned in military school. The stuff he was good at, not all the combat junk that Mads excelled at and liked to lord over him. The signal repeated, "Distress... Distress... *Hope* taken damage... forced landing... New Varhus southeast... refugees and Void..."

The signal cut out.

"We need to go back," said Macq.

"You're kidding, right? You saw that place. It was a slaughter."

"My mom. The signal said hope. As in *Xandraitha's Hope*."

"I dunno, coulda meant something else like 'I sure hope we don't run into any Void.'"

"Seriously? That's what you think they were saying in the middle of a crash landing?"

"That's what I'd be saying."

"Yeah, you're right. I'd be saying that too, but I don't think that's what *they* were saying."

"For the record, I'm not okay with this."

"But you're coming?"

She nodded. "But I'm not going back through the tunnel. We don't know if any more of the Void, or even those flying centipede thingies, are back there."

"Alright. Topside then. Let's get a move on."

He grabbed her hand and helped her up onto a sloped slab that looked like it led to a reasonable path to the surface.

The signal crackled through again. This time, it was indecipherable but sounded more desperate. They doubled their pace and reached the surface just as long shadows overtook the valley and the sun slipped behind the coastal mountains.

CHAPTER 27
GOING DOWN

D'avry was still basking in the afterglow of what he and the others, with Seda's help, had accomplished, raising something that size from the bottom of the ocean... he'd never heard of magic that powerful on E'rth.

There'd been impressive feats, for sure. The fortified walls of Kel'Adur, forged from the very rock of the mountain. That was Zamph Ak-Agarra and his Nine of Bloodthistle that had concocted that gem of defensive arcana, saving their school and supporting village from bloodthirsty borderlanders.

Of course, they all died of starvation and disease after that. Such expense of arcane energy left the mages and students depleted and incapable of taking care of even the most basic necessities. Plus the hundred-foot-tall wall of rock and army outside made trips outside for food and water impossible. A cautionary tale, to be sure.

There was the Fugue of Madness—one of D'avry's personal favorites. Chelebrum D'Saul, the Vizier of Magh—also a Once-Brother, same as D'avry—had fashioned a good ol' charm spell into something that had caused the combined armies of Nur Al'Sandes and Glyffe to turn on each other. Not a soul stood to fight the Maghians that following day. They say the stench of the slaughter never wore off, and to this day no one has built in the plains of desolation for that reason. Kind of gross, but a clever use of magic, and on a scale that was undeniably magnificent.

But what he and four others had done today? The partial raising of a hunk of ceramo-metal larger than any city on E'rth. He was struggling to get his mind around it. He had done this. He didn't have the Astrig Ka'a to guide him. It was Chareth-Ul magic, combined with the ancient Sylvan magic of the Gefkarri hive mind.

His grandiose feelings of achievement wobbled a little as he remembered the way Seda had spoken to him afterward. She had pulled away after such an amazing experience. There was a niggling thought that he could not quite put a name to. The way that she looked at him. The way that she'd been willing to fudge the storyline about allowing the *Xandraitha's Hope* to enter the atmosphere for just a short time, when, in fact, the whole of the Arcfire was essentially disabled. The tension she'd had with Theal. And that word, 'assigned'. She was bound to him in a way that went, he was certain of it, far beyond an assignment.

He realized in that moment that he'd barely thought about Deven and how she was doing in all this time. He'd sent her off alone. Well, not really alone. She had Volkreek and Liggo to look after her.

They were two of the original companions on the quest to save humanity from the invisible hand that enslaved it, during that tiny slice of human history he called home. He'd almost forgotten he was still on *that* mission. He'd been so caught up in the events that'd transpired since he'd met Rutker, the soldier from a time before E'rth. And now, here was D'avry, smack in the middle of Rutker's people's—his ancestors'—existential drama.

Humanity, it seemed, was always embroiled in one existential threat or another. At least he was beginning to see a common thread for the woes on E'rth—the Gefkarri.

He glanced in Seda's direction. She was still blocking her mind from him, standing aloof in the corner of the bridge. For a fleeting second, he almost wished to see that flash of emotion behind her almond-shaped eyes. They had connected in some way.

He shook his head to clear the thought. *She's a tree. And she tried to kill me. And I have another burgeoning romance ... with a woman from another time, eons and eons in the future, who's hunting down an artifact for me whilst being hunted herself by the Void and who knows what other dangers.*

Too many thoughts. Too many questions. What he knew was that the Gefkarri were core to humanity's dilemma, in this time and the ones to follow. He needed to get back to E'rth to get to the bottom of how. And he needed to bring these people, the Epriots, with him. He looked around the bridge at Mads, Katherynn, and the magically inclined Ensign Presche. He would need these people and many others besides in order to do it.

Now, *how* to do it? That was the question.

"Ambassador Novak. Trouble," the captain said with urgency.

Katherynn was already staring at the map table. "I see it. Another Defiler?"

"Appears so, but we won't know more until we get closer, which is the other problem."

"Explain."

"We'll need all that distance to slow down. We're going to be right on top of them in thirty seconds."

"Shit."

"Affirmative."

"What do we do?"

"We can try to blow on by, but..."

A voice came over the ship's intercom, "Interstellar craft, *Xandraitha's Hope*, you will stand down and allow Chareth-Ul assumption of command of your vessel. Epriot Prime is now..." Some commotion could be heard over the signal or in the background, "...standby."

The transmission ceased.

"What do we do now?"

On the view screens surrounding the fore section of the bridge, a valley unfolded beyond low peaks. Long shadows cast eastward across shining lakes and rivers and in the middle, a shelled-out city sprawled with a massive mech looming over it.

D'avry's mouth dropped open. It was so much bigger in person than he imagined. And then details began to emerge. Fires, smoke, movement, mechs, and dark flying creatures leaping from the top of the structure, which had two temple-like structures atop it. As they magnified the scene, he could just make out small figures atop the temples with their arms wide. Arcana, if he'd ever seen it. Little good it seemed to be doing.

Black creatures were blinking back and forth, crawling over every square inch.

"The Void," he uttered in shock.

"Oh, frag. The people," Katherynn cursed as she looked down at the field below the mech. A miles-wide park within the city sprawl and upon it he could see figures in white running in every direction amongst the chaos. Many ran for the safety of the city's husks of rectangular buildings, but it was a long run.

"We have to save as many as we can," Katherynn told the captain.

"Ma'am, begging your pardon, but setting down anywhere down there would be suicide."

"There," she pointed to a spot on the far side of the field. There was an oval-shaped arena with large paved fields surrounding it. It was directly in line with the exodus of people and well enough away from the battle unfolding before them.

The captain made a tight-lipped face and nodded. "Make it so," he said to the pilot, who nodded in return. Just as a swarm of low sirens erupted from consoles throughout the forebridge.

"Shields to port—"

The captain was saying just as the ship bucked and loud booms rattled it end to end.

"What the..." D'avry was saying when he was thrown into the air and the floor tipped away beneath him before he came crashing down.

"We're going down. We're going down," the captain yelled from the floor as he held to the railing post, scrambling to get to his feet. "To your seats everyone. Buckle up."

"Distress. Distress. This is the *Xandraitha's Hope*. We're assuming a forced landing," the co-pilot repeated into his comm set. "New Varhus. Southeast. I repeat..."

Another boom shook the craft, and D'avry felt it lurch sideways and assume a slow spin. They were headed for the arena alright. *A lot* faster than they expected. The ground flashed by beneath them. Broken buildings flashed by and the ship shuddered as it clipped more than a few rooftops and walls.

"Shields full forward!" the captain yelled as time seemed to slow down. He was immediately aware of Seda, her eyes blazing bright. He reached out to her telepathically, and they connected.

Instantly, he pulled in the other three, Mads, Katherynn, and Ensign Presche. He imagined the exterior of the ship, saw it burst through a mid-sized building skinned in metallic yellow and glass as it careened toward the ground and the arena beyond. He touched the talisman at his hip and the world exploded into rushing wind and chaos. The five minds all settled on the ship, slowing it and settling it peacefully on the ground.

Well, that didn't happen. But they did stop, and they were all in one piece. And the arena would never be the same. Its nearest side had blown across to the far side and nearly disintegrated it.

The five collapsed in their seats, and the rushing wind ceased. The link dissipated and D'avry looked for Seda. She was frozen in tree form, her branches arching upward and sunk into the ceiling, her legs a mass of roots penetrating in a broad swath into the floor. She didn't move until the ship settled off-kilter on the ground.

"Well. That was ... something," she said as her body slithered back into the human form he was more familiar with. Her eyes were still cool, and she still kept herself mentally at a distance from him. "Now, I assume we are to round up your species while not getting killed by Void or Chareth-Ul in the process?"

D'avry answered first, "Yes. I think that would be the plan."

"And then what, D'avry, of the All-Magic? Form a circle and wish our way to some corner of the galaxy where no one can ever find us?"

D'avry was ashamed to admit it, but that pretty much was the plan he had in his mind. But then he was struck by something odd in the way she'd said it.

"You're speaking like you're one of us."

She didn't say anything at first, but after a moment, he heard her in his mind, a faint whisper. *Do you really think I can go back after what I've done? The choice I made ... is final.*

He couldn't begin to understand the gravity of what she just said, but was interrupted, thankfully, at least for the time being, by one of the others.

Mads was at the mapping table. He swiped the map up onto the main screen.

"The first waves are nearing the edge of the parade grounds. Do you think Dad or Macq are with them?"

His mother answered, "I pray to Maker they are. But we'll take all we can."

"There are too many, Ambassador Novak. We can take a few hundred. They are thousands."

"Then we fight."

"Ambassador... Katherynn. We were never able to replenish our armory after Gellen III. We have nothing to fight with."

She glanced over at D'avry and then at Seda. "We'll think of something."

CHAPTER 28
ASCENDING

Chareth-Ul Reality Zero, Enclave at Ak-Umbrech
[Three months later in Chareth-Ul Time]

Galas rolled onto her back and heard the clinking of chains. She breathed in deep and let it out. She was staring at the ceiling of the arena.

Again.

She heard and felt the thudding of heavy feet on the sand. She closed her eyes, felt the sutures bite deep into her flesh as the ceiling above fell away into a spectral display of a kind of heavenly arc that Chareth-Ul would never see again.

She hinged on her heels, flat from her back to fully upright as she drew on the broken magic of the tortured planet. Her head snapped in the direction of her adversary, whom she saw through the arcane sight of her third eye, something like a Makrit bully but larger by times in both height and width and weight. A true juggernaut.

A scream burst from her lips and a multitude roared with her as a wave of sonic energy like a scythe swept out of her, slicing the Makrit Thunderer open from shoulder to opposing thigh. Its slick gray insides bulged out as it roared before dropping its head and blasting its own attack, a concussive wave of psionic energy.

Galas was swatted like a fly across the arena floor.

Someone or something grabbed her wrist and hauled her to her feet. She blearily stared across the arena sands at no less than five of the thunderers issuing from cavernous openings below the stands filled with jostling acolytes, initiates, minions and others.

"Righteous kill. But can't you stay on your feet for more than a minute without losing consciousness?" a tall, gray, forken-horned Chareth-Ul asked her as she set her down on wobbly legs. She looked like a younger and somehow thinner version of Wahr-Zen.

"Where'd the fun be in that, Noor-Andra?" Galas asked her fellow priestess initiate.

"You two, get a room. We've got work to do," a heavy-set forken-horn spat out while dipping low into a fighting stance with her fists raised in a U-shape before she brought them forcefully together. Her third eye glowed a deep purple, rather than the crimson color that Galas and her sponsor, Wahr-Zen, sported.

Galas flicked a glance toward the middle of the stand where a booth held the highest-ranked Battle Priestesses. Wahr-Zen was there in the middle of them. The look on her face was borderline disgust.

Galas cracked her neck from side to side. No getting back to Epriot Prime without getting out of this arena alive and in one piece.

The thunderers were growing smarter. They fanned out as they converged on the trio of initiates. The ground literally shook with the sound of the creatures as they bore down on them.

Galas closed her eyes, and the world swam. The sutures wouldn't come. She was too scrambled. What would Raphael do? The thought came unbidden, and a pang of loss struck through her. She missed him. She missed Jinnbo. She missed her baby girl, who she knew probably wouldn't even recognize her or know her name. And if she did, would she feel as ashamed as Galas felt right now? Dead-beat mom. Monster.

This arena was step one. She had to survive to get to step two. She had to survive to see the ones she loved. She was thankful for the sped-up time that the Chareth-Ul's defensive bubble provided. It meant that the months she spent here would be just days at home. But the big question still remained. Would she even be human when she got there? The things she had to do to get this far...

It was one thing to kill to survive. Another thing to extract suffering from your prey to feed your magic.

Quite another thing indeed.

Her lips quivered with hunger. She stared across at the thunderer she'd already defeated. It lay on the floor, not quite dead. It's breathing shallow. Hunger welled up inside her.

She knew what she had to do.

"I can't ascend. Noor. Zaha. Cover me," she yelled as she sprinted for the wounded creature...

...to feast.

CHAPTER 29

RUTKER AND THE OTHER REMNANT

Epriot Prime, The Spires—Alpha Tep

Rutker peeked around the corner. Two guards wore the same uniform that he normally wore. However, right now, he was bald from head to toe—and everywhere in between—and he was wearing the filthy black robes of the traitors who'd sided with the Chareth-Ul.

He leaned back against the wall to calm his nerves and sort the maelstrom of thoughts and worries swirling inside him. The city-sized Chareth-Ul Defiler mech would be here within the hour. He didn't know if it'd be a full-scale attack, which they certainly weren't ready for. All of their defenses were stacked up at the base of the Spire facility. And due to its size, the mech could launch the attack from nearly halfway up.

The other possibility was a simple handing over of the keys by the traitors in power, specifically Head of Houses Reddum. Rutker wasn't sure how many of the members of the council were onboard with this plan but it was clear that Reddum and Colonel Dexx had been conspiring for some time.

Rutker's blood began to boil as he thought again of the bastard who had sacrificed a squad of marines, scuttled the peace treaty, sent him on a snipe hunt on a foreign planet for jettisoned diplomatic packages that turned out to be empty, causing him to risk his life for nothing, and then, most recently sneaking away during their orbital HALO drop to the planet's surface which resulted in Rutker's son Macq getting lost in the descent.

Dexx feigned ignorance, but Rutker knew he was lying. His only solace was in the fact that if he had done something to Macq, Rutker would be able to see it in his eyes. Or he'd come right out and say it.

Rutker rubbed his stubbled cheeks and face before sucking in a deep breath and letting it out slowly. He was a fighter pilot after all, stress was no stranger. But then, there was his wife Katherynn, and his other son, Mads still on the diplomatic vessel the *Xandraitha's Hope*. They had been safely in orbit, outside the range of the planetary defense system but for some reason, had come down planet-side.

First off, how?!? Secondly, why would they do that? This place was ground zero for a five-sided war and the outlook for humanity was, well, humanity wasn't even a player, really. They were a commodity to be used by the powerful hive-mind known as the Gefkarri Pentarch and the creepy-as-hell Chareth-Ul with their Defiler mechs, powerful and twisted battle priestesses, metric shit-ton of Deathhound mechs, and host of insectoid creatures that appeared to be built to destroy.

Next was their old nemesis the Delvadr—the ones that were left after Colonel Galas annihilated their fleet, anyway. Still, their mechs and jump marines were formidable.

Lastly, there was the Void. Interdimensional. Innumerable. They had no desire to negotiate, just to take over, wholly and completely, and move on to the next galaxy, or dimension, or who knew what they were actually after.

Rutker sucked in another breath. How did things get so fragged? Humanity hung on long enough to win the war with the Delvadr and now this? It was a cruel joke. Humankind used to number in the billions and spread across the entirety of the solar system. Now there were less than 250,000, split up between those huddled up in the detention center at New Varhus and those holed up here in the Spires.

He peeked around the corner again and was certain that one of the guards saw him. *Shit.* Footsteps heading his way. He hoped Monster Mind was having better luck gathering up the refugees one level down. The old marine had certainly saved Rutker's bacon, both during the escape from New Varhus and here, when he was being ushered to his new quarters to "freshen up and relax" which were really just words for detain and pacify.

The steps drew closer. One set of boots. *Dammit.*

"Hey, whoever's over there, you should just come out. You shouldn't be down here."

Rutker didn't say anything. But there was indecisiveness in the young man's voice. He regretted having to do this.

The steps drew close and stopped. He did some quick math—fifty feet to the hanger entrance where the other guard waited. *Okay, relax.*

He heard the sound of the guard's sidearm sliding from its holster. Rutker stepped out into the corridor with his hands up,

"No need to shoot." He decided to lean into his scroungy appearance. He looked like a refugee.

The guard stepped forward, weapon raised. "Are you alone?"

Rutker cast a glance toward the corridor he'd just exited from,

"Guys. It's fine. This doesn't look like the galley anyway," he said to his imaginary cohort. The guard pied the corner wide to keep Rutker and whoever these unseen people were in his line of sight, which was smart. It was the right thing to do. But he got a little too close to Rutker in the process.

Rutker noticed the other guard had brought his rifle to the ready, just before Rutker's hand flashed out, grabbing the first guard's wrist and pulled him hard into the wall. His other hand followed and as the man's head bounced off the wall—just hard enough to stun—the second hand connected, open palm, and this time the man's head bounced off the wall much harder. He crumpled on wobbly legs.

Rutker peeled away his firearm, slipped around behind him, confirmed with a glance the weapon held a non-lethal colored magazine and whipped the guard and gun around to face the man with the rifle.

"Drop it!" the guard yelled. Rutker pushed forward to close the distance on the shot.

"I said, DROP IT!" But, Rutker was still pushing forward, pistol extended, the other man stumbling and stunned ahead of him, blubbering something unintelligible,

"I don't want to hurt anybody," Rutker said as he continued to close the gap, the man craned his neck to speak into his comm device while he maintained aim. Just as he started to open his mouth, Rutker fired, knowing it'd be difficult to initiate a conversation and maintain situational awareness.

Rutker fired again and finally hit on the third. The guard got a shot off just as he dropped. Rutker hadn't felt the impact but the young man he was holding groaned and started to fall to the floor.

Dammit. Dammit. Dammit!

He flipped the kid over. Shoulder wound. Probably he was in shock more than anything. Maybe a broken collarbone, but he wasn't going to bleed out. The kid groaned again and reached for his comms. Rutker struck across the temple with the butt of the pistol.

"Sorry, kid." He was little more than a year or two older than Mads. "No time to explain. But the Chareth-Ul are on their way and our government has given up. I need these transports," he said as the door to the hangar opened up and two more guards walked through.

"Supposed to be here any time..." one of the guards was saying as he looked down on the scene before him and his mouth fell open. He was reaching for his sidearm when Rutker, still bent over, attending to the fallen guard, slid the muzzle of the pistol underneath his armpit and fired off two rounds into each of the men at less than three meters.

Rutker stood up and looked at the mess. Three unconscious guards and one in shock. He didn't have time to clean up this mess, but what was this newest guy saying? That they were expecting the Chareth-Ul to show up?

He considered all the people gathered on the lower level and a terrible thought occurred to him. *Was this a trade of sorts? The politicians and the military hand over an offering of warm bodies to ensure their continued existence? Unable to negotiate a truce they just cut their losses?*

Through the doors in the distance he could see four transports. Running lights on, shore power cables removed, they appeared to be getting ready to go. He looked back at the kid, lids heavy, head lolling on his shoulders,

"Hey! Kid!" He slapped his cheek a couple times. "Kid. You in on this? The Deathhounds coming to take our people?"

The young guard looked up in confusion and then around at the other guards sprawled all over the ground as if seeing them for the first time. He looked back up at Rutker in outrage and fear.

"Look. The Deathhounds are coming to take over and I don't know who's in on it. We gotta get our people out of here. The council already has transports warmed up and ready to go. Did you hear an all-hands to retreat?"

The kid shook his head, eyes wide as he struggled to take in what Rutker was saying along with the shock of being shot and of having his comrades taken out.

"Kid. Look at me. I'm one of you."

The confusion on the guard's face was evident as he flashed a glance at Rutker's tatty robes.

"No, no, no. I was grounded and went through the intake at the New Varhus detention center. I escaped to warn everyone up here that the Chareth-Ul were on their way in the Defiler mech, but the council already knew. They were in on it.

"I think they're planning on handing over the refugees and running out. I don't know where to, but I intend to take those transports," he grabbed the guard's jaw and pointed his face toward the hangar, "and fill them full of our people."

He looked the kid in the eyes. "You with me?" He glanced over at the incapacitated guards. "Or are you with them?"

The young man gulped and nodded. He went to lean on his arm to get up, but Rutker stopped him. "Hang on, kid. That thing might be broken."

He grabbed his other hand and pulled him to standing. The kid almost toppled again, but Rutker held him up until he was stable.

"Alright. There's gonna be a bunch of folks headed this way. Guy in charge's name is Monster Mind, he's an old gunny. You let them through, but no one else. Can you do that?" he asked, handing the kid one of the pistols.

"With this?" he asked incredulously, before grabbing his partner's rifle, charging it, pulling it up to his offside shoulder with his left hand, and sighting down the corridor. He wobbled a little and then straightened. "Yeah, I got this. Gave us up, huh? Fragging Reddum."

Rutker nodded. "Yeah."

He bent over and took the first guard's clothes before binding his hands and those of the other two. He dragged them across the hall and propped them up so they were easy to watch.

"What's your name, kid?"

"Corporal Reddum," he said with a grimace. "My dad. Step-dad actually. Hope he gets what's coming to him for this."

"Sorry kid. Sounds like there's a story there. I want to hear it sometime. Hold down the fort, alright? I'm gonna go sneak onto a ship and find out where they're headed since everything's all ready to go."

With that, Rutker trotted off across the open floor of the hangar. It only took a couple of minutes for him to board the closest vessel, locate the cargo bay interface, and conduct a query on the flight plan. He was lucky it didn't require credentials because the system was AI-based. He found what he was looking for right away,

"Guisse IV. That's where the cowards are heading?"

The abandoned planet had been taken over by the Delvadr almost three decades prior, still in the first wave of the invasion. It made sense. If there were still any Delvadr there, it was an easy environment to get lost in, with all the oceans, lakes, rivers, and perpetual rainstorms.

It was a good hideout, but nothing that made sense to colonize for anything but commerce and research. Still, in the short-term...

"Excuse me, soldier. What're you doing down here?"

Rutker looked up to find a woman officer with her sidearm leveled at him. Probably from engineering or operations.

"Don't make me repeat myself. I really don't mind shooting someone lurking around my ship."

Rutker looked at her brutishly pretty face. The set of her eyes told him she wasn't bluffing. She was smart and kept about five meters between them. More than enough space to react if he bolted or went for her,

"Do you know who I am?"

"Yeah. SortieNet facial recognition says you should be in a detention cell."

"Then it should also tell you that I was on the sabotaged diplomatic mission to negotiate a treaty with the Delvadr. And that we're back here, with an alien super-entity parked in far orbit. The mission changed. We came back to negotiate between the Gefkarri and the EDC."

"No, it doesn't say anything about that."

"Well, it probably doesn't say anything about the Chareth-Ul, or Deathhounds as we know them, showing up and betraying the alliance with the Gefkarri."

"We heard about the Chareth-Ul. How they've taken over New Varhus and captured most of the citizens."

"Did you hear how they plan on using them as magical batteries or something like that for their mechs and that they're on their way here?"

"Let 'em come. We're prepared."

"No, you don't understand. The mechs they have, they're so big they can breach our defenses a hundred stories up. They're also loaded with Deathhound mechs and creatures that look like they're genetically modified for just such a mission, to seek and destroy in caves and tunnels."

Her gun wavered, but then she readjusted her grip and pointed it at Rutker's head again.

"Look. We don't have much time."

She held up a hand to shush him and looked as if she was listening to something through her neural link. That's when he realized she must be part of the executive crew or even a pilot.

Her face went blank and then screwed up in confusion. She glanced back at him.

"I don't know what's going on, why you're supposed to be detained, or why you're here on my ship. But I just received what sounded like a distress signal ... from a ship claiming to be your diplomatic vessel, the *Xandraitha's Hope*."

CHAPTER 30
MACQ & SERAF

Epriot Prime, Somewhere East of New Varhus

Macq and Seraf sped down the road toward the cloud of smoke and dust illuminated by fires in the distance. For a kid from a boarder, Seraf had taken to the power armor in a hurry. Maybe she was related to Colonel Galas after all.

Macq desperately hoped his mom and the rest of the crew of the *Xandraitha's Hope* were alright. But even if they had managed to survive the crash, there was plenty of danger still out there. His attention went to the city-sized Defiler mech looming over the west end of New Varhus, the nearly decimated planetary capital of Epriot Prime. It was also on fire, smoking and bathed in bursts of plasma and the brilliant poofs of light from the Void creatures as they were vanquished.

And then, somewhere behind him in the darkness, were the Spires. The even larger Defiler mech that had headed that way earlier would be showing up any time now. He prayed his dad had made it in time to warn High Command of the imminent threat.

He was sure his dad had made it. He told himself over and over that was the case.

Up ahead, a light in a window of a broken-down three-story building caught his eye, but when he looked again, there was nothing there. It was spooky out here at night. His thoughts went to the Void creatures or even the flyers that had descended from the Defiler—no face, black armor, and wings, and then there was the way they formed up into hunting packs. He wanted nothing to do with any of them.

His thoughts went back to the men they'd found in the tunnel. How he'd left the two survivors to their fate as he ran away and hid with Seraf. His stomach churned. There was nothing he could have done, right? The bile in his throat told him differently.

Another barely perceptible light flashed. This time from the opposite side of the street. He had a bad feeling and was about to warn Seraf, who was jogging next to him when a line whipped up from the road. He and Seraf both took it to the chest, but he didn't see what happened to her after his feet flew up and he spun end over end before hitting the ground on his head and tumbling with the momentum of their thirty-kilometer-per-hour pace.

Macq was struggling to get up to find out if she was okay when a very large rifle muzzle pressed to his face shield.

"Stay down or you'll regret it, Delvadr pig."

His mind spun as he struggled to gain his composure. "Whoa, whoa, whoa. Just wait a second. If I were Delvadr, do you think I would understand what you're saying?" He focused on the bore of that muzzle. "Also, side note, that is the biggest gun I have ever seen in person." He leaned back so he could take it in. "Is that a Slair Six?"

The man holding the gun stepped back and looked at the side of the oversized railgun that made him look tiny in comparison. He looked back at Macq. "Nah, it's a Slair *Two*."

"Really? That's a verifiable antique," Macq said, attempting to stand up, but the man with the gun tapped him back onto his butt with a muzzle to the face shield again,

"Maybe take it slow, hotshot," said the man.

Two guerillas came in from either side of the avenue, holding similarly large and antiquated weapons. *These are Hillmen*, he thought—a band of disgraced snipers from the northern foothills of the Merrat Valley. He didn't recall the details, but he remembered they weren't good.

Whether they'd left their post or just got lost in the chaos, there were a lot of questions. But one thing was certain: there had always been questions about the ethics of their activities. He racked his brain for details and came away with little. Just that unnecessary brutality was a recurring theme. Hopes of him and Seraf getting back on their way without trouble were diminishing rapidly.

Seraf sat up. "Look, I don't know what you guys are after, but we're trying to get to that downed transport. His family is on there," she interjected. "It's an emergency."

The man, whose face was shrouded by a dingy, multi-colored scarf and metal goggles, tilted his head. "I don't think anyone on board that ship made it. It split the arena in half when it hit. I'm shocked it didn't blow right through and leave one big crater, to be honest."

"You don't know they're dead," Macq protested as he tried to stand up and was pushed back once more.

"Let's try this again," the man said. "If you're not Delvadr, who are you and where'd you get those suits?"

An explosion far off in the distance lit up the sky in pulses and was followed several seconds later by multiple dull booms.

"Sounds like that big Deathhound's gettin' what's coming to it," he said and Macq could tell he was grinning under his face covering.

"Brother, you don't know what you're talking about. If you've seen the Void creatures, I don't think you'd be cheering them on," Macq said, finding the release for his face shield on the helmet heads-up display and activating it. It slid up and out of the way, exposing just his face to the crisp night air. His breath caught. It was a *lot* colder out than he'd realized. Suddenly, he felt for the refugees fleeing the detention center out there in the darkness. With actual monsters running around, no less.

"What's a *Void* creature? Is that one of them flying do-dads, look like centipedes with wings and big hopper legs? Pasted a few of those nasties earlier. They go splat real good," he said, patting his rifle as he cradled it across his chest.

Macq noticed that it was on a multipoint gimble mount attached to some sort of body harness under the man's poncho. The poncho was split on the sides to accommodate the flexible armatures that supported the gun's heft. The setup looked familiar, and further confirmed his suspicion about the men being part of that infamous band known as the Hillmen.

Macq shook his head, "The centipede things are from the Chareth-Ul Defiler mech, the mother ship, for all those five- and ten-ton Deathhounds. The Void creatures are just like they sound, black as night, bigger than a man with talons and claws, and they're, I don't know... they blink in and out of physical space, skipping from one spot to the next in bursts. They cover ground really fast and it takes a lot of rounds to take them down."

The man tilted his head forward, eyebrows lifted. "And how would you know?"

"He killed two of them. And one of those flyer things in the tunnels below the city. We were on our way to the Spires to warn High Command about the Defiler headed their way, but then it crushed the tunnel, and we were forced to either try to outrun it or, when we heard the mayday signal from the *Xandraitha's Hope*, to come back and help," Seraf blurted out in a rush. "Now, we've really got to get out of here to help his mom and his brother. Not to mention all the refugees, if there are any left."

The man paused. He seemed to consider the veracity of their tale. One of the other men stepped up and whispered in his ear, and he nodded.

"Quite a tale, little lady. We did see that big ol' mech go by, but then, who didn't? But I still don't know where you come from or how you got a hold of two sets of power armor."

"Ah, I get it. You're looking for an armory in the city, is that it?" Macq asked. "Unfortunately, these suits came from that transport. It's kind of a long story and we don't really—"

The man stepped forward and leaned over Macq while his two friends raised their weapons. "Please ... continue," he said in a low and dangerous tone.

Macq heaved a sigh. "Alright. Look, I was on the *Xandraitha's Hope* with my family when the peace talks were sabotaged and we lost our contingent of Marines."

He told him about the Gefkarri super-carrier currently residing in outer orbit, the incursion by the Void, and how Colonel Galas was threatening to blow up any ship that got near the planet no matter who they were.

"So, we had to HALO drop to talk to her face-to-face. But, halfway down, the saboteur, Col. Dexx tried to escape, and I chased after him. This is my suit from that drop and the one she's using is the one that Dexx had been wearing. Only ... after we got down here, he split. I don't know where to, but I'm betting it's the Spires. I think that's where my dad went, but I don't know if he made it or not. So that's why it's so important for me to get to that transport. I may not have anyone left. Oh and one other thing. We brought someone back from that planet. He may be our secret weapon for beating all of them, the Gefkarri, the Chareth-Ul, the Delvadr, maybe even the Void. He's on that transport too."

The leader of the gang of snipers stepped back, shaking his head. "Kid, you are either the biggest badass or the biggest liar I have ever met and I've met a lot of both. More of the latter."

"Well, you're not gonna like this part then. That guy, a human just like us, he's not just from that planet that we crashed on, but he's supposedly from the future. And as crazy as all that sounds, he's some kind of magician or sorcerer or something like that as well. I've seen him levitate and do a bunch of freaky stuff like that, so…"

The men snorted and then started laughing. "You're right, that's definitely the biggest pile of ox shite I've ever heard."

The lead man lowered his weapon and looked intently at Macq. He looked like he was about to get to the point, which Macq was certain was not going to be good. He texted one word to Seraf using eye movement commands and his suit's heads-up display.

[Macq: Repulsors.]

The man pulled down his handkerchief to reveal stubbled cheeks and a couple of missing teeth. He spat a wad of tar leaf in the dirt and then looked at Macq. "Now, it's been fun, but I'm going to have to kindly ask you to step out of your suits before we have to pry you out."

Macq spread his hands to the side in a gesture of surrender as he lifted a boot and engaged its repulsor. The man blew backward like he'd been swatted by a mech. Before he even hit the ground, Macq was up and grabbed the muzzle of the other man's rifle as he side-kicked that man in the chest, ripping him free of his weapon.

Macq was fumbling to bring the unwieldy weapon to bear on the last man but was a fraction late. The man's rifle came up, and Macq expected to die, but then he was cartwheeling away as Seraf initiated her own repulsor-aided kick.

"Go!" Macq yelled as he ran toward her, grabbed her wrist, and yanked her up into a run.

Their power suits burst forward and they careened toward an alley just as the wall of the building next to them exploded into shrapnel, peppering their armor.

"Shit!" Seraf yelped as they slipped into the narrow street, with broken walls and debris speeding by.

"Couldn't have talked your way out of that one, huh?" she asked, breathless.

Macq hazarded a glance her way and then yanked her up another street just as a boom echoed behind them. He heard more destruction from the direction they'd been running just a second before. They'd gotten lucky twice now. And they couldn't be certain that there were only three of those bad guys running around. For all he knew, they could be running into another trap.

He yanked her right onto another street that paralleled their original route. Best to stay off the main avenue but they needed to not get shot in the back in the process.

"Keep heading up this block," he told her as he darted into a doorway vestibule and spun to sight down the street with the massive rifle. *Now, if I can just remember how one of these works.*

"What do you mean? You're not leaving me, right?" she asked, desperation clipping her words and sending them an octave higher, but to her credit, she kept running.

"No, just trust me," he said as he scanned the side of the rifle where the mag assembly met the power cell. There was the safety. *Off already, of course. Charge? Ninety. Good.* He dropped to a knee, braced against the wall, and zoomed in with the suit's HUD. This armor set was not full mil-spec, so it didn't sync up with the rifle as he'd read it would have. Instead, he had to draw a virtual line down the length of the barrel between the manual sights. It was a clumsy work around.

This is taking too long! He worried as he lined up that augmented reality benchmark by pulling the gun up to his shoulder and laying his helmet as close as he could against the stock. Manually sighting a rifle ... talk about antiquated.

He didn't even know if it was safe to fire one of these things. Those Hillmen must have had neural augments or their goggles were tied to the weapon. That made sense. Oh well, he had to make do.

He enhanced visuals to pull movement off of any reflective surface, but nothing came up. He hoped he wasn't wrong about this. Seraf's white cursor was continuing up the street at a good pace and he still hadn't seen a sign of his pursuers. They weren't showing up on his sensors, which was weird. But then the tiniest flicker of movement caught his eye from the lower left, two blocks back.

With no time to sight in, he dropped the barrel slightly and fired into the street, counting on the ricochet to blind or injure the other sniper. The rifle kicked savagely. He almost gasped as he bolted across the alley to another vestibule with a better angle on the enemy's position.

He pulled up and braced against the wall but was firing off his weak side this time. It was awkward, but he'd practiced with battle rifles for years and knew a thing or two about engagements. None of it from real experience, of course.

He saw motion again as the sniper re-engaged, only this time Macq had a bead on that pocket and fired. The gun kicked hard, but he held tight and kept his eyes on the target. The low corner of the building disappeared in a cloud about two feet back. Anyone hiding behind that wall was red mist now.

His chest caught as he realized what had just occurred. He'd killed a man. One of his own kind amidst a battle of alien and interdimensional races. After a moment, he remembered to breathe and barely registered a subtle shift of scenery farther down the street. Reflexively, he spun and dropped just as the back end of the vestibule exploded away into the building. Macq didn't wait but bolted into the cloud of dust and debris, hoping the building didn't open to a lower floor.

He felt something solid beneath his feet. Heard the pounding of boots on wood and finally the dust cleared to reveal broken walls and the inside of a darkened warehouse ahead of him.

He enhanced night vision and sprinted for a door at the far end as he checked his HUD.

Seraf's white cursor was holding three blocks up. A blue cursor highlighted the last known position of the sniper that'd fired on him and another where he'd most likely killed the other one. There was nothing else in his map.

He yearned for a SortieNet with a Battlespace model to keep him up to speed on the environment, but there was none of that with his borderline civvy armor. To be honest, he'd probably just hurt himself with a real unit with plasma blades, laser cannons and rocket nacelles. Still...

Then he flashed back on the man he'd just outgunned and the gargantuan rifle he was hauling with him. And then there were the creatures in the tunnels he'd dispatched with a regulation battle rifle.

Well, he shouldn't sell himself short yet. He'd gotten this far. But, there was still a bunch of work to do. He needed to rendezvous with Seraf and get to the *Xandraitha's Hope*. A hollowness was building in his gut. His mom and his brother—one thing at a time.

Macq exploded through the warehouse door out, onto the street and bolted for the deadman's alley, the shooting gallery he'd just come from. He could blow past it and up to the next or...

He looked up and saw a way. Slotting the Slair Two into the magnetic front holster across his torso as he ran, bounded off the wall, and launched up to an old-style fire access. He couldn't fit through the lower section, which was built to restrict access, but he could climb up the outside from landing to landing until he got to the rooftop. Then, well, he just had to jump from building to building. *No sweat.*

"Seraf? You okay?"

No response.

He let out a breath as he jumped up to the building's edge and pulled himself over the lip. He sized up the distance between buildings with the street five stories below. On his own, there was no way. In the power suit? It was dicey, but as long as the roof held on the other side, well, he didn't want to think about what would happen if it didn't. And, if he were being honest, the state of the city in general told him it was questionable.

Macq ran back fifteen meters, turned, and before he could talk himself out of it, started sprinting. The edge came up fast, and he launched himself out over the street, landing on the other side with little effort. Carrying momentum, he kept on going.

The rooftops weren't aligned in any sort of way. He had to jump down and then up again as he covered building after building along the block. He launched another street and then he came to the real problem: up ahead, the last building was several stories taller. He'd have to cross the deadman's alley. He hoped they weren't expecting him to take the high route.

Macq blasted off the ledge and felt it crumple a little, but he still had the velocity, just maybe not the angle... it was going to be close. A loud crack echoed through his audio as he barely slipped over the parapet of the other building's roof, but it wasn't the roof buckling as he landed. The suit's HUD located the noise and placed a blue cursor. It was one of the Hillmen; he didn't know which. but they'd moved up a block or two.

Suddenly, the roof exploded into splinters just a meter away and started to sag. The HUD located another loud bang behind him and a couple of levels up in a building across the main avenue. He was just realizing that there must be more of them when the roof buckled beneath his feet and he was free-falling. His last thoughts were of his brother and his mom in the crashed transport. And of Seraf.

CHAPTER 31

THE CIRCLE OF FIVE

Epriot Prime, New Varhus, The *Xandraitha's Hope*

"Damage assessment?"

The bridge of the *Xandraitha's Hope* was mostly dark after its second crash landing in as many weeks. A few instruments flickered holographic gibberish above their consoles. The main screens overhead were blacked out. One was hanging precariously, looking as though it could fall at any second. The silence was total, which for anyone familiar with working interstellar craft, was a sound as loud as a blaring klaxon.

"Damage assessment," repeated the Captain, weakly. It sounded as if it were more of a knee-jerk reaction than a coherent grasp of the situation.

The situation was that they were alive. At least, everyone on the bridge that D'avry could see from where he stood at the map table. He was still holding hands with the other four; Katherynn, Mads, the dark-haired, dark-eyed, closet mystic Ensign Presche, and Seda, aspect *of* the Gefkarri Pentarch and also, he realized, his ally. He didn't know why, but she'd chosen a side and despite all reason, it happened to be his.

He let go of Seda's and Katherynn's hands and realized that the aspect had extended her vines to encompass the five, shielding them from damage and from the impact of the crash. He didn't know what that effort would have yielded if they'd not been successful in arresting the ship's impact, but they had. They, the five of them in total, had slowed an interstellar transport and shielded it from creating a very long and considerably deep valley through the Epriot capital city of New Varhus.

One monumental crisis averted. Next...

He reached out with his senses to encompass the area around them, riding an invisible bubble of consciousness through the ceiling of the bridge, through layers of ceramo-metal hull, and up into the dust and smoke of the crash site. The sun had set. The valley was shadowed, and there were fires and smoke and dust in every direction. Behind them was a path of destruction through the buildings of the city. Farther beyond that was a large park and looming over roughly a quarter of the urban center was one of the Chareth-Ul Defiler mechs. As if there needed to be more than one.

The monstrosity looked like it was struggling to hold up its own weight. In the waning light of dusk, he could see mechs and creatures fighting both on the mech itself and on the ground surrounding it. There were other shapes in the darkness—clots of moving figures. Some were too dark to discern. The creatures most likely. The Void or even some of the Chareth-Ul's flyers. But then amongst them were clearly human figures in robes of white covered in ash and mud and invariably, their own blood and the blood of their brethren.

It was a trick of the magic, the amazing level of detail that he could pull from visions like this. He was blending Gefkarri and Chareth-Ul magics freely now. Just feeling his way around.

To his knowledge, this had never been done before. By anyone. According to what he'd deduced, only humans were capable of fusing alien systems of magic. It was what made humanity Pan Arcanum or All-Magic. And that fact was both their greatest strength and the single greatest threat to, if not their continued existence, then certainly their sovereignty.

The Gefkarri needed humans to facilitate the neural net that would harmonize the efforts of the various armies fighting against the Void. The Chareth-Ul—who no longer wished to join forces with the Gefkarri but to claim Epriot Prime as their own—needed humankind as pilots for their mechs and as magical conduits to transfer energy from their home dimension to power the reactors and weapons systems of the Deathhound mechs.

Humanity's role in this battle against the Void was not as another army, but as ammunition—a commodity to be expended against an unending horde of enemy combatants. And there weren't very many humans left to do it with. Less than 250,000. Certainly much less after today.

To D'avry, this was a travesty on multiple levels. The slain Epriots weren't just fallout of a foreign conflict. They were the very seed of humanity's existence on E'rth. Somehow he'd graduated from carrying the future of his species on his shoulders back on E'rth to fighting for its very existence here in its past. D'avry decided he didn't much care for time travel. More trouble than it was worth.

"What are we seeing right now? D'avry, what is this? We're not holding hands and yet I'm seeing the area outside the ship," Katherynn said, confusion and bewilderment tinting her normally smooth and confident ambassadorial delivery.

The observation was a surprise. "Uh ... well. You can see that?" D'avry asked.

"You're projecting," Seda provided. "All of us can see what you're seeing right now."

"Yeah, I can see it too," Mads offered. Ensign Presche nodded, smiling at the pure novelty of the experience. For her, having been raised embracing the esoteric on a planet that was blocked from its magical wellspring, it must have been an immensely satisfying acknowledgment.

"Well, I can't," said the Captain sourly. "What's going on?"

"Refugees from the detention center are fleeing the battle," Katherynn answered. "Deathhound mechs and Void creatures are continuing to fight it out on the ground and aboard the Defiler itself. I don't know how long it's going to last, there's an awful lot of damage. Additionally, there appear to be Void creatures not actively engaged in the fighting but prowling the grounds. And there are other creatures as well. They're large and somewhat bug-like, with wings. When they're not fighting, they seem to be hunting our people." Her hand went over her mouth as she saw something horrible. She shook her head. "We have to do something."

"I don't know if you noticed, Madame Ambassador, but our ship is barely intact—"

"That is enough! Captain." Her typical poise burned away by the suffering and injustice she was bearing witness to. "It is *our* job to protect our people. We were unable to do that through a truce. We will accomplish it through battle if we must. Those people need refuge. They're cold, they're hungry, they're terrified ... as they should be. What's out there in the darkness is..." she swallowed, "...their terror is justified. We have to do something. That means getting ship's weapons online. That means finding weapons within the city if we can, and..." She looked at D'avry. "What can we do? Together. With magic? Can we fight?"

D'avry nodded. His whole focus since leaving E'rth had been reconnaissance and when that failed, had been on running away—gathering who he could and retreating to E'rth. Some way, at least. He hadn't figured out how. But now, he realized ... they just needed to figure out how to survive through the night.

And if they were lucky, the days to follow.

He looked around at the others within his circle of five. They had fumbled through raising a portion of the *Righteous Fury*. They had fumbled through, stopping the *Xandraitha's Hope* from punching a hole in the ground. But could they fight the overwhelming hordes of Void creatures? Or stand against the might of the Chareth-Ul and their city-sized fortresses on legs and their hundreds upon hundreds of Deathhound mechs and legions of flying creatures?

D'avry and his company of magical apprentices didn't just need to save the refugees, they needed to *enlist* them. The same way that the Gefkarri and Chareth-Ul intended to. He didn't know about the Delvadr; they were as much pawns as the humans were, but still, they were dangerous and they hated the humans with a passion. One problem at a time though.

Everyone was looking at him expectantly. He turned to the Gefkarri Aspect, her almond-shaped eyes glowing a soft jade, her perfect features cast in pale birchwood. His stomach jumped a little, the way she looked at him. It was jarring, the intensity of the connection between them, members of completely unrelated alien races. But he felt like he knew her in some incomprehensible way. He'd known she would betray her people for him when he'd asked for her help. He didn't know why, or how, but he knew.

"Seda, will you teach them? To use the Gefkarri magic?"

"I cannot." She looked away. "We," she motioned, "you and I ... were bound together. It is what the greater mind had chosen. I know you don't understand it, but I cannot just share that bond." She turned back, eyes cast down, but, after a pensive moment, brought her eyes up to meet his. "I can *prepare* them. Either to use humankind's own inherent magic or some other source. But I'm unable to allow the kind of access that you..." her breath caught, and she shook her head, leaving the sentence to dangle. This topic was deeply intimate. He felt like a heel for suggesting it. Why did he keep getting caught up in all this emotional weirdness?

D'avry flashed on Deven, his most recent romantic debacle, and forced his attention away from the idea, not willing to share on that topic so openly in the moment. He instead focused on the artifact at his hip. The Chareth-Ul talisman he'd liberated from the corpse at the Sanctum within the mountain here on Epriot Prime. The one that looked and felt just like that which was used by the battle priestess, Wahr-Zen, before Colonel Galas pulled her through the portal and the two of them had disappeared. For good, he'd thought...

There was no way he'd allow the uninitiated, such as the people around him, to channel the malevolent force attached to it. Who knew what kind of mayhem that would unleash? Or whether their minds could handle it. The Chareth-Ul magic was wild and twisted. Corrupt. It was dangerous for even someone with as much experience with different magic systems as himself.

In fact, if he was being honest, he'd admit he'd just as much prefer to huck the talisman into the ocean as try to master it. But he had no choice. The darkness within the artifacts inside his chest, beneath the golden lantern door that resided there, bristled with energetic excitement when he used the talisman. That was reason enough to avoid it. What a magical orcish arrow had to do with another-dimensional necromancer cult was a question for another time.

Evil knew evil, he guessed. His hand traced the edge of the lantern door beneath his tunic, as it often did when he puzzled over something. But it wasn't just an unconscious habit. Something had caused his attention to rest on it.

He closed his eyes and felt a gentle tug. Something subtle, like the pull of a river current close to shore. It was little at first, but the farther that one strayed from the edge...

He felt an invisible force pulling him toward that huge mech. He was tired from earlier, but this energetic pull... it rattled in his veins. His mind slipped into the flow state he was so used to, and it was like submerging himself within the freezing river's flow.

The perception that had engulfed the area around the *Xandraitha's Hope* pulled him toward the Defiler. Rising up into the sky as it did so, the faint glow of the setting sun over the coastal mountains. The monstrous silhouette, illuminated by fire and explosions, grew in size as his mind's eye drifted nearer. The perspective of the vision floated higher and higher. Darkened hills and streams below drifted into obscurity.

His view opened up to the top of the mech. It was a city in its own right, dominated by two temple ziggurats bordered by vast plazas. The plazas themselves were covered in bodies of flyers and other forms he was unfamiliar with. The battle raged between Deathhounds, Void wolves, and yet other creatures who hurled balls that burst into rift holes.

And beyond and above all that, atop the stepped pyramid temples were other forms still—those of the battle priestesses. One was taller than a human woman and she had large forked horns. Not the huge rack of antlers like Wahr-Zen had. Maybe she was younger? The other priestess was shorter still and had no horns, but she fought ferociously.

His attention flowed to this closer priestess just as Void creatures burst through the line of Deathhounds below. They sprang up the block steps, taking several at a time as they blipped forward. The priestess' attention was elsewhere. She hurled crackling plasma down onto the deck, wiping out dozens of the Void wolves along with flyers and at least one of her own mechs.

D'avry watched as the Void wolves bounded closer and then, before he realized it, he'd assumed his raven form and was bearing down on the trio of creatures. He mutated at the last moment, materializing his staff as he pierced one of the creatures from behind. It exploded into blinding energy and he felt that energy roll over him. The scent of it, the taste of it, was foreign and acidic.

He stared in horror as the two remaining creatures burst forward, a mere blip away from taking the battle priestess by surprise. He bent space himself and brought the staff down upon the closest creature. It turned and looked at him, and he could swear that there was recognition in its eyes before it exploded into a blinding white burst of light.

He blinked away the stars and just caught the battle priestess as the remaining creature lunged.

His mind must have been addled because, for the briefest moment, he could swear the priestess looked like Colonel Galas but gaunt and gray, like the Chareth-Ul. But then she was gone, over the far side of the temple. The Defiler lurched beneath him. He stared across to the other temple, and the priestess there was looking his way.

The mech lurched again and started to sway. He didn't know what to do, so he did the only thing he could think of, he stepped up to the top of the temple and assumed a low posture, his palms opening upward and out as his arms extended, scribing an arc around him before settling palm to palm at his center. He extended his right hand and his staff sprang into existence and thudded as it touched down on the temple stone.

As expected, the temple was a channeling tool for the mech itself. Because of its sheer size, it required two. And this wasn't even the biggest he'd seen. The one that had occupied New Varhus before had *three* temple structures. Now he realized why.

He opened himself to the roaring rush of Chareth-Ul magic and he heard a booming but decidedly feminine voice. "Who are you?!? And why are you here?" The voice was so loud in his mind he could barely think.

"I'm Avaricae D'avry. Sorcerer of the Pan Arcanum. And I'm here because you need me."

There was a desperate silence and then, "Very well."

He felt control of the massive mech flow to him—only pieces of it, operational components, logistical components. Below his feet, a city lived and breathed and he was part of it now. But this city was under siege. What about *Xandraitha's Hope*? The Five?

He realized this was their only hope. If the Defiler fell, the Void would consume everything that was left. The refugees fleeing to the relative safety of the downed transport.

His friends. All of a sudden, leaving them was the best thing he could do for their safety. He felt the last vestiges of Seda's presence in his mind slip away and then all he could think or feel was the metal beast that was the Defiler. And the threat against it.

Void broke through the ranks below and he lashed out with arcane fire, sweeping the plaza clean of life. The power of the Chareth-Ul surged within him and he smiled darkly. *Oh, this will do ... this will do nicely.*

A note of alarm came from the other temple, the priestess, he realized, but he couldn't be bothered. He was digging deeper into the bowels of the mech, tracing its conduits of power, reaching out to the denizens piloting the mechs, reading the thoughts of the Makrit—that's what the large humanoid forms were, acolytes of the indigenous people ruled by the Chareth-Ul, and their pets, the flyers he now realized were called Umzat.

He delved deeper and the battle priestess tried to stop him, but he flicked her aside effortlessly. She was no Wahr-Zen, just a pup amongst the Chareth-Ul.

He read her terror, realized she'd been a newly ascended. Just like the priestess he'd seen toppled on the temple he commanded now. This Defiler, no Heretic, had been pulled from the Chareth-Ul domain, Reality Zero, they called it. The home they were abandoning in hopes of slamming the door shut on the interdimensional cancer known as the Void.

Now he understood. The Chareth-Ul were in retreat. They thought they could stop the Void here because of the resources indigenous to this planet, namely the human commodity. This mech had come from the battle on Reality Zero. Had fled actually. But there was more to it. He couldn't quite decipher the details.

They didn't matter. What mattered ... was power. And with this machine, he had true power. Maybe it was enough to create a rift back to E'rth. But then he realized that wasn't what he really wanted. What he *really* wanted was for someone to pay. For now, the Void would do, but then his eyes drifted heavenward. Next will be the Gefkarri. For the people of E'rth, locked in a perpetual cycle of stifled agency, destined to be brought low whenever they reached too high. For them, the Gefkarri Pentarch was the source of their suffering.

D'avry shook his head, trying to clear his mind. The rage inside him was roiling with every injustice, all the suffering. He fixated on images of refugees fleeing in the darkness and being consumed by the creatures that lived within its shadows.

Now I am the shadow. His mind flickered. He struggled to grasp a shard of light within the madness. He felt the purging cold.

Here was the true price of the Chareth-Ul magic, losing oneself to hatred.

He stepped back, and it was like hooks of piercing ice were embedded in his flesh, dragging him forward. Back into the place of control. Perceived control. He hesitated, he'd thought, but realized he'd stepped forward yet again. But he did everything he could to remain separate and distinct from the magic. He was here to save humanity. Not to exact justice. But the craving inside him grew and grew. And grew until it was all he could see or hear or feel.

He lashed out. Wicked arcs of purple-white plasma crashed over the deck, wiping out foe and friend alike. His battle priestess comrade recoiled at the display. But then, after a moment, she reached out and connected with him.

He felt her ... character, the person within the gray skin and forked horns. She was so out of her league here—had made a decision that was irreversible. And then she betrayed a name. Prima-Caz. It was unfamiliar, but still...

D'avry's mind whipped to the priestess who'd been attacked earlier, struck down by the Void wolf.

"She's gone," the priestess acknowledged. "Now, it's you and me. Whoever you are."

"Where is Wahr-Zen?" he asked.

There was hesitation on the other end of the connection. "Why?" she asked suspiciously.

"We have unfinished business," he said and left it at that.

"She's gone to the Epriot base at the Spires to accept their offering."

"What offering?"

"Well ... their people, of course."

CHAPTER 32
THE OUTSKIRTS

Epriot Prime, Somewhere East of New Varhus

Macq blinked away stars as he struggled to suck air into his lungs. Panic surged as the air wouldn't come fast enough. What had he done? Where was he? The questions rattled around without answer. He stared past the blare of data flashing at him from the suit's HUD. There was nothing but darkness beyond those lights.

"Seraf?" he groaned, his voice breathy and coarse. "Seraf?!?"

No one answered back.

He tried to move, and his body screamed at him in one big drunken chorus. Every cell everywhere all at once was on fire.

Not good!

The panic was threatening to take over again. He settled back and breathed to calm himself,

"Okay, Macq. Just take it easy... pain is good, right? Pain means at least your spine's probably not broken. Now what the hell did you do?" he asked no one. It was just soothing to hear a voice in his audio, even if it was his own.

He flicked on the night vision filter using eye movement commands in his suit's HUD. The scene beyond the display resolved into gray and green smoke that he realized was the filter's visualization of the dust from the fall he'd just taken *through* two floors and a roof.

"Thank Maker for power suits," he chuckled weakly and regretted it.

Now the pain screaming at him from everywhere made a little more sense. The dust began to dissipate visibly, so he felt reasonably confident that the fall had just happened and he hadn't been lying there for hours.

Then some of the details began to percolate into his memory. He hadn't just stumbled, the roof had opened up ahead of him. Then he remembered the crazed Hillmen that were after them. It was clear now that there were more than just the original three. That or someone else was shooting at them with a gun big enough to blast a hole in the roof and two subsequent floors.

That told him a lot about the angle of the attack. The sniper was above and behind as he leaped across the deadman's alley. That was important information, but it didn't mean they were still there. Or that they didn't send someone else to make sure the job was done.

He tried to move again and some of the intensity of the pain had dulled. He cautiously sucked in a full breath and felt a little more comfortable about the state of his body. His ribs ached, but the net result was that he'd just taken a hard fall. Maybe nothing was badly broken. Again, he wished for a full mil-spec suit. One that could diagnose and triage damage to the operator. Some could even sense a freefall and auto-orient so that you always landed on your feet. That would have been nice.

But now, the danger was out there. And it was on its way. He needed to put distance between himself and his present location. And find Seraf, ASAP.

He brought up his map, but just as Seraf's last location populated, something on the floor above jogged his memory. It was the tapering rectangle of a butt stock. The Slair Two sniper rifle.

"You gotta be kidding me."

It was the rifle he'd appropriated from the Hillmen and it was lying halfway over the edge of the opening two floors above. He sat up, muscles and joints screaming in protest. Then he worried that he might still be within the sniper's line of sight.

If the Hillman's rifle had blown a hole through the building and he'd fallen into that hole, he probably was. He quickly rolled to the side before standing up and returned to that same line of reasoning. Trying to reclaim the weapon would also put him in within that window. However, the idea of running around the countryside without a weapon was equally discomforting. He needed to retrieve it, and he needed to do it quickly.

A quick scan of the floor he was on showed a hallway off to his right. He rolled his head, flexed his fingers and gingerly shook out his arms before padding toward it. All of his nerve endings were still buzzing, but it was more of an agitated grumble now than anything. He'd live. As long as he kept moving, that was. But what had happened to Seraf?

Get the gun. Then get the girl. Then ... get to the transport and hopefully don't get shot along the way. His thoughts were heavy again as he remembered why they'd been heading this way and what they were heading away from. How did it all turn to shit so fast? Nothing was ending up like it should. The treaty, getting back to the planet, contacting the EDC ... everything had turned to shit. And now, he didn't even know if any of his family were alive.

He was so consumed with all of these fears he'd stepped right out into the hallway and had to quickly duck back in when he saw a shape at the end of the hall moving in his direction.

"Shit."

The red cursor popped up in his HUD, and the map spun to orient himself to the floor and to this new threat. He didn't hear any yelling, and the sounds of footsteps he was now tuned to, didn't pick up or slow down, so most likely, they hadn't seen him.

He scanned the map. There was another door from the corridor into the large open room he was in. The person might enter from there or they could continue down the hall and enter through the open door where he was standing, frozen in fear. He used the HUD to crank up the external input to the audio circuits as he positioned himself to either slip through the door to the hallway if he heard the other door open or slip toward that door if the person continued down the hall toward his present location. It was a toss-up.

He watched as the cursor creeped forward and then he heard the jiggling of the latch. He zoomed in to the door and watched as it slowly crept open a few centimeters. He shifted toward the opening to the hallway. The other person pushed the door open more fully with what he saw now was the fore-end of a rifle. Macq slipped out into the hallway just in time to see the Hillman's foot before it disappeared into the room he'd just been occupying.

He scanned both ways. It looked like there were stairs at either end of the long corridor. He quickly made his way toward the stairs farthest away from the person searching for him. As quietly as he could. The cursor grew jittery and spread out as his movement made it more difficult for his suit to track the other person, but it was close enough. He could see that they were moving toward the place where he'd fallen through from above.

They'd see he wasn't there and the search would be on. Hopefully, they wouldn't notice the rifle on the floor above and go to retrieve it. He made it to the end of the hall and was faced with a closed door to the stairwell. He hoped it wouldn't make any noise when he opened it. Prayed it wouldn't.

Macq twisted the manual release, and the door started to squeak. He stopped. Then he lifted as he pulled to relieve the friction on the hinges, only opening the door as much as he absolutely had to in order to slip inside.

The cursor started moving his way, and he moved to the stairs as quickly and quietly as he could. The cursor grew large and transparent again, signifying that the suit wasn't a hundred percent certain about the target's whereabouts. But it was clear they were moving quickly in his direction.

He rounded the corner, skipped a couple of steps, and heard someone yell from the bottom of the stairwell.

"Dammit!" He bolted through the door and sprinted down the hall, but there were several doors here, where below there'd only been the one. He didn't have time to figure this out. He crashed through the first and it was an empty flat. Fully intact.

He ran back into the hall and crashed through the next door. Same thing.

"Shit." He lurched back into the hallway again, only this time one of the figures was just entering the hall from the stairwell. He heard a shout and gunfire just as he smashed into the third door. This too was empty, but there was an interior door leading to the next room and this one had a hole through its floor and the far wall was partially gone destroyed.

Best of all, the Slair rifle was lying there on the floor. He grabbed it, checked the charge, and cycled the next round. Everything functioned.

"Thank Maker!"

He heard heavy boots pounding down the hall. There were two cursors heading his direction and the first one was nearly to him. He lunged through the hole in the floor, dropping to the next and letting the suit soak up the fall, which it did with ease. And then he started sprinting again.

"Let's see how they do with that," he said to himself as he ran for the far end of the room. He didn't know what floor he was on. All that running from roof to roof, up and down, he just couldn't be sure how tall this building was. He knew he was two floors down, but beyond that, maybe he was on the fourth, maybe the third? How much of a drop could this suit take?

Gunfire crackled behind him. He saw the floor chewed up to his left and veered right. There was a window. One of the pursuers dropped down to the floor behind him, or so it appeared in the model. It was either drop, turn, and fire, knowing that aiming with the armor and rifle required some finessing, or jump for it.

The window ahead of him shattered before he got to it. He registered the sound of automatic fire as he leaped through, out into the gray-green of Nightvision-filtered darkness beyond. He was much higher up than he'd expected. It had to be five-stories, but the HUD painted the landing area green. Then he felt and heard the pinging of gunfire across the back of his armor. The area below turned red, and he realized in terror that his repulsor pack had just been damaged. This was not going to be a soft landing.

His boot-mounted repulsors may not be able to soak up all the energy from his fall, but they sure as hell could guide him. He aimed for a full-height window and balcony on the building across the street and maxed out his repulsors. His downward velocity diminished a little, but his forward velocity increased a lot. He made a last second adjustment and came in high and hot, crashing through the plas and then bouncing off the floor before slamming into couches, chairs, a table, and who knew what else.

Stars were careening around his vision as gunfire peppered the floor where he'd landed. They couldn't get the right angle on him. He was safe, for the moment at least. He had to beat them to ground level and continue his search for Seraf. He thought he was on the second floor now. And he was only a block away from Seraf's last known location.

"Seraf?" he called through the suit's short-range comms, but nothing came back. What had happened to her? She'd just run a little ways farther on when he'd stopped to take out their pursuers. Macq got up and headed across the hall, through an open door and into an office suite with cubicles and a conference room. The color scheme was bold, with black and red and lime-green. It was horrible. He had no idea what kind of business it had been, but he certainly hoped it had not been interior design. A painting on the wall was of a circle penetrated on one side by a trapezoid shape reminiscent of a transport ship like the *Xandraitha's Hope*. The far side of the circle exploded outward with geometric shards of the same black as that of the circle and the ship.

If they'd been a spacecraft design firm, that was horrible, horrible marketing. He jogged to the window and looked down. Of course, it couldn't just be a flat street below, but instead was the edge of a crater filled with rubble from the building that had once inhabited the space. Large portions of it were still intact. He had planned on jumping down, but this maybe wasn't a prudent tactic. That meant he'd have to take the stairs and his pursuers were most likely heading up them at any moment.

From this vantage point, he could see physically where Seraf's last-known-location pin existed. He switched to augmented reality mode, and the HUD overlayed the model with his perspective feed. The blue pin populated near a large overturned trash bin. There was nothing there, but movement fifty or so meters farther on caught his attention.

There, two people were crouched over a third. He realized the form on the ground must be Seraf and zoomed in to confirm. The two figures were trying to pry the face mask open. He whipped up the Slair 2 rifle and sighted down it. It was no good. He'd only gotten close enough the last time he'd tried to sight in using his suit's HUD. He'd have to do this without his helmet on.

His pursuers were certainly closing in by now. He had very little time. Macq ran back to the door and pushed the reception desk in front of it. Without the armor, he wouldn't have been able to move it at all. That might hold for a minute or two. He ran back to the window, kneeled down, and removed his helmet after sending a text to Seraf.

[Macq: Keep your head down. I'm coming for you.]

Macq propped the long rifle on the ledge and aimed down the fixed sights. He wished he could use the magnification built into his suit, but this would have to do. The sight post lined up on the closest figure. He aimed slightly high, not because he was worried about drop or windage, he was firing from above and there was very little breeze—he knew the velocity of the round passing by was so great that if it passed within fifteen centimeters, the air turbulence alone would likely kill the target. He just didn't want to subject Seraf to that impact. Thankfully, she was in her body armor.

Then, as luck would have it, they levered her face shield open. The closest person bent down to work on it. Macq shifted aim to the second target, who was still kneeling upright. He heard someone jiggle the handle of the door behind him as he pulled the trigger. The rifle kicked hard, but it was the sound of it with his helmet off that split his head in two. It was like being inside a lightning bolt.

Everything was buzzing and muffled. He couldn't tell if the people coming after him were pounding on the door, shooting, or what. What he did know was that his shot had taken the upper half of his target clean away and the rest of them was sprawled in the street a few meters away. The other one had bolted upright, saw what happened, and dove behind the dumpster.

He saw Seraf stir and reach for her head. The person behind the dumpster had a gun and Macq just saw the barrel of it poke out from behind cover, pointed at Seraf. He brought the rifle to bear on the point behind the dumpster where he knew the attacker had to be and pulled the trigger just as gunfire erupted from behind him.

The rifle punched him in the shoulder and the deafening crack of the railgun slammed his ear canals again, sending everything into a muffled buzzing. He saw the dumpster blow backward and was confident Seraf's assailant was neutralized, but his own situation was now dire.

Projectiles zippered across his chest and a flare of pain slashed across his cheek. *Shrapnel*, he thought. *Lucky it wasn't my eye.* But it was a good reminder, "Get your helmet on, you idiot."

He grabbed it just as he heard a loud thudding on the door outside.

Alright, enough's enough. He sprinted for the door, jumped up into a two-footed kick and hit his repulsors. The door exploded away, and he fell onto the reception desk. A startled soldier peeked around the corner and was just bringing up his gun when Macq slammed the end of the Slair Two rifle forward with all he had.

With the suit's augments, the man's head made a crunchy sound as he crumpled. Macq didn't wait to find out if there were more. He rolled backward of the desk, turned and bolted for the window. He'd deal with the drop. It was just two or three floors.

As he leaped, he saw movement in the rubble-filled crater below. Creatures. They were all black. He caught the flutter of wings as they turned at the commotion from above and gathered into a formation of three. He was heading right for them.

CHAPTER 33
REALITY ZERO

Reality Zero; The Keep at Ak-Umbrech
(Months prior in Chareth-Ul time)

Galas awoke to the feeling that someone or something was standing over her. She calmed her racing heart and didn't flinch a muscle to give away the fact that she was awake. And most of all, she didn't allow herself to ascend into the deepening of the Saine'ril to gather her full power. Instead, she pulled on the finding energy of the Duine'at. With enough of it, she could be dangerous. She did this now in the same way she'd slip on a robe, gathering it about herself and preparing to strike.

"Don' even dink abowd eh, pup," a low, husky voice growled as she felt a blade at her throat. "I gwine teh cut you real quiet, or yer fren gwine ta bleed instead."

Galas's eyes opened to lock on to the sewn-shut lids of Muhd'e Vains, a Chareth-Ul initiate like her but two years her senior. She should have been promoted to acolyte already with these last games, which was shameful. But then Galas, a novice initiate and human to boot, had outperformed her in the arena, pouring salt into the wound and mashing it down for good measure.

Galas glanced over at her roommate and training partner Noor-Andra. Another older initiate Galas didn't recognize held a blade to her throat. The blade like the initiate's eye burned a pale yellow. A yellow haze bloomed near Galas's face and she watched as Muhd'e ascended fully. Now she could tap into the Chareth-Ul magic at will. Snap Galas's neck with a thought.

It would be against the laws of the priesthood, but then, it was expected that they'd be broken. One just mustn't get caught. Galas's mind raced desperately. Why would she do this now? And in this way? It'd be easier to pull a dirty trick in the arena or even in the training drome, but sneaking into another initiates dorm while they slept? There was no honor in that, and honor was what it was all about. Anything could be forgiven if it was done for prestige and glory. *Ad dignitatum et gloriam*, she remembered seeing stenciled on the back of a Marine's helmet. It seemed a common sentiment amongst the warrior races.

"Are you so afraid of me, Muddy? To kill me in such an honorless way."

Her pale yellow eye flared. "Yeh know nuttin' of our ways, filth," she spat.

"Oh, so you're not here to kill me then?" Galas realized as she spoke. "What's this about then?" she asked, just as a faint jingling sensation ran up her spine.

It's about Wahr-Zen. There's a coup underway. Her senses told her that her patron was in trouble.

Unlike many of her contemporaries who kept dozens of acolytes, the chief battle priestess only kept a handful of carefully chosen women to be her honor guard. Each was bonded to her. Even though she was just an initiate, Galas had this bond as well, but only because it had been Wahr-Zen herself who had turned her.

Galas's stomach still twisted at the thought, at her monstrous transformation. Not quite human, not quite Chareth-Ul, some kind of wraith inhabiting the space between. Only half-living, but something much, much more than dead.

Stuck in a dimension that looked to her pretty much like what she'd imagined as hell, bonded to what she imagined being some kind of demonic necromancer-like embodiment of pure evil, and being forcefully enrolled into undead necromancer school by being partially turned into one of their kind—her outlook was decidedly bleak. But nothing was impossible. It was just much, much worse than anything she could have possibly imagined. But not impossible.

She looked again at the initiate with the glowing third eye holding a ceremonial dagger to her throat and that whole idea about things not being impossible, wilted for a moment.

No. Not acceptable. This pathetic waste of pasty skin and antlers isn't going to get between me and my daughter. It's going to take a hell of a lot more than this to keep me down.

"Muddy, you should remove the blade from my throat before someone gets hurt," she said in the sweetest voice she could muster.

The woman sniggered and smiled. "What'r yeh gwine to—" she started to say before Galas's blade came from beneath her fur blanket and into the woman's diaphragm.

Galas channeled the minor, ambient arcana into a gleaming point that rode the edge of her blade deep inside the initiate's rib cage. Her scream was cut off with a gurgle. The other initiate turned in surprise and that's when Galas's trap snapped shut.

Her aura-imbued blade siphoned Mudh'e's Sain-ril in an instant. Mudh'e collapsed and the power that flooded into Galas's veins burst from her outstretched hand in a crimson bolt that struck the Chareth-Ul woman, crackling around her chest and throat, and escaping from her eyes, ears, and open mouth as she attempted to scream.

Galas saw all this through her energized third eye, the spectral light flowing from the hewn-rock floors, walls and ceiling through Galas and into the other woman. The energy splayed out in wild miasma before Galas drew it all back into herself, the same way she'd done with the now lifeless husk of the initiate formerly known as Muhd'e Vains.

Noor-Andra bolted upright, clutching her throat. She turned in horror to find Galas, fully energized by the Saine'ril of two initiates, her eyes sewn shut with black sinew, her third eye a piercing crimson and her face, Galas was ashamed to admit, a mask of ecstasy.

She bit her lip until the all-consuming feeling of pleasure subsided. How was she going to maintain her sense of right and wrong when the rules of this dimension and this magic system made doing wrong feel so good? Her tendencies toward vengeance and the love of fighting were constantly being exploited to turn her fully to the darkest version of herself.

"Galas, what have you done?" her roommate asked as she surveyed the bodies of two dead initiates on the dorm room floor. "This is forbidden."

The jangling sensation in Galas's spine spiked once more, and she turned for the door.

"No time, Noor. My patron's in trouble."

Noor-Andra slipped from beneath her blankets, every inch of her slender gray form shamelessly exposed. Her hand casually stretched toward the wardrobe and its doors sprang open as her robes flew out and wrapped themselves around her.

"Then I'd say we must make haste. I, for one, will not abide the slaying of a mother. Even be she not of my line."

She, too, drew on the Chareth-Ul magic, sinew growing from the skin around her eyes, piercing the flesh and drawing tight as her third eye bloomed into an effuse purple. The two ran down the corridor to the grand stairs leading to the upper chambers. Other acolytes stepped out dazedly from the quarters and were blown back as Galas and Noor flew past, the magic aura around them barely contained by the hewn-rock walls.

As they entered the common area where each wing of the dormitories came together, the vaulted rock lit up with deep reds, purples, and yellows while wicked crackling and thunderclaps echoed through the ceiling-less chamber.

"It's already begun!"

"What?"

"The coup. Follow me," Galas yelled back to Noor as she sprang three floors to an overlooking balcony cast in the same smooth black rock of the rest of the Keep. Noor leaped but could only make it to an opening on the second-floor corridor that ringed the chamber.

"Go. I'm only working with Duine'at, you've harnessed deepening power. I'll catch up."

Galas nodded and leaped another three floors, to a balcony on the far side of the open chamber and then to the top of a massive iron chandelier before leaping to the final floor and the source of the fantastic display of lights. Lights that she knew were the residual effect of ungodly amounts of power being cast about by women with many times her strength in the Ahk'menaim—the Chareth-Ul arcanum.

The upper levels in general and the upper commons chamber in particular were off-limits to initiates so she took a brief second to take it in. The area, like below, was a central hub to wings of the various lines, but within those wings were the dormitories of the battle priestesses and only their most superior acolytes. There were darkly intricate tapestries hanging on the walls and adorning the floor.

At the far end, away from the vertical opening of the common chamber with its huge iron chandelier, aglow with a nebula of ancient candles, was a wide dais made up of thirteen broad steps.

Atop those steps rested the Seat of the Grand Mother, empty for these many decades since she had been slain in battle against invading Void armies. As far as Galas had learned, no one had been able to claim the gold, silver and jeweled throne. Its lines mimicking the branches of a tree, interwoven with the horns of a great elk and the skulls and bones of all the foes that had fallen before the might of the Chareth-Ul.

Galas shuddered as she looked upon it. She felt like she couldn't take her eyes away, even as the bolts of crackling energy in a multitude of colors splashed this way and that, taking the lives of acolytes as the battle priestesses looked on from the flanks of the grand dais.

The battle priestesses were unable to engage in the fighting themselves, but once a priestess was without her honor guard, she was free game. And as strong as Wahr-Zen was, standing against a dozen ascended acolytes, whipped into an ecstatic frenzy, their Duine'at and Saine'ril reserves bloated with the conquest of the fallen, the odds were less than favorable.

The other battle priestesses wouldn't interfere for fear of being turned on by the slavering horde. Who could deny them in such a moment?

Golden light pulsed and grew into a brilliant sun as streams of energy shot from six of the women on the dais toward an energetic sphere on the upper dais. Within that diminishing ball were three of Galas's sistren. The only acolytes left to protect Wahr-Zen.

Galas could have cared less about the woman herself, but what she represented was Galas's freedom. It was only by ascending through the ranks of the priestesshood that she would be able to command a defiler. And it was only by commanding a defiler that she'd be able to return to her realm. Albeit in order to subjugate the people of Epriot Prime, defy the Gefkarri and continue the battle against the Void, but one thing at a time.

She needed to ascend the ranks to escape, and for that, she needed a patron. The fact that she was a human meant no other battle priestess would touch her. She was only good for Deathhound duty, but having become an initiate meant she was too capable within the Ahk'menaim to be subject to the soul-bonding that all Deathhounds underwent. She was unsuitable for both and would be terminated right behind her patron, Wahr-Zen.

One of the women within the sphere shrieked as she flamed out. She had tried to control too much of the magic and it consumed her. The sphere shrank and the crackling golden light grew in intensity, making it impossible to see the other two women within it.

They could not hold on long. Wahr-Zen looked on in horror and fury. Her shoulders rising and falling as she took in a shuddering breath to calm her rage. Then her gaze drifted to where Galas was standing near the railing to the shaft beyond, and her eyes flared with puzzlement and then contempt. She turned away, resigned to her fate.

Galas marched forward. One of the other battle priestesses saw her, recognized her as a lower-level initiate, and pointed at her. "Get her out of here. She doesn't belong—"

One of the acolytes on the lower steps of the dais, one with a glowing yellow eye in the middle of her forehead, stepped in her direction, but Galas swatted her away with a sweep of a hand. The woman flew across the dais, crashing into a wall and taking down one of the tapestries.

This brought the attention of others of the battle priestesses as they watched. They called out to their respective acolytes, who turned to take in the new threat. Galas strode forward, still charged with the Saine'ril from the slain Muhd'e and her partner in crime. Two of the acolytes stepped forward into a low stance, their arms arcing wide, scribing a dramatic circle that, Galas supposed, would be a powerful spell, but she didn't much care for dramatics. She pushed out with two black-taloned hands and waves of energy pulsed out, crumpling the two women and smashing them into others farther up the steps.

Galas twisted her gnarled hands, and the women lurched into the air as she swung them around like a chain flail, wielding their bodies like a weapon against the other acolytes who were now turning, not in anticipation of a fight but in surprise and fear.

Gold and orange and green streams of crackling energy lashed out, but Galas had grabbed two more of the fallen women and now held them in energetic streams of her own as she siphoned their energy into her own Duine'at and Saine'ril stores. The multi-hued assault splashed against her own sphere of defense.

She felt the energy coursing through her like never before. The priestess initiates at the end of her tethers shrieked as they wilted, Galas sucking the life essence out of them like she had the Makrit Thunderers in the arena. The battle priestesses on the flanks shrieked with outrage, but Galas couldn't be bothered.

The sensation of ecstasy pouring over her, energizing her from within, was undeniable. Even as they pleaded, she powered forward, taking the next step up, grabbing yet others as they fell to the floor, depleted. By now, there was only one of Wahr-Zen's acolytes left on the upper dais. The three women who'd been perpetrating the attack pressed forward, sensing victory. They were struggling now, but so was the acolyte underneath the barrage. How she'd held on this long was impossible to say.

There were still a dozen between her and the remaining acolyte, a woman she thought she recognized but didn't know her name. There wasn't enough time. She cast the lifeless bodies of the acolytes she still held at the women and they scattered in disarray. One of the bodies struck the three golden acolytes and their streams ceased momentarily.

Galas saw the woman within the shield. She was down on one knee, panting, one arm outstretched in defense. The sutures in her eyes bleeding dark crimson streaks down her face. It was the woman she knew. A once untouchable acolyte, next in line to assume Wahr-Zen's place amongst the line. She was so close to failure.

Galas paused to collect herself. She was teetering on the edge of complete burnout, but she needed to press the attack. Now was her only chance. Just then, she felt a disturbance in her shield spell and she spun. A knife blade burned her belly as she stared up at the yellow-eyed woman staring down at her with a cruel smile.

This was the priestess behind the attack. Kada-K'thul, a particularly nasty woman amongst a cadre of particularly nasty women. "I said, initiates aren't welcome in the upper commons, whelp," she growled and the blade pressed into Galas's stomach. She felt blinding pain and smelled burning flesh. Galas's hand lashed out instinctively, but the priestess caught it with ease and turned it cruelly. Galas cried out with the pain but brought two of the acolytes she still held with her energetic tethers flying in from either side. Kada-K'thul let go of Galas and, with hands extended to either side, caught the women while they were still yards away.

Galas saw her opening and pushed with as much of the Saine'ril power as she could muster, but the battle priestess stood steadfast and, instead, Galas was sent flailing into the crowd of acolytes watching from the steps above, sending them flying in every direction.

Everyone had stopped to watch, even the golden acolytes who had been assaulting Wahr-Zen's one remaining honor guard. Galas struggled to her feet and found help from her training partner Noor, who had finally arrived, and who also should not have been allowed into the upper commons and definitely not on the thirteen steps.

The remaining acolytes gathered their wits and stepped in to seize them,

"No! Leave them to me," Kada commanded. "Such insolence must be punished swiftly and without mercy. No initiate has ever disgraced the chamber of the Upper Commons, let alone assaulted an acolyte and even more audacious, a battle priestess.

"These two shall be made to suffer so that none who follow will make a similar mistake. Though I can scarcely imagine anyone so stupid. Perhaps it's her atrophied human brain that caused her to do it."

Kada drew back a taloned hand to strike them down, her third eye glowing a fearsome gold and her voice filling the room with like fearsome thunder. But then Wahr-Zen stepped in before her, and without saying a word, stopped her in her tracks.

"No one shall be punished by your hand, Battle Priestess Kada of the Golden Line. Your coup has failed. It is to your own disgrace that it was accomplished by a lowly initiate. But the fact that

Reality Zero

you, as a battle priestess, stepped in personally to do what your acolytes could not just confirms even more that you are without honor and are not worthy of the position."

"You shall be removed. In fact, the entire Golden Line shall be set under review until it has been deemed apparent that it is not just as corrupt and honorless as its patron. And these two, for their part, shall be exiled. It is unforgivable that they have come here and intervened, regardless of their misguided attempt to protect their patron mother."

Galas was relieved that Wahr-Zen had stepped in but felt a sudden terror that she was to be removed from the enclave. She couldn't care less about what happened to her ... but falling short of her mission to return home?

She began to step forward to confront the chief battle priestess, but Noor's hand rested on her forearm, gently but unmistakably fixed.

"Forgive us, Mother. Initiate Galas felt the call as she is bound to you through the turning. I ... came to stop her, but she was already fully charged from an altercation with initiates of the Golden Line who had broken into our dormitory. Most likely to prevent such an outcome as what has unfolded here," she said, nodding first in the direction of the scattering of acolytes and then at the disgraced Kada K'thul.

Wahr-Zen's eyes drew into slits as she took in the information. She didn't turn to face the woman but asked, "Is this true, Kada? Did you send initiates to harm the women of another line?"

The battle priestess didn't answer but stared ahead, barely able to contain her fury.

"An initiate is unable to provide witness against a battle priestess. Who among you can corroborate this statement?" Wahr-Zen asked the remaining women gathered in the upper commons. "Anyone?" There was a breathless pause for a long moment.

Galas saw the tiniest shift in Kada's gaze and then a dark-haired acolyte with green eyes, thin by even Chareth-Ul standards, stepped forward to speak. Kada's hand flicked out as she cast a ball of crackling dark energy at the woman but Galas, anticipating the attack, leaped in the way while hastily pulling her shielding about her, but it all happened too fast.

She realized too late that was down to her Duine'at reserves, the deepening power fully depleted. She took the full brunt of the blow, which sent her spiraling through the air and fully engulfed in darkness.

CHAPTER 34
CHRONOSHIELD

"There you are. I hope you got your beauty sleep," Noor-Andra said. "We've been promoted." She spread her hands to either side and smiled a trite, mirthless smile.

Galas squinted against the driving sand, harsh sunlight, and freezing cold. She had a very bad feeling about this promotion. Slowly, she made out the shape of one of those dragon wasp creatures flying away. Up and away. Back toward what she recognized as the Keep at Ak-Umbrech high atop a vertical spine of rock in the haze of volcanic off-gas.

"Oh, no."

"That's right."

Galas spun around. Fractured earth stretched for miles to the north and the south, resembling massive veins in the valley floor. Luminous vapors drifted from the molten flow within.

She turned to face the inevitable reality and there it was, stretching up and out of sight—the amber chrysalis of the Chronoshield. While Wahr-Zen returned to Epriot Prime in a newly outfitted Defiler, Galas would be here, manning the useless and dilapidated two-temple heretic, just in case any Void managed to slip through the non-existent cracks.

Just then a Makrit acolyte mounted the steps to the raised dais where Noor and Galas were conversating. He gave a trill, which Galas understood to be the bug equivalent of clearing his throat.

"My humblest apologies, Acolyte Prima-Caz, but the guild awaits its orders," he said in a dry raspy tone. The creature tried not to stare at what Galas assumed was her scandalous lack of antlers.

Catching his attention with a raised eyebrow, she offered, "I'm a late bloomer. What can I say?"

The Makrit, which Galas now realized was head of battle ops for all things bug-like on the mech, cocked its faceless black shell. The Makrit acolytes, Galas's opinion, resembled the second dude from the right on the Chareth-Ul bug people's evolutionary chart. The Umzat or flyers were farther left and the Thunderers, well, they were ... to be honest, that's where the analogy broke down. They were just bigger, uglier, meaner, and dumber, but in a cagey sort of way. She guessed by Chareth-Ul standards that made them the farthest dude to the right. Yeah ... this was a broken planet and the Chareth-Ul were the ones that broke it.

But at least Galas was in charge of a mech again. She caught sight of her gaunt, gray hand with fine traces of black veins and curved black talon-like nails. And all it cost her was ... she wouldn't think about that. All for the greater good. She told herself. All to get back to Seraf and Epriot Prime. She'd worry about what to do when she got there, well, if she got there. First, she had to get out of this hellhole. Literal. Hell hole.

"Acolyte, what do they call you?" she asked.

He paused as if he'd never been asked that before. She thought it was strange how, for a faceless bug, she could read his body language with ease. It was saying, "No one's ever asked me that before."

"Ooohzma-Teklat-M'randkr."

"Mmhmm. Oozie. What would be a customary first command for a brand new battle priestess-in-training?"

He looked at her with that face again. The blank one that suggested she was completely insane.

"A traditional first command would be to order assembly."

"Sounds good."

"Followed by a proper sacrifice."

"I'm listening," she said, and she was. Her stomach was getting excited, but her head was lagging behind. She didn't like where this was headed.

"After that, an inspection of the Heretic from top to bottom. Typically performed by your second in command," he nodded toward Noor, "as you will most likely be resting after your state of..." He looked about nervously. "Uh ... satisfaction."

"Mmm, yes, this all sounds quite satisfactory, Ooze."

"Would you like me to order the assembly then?"

"No, no. Not quite yet. Tell me more about the heretic. Do we see much action?"

"I'm sorry, action?"

"I mean incursions. From the other side."

He shook his head perplexedly. "No. Never. Ours is to stay ever vigilant, madame Acolyte."

"Yes, of course. And of the machine itself, is it ... fully ... functional?"

"Well, of course."

"But, I mean, armaments, and defenses, temple energetics and ... displacement?"

"Displacement? You mean the transport apparatus? Well, yes, quite functional in all respects, but I hardly see how that would matter-"

"No, no, of course, it's merely an academic inquest. For ... information's sake."

He nodded slowly.

She turned to Noor-Andra. "My dear, you've been ascended as well, have you not?"

"Well, yes."

"Very good. What am I to call you now?"

"Noor-Andra?" she offered, nearly as perplexed as Oozie, the head Makrit-in-Charge.

Galas shot her a puzzled look. "Well, then why am I the only one to get a new name?"

"Because your name was stupid. It sounded weak and silly."

"Oh, thanks for not sugar-coating it."

"You're welcome."

Galas took inventory of her present Noor'at stores and found herself truly depleted. Not even her long nap was able to restore her after the evening's activities. Her stomach grumbled in that way that would only be satisfied by feasting. She tried to distract herself.

"Noor, dear, how long have I been ... you know." She twitched her head sideways, feigning sleep.

"Eleven days. We weren't sure you were going to make it. That is, until yesterday, when you woke up screaming that you were going to take Kada's head off and," she coughed politely, "um, defecate ... down her oozing black throat hole, I think it was." She smiled thinly. "Typical Galas. The consensus was that rather than waste a perfectly good portal of exile on the two of us, Reality Zero would be better served to have you defend her from the Void threat. Here. At the Chronoshield. Lucky us. I was rather looking forward to exile," she said, sighing wistfully.

"Eleven days! Wow." She turned and yelled in the direction of Ak-Umbrech, "Kada, you duplicitous bitch, I swear by all that is depraved and twisted that I will most definitely not evacuate my bowels until I've made good on that promise!"

Noor reached for her arm. "Careful warrior, you may be holding that for some time. As it turns out, the day following the pronouncement of our exile by Wahr-Zen, Kada was found hanging by her own entrails from the great chandelier." Galas blanched. "There was a note. It said, 'I do this by my own hand.'"

"Bold move..." Galas breathed out in surprise.

"Yeah, but nobody believes she did it."

Galas looked at her, "They don't?"

"Of course not. Battle priestesses are hard, but that's, well, I don't even know if that's possible. At first, people assumed it was Wahr-Zen."

"Yeah, well, that makes sense."

"Until they divined the author of the note."

Galas snapped to Noor, ears perked. "Go on."

Noor looked down at her with her most serious expression. "The handwriting..." Galas nodded for her to continue, her mouth going dry in anticipation. "...was yours."

Her mouth fell open. "H-h-how? You said yourself that I was incapacitated. You didn't think I was going to make it."

"Right. No one knows how. They speculate astral projection from within your comatose state."

"No effing way."

"Yes, effing way. What does effing mean?"

"Nevermind. So that's why they put us down here? Because my outburst confirmed a suspicion, no matter how impossible?"

"More or less."

"Wow," Galas said, her brows knit. "But there's one thing I don't get. If I killed Kada in my sleep, wouldn't my Saine'ril or Duine'at stores be full? Wouldn't I have sucked her dry? I mean, that's what I think I would have done."

"No, you woke on an empty stomach because when you cried out, you expelled a telepathic wave so strong it ripped the chandelier from the ceiling and split the thirteen steps all the way to the throne. The throne bled."

Oozie made a series of gestures with all four of his hands, covered his head and ran back down the steps.

"I'm sorry. Come again?"

"The throne? It bled? Did I stutter?"

"No, I just..." Galas sighed out a long, stuttering breath. "I just don't understand, I guess."

"No one does. And I'm stuck with you."

"Sorry."

"Me too."

"You don't have to agree with me."

"But I do."

"Nevermind. This is too weird." She looked again her at hands and realized that they more fully appeared Chareth-Ul-like than before the events of the coup. And then the hunger hit her. It felt like her insides were twisting and convulsing. She groaned and clutched her stomach. "Dammit." She whispered.

"Too late for that, kitten. You're already damned," she looked around, "in case you haven't noticed."

There was going to be none of that. Damned or not, she wouldn't stay down just because some puffed up priestess ordered her to watch the back door.

"Oozie!" she screeched. "Assemble. Now!"

She walked to the edge of the dais where there was a banister she could lean on so she wouldn't look so pathetically weak. Noor-Andra pulled up beside her.

"Time to feed, Prima-Caz?"

Galas nodded slightly, barely able to acknowledge what she knew she had to do.

"Can't do it, can you?"

"What do you mean?" Galas asked, feeling suddenly concerned.

"Feed," Noor squeezed her freezing hand. "Don't worry. I know how much it tortures you. A thunderer is one thing. Little more than brute. But a Makrit like Ooozmah?" She let the question hang. Then she slipped something into her palm. It was a small satchel.

"What's this?"

"A talisman? It's, well, let's just say I've been saving up for a little while. You store Duine'at there. In some cases, it can act as a channel for Saine'ril, but I've never used it that way. That only applies off-dimension. If you'd had one of these during the coup when you took Kada's full assault against Yon'di of the Green Line when she was about to come forward and name names, a talisman like this would have saved your pasty, human ass."

Galas looked down at the small leather satchel. Very few things on Reality Zero had skin. She shuddered at what it could be made of, but accepted the offering.

"Thank you."

"No. Thank you. What you did by standing up against Mudh'e and her partner ... you saved my life. Even if you ruined it by getting me stuck here."

Galas nodded. "Well, don't worry. I don't plan on being here long."

Noor looked at her sidelong for a moment as the Makrit, and Umzat assembled before them in the hundreds and then thousands. After a while, the regiments were all formed up and the blazing sun had shifted south, casting long shadows through the crowd.

A trill went through the crowd and, as one, they all turned their attention to Noor-Andra and herself. A shudder ran down Galas's spine. No matter what she thought of the creatures before her, they were under her command now. Their lives were in her hands. Her stomach grumbled as she remembered the customary tribute and struggled with what to do next. She couldn't run a Heretic without full reserves. Noor's talisman could get her through a pinch but, not long term.

She brushed the satchel with the back of her hand after tying it to her belt and a shiver ran through her; a knowing; the gold line... a retaliation.

She was just reaching for Noor when an explosion rocked the mech, but it'd come from behind them. Her stomach dropped as she realized it was from the direction of the time shield that held back the flood of Void creatures from a dimension beyond.

"Breach, breach!" Ooozie shrieked, followed by sirens blaring seconds later. The whole of the assembly flooded to the exits to the sides as well as elevators routing into the mech's interior. This was the worst possible situation. No one was at their battle stations.

"How did you know?" Noor shouted over the chaos.

"I felt it when I brushed the talisman. Gold line. They've sabotaged the shield, so that it'd look like I did it or at the very least that it was due to my ineptitude. And they waited until they knew everyone would be away from their stations. We'll be punished, but I don't think they expect us to survive."

"They're right!" Noor yelled as she rushed to the edge of the temple dais and launched herself through the air toward the other temple, hundreds of meters away. She needed to be there to operate the mech's defenses. Perfectly planned. Galas had to hand it to them. But why?

Galas gripped the talisman again and sent a force wave after Noor to carry her the full distance. Once she saw her land atop it, she stepped back to the center of her own temple mount and sank low into a wide stance. No one had taught her what to do, but she let the ethereal flow of the Ahk'menaim wash over her. The temple would show her.

She hoped.

Thousands upon thousands of Savages flooded the visible part of the breach. They penetrated deep into the hordes of Makrit, Umzat and what few Thunderers they had. Her retinue of Deathhounds was limited to begin with, but now all the pilots were scrambling to get to their mechs. Some probably wouldn't even make it.

Galas searched the Heretic's arsenal for Deathhounds. There were twenty. She should have five times as many. They must have all been deployed to Epriot Prime already. She'd have to make due.

She reached out to Noor via mind link. "Is Wahr-Zen still in dimension?"

"What? Why would that matter?"

"In case we need backup."

"Oh, we're going to need backup."

"Yeah, that's my point. Is she here?"

"Sadly no. She left directly after ordering your ascension and commission."

"That bitch. She knew I wouldn't go down easy."

Screeches and flashes of light moved in a flood between buildings and then entered the temple plaza, streaming in from first the shield area and then slowly from the sides. Her forces were massive, but the flood was overwhelming. How could they seal the breach? Answer: they couldn't. This was the beginning of the end.

"Those Gold Line traitors must have a plan, or they wouldn't have done this. This is suicide!"

"Oh, they've always had a plan," Noor boomed within the mind-link now that she had achieved full immersion, her A'ta visible even from this distance. She lashed out a wicked wave of psychic energy down the temple steps. It collided with the wave of Void pushing through her scattered Umzat guards, taking out the whole lot. "Their plan has always been to hole up in the Keep and blow the portal, killing the greater half of our people, our ancestors, and millions of Makrit besides. But," she lashed out again, and the Void made it farther up the temple steps before disappearing in a flash of energy, "from the looks of this breach, I'd say our people have been gone for some time."

Galas drew Duine'at from the talisman and tapped into the well of deepening energy within the mech. Her eyes stitched up, and the world sprang into the spectral light provided by her own A'ta. She knew it would be blazing a brilliant crimson like it had the night of the coup. She struck out with crackling lightning that sought out the Void and popped them like overdue pimples. Dozens of enemy combatants burst into oblivion across the deck.

"Ooh, I like that," she said before looking down at her scorched palms. She willed healing Saine'ril energy from the mech into the wounds. The smell of burned flesh began to diminish, but she still had to choke down bile in her throat. "Maybe I don't like it that much."

"Moderation, Prima-Caz. That weapon is impressive, but it is typically used as a last resort. Though, I've only ever heard of it being used a few times in all of Chareth-Ul history. Why we haven't tapped into the human resource for more than just Deathhounds is beyond me."

"That makes sense about how and when to use that chain lightning," she said, shaking out her hands. More of the Void pushed in from the sides of the plaza. Umzat bubbled up from below out of openings in the plaza, where elevator platforms would usher Deathhounds to the topside of the mech. Still, none had joined the fray.

Next came Makrit grenadiers. They launched volleys of the rift, opening grenades over the heads of the flyers, that exploded just above the deck. That must have been armed with prox sensors. Portals ripped open and sliced the Void Savages apart, but many blipped out of the way.

The waves kept coming.

"Noor. We only have one option. The Void will overtake us, but even if that doesn't happen, if what you're saying about the Gold Line is true, then we're sitting at ground zero of an atomic-level blast."

Noor-Andra's attention was on Galas through the mind link. Galas could tell she got it.

"We need to leave. Do you know how to initiate the displacement mechanism?"

"I've read the texts. It's all theoretical, no practical experience. But we'll still need coordinates. That's how they keep newly ascended like us from screwing up the multiverse. You don't happen to have them, do you?"

"Is there any other way?"

"I don't know." She lashed out with another wave that rolled out across the plaza, but the Void blipped past it. She lashed out twice more and caught several of them, but not all the creatures, with that ploy. "Galas, a little help," she yelped as the pack of Savages reached the steps of the temple.

Galas lashed out with lightning once more from her newly healed hands and the creatures lit up one at a time until the last one blew up within meters of the top. Galas pulled her smoking palms back to her body. "Damn, that hurts. We need to evacuate now, Noor. I'll work the deck. You get the displacement mechanism charging."

"Okay, but we still need to figure out how we're going to navigate to Epriot Prime without a guiding artifact."

"I'm from there. Can I be used as a reference?"

Noor paused. "Maybe? I mean, I guess. I don't see why it couldn't use you. I mean, it might kill you in the process, but it *could* work."

"We'll have to try," Galas said as she drew up Saine'ril from within the temple and expelled it in a wave that took out handfuls of Void and Makrit alike. At this rate, she was going to wipe out her entire crew and there'd still be an endless supply of the enemy pouring through the breach. Time was running out.

An explosion ripped through the heretic from below. Smoke billowed out from one of the elevator shafts as a Deathhound emerged from below. It had Savages attacking it from all sides; the pilot was swinging dual rotary blades maniacally. One of the creatures exploded into light just as another blipped up to the canopy of the mech and plunged a taloned fist inside, ripping out a large chunk of the pilot's chest. The Deathhound sagged and then toppled.

The Void were clearly inside the Heretic now, but was it them who were causing the explosions or was it more Gold Line sabotage? Or was the plan all along to blow up the Heretic itself and let the mech's reactors wipe out the Chronoshield?

That rang true. And it also meant that it was possible that Galas and Noor-Andra could displace the Heretic to Epriot Prime and then just blow up there.

She was suddenly glad that she'd killed Kada in advance. It'd save her the hassle of having to come back here and do it. As for the rest of her ilk, it'd have to be enough to know she was leaving them here with an open portal to the Void realm.

Noor-Andra broke her stream of thought. "Prima-Caz, we're spooling up. We need to project the portal seed!"

Galas understood. She'd need her help to do it, and their defenses were dwindling. Multiple problems with competing resources all at once—this was very much like piloting a mech. And then she realized it was actually piloting a mech, only much, much bigger. And if possible, even more alien than piloting a Delvadr Elite. Suddenly she missed Raph. Soon, maybe, she'd have him back.

"Let's do this." Galas looked around for something to use as a defensive shield and she spied the glowing cracks in the valley floor. "I'm building a wall around the temples. It'll be temporary."

Galas reached into the machine and delved into the deepening power. She'd found that while she was stationed atop the temple, the Duine'at buy-in to channel the Saine'ril was significantly diminished. Good thing, but it was still exhausting channeling that much energy. She dug deep and scribed a line around the temples with one hand while the other stretched toward the valley and the fractured fault lines with their toxic gas.

Sometimes you had to use what you had at your disposal, and Reality Zero had a lot of this, whatever it was. She siphoned the luminescent vapors away from the chasm and into the waiting channel she'd created. It wasn't a physical vessel, but a magical one, and, as she'd mentioned before, quite temporary. A sand castle holding back the sea.

For a moment, it seemed like the Heretic forces were gaining the upper hand and pushing farther toward the breach in the wall, but then an equal number of Void burst forth. The numbers on the side of the Chareth-Ul that had been pouring from below decks were growing noticeably thin.

Galas continued to draw on the vapors and soon a vaguely glowing barrier grew up, becoming deeper and more dense. At first it was just on the side facing the breach, but slowly it began to extend around the edges. She still had a long way to go.

"Neat trick, but is that going to do anything?"

"I don't know. I hope so. Are you ready?"

"Ready and waiting."

"Okay," Galas said, turning at least half of her attention on her second-in-command. "What now?"

"Follow my lead."

Noor stepped forward into a low stance and drew her hands down and then up to her chest before stepping forward again and pushing them out toward the front of the mech. Galas followed suit. Somewhere in the midst of the motion, she realized she had to choose the nature of the summoning and she chose displacement. The melding of machinery and magic was bizarre, but she guessed it wasn't all that different from the virtual reality interface of the Antiquity cities back on Epriot Prime.

A small shimmering dot emerged between the temples and then sped forward out beyond the massive deck. As it did so, it expanded into a larger and larger disc of light. Then she was prodded to provide the artifact. She felt Noor defer to her in the telepathic space. Galas imagined stepping into the space where the artifact was to be placed.

There was a pause and a vague ripple shook through the machine as if it were offended by the suggestion but then it took hold of her and somehow she was in two places at once—half on the temple dais and half inside this magical interface between mind and machine, and then the bottom dropped out. She couldn't tell if she was falling down the temple or falling into a hole inside the link.

Suddenly a burst of light lit up all around them and she realized they were ripping through some kind of transient space between dimensions. Noor let out a pained grunt as the requirements of the displacement spell ripped more and more Saine'ril energy from the mech's stores, and through her to feed the displacement mechanism.

Galas realized she wasn't pulling her weight and stretched into the machine to do the same, only she was also holding up the wall of noxious gas to keep the void creatures from slashing them apart. She tried to shift some of her attention to how the Makrit and Umzat were doing against the enemy but found she couldn't. The machine demanded her total attention in order to arrive where she'd instructed it.

Then the world around her started to shimmer, and she realized she needed to provide finer navigation. Where in Epriot Prime did she intend to go? They could end up at the top of a mountain or the bottom of the sea if she wasn't careful. She focused on the northern continent, then on the Merrat Valley, and finally on the capital city of New Varhus.

But this was a massive machine. A city in and of itself. She'd destroy the city if she just landed anywhere. She navigated north at the last second and, with a massive concussive boom, the Heretic found the space previously inhabited by a Defiler mech. That would do.

The bottom dropped out again and suddenly the air was crisp and it was night. The fires on the deck, which she'd barely recognized in all the chaos before, now lit the low clouds above them. And the Void were breaking through the dissipating shield.

"Is this it? Did we make it?" Noor asked, desperation saturating her voice in the telepathic link.

"Yes, but we're not out of this yet." She drew from the machine again and realized that it had massive stores, but she did not. She was near exhaustion after the dimensional travel and the constant fighting. But then, the fighting started to shift as well. Now that the Void were cut off from their source, they became cagey. No more frontal assaults. They shifted down into the interior of the Heretic.

Galas breathed a quick sigh of relief. At least she could pause to catch a breath, then a ripple of alarm ran through her system, but not one of urgency. In fact, it was several levels lower on the shit's-exploding-everywhere-meter in her mind. It was a warning of a fast-approaching ship.

An acolyte still manning his post notified her that it was a transport vessel called the *Xandraitha's Hope*.

"No fragging way. That's great. Flag them down," she told her bug-like staff. In the time-honored tradition of the Chareth-Ul, he interpreted that as "Bring them down."

She was trying to hail him again as he broadcast to the ship that they needed to surrender and promptly fired missiles.

Galas watched in horror as they arced up and away. She waited for them to explode uselessly off the transport's shields, but that's not what happened.

CHAPTER 35
RUTKER AND 'ZERK

Epriot Prime, The Spires—Alpha Tep

Rutker heard the words and all the plans and ideas about the mission faded.

Katherynn. Mads. How could he get to them? Were they alive? Were they injured and alone? His mind raced with possibilities, none of them good. He felt short of breath, felt like an invisible hand was clutching his throat.

"Captain Major," the woman said, still pointing her sidearm at him but with noticeably less conviction than before, "... Captain Major."

Rutker snapped to her from his harried thoughts. Her countenance had softened too, but he couldn't care less about any of that. He was desperate, and all he could think of was his family.

"I have to go to them. Find out if they're okay."

"We're trying to hail them now, but there's no response."

"I have to see for myself."

"What about the people? You said that the refugees are going to be handed over to the Chareth-Ul. That's why you resisted arrest. What about them? If that's all true..."

He wavered, his knees felt weak, and he still couldn't breathe. He was underwater, held inches from the surface. What about the people? His people? But what about Katherynn and Mads? And the kid ... the all-powerful and enigmatic mage, D'avry? Where was he? He'd just skipped out in the middle of everything. Had he just gone back to his world and time? Could he even do that?

No. He knew better. The kid was a pain in the ass, but he had the right motives. And, given the right circumstances, he would probably make a difference. But right now? With his family in danger... Rutker's mind was swimming.

"Capt. Major Novak? What about the people? Do you really believe the council will hand them over—"

"Yes. Yes, I know that Reddum and the rest of the council will hand them over. That's why they're all holed up on the lower levels and aren't able to roam freely. That's why there are four ships ready to go with the Defiler mech on its way. Have you heard anything about it? Has anyone mentioned anything about that mech?"

"Surely it must be getting close. It was only going to take a couple of hours to get from New Varhus to here. It's been a couple of hours. They should have been able to track it the entire way. Have you heard anything about that at all?"

The look on her face told him everything. She knew she was supposed to be ready for something, to transport someone, but beyond that, she'd been kept in the dark. He looked at her uniform lapel and insignia. She was a Captain. He'd missed that initially. Probably the surprise of being caught. He'd been too intent on what he was doing. Big mistake.

The name on her lapel read Juul.

"Captain Juul. Will you get the other ships to take the refugees on board? It's humanity's only hope of survival. That and maybe the refugees at New Varhus."

"There's been more about that. I doubt you've heard."

"What? What haven't I heard?"

"There are unsubstantiated accounts of a skirmish at the detention center."

"Yeah, yeah, I know. That was the slaughter that happened when I a dozen others tried to escape. As far as I know, only two of us made it out."

"I hadn't heard that. But no, this is bigger. Something about the Void attacking a Defiler. But it doesn't make sense if the Defiler is on its way here."

"You're right. That doesn't make sense. Who was saying this?"

"One of the guys manning the sensor arrays in Charlie Tep. But, there was a lot of speculation and conflicting data. The Defilers scramble the hell out of our sensors."

"Yeah, well, that tracks. I was in a shuttle and it was commandeered remotely by the Defiler that's on its way here now. So, maybe it's possible that their tech makes it so we can't see it. Still, it doesn't change the fact that I warned the council, and only a few of the members seemed surprised. And then they sent me to my quarters to freshen up and get some rest. Escorted by military police."

"I'll do it."

Rutker looked up in confusion. "I'm sorry? You'll do what?"

"I'll talk to the other pilots. There's been a lot of weirdness going on for weeks now. A lot of under-the-radar bullshit. If your guy makes it up here with all those people, we'll load them up and get them to safety." She shook her head. "I don't know where we'll go..."

"I do," Rutker blew out a sigh, "I do. Gellen III. E'rth. It's not in any of the maps, but the Xandraitha's navigational computer will have it. If it's still intact. I can go retrieve it, and..." he sighed again, and it came out in one long shuddering breath, "and see if my wife and son are okay, but in the meantime, we need a rendezvous point. It has to be somewhere rocky so the Chareth-Ul can't get there in their Defilers ... or teleport or whatever it is they do with those things."

Captain Juul looked up quickly. "The Eldomitik. Base Fahl. It's a rugged island on the other side of a deep channel, but it's not all that far from shore. Or from here."

"Sounds good. Now I just need a way to get back to New Varhus. Are there any fighters left? Maybe a Phalanx transorbital?"

"Really? You think we have any of those lying around after the last invasion? If we did, I wouldn't be piloting this hunk of shit." She patted the bulkhead. "Sorry, baby."

"Yeah, too much to ask."

Juul brightened. "We do have a reconner loaded in back. Part of the deployment package. I never asked what it was for, but it makes sense if we were hightailing it for uncharted parts on Guisse IV."

"Great, but what's an aging recon mech going to do for me? Does it even have guns? I'll be easy prey for those Deathhounds. That's if I even make it to the valley floor."

"That's the cool part. Repulsor pack. I've never seen one on an older-style mech like that. Especially not something as one-off as a Skatuul class. The other cool bit, it's a reconner. You'll be able to slip right by their sensors. And it does have a chain gun." She shrugged. "Better than nothing."

He was beginning to feel like it was the Long Rifle all over again. Flashbacks of fighting—and mostly hiding from—Dragoon and Osiris mechs back on E'rth flitted through his mind. His mind jerked back to the reality of the moment. The real crash-landing of the *Xandraitha's Hope*. The likelihood of what had happened to Katherynn and Mads.

Crash landing was a misnomer. Interstellar craft only did the landing part under very specific circumstances. The odds table that was running in the back of his mind told him what the most likely scenario looked like, but he had to see for himself. And, he acknowledged morbidly, that he needed to extract the AI core with the nav module. That was the real mission. But he didn't let his mind go there. He would focus on one thing at a time. Mount up the reconner, ride the repulsor pack the three kilometers to the valley floor, evade the Defiler and, he was sure, its contingent of ground forces, then make his way as quickly as possible back to New Varhus. He would worry about what to do next when he got there.

"Okay. Base Fahl. If we can't make it to the island, we'll signal from shore."

"Preta airfield."

"Ran counterstrike outta there during the Yanz Defense. Makes sense if it has crumbled in on itself. Okay, Captain. Good luck. And..." He swallowed a lump that was forming in his throat. "Thank you. Humanity thanks you. And I thank you."

"Good luck to you too, Captain Major." She snapped a salute. He returned it, nodded, and then made for the back of the cargo bay. He turned back once, and she was gone.

Good. At least there are some of us left, patriots, good people like Monster Mind. He chuckled at how odd that sounded. Rutker scanned the stowed pallets and found the only one that could be it. By mech standards, it was a runt. But standing there, looking up at it in the relatively low-ceilinged space of the ship's cargo hangar, it was positively huge.

He felt that familiar rush of adrenalin before a fight and that pang of fear. He hated mechs. A thousand times out of a thousand, he'd choose a fighter, but ... no sense in complaining. His family was out there and this, well, it was better than power armor, anyway. He looked again at the skeleton in front of him. Well, it was a little better than power armor.

Rutker tapped the control panel on the stowed mech and it beeped loudly before shifting forward into the main aisle on its cargo repulsor pad. The pad followed a painted channel toward the very back of the bay and then flashing lights and still more beeping noises ensued as the cargo bay door slid apart while a ramp lowered to meet the floor of the main hangar.

Once the stowed mech's cargo module had come to rest, he approached it and entered the instructions to activate and detach. A few pneumatic valves activated as restraints disengaged, but that was it. There was a low whirring as the mech's internals came online.

It was gunmetal gray and did resemble a tall, skinny skeleton curled into a sitting position with its knees to its chest. The chest itself was fused with the head structure so that it resembled a vertical torpedo shape. On its back was a slim repulsor pack. To the left of its head was a bristling array of sensors and on its right, mounted atop the shoulder, was its chaingun.

Rutker had a hard time imagining a more utilitarian form. It looked like an old-school robot, which, he guessed it was. Except it was big enough to hold a human pilot. It was going to be cramped. Just like the Long Rifle.

He rolled out his neck. Time to go.

"Skatuul 808TL. Attention. Prepare to mount."

"Confirmed," a thickly digitized voice emanated from the mech's external speakers as it shifted its weight forward and rose up to its full height of six meters. He slipped around its Y-shaped foot structure, climbed the inset steps inside its leg, and found the entry portal underneath. It was a tight fit, but soon the hatch was closed and he'd navigated the dim, awkward space behind the pilot's chair and slid into the gel couch.

Not all that different from a Phalanx trainer, he conceded. The view through the forward screen was adequate, but there was little else that didn't rely on cameras that would populate the dashboard once he linked up. Here was the moment of truth. The link up. Just how antiquated was this machine?

He placed the helmet on his head and instantly felt the bee hive buzz of neural hardware integrating with the helmets connection to the beast itself. He smelled ozone and a harsh twinge of metal before everything cleared up. Once it did, the heads-up display was clear and lucent, splayed around his periphery in an intelligent fashion. All the cameras were online and contrary to his expectations, also clear and considerably high-res.

He navigated quickly through the menus and systems, and everything was up to speed with current Epriot systems. Well, this was retrofitted for a new mission, wasn't it? A feeling of happiness at screwing up Reddum's plans washed over him. It was a good feeling, but it reminded him all the more about the mission at hand. Find Katherynn and Mads. Get the AI core. His gut churned, and he nestled down into the familiar steel saddle of duty.

"Skatuul 808TL."

"I prefer 'Zerk."

"Oh, really?"

"Call sign, Berzerker. He and I were paired for many years. I prefer 'Zerk."

"Fair enough, 'Zerk. You ready to get some?"

"Infinitely."

Rutker smiled. Maybe he was going to like this. He initiated the foot and pack mounted repulsors to gauge thrust and the light mech lifted off the hangar floor with ease and dropped back down with balletic poise. Not the clumsy clunk he'd expected. His smile broadened.

"Okay, well, we have a Defiler mech on its way here that we need to avoid and we need to cover a lot of ground quickly without being seen or heard."

"Excellent. You've come to the right mech. Active jamming engaged. I've hardened comms against infiltration and with this repulsor pack, we shouldn't have to touch ground for several kilometers. It can operate at 150 percent max for 240 seconds. I can calculate an appropriate glide path to navigate us out of harm's way from there. Ready when you are, Captain Major. One thing. My data feed has you flagged as AWOL. I assume this is a mistake. This won't be a problem, will it?"

"'Zerk, this will most definitely be a problem. But we have bigger problems right now. A downed transport with my family on board and an incursion by the Void and Chareth-Ul within kilometers of the site."

"Say less."

Rutker nodded and guided 'Zerk toward the opening at the end of the large, red rock hangar. They built speed quickly and were flying past the other transports at nearly 80 kilometers per hour before the opening loomed before them. Other spires in the distance were faint traces of vertical light. Some vague mist in the foreground were clouds, but beyond that was darkness.

As they leaped out into the night air, they arced slightly west. He intended to slide out near one of the farther, uninhabited spires so he didn't stumble directly into the Defiler, but as he looked down, he realized that wouldn't be a problem. His stomach clenched. The Defiler was already here.

"'Zerk, send a cargo maintenance record for yourself to Capt. Juul regarding your Ops and Comms hardening effort. Channel Five Priority. Make sure to note 'Arrival Procedure, Status: Engaged'. Hopefully, she gets the hint. Otherwise, it's going to be a short flight. And that's *if* Monster comes through."

CHAPTER 36
SERAF AND THE VOID

Epriot Prime, Somewhere East of New Varhus

Seraf woke with a start. There was a racket going on. Something large to her right was clanging around. Her brain felt like the inside of a dirty wash bin. She fought back the urge to puke. What was up with that? She'd been doing that quite a bit lately. Then she remembered the flyers with their stun attack. She almost threw up again. At least her visor was open.

Her visor ... she was in an armor suit. Cool. Okay, things were beginning to come back together. Macq. The nice guy with the cute butt. She tried to shake the image out of her head, but it hurt too much, so the image stayed. She tried to think around it.

"Okay. Bad guys. Bugs. Trying to get back to the ship that crashed. That thing's probably toast. I hope Macq's family is alright." She said all this in a stream of consciousness. The thoughts needed to come out. If they had words attached to them, that was just part of the package. She was in no shape to be picky.

She rubbed her face but only managed to poke herself in the eye with her gauntleted hand and clang around the edges of her open face shield.

"Ugh. Right."

Seraf turned to see what the ruckus had been about earlier but just saw the twisted metal of a refuse container and some boots. And also a rifle that was bent nearly beyond recognition.

"Huh. Wonder who left that lying around?"

She panned left and nearly threw up again. Scattered across the pavement was the lower half of a person. She convulsed painfully as her last meal came up, in projectile fashion, coating the ground and another rifle. That one was in surprisingly good condition. Well, at least it had been.

She thought again about the half a body on the street and her brain, which was just now beginning to get some traction in reality, told her not to turn around. Those boots were probably not empty. Whatever had ruined the dumpster had absolutely wrecked the person wearing them.

Her thoughts raced back to Macq but were mollified by the realization that he had been in power armor as well. Suddenly, she was feeling very alone. And very afraid. Lying around in the middle of an alley on the outskirts of New Varhus was not a safe place to be. Even the humans weren't safe.

She reached for the rifle, puke and all. It wouldn't hurt the gun, she was sure. She didn't bother cleaning it off, she just checked the projectile mag, the energy charge, and the safety. It was a BR3. She'd seen enough holos to know how it worked and, having used that other rifle in the tunnels, it was all beginning to make a lot more sense. This was the new normal.

Okay, now for the hard part.

"Let's start with sitting up, shall we?" she asked herself as she attempted to engage her abs to draw herself upright. Surprisingly, it worked. "Oh, that's better—" she began, but then another wave of nausea hit and she vomited again. This time it was more of a dry heave, thankfully. She convulsed with another wave and then was finally left spitting what little moisture was left in her mouth into the dirt.

She grimaced. She didn't like the new normal. What had happened? Something about those flyer bugs. She'd been running from those degenerate hillbilly snipers and then Macq had told her to keep going while he, what? Held them off?

She'd kept going for a block or two and then run right into one of those bugs. She vaguely remembered dropping a shoulder and tackling it at full speed. Probably a stupid move in retrospect, but, then again, she was alive, and it was nowhere to be seen. Had it survived? Seemed unlikely.

Seraf looked up and down the street, deeply concerned that she would find yet more imagery to empty her stomach to, but was blessed with empty war-torn cityscapes in either direction. Dark, empty, war-torn cityscapes barely lit by the pale blue light of Cyclopedae. She wasn't sure if she was happy or sad that the smaller brighter Skleetrix was hidden behind it. Still, she needed to assess her situation.

This prompted her to slide down her face shield, which only connected vaguely. It didn't seal properly, but it stayed shut. The scene around her melted into grays and greens, and suddenly, the whole area took shape as the suit's virtual dashboard came online.

There was a tall building to her right and a crater where a building used to be directly ahead. Her HUD perked up, and three red shapes populated the suit's minimap.

"Oh shit. There's more."

She remembered how many rounds it had taken to drop just one of the creatures. You had to hit them in the underbelly. That was fine as long as you could get to it. They usually kept them pretty well guarded. Another thought struck her, "Where's Macq, anyway?"

Just then, the sound of shattering plas came from high up above. She watched in surprise as someone in a power suit flew from a window and out into the open air, arms and legs flailing purposefully, almost as if the flight was on purpose. Which, how could it have been?

She did the quick mental math and realized they were going to land in the middle of the debris-filled crater across the street. Which would probably kill them. But if it didn't, the pack of creatures definitely would.

"Shit." She realized that was probably Macq. She stumbled forward and promptly tripped over the pair of pants, hitting the ground just at about the same time that Macq hit the crater.

Seraf willed herself to her feet and started across the alley as fast as her head and her stomach would let her. She brought the rifle, and the middle area of the crater was a cloud of dust. At least she knew roughly where he'd landed. A dark shape darted through the rubble, and she recognized it as one of the flyers. She opened fire while pressing forward on reluctant legs.

The scene before her swam in the monochrome light of her night vision display, each muzzle blast devouring her visibility. She'd only let off a few bursts, and now she struggled to pick out the creatures in the broken landscape. They were completely lost in the shadows. She felt her stomach drop. Just like that, she'd gone from hunter to prey.

"Bad move, Seraf. Dammit," she cursed herself.

"Seraf? Is that you?" she heard Macq respond, though she wasn't sure quite where from since the dust kicked up was spreading out and obscuring a larger and larger area.

"Did you just land in the middle of that pack of flyers? And are you okay?"

"Yeah. Felt like a head-on with a transport, but I'm in one piece. My repulsor pack took a bunch of rounds up there. It's dodgy at best. I won't be able to jump out of here."

"Can you make your way to me? I'm up in the alley, left of where you landed. I'll keep an eye out," she assured him.

"Yeah, I know where you're at. Heading your way now."

Seraf scanned the slowly dissipating corona of dust with her rifle's targeting display. She caught vague ghostly shapes slipping between the rubble, but she couldn't tell what was Macq and what was not. She became aware of red and blue cursors moving on her HUD and realized she could track them that way, but then the numbers were all wrong. She expected to see just three of the red cursors and just in the crater ahead. But there were easily three times as many and they were scattered about the minimap. And they were converging on her location.

"Scratch that, Macq. Don't come to me. Go the other way. Fast."

"Yeah, I see what you mean. I'll try to draw them off."

"You'll what??? No!"

A large boom issued from within the dust cloud, and she realized he'd fired his stolen sniper rifle. Instantly, the red cursors on her map changed direction to investigate. The creatures that had been zeroing in on her were now headed for Macq. He had that high-power rifle, but she doubted she could handle the creatures in number.

Another boom echoed through the area, and one of the red cursors turned gray. Great, but that's only one of nine. She tried to pick out a path on the minimap that would take her to Macq, but she just wasn't familiar enough with the system to get it to work. She'd just have to make do.

Two of the creatures burst into the alleyway to her right. She spun and started firing. The creatures put their heads down and charged. She knew from experience that the rounds from the rifle would do little against their outer shell, so she sprayed the street ahead of them as they half-flew and half-leaped forward.

Either a shot or a ricochet clipped one of the creatures and it stumbled off to the side. The other one kept charging forward and Seraf instinctually leaped away toward the crater. She maxed out her repulsors and carried enough momentum to land her nearly to the edge of the dust cloud.

That's good. That's a good thing.

The creature followed, but now she was below it. She brought up her rifle and fired wildly, decimating her night vision again, but she heard a screech and the sound of the creature hitting the ground several meters away. Its red cursor turned gray and she let out a whoop.

"Yeah, take that!"

Another boom of Macq's rifle came from the far side of the building crater. She saw three red cursors between herself and Macq's location and there were still three more scattered around the area.

No. There were more than that. All of this activity was drawing them in from farther away.

"Dammit. There's more coming Macq."

"I know. I know—"

And then she heard a scream.

"Macq! Macq!"

No response.

She leaped and boosted her repulsors again for several long seconds as she headed toward the solitary blue cursor on her map. It was surrounded by red and they were closing in.

Seraf picked one of the cursors near the back of the pack, flew right for it, and cut her repulsors. She plummeted toward the ground at speed, but at the last second kicked them on again and the flyer took the brunt of her fall. There was no shriek this time, and she didn't wait to see the cursor turn gray. She knew. She'd felt it crunch beneath her boots.

She leaped over the creatures, spun, and fired her rifle, careful to avoid Macq's blue cursor. She was pleased to see the red cursors follow. At least she was pleased for a moment. That was until she landed on the road and all the creatures were bearing down on her in the darkness. Across the crater was the alley she'd awoken in only minutes before.

She needed a plan. Seraf scanned the minimap and the number of red cursors heading for her was even more than before. There was no way she and Macq could take them all out. And then she thought about Macq. Her friend. Was he okay? Had he just been knocked out like she had? Or worse? His cursor was still blue, so at least his power armor could sense a pulse.

Through her audio, she heard the clattering hum of the creatures as they jumped and flew with their beetle-like wings. Maybe she could draw them off?

One of the creatures skidded to a halt on the roadway. And then another and another. She stepped back, rifle at the ready. The talons on their toes clattered against the street as they twitched with anticipation. Several more drew in from either side and, as one, they pressed slowly forward.

She remembered how badly her head hurt from running into just one. There was no surviving this. She stepped back again and her back bumped up against a wall.

She just wished she could have done more. If she could have helped Macq find his family. That would have meant something. She could have returned the favor for saving her life back at the detention center. Without him, she would have been fleeing from the Void and flyers and the Deathhounds, alone, unarmed.

At least now she could go out with a fight. She brought up her rifle and suddenly the row before her exploded into bits of shell and goo. She looked down at her rifle and then at the remaining creatures. They'd all turned to their left to face something. And then the sky lit up with fire and the roaring whir of a chaingun muffled the screeches of the flyers as they scrambled for cover. Only a few made it off the street.

Whatever it was in the air followed quickly and the chaingun erupted again and again until there were no more red cursors on the map. She didn't know who or what it was that saved her, but it didn't matter. She was racing over the rubble and debris to where she'd last heard Macq.

Amongst the broken plas and twisted columns, she saw an arm and a boot. She flashed forward and within a second she had him pulled out of the rubble and was working to remove his face shield.

"Macq. Macq!" she pleaded as she gently patted his helmet, remembering how fragile her own head had felt upon waking after receiving that psychic smackdown just a little earlier.

And then the ground shook with a loud rumble as something massive set down behind her. She spun, weapon ready, and aimed at the kneecaps of a huge robot. She slowly moved the muzzle upward until it was aiming at the opaque plas of the mech's cockpit. To the left of it was that chaingun that'd mown down all the flyers that she was certain were going to be the end of her.

Her rifle faltered. But she didn't know who they were and so far that evening, no one had proved to be trustworthy.

"Never aim at something you don't intend to kill," boomed the slightly digitized voice of the pilot through the mech's external speaker.

"Yeah, well, ya never know," she hollered back. "Who are you and what do you want?"

The cockpit plas turned transparent, and inside, she could barely make out the pilot, but his hands were up, palms open, which she knew was just a gesture. He could kill her with a thought right where she stood. Still...

She kept her rifle, worthless as it was against a mech, trained on the pilot.

"Who are you?"

"I'm Captain Major Rutker Novak. And that's my son."

Seraf almost collapsed from relief as she struggled to choke back tears that she didn't understand. She nodded and dropped her rifle, letting it magnetize to its holster diagonally across her chest before removing her helmet.

"I'm a friend of your son's. Name's Seraf," she said as she ran a gauntleted hand over her chin-length auburn hair.

She could swear the pilot's mouth was hanging open, but it was hard to tell in the low light.

After a moment he responded, "Well, Seraf. You don't know how happy I am to meet you."

She thought that was an odd comment to make considering the circumstances, but then she remembered what she and Macq were doing before everything went sideways with hillbilly snipers and then the flyers.

"Oh, shoot. Capt. Major, there's something I need to tell you. About your family."

"I know. I was on my way to the crash site when I saw the battle playing out on my SortieNet. Thankfully, I could identify Macq in the system through the power armor's computer when I got close enough to link. I didn't recognize you though. But now that I see you in person..."

"What?"

"Well, let's talk after we figure out what's up with Macq. The suit's systems say he's stable. It's like he's knocked out, but it's different from that."

"The flyers. The beetle thingies. They stun their prey. We need to keep his face shield open cuz when he wakes up, he's probably going to puke all over the place. In fact..."

She turned to put him on his side, but then he started to groan. Seraf stepped forward quickly and nearly received a face-full, but got him facing the right way just in time.

"Ugh..."

"That's right. Just take it easy. It'll take a couple of minutes."

"Wha—"

He started and then puked again.

"You got smacked by one of those flyers."

He reached for his head and then rolled onto his hands and knees, dry heaving a few more times. After a moment, he seemed like he was beginning to stabilize.

"Macq, someone's here to see you."

He turned slowly toward the sound of boot steps on gravel. He saw the mech first and was about to say something, but then saw his father, and his eyes welled up as he tried to stand but faltered. Seraf swooped in and caught his arm, but then Rutker was there, crushing Macq's power suit with a huge hug in spite of the danger of it and its weight.

"I thought you were dead," Macq whispered, his voice tight.

"I never doubted you. I ran into Dexx and he tried to suggest otherwise, but I never doubted you."

"That snake. Did you put a fist down his throat?"

"Not yet. But don't worry. That day will come. I'm guessing that's Dexx's power suit Seraf's using?"

"Yeah. Lucky thing too."

"You'll have to tell me all about it. After we find your mom and your brother."

"Yeah. We were heading to find you, but then the Defiler crushed the tunnel and then we heard the mayday transmission. I don't know what to think, Dad."

"Yeah. One thing at a time. How are you feeling?"

"A bit groggy still, but—"

"Just take a minute," Seraf interrupted. "It takes a couple of minutes and then it gets better from there."

"No. I'm good. Let's just move slow for a minute maybe."

Rutker and Seraf exchanged glances and then Rutker stepped back. Seraf could see the competing concerns play out across his face. He nodded.

"We'll go slow for a few minutes. But we need to stay together. I'll work point. You just tell me when we can pick up the pace."

"Deal. I just need my gun."

Rutker looked over into the shadows. "This it?" he asked as he pulled the massive rifle out from under some rubble. "What is this? It's a beast."

"Slair Two," Macq said, beaming with pride.

"Ooh, that's an antique, but," he nodded, "probably a great tool with these flyers and Void, and even Deathhounds maybe. Nice choice."

"Wasn't a choice, but yeah. Thing's badass," he said and grabbed it from his father. "Let's go find our family. And D'avry. I think he's our only hope anymore."

"Yeah, well, we'll see. I hope you're right."

With that, Seraf pulled on her helmet, and they started up and out of the crater. There were still hours before the sun came up and about forty kilometers to the crash site. They started to jog but within a minute Macq was already pushing toward top speed. She looked over at him as he ran. He looked her way and nodded.

"Thank you, Seraf. I know you looked out for me."

"Yeah. What are friends for?"

The trio raced down the avenue, bordered on one side by a riverwalk and the other by buildings stacked along a short cliff that rose gradually into the distance. Looking ahead, Seraf wondered if they were headed for the crash site of the *Xandraitha's Hope* or back to the detention center. The Defiler mech was a massive dark shape bordered by a dark sky. She didn't need the night vision filter to see it though. The fires and random explosions accomplished that just fine.

"Um... where we headed, exactly?" she asked.

"The terrain is forcing us north. The next bridge doesn't look good though. I'd rather roll the dice that there's a more suitable option ahead. We'll have to push on farther or risk a water crossing. I don't know how you guys feel about that. I won't split us up again."

"Yeah," Macq agreed, "Let's not do that. I wish my repulsor pack was still working, but it's too intermittent to count on."

"No sense getting hurt trying a shortcut. We've still got a few klicks to go before we have to—" he was saying when a bright flash lit up the night.

Seraf looked up and, for the first time, wondered what would happen if that thing fell over. A quick estimate in her head told her a quarter of the city would be crushed and who knew what the impact would do to the rest of it?

"Capt. Major? Should we be concerned?" Seraf asked.

"Yeah. That's not good. We should cross over now."

She looked up at the massive mech and could swear she saw it shudder. Fires atop it caused the low clouds to glow an eerie orange.

Yeah, good idea...

CHAPTER 37
THE CRASH SITE

Epriot Prime, New Varhus, The *Xandraitha's Hope*

D'avry seemed to vaporize into a thin wisp of coal and diamond dust. As one, the other humans turned to her, their eyes asking the question, "What have you done with him?"

"Don't look at me," Seda responded. "I may be his mentor, but only in things Gefkarri. As guileless as he appears to be at times, he operates as one who is a free agent amongst a matrix of magical systems. Once I presumed to keep him on a leash ... clearly that notion has expired."

She drew herself up, steepling her fingers before her, and closed her eyes, intending that to be the end of the one-sided conversation.

"You saw what happened though. Didn't you?" Mads said, stepping forward, concern and confusion warring on his face.

Ensign Presche spoke up next. "He's on that mech. The Defiler. It looked like he joined their side."

Seda acknowledged the fleeting emotion of annoyance, bundled it up, and sent it off to the greater collective. She was careful to mask the desperation and fear gripping her insides over D'avry's well-being.

It was a delicate game, her connectedness to the greater entity of the Pentarch. Simply withholding emotion was tantamount to treason. And she'd done so much more than that. Helping the humans. Helping *him*.

"I will not speculate as to the motivations behind D'avry's actions," she said without opening her eyes or moving a finger, "but yes. Of course, I saw."

Katherynn stepped closer but hesitated at the space where D'avry had just disappeared, as if he'd return at any moment. Given the events of the last several hours, it wasn't entirely unlikely.

"Seda, we must do something. D'avry has left and we don't know when or even if he's coming back. The refugees, our people," she motioned between Mads the ensign and herself, "...the few that remain, are headed this way. You saw for yourself that they're being tracked down and slaughtered by monsters and Deathhound mechs."

She opened her eyes and Katherynn recoiled, looking as though it was everything she could do to hold fast.

The woman has a spine at least, Seda thought as an unfounded maelstrom of anger and frustration washed over her. Holding her emotions back from the collective was much harder than she had anticipated. And these simple creatures could feel it, even if they didn't understand how. She had to tread carefully.

When she saw both Mads and Ensign Presche, eyes wide, posture tense and alert, she realized her eyes were blazing intensely and her long hair was radiating out like undulating tendrils. This was going to be harder than she thought.

She drew herself inward, gathering and then twisting the emotions into a tidy little packet of anger—something that would be easily understood by the collective—and sent it away.

It wasn't easy. The connection was tenuous, but she needed to keep at least some small portion of it viable. Just enough to allay concerns that she'd lost control. Of what? The situation? Her perspective? Her emotions?

"I *must* do nothing," she said, cutting off every word. "But, I *will* do as I promised and instruct you how to tap into that which you already possess."

The humans cast nervous glances at each other. Without having D'avry here as a buffer between them, they were growing less trusting. Very well. She would have to do it *without* trust.

She placed her hands on the map table. Contemplated the smooth graphite surface of it. The lines were so rigid. The same

The Crash Site

with the rest of the bridge; slick, dark surfaces with red carpet and leather-esque seating along the walls.

Ordinarily, it was so clean and orderly. So contrary to her world, where utility flowed from within each living being. Even the flagship, which was part Thune-built ceramo-alloy and part living flesh of the collective itself.

Here, everything seemed like an afterthought.

Now though, the bridge was in disarray. Monitors hung from the walls precariously, cabling bulged from between panels, and the whole of the room was canted at an angle as the craft rested in the earth where it'd carved a crater out of the cityscape. That explosion of energy from the collision cast into the very structures around them.

This, at least, was honest. A real assessment of how little agency this ignorant little race possessed. Soon they'd know their place in the universe. The look in their eyes now alluded to the fact that they were beginning to get it. She felt a twinge of pity.

She would not be sending that little packet of emotion back to the greater being.

Seda turned so that her eyes met Katherynn's. A world of emotion dwelled within them. Pain, suffering, longing ... hope—all greeted her. She thought again of D'avry and the swelling feelings of disdain toward these people began to waver.

He was one of these, was he not? Crude. So ignorant of what he asked when he used her as a conduit to the Gefkarri source. She suppressed another emotion, one the collective would most certainly not comprehend ... a longing of her own.

She couldn't describe what it felt like to be connected with him that way. The power. The assuredness, even when he had no idea what he was doing. The irony of it was delicious, that she had been assigned to his case as a sort of penance. But what she'd gained ... a kind of wholeness that she hadn't experienced, even within the collective.

She breathed in slowly and out again. She realized she was smiling now. The humans seemed uncertain as to what to do with that. Mads was fiddling with a ring on his index finger. Ensign Presche looked at her with a knowing expression. Odd one, that.

Katherynn stepped forward and placed a hand on Seda's arm. Seda flinched and stared at her with a raised eyebrow. There would be none of that sort of familiarity.

She shot out tendrils along the floor and they came up beneath Mads, Ensign Presche and the Ambassador. They wrapped around their bodies as they struggled, holding them firm, and then the tendrils swept up to cradle their heads.

"What're you—" Mads began to ask before she clamped his mouth shut.

Maybe she'd reacted harshly. Withholding her thoughts and emotions from the greater being was much, much harder than she realized it would be.

She was about to set them down when others from the bridge ran forward to help their fellows, but they met similar fates.

So be it. She'd need them too. Seda wouldn't willingly share her magic the way she did with D'avry. Their relationship was ... complicated. Special.

After all, it'd been he who had helped her unlock the greatest discovery in millennia—the existence of an entire race of Pan Arcanum. Not just individuals with the rare power, but every last one of them.

A door whisked open and more of the humans entered the bridge with weapons in hand. She snatched them up and separated them from their tools of destruction. It was to be a party then.

Many still struggled, but it was only a matter of time before they realized the futility of their efforts or ran out of stamina. Once things quieted down, she'd decided it was time to get to know what she was dealing with.

She created a psychic node—a local network where she could speak to them telepathically.

"Allay your fears. This ... connection, while foreign to most of you, is not so with me. I've been doing this since before your earliest recorded history. And if not I as an aspect of the greater being such as I am now, then certainly as one who is connected to that ageless being. In that way, I am as old as the earliest forms of sentient life in our galaxy."

"What you need to know is that you are nothing. Your concerns. Your hopes. Your dreams, your reality ... are nothing. And if you cannot grasp this, then soon, you will truly be nothing. You will be consumed or used up, either by the Chareth-Ul in one of their soul-bound machines, or by the Void, or possibly even the Gefkarri, though our designs could be to your benefit."

She paused, waiting for all of that to sink in. She felt their anger, their outrage, their denial, but under all the bluster was acknowledgment. They knew she was right, that humanity was at the end of the line, and they were surrounded by races far greater than they could even comprehend.

But there was more. And this was what she needed them to hear,

"But for today, this moment, you may have a different path. If you would seize it."

She reached into the connection, into their minds, like she had done with D'avry when he'd first boarded the flagship. Her only concern at the time was that he should live long enough for her to extract the information the hive mind needed to assess the threat he and his partner Rutker presented. Which was assumed to be nothing.

How wrong they'd been. Now, however, she needed these aliens as much as they needed her. The truth of it was that she was on an alien planet, surrounded on all sides by combatants and even her own race was a threat, for surely the Gefkarri would find out what she'd been up to. And there'd be hell to pay.

Seda reached further into the connection and the humans, twenty strong at this point, as a whole, recoiled at the intrusion. But, they didn't really have time to lollygag, did they? Katherynn had said it herself. The refugees were on their way and with them Void and Chareth-Ul minions and Deathhounds.

She brushed past their inhibitions. Some put up more of a fight than others, and she took note. The ensign was one of them. But then she found herself standing in the midst of an overlapping consciousness like an unopened flower, the layers folded in around her and she could feel all and nothing of each of the members of the node.

She kept them partitioned from one another until she could spread things out a little bit. Their minds were too unfamiliar and would struggle in vain to make sense of each other's thoughts. Here, she had to be the most careful. One misstep and she'd be surrounded by vegetables or bodies. D'avry would never forgive her. She imagined that neither would anyone in this room. Not that it mattered if they were in such a state.

There was a general unrest amongst the people and she realized that she was projecting more of her inner thoughts than she intended to. *How embarrassing*, she thought, ironically, and realized that on at least some level, she was. Managing her feelings outside the collective of her species was wearing her down. She practiced it now with the humans, offloading some of her concern, and it dissipated quickly.

"Do you feel that? I exported some of my unpleasant emotions to our small collective."

There was a general murmur of understanding tinged with bewilderment. "Now, I want you to do the same, but one at a time. Focusing on playing out the emotion smoothly. Feel it, isolate it, send it ... gently. Katherynn, you go first. When you're ready."

Bitterness, frustration, fear, and betrayal all came barreling at her in truckloads. She tsked, "My dear, I said to share it with the collective," she said and gestured to the crowd surrounding her, "and please remember to be gentle. Everyone will get their turn. You may not trust me, but right now, you better believe that you need to trust one another."

There was a pause and then Seda could feel it. Compassion. Comfort. Benevolence. It was kind of beautiful. Maybe there was hope for humanity after all.

"Very good. You understand that you can share the good as well as the bad. Every day we do this, but you humans have such little sense of the greater being that you represent. It is stifled, but it's there, nonetheless. With my assistance though ... now you feel it."

Her thoughts turned to one of the others. The Captain. Perfect. He understood immediately, but hesitated. He couldn't bring himself to open up to his crew or passengers. He was just too used to holding it all in, presenting the image of the stalwart and stoic leader. She didn't have time for this.

"Captain, if you are unable to lead in this small way, how can anyone in this room expect you to lead ever again? Now that we know who you really are. Will you hide in shame behind your position, garnered through favor for your family, or will you step into that which you've always had but suppressed for fear of failure

The Crash Site

in the eyes of your father? And mother. I see. It's her you truly fear. And I sense that she isn't even with us anymore.

"Now the acceptance you failed to gain while she was living is even more impossible to achieve. That's a sad story. But, as you are beginning to become aware, this room is filled with similar stories."

She began to let down the walls of separation. Slowly. It would never be possible to let it down all the way. Fear, uncertainty, shame, and guilt all exploded through the connection and she realized, along with everyone else, that he'd known what Colonel Dexx was up to when he'd sabotaged the peace treaty between the humans and the Delvadr and sacrificed his contingent of Marines in the process. And now the cat was out of the bag. No wonder he'd been so reluctant. She'd never been able to understand it. Secrets, that was. But now, she was keeping secrets of her own. Equally treasonous, she realized. And yes, there was shame and guilt on her part too. But there was more. There was what was right. D'avry was many things, but one thing was certain, he could always be trusted to find the right path. That, above all else, was what drew her to him. Somewhere along the way, the Gefkarri had strayed from this.

She sensed it in the deepest recesses of the greater being. That ancient presence. When it had spoken, it had revealed something of itself and in that moment, within her were born the seeds of doubt.

A grumbling within the node rose into a clamor. The whole of the human collective erupted in anger, betrayal, and disgust at what they'd just learned of the Captain. But even as the feelings of outrage and hatred bloomed, there was an undercurrent. Slowly, hesitantly at first, there were other emotions. Some within the node extended, if not forgiveness, then at least a tentative acceptance.

It had been a complicated situation. Colonel Dexx was the ranking member of the delegation and was operationally in charge of the mission. He hadn't known about all of Dexx's plans, that they would have such a horrific cost, but he'd had foreknowledge and therefore, he'd be considered complicit.

The man collapsed within Seda's grasp. Tears of shame streamed down his face. She was stunned by this turn and before she knew what she was doing, she lowered the partitions and enhanced the connection so that all the collective could feel his anguish. Not just at being found out but at being wrong and having to hide it.

The mood of the entire network softened, and then something beautiful happened. The humans let down their own partitions. Their reluctance, their inhibitions crumbled. It was an organic, almost unconscious response to the Captain's vulnerability. Just the acknowledgment that he was responsible for the deaths of those men and the guilt he felt over it was all the argument in the court of public opinion that was needed.

She realized it was because they couldn't trust one another. In a normal environment, everyone was holding back secrets from everyone else. But in this environment, that was impossible. The human response to honesty, vulnerability, and raw and unfiltered truth-telling was instantaneous. She made a mental note.

"Now you begin to understand why you cannot compete with the Gefkarri. It is single-minded of purpose and within it, there is no wasted effort. What it seeks, it will find. What it desires, it will obtain."

A thought floated above the general murmur of the working collective. "But now?"

Seda considered this. It was not the thought of a single person within the collective, but truly a product of the network itself. An entity unto itself and of the many selves that constituted it. She hadn't realized it at the time because it wasn't so overt, but when D'avry had united the five, it had been the birth of a new entity in the universe. A human collective.

But now. Those words echoed within her. The universe might never be the same. Could they fight back? Maybe. Maybe they could.

The node hummed with a thought, "Yes. But we must be more."

She nodded her agreement. Yes, the humans may be able to fight back. But there must be many, many more. The Pentarch was made up of billions of aspects. And that was just the one being. There were many more beyond that. That was if they were still engaged in their campaigns against the Void and had not yet lost.

Yes, humanity would need more.

The Crash Site

But then, in that moment, she felt something ... terrible. A knowing. The presence of the ancient one had never truly gone away. It had merely obscured itself.

Secrets.

Of course, why hadn't she realized this? If there was a connection to the collective, the ancient would always be there. She'd been a fool to believe she could hide herself. Her true feelings. And now she realized it had been no accident that she'd been assigned to D'avry. In that moment, she realized that the collective had its own secrets, and she'd been a fool to believe otherwise. Fear clenched her insides and her throat, threatening to blow up into full panic.

A tremor ran through the node. They sensed it too.

They pulled her back from the edge. Back into the fold.

"You're with us. One of us."

And the collective turned that partition that used to be focused internally, separating them from one another, out. It enveloped them. This was a magic but not a Gefkarri one. Something new. There were still traces of the Gefkarri source, but now there was some kind of firewall built up around them.

She felt the ancient slip away, but its attention was on her now. On them all. And ... it would be coming back. They had little time.

Her thoughts turned to the refugees. They needed to gather as many as they could. Just then, a sound, like scraping and clattering, could be heard just beyond the door that led to the operations and the cargo bay. What was it?

Her imagination went wild. She had heard that noise before, but she couldn't place it. Then a thought percolated from within the human collective: "The umzat." The Chareth-Ul flyers. There had been so much going on when D'avry had guided the five astrally above the city and up to the top of the Defiler, but she had heard it there.

She stilled the panic suddenly coursing through the node. "Be still. Wait for the opportunity to present itself. We do not yet understand our capabilities—" she was saying when the door slid open. She didn't turn to face the disturbance, but one of the members of the collective had a direct line of sight and the entire group could see two featureless black shells bobbing in the corridor, attached to long legs and arms ending in talons.

The creatures' claws clacked with anticipation, but they didn't attack. Instead, they stepped forward, their heads swinging from side to side as they inspected the area with sensory organs she could only guess at.

The lead creature drew close to one member of the crew who'd come in later than the others. There was a tense moment as it prodded the man telepathically. Seda slid in between the two in the psychic space, obscuring the energetic signature as she'd learned to do in similar events against aggressors with these kinds of powers.

The creature bristled. The other one swung its head in the direction of the man, who was now emanating massive amounts of terror as the creatures drew up on either side of him. It was almost more than Seda could do to mask her psychic presence, but then the rest of the collective shifted to join her, drawing away the emotional energy and dispersing it amongst themselves.

The two creatures drew closer still and she could feel their power building for an attack when one of the other doors slid open. The two creatures turned and charged for the opening just as a shape, black as night and taller than a man, appeared in the corridor beyond. Its glowing red eyes grew large as it took in the pair of Umzat lunging forward to attack.

The creature blipped away just as the two flyers collapsed on empty air, discharging a combined psychic disruption that rolled over several of the closest members of the human collective. The effect on the node was something like having an appendage fall asleep.

The crew members collapsed in Seda's grip as the Umzat shrieked and tore off down the corridor after the solitary Void creature. Individual voices rose from within the telepathic network.

"What's happened to our team members? Are they okay?"

"Are we safe here?"

"The ship has been breached, but how many creatures are out there? And what of the refugees?"

Seda placed a calming effect on the node. "All good questions. I sense that our team members are okay, but they've been incapacitated. Knocked out, effectively. Regarding the breach of the ship and the state of the refugees, we will need to explore to determine this."

The Crash Site

The Captain's thoughts lifted out from the group. "The ship can help if we can interface it."

"No," she replied. "We should not draw attention to ourselves by manning the consoles. I will project our presence the same way that D'avry did with the Five. Follow along."

With that, the viewpoint of the collective flew from the bridge, splitting down each of the corridors. The humans struggled with the tandem views, but within each corridor were more of the Umzat and Void, and there was carnage too. Some of the refugees had sought refuge within the ship and been found. The emotion level of the collective spiked. It was a mix of concern for the refugees and concern for the collective itself.

Seda extended tendrils to the doors that entered on the bridge and blocked them so that even if the doors were forced open, it would keep at least the Umzat creatures out. She was getting low on resources now, having expended so much to capture and hold the crew members. She was going to have to loosen her grip, but at least now, there was an understanding that she was here to help.

Of course, her blockade would do nothing against the Void creatures. They'd just have to deal with that when the matter arose. The collective felt unsettled about that prospect but didn't know what else to do. She continued her projected journey through the ship.

Part of her projection continued through the crew quarters while the other entered the cargo area. Here was more of the same; creatures scattered around the space and clusters of bodies of refugees. But there was something different here than in the corridors. Not all the refugees had expired. The collective sensed their weak psychic presence.

Like the members on the bridge who'd been knocked out, they were merely unconscious. One couldn't guarantee that was the extent of their injuries, but maybe some could be saved.

Katherynn's voice rose above the group,

"We must gather them up and expel the Umzat. The Void, we will have to fight as they appear. There's no way to keep them out."

Seda was about to respond, but the collective had already achieved a quorum. The members of the node were trying to move toward the corridor but were unable to because she still held them fast. She felt the ire of the node turn on her and she grudgingly submitted. This was her collective now? She might be the leader, but she was no longer an authoritarian one. She felt anger at first, and then exposed, but the collective helped her process those feelings until there was a level of comfort that bloomed in its place. Belonging. The collective was growing up ... fast.

Within seconds, they were up and on the move. The security contingent setup ahead and behind. The rest moved along with Seda in the middle. She kept a tendril in contact with each, except for the few that had been knocked out earlier, whom she still cradled as she glided along with the crowd.

She'd meant to move to the front so that she could use her tendrils or her magic against any creatures in their way but the collective was opposed to this. The entity now meant to stay one. If Seda was compromised, then so was the collective. This was more than a little disturbing. Was she a captive now of her own creation?

Better to play along than find out. For now.

They had only just moved to the lower level when a trio of Umzat skittered into the corridor before them. The security detail opened fire with little success. The Umzat lowered their heads and charged. Seda's tendrils shot forward but at the same time the collective gathered psychic energy, feeling out the possibilities of what they could do.

The creatures collided with ironwood vines and were caught up, but they thrashed with strength many times that of the humans she'd dealt with so far. The creatures ripped away but the security team fired at the exposed belly of one of the creatures and it shrieked as the projectiles tore through its body.

The other creatures turned to flee, but the collective was energized now. Seda paused momentarily, uncertain whether or not it was safe to show the collective too much, but now was the time for fighting and soon, their lives—hers included—would depend on it.

She lashed out with a psychic wave that burst down the hall, blowing out lights, and cracking the outer shells and inner organs of the fleeing creatures. They collapsed without a sound.

The collective took a pause as they saw this and realized what it meant. They could fight back after all. They could go on the offensive. Individually, even in small groups, they might not stand

The Crash Site

a chance against the creatures outside and within the ship, but like this? They were a force to be reckoned with. And the more refugees they saved ... the more powerful they would become.

The collective moved forward. Two of their wounded team members awoke and the collective gently brought them back into the fold. The third member, the group realized, would not make it back. Seda was going to let her go, but the collective wouldn't have it. She carried her along until suitable arrangements could be made.

Within minutes, the doors opened on the high ceilings of the cargo bay. It spread out, forty meters across, and nearly 200 meters deep. The area near the entrance was crowded with cargo and supplies that'd broken loose with the crash.

They slipped through the gap and watched as a skirmish between Void and Umzat unfolded. Three packs of the flyers bounded, skittered, lunged, and broke away in a concerted effort to corral the five void creatures that remained. It was impossible to tell how many had died since they disappeared when they were killed but there were nearly a dozen Umzat bodies littered across the floor.

This battle had been going on for a while.

Seda took over now, racing feeder lines across the floor, searching the human bodies for survivors and then pulling them back to the fold. She rescued a half-dozen people of various ages and physical conditions before a ripple of fear emanated from behind the group.

The image of a pair of Void creatures within the corridor percolated into the collective eye. Her tendrils pulled back of their own accord and then burst through the back ranks as the creatures surged forward.

Seda's tendrils pierced the first creature, and it exploded into blind light. When their vision cleared, the other had disappeared, but it was impossible to tell where to. Seda pulled all the components of her body back. She'd become too overextended and the collective taking control like it had was too much.

A tug of war ensued, and within a few seconds, a quorum was achieved. The collective would not encroach on the sovereignty of Seda and she would not, ever again, do the same to a human unless it was ordained by the collective.

It was an acceptable result.

Soon, the new members of the collective joined the psychic space. It grew more substantial. It became a place as real and not dissimilar to the ship's bridge. The members gathered around it.

And the node itself became something greater. Soon it decided on a name, drawn from mythos, the embodiment of human virtue and the namesake of the ship from which it was born; Xandraitha.

CHAPTER 38
HOPE AND THE HERETIC

Epriot Prime, New Varhus, Atop a Heretic-Class Mech

Galas watched in terror as fire erupted along the belly of the *Xandraitha's Hope* and then secondary explosions ensued. Portions of the back end ripped away in fire and smoke. The ship began to descend as it sped past and toward the center of the sprawling urban landscape.

"What have I done?" she asked, but her grief was cut short as a ripple of alarm raced up her spine. She spun to see a handful of Void Savages racing up the temple steps in their spurting, lurching manner, blipping in and out of reality. Their eyes glowed bright crimson and she could read the hunger in them.

"Feast on this," she said as she dredged Saine'ril energy from within the mech up into a ring of fire around her and then timed a leap up at the last second.

The Savages burst past the wall of arcane flame, talons extended, and skidded to a halt where she'd been a fraction of a second before. She filled the circle with that same arcane energy, ripping the creatures apart.

The flames dissipated as she touched down on the temple once more. There was nothing left to suggest that she'd just destroyed five of the Void Savages. Nothing to feed on.

That was the great advantage of the Void, she realized. That's what made them different from other enemies. When the Chareth-Ul won an encounter, it would boost their power. But not so with the void. To stay energized, the Chareth-Ul had to cannibalize their own.

Galas realized that even now her body was shutting down. She'd expended so much, channeling massive amounts of power to fight and then to flee and fight some more, but it was too much. The laws of the Chareth-Ul system demanded sacrifice. She needed to feed or she wouldn't live through the day.

And there it was, the dilemma she'd been unable to articulate, even to herself. In order to see her daughter again, she would have to sacrifice her own humanity. Her soul. Hadn't she said that she'd gladly make that trade?

But how could she? Seraf, when they met again, could only ever see her for the monster she'd become.

Galas collapsed to her knees, head hanging low. After all this, she'd gone to hell and back, just to lose her once more. She stared down at her gaunt gray hands, the fine black veins coursing within, the charred black palms oozing liquid ash, and curved black talons where her nails trimmed to a soldierly length her whole life had been.

Another explosion racked the massive machine, and it shuddered with aftershocks. She felt within the mech that it too, was shutting down. The Gold Line's sabotage would culminate soon and the reactors would collapse.

She'd traveled through dimensions to what, deliver a time bomb to the final refuge of humanity? *Nice one, Galas. Less than a Chareth-Ul year ago—weeks on Epriot Prime—you saved your people from the Delvadr threat, turning their armada into a glittering cloud of dust in low orbit, and now? You would do it again. Only this time, it was your own people you were destroying because you couldn't see past your own selfish desires.*

"Congratulations. Wahr-Zen was right. You really are one bad bitch."

"What was that, Prima-Caz?"

"Oh, nothing. Just having a little existential crisis during a battle. You know, normal stuff."

"You're scaring me. We made it to your gross little planet, and now you're all moody and stuff. Can't we just deal with the Void and go about the business of whatever you had intended to do once you got here? That was the plan all along, wasn't it?"

Another incursion of Void sprang up from one of the entry buildings of the plaza. Umzat flyers were scattering in all directions, reforming into packs of three and charging back into the midst of the blacked-out creatures. But as they converged, the Void would blip away and back again, to slash the flyers apart.

Sometimes it worked, sometimes it didn't. Flashes of light erupted as Void got caught by the flyers or Makrit, or bodies of the Chareth-Ul defenders fell to the floor in shreds. It played out over and over again.

"I don't know how long we can last. We're so evenly matched, but I'm running thin. My body is exhausted."

"You need to feast and so do I, but we cannot leave the temples for fear of leaving the mech unattended. We need to call for tribute."

Galas nodded grudgingly. She knew Noor-Andra was right. "Very well. But, there's more. Even if we win this battle, the Gold Line have sabotaged the Heretic thoroughly. Eventually, the reactors will succumb and this thing will take out the entire city. Us with it, of course."

Galas reached out through the mind link to Ooozmah but the connection came back empty. He was gone. In contrast to the Ahk'menaim Priestesshood, the Makrit used a relatively flat chain of command. That meant that the remnant of Makrit, Umzat, and Thunderers were just fighting on instinct. No wonder the fighting was so sporadic.

Explosions deep within the mech reminded her of the dilemma at hand. She reached out through the internal well of Saine'ril of the machine. Reached through it to the minds of the Makrit acolytes that still lived and to their minions, the Umzat flyers, but found she couldn't decipher much of anything. It wasn't like her mind link with Noor.

"I can't communicate with them, Noor. Their minds are too foreign."

"It's because you're too depleted. Can you use the satchel?"

"I'll try, but I need you to reach the Umzat and Makrit. They need to hunt for whatever the Gold Lines have used to sabotage the Heretic. It's been hours and we don't even know what they've done yet."

Galas tried to reach through the mech again and found nothing. The well was gone. The interface that showed up when she engaged it was completely absent. Galas's legs grew weak, but then a thin ripple of energy reached out to her and she grabbed, desperately pulling on the power.

"Take it easy, warrior. I'm sending a little Duine'at your way. Enough to get you going," said Noor.

Galas felt ashamed for being so desperate. She knew it was no small thing to share power. In fact, it went against everything that the Chareth-Ul believed and taught. Survival of the fittest. Take what belongs to you, and oh, by the way, everything belongs to you. Charity is weakness. Galas knew that Noor was making the smart play. If Galas fell, she'd likely die as well. And besides, Galas would forever be in her debt. Still, she accepted the offering as something deeper.

"Thank you, Noor."

"Don't thank me. Get down there and feed and don't make me ever have to disgrace myself in this way again."

Galas nodded. She turned away from the other acolyte and leaped out into the plaza dozens of meters below. There were bodies everywhere, but few were fresh enough to give her what she needed. She wandered among the carnage until she found a faceless carapace that, though identical to all the others, was vaguely familiar. It was Oozie.

She could make his sacrifice mean something more by taking his essence and turning it into destructive power against their shared enemy. She shelved her inhibitions and drank, the shuddering ecstasy of it turning her stomach in self-loathing and disgust.

The mech rumbled and dropped beneath her. It was happening. Suddenly the deck listed to the side, tipping in the direction that the *Xandraitha's Hope* had gone and the direction of the Spires—the only other place where her people might be seeking refuge.

"Prima-Caz, are you done? I need your help. The Heretic … it's failing."

With her stores at least slightly replenished, Galas sprang up the steps. It was a far cry from the power she'd wielded after killing Muhd'e and her partner, or the other acolytes, the night of the coup, but it was something at least.

She mounted the last couple of steps and could see just how depleted Noor was as well. She could see it in the way she stood as if she was straining to stand up herself.

"Your turn Noor-Andra. I've got this."

The woman didn't waste time but staggered down the steps of the temple as Galas reached into the machine. The well was there, and the arcane mechanism as well, but pieces were missing. Whole swaths of machinery that had been there before. This was not good.

As she held the image in her mind, another section went dim. She had to find what the source of the Gold Line women's retaliation was. It was a spell, of course. But what kind?

She settled into the machine, seeking, searching, but there was nothing there and then she sensed alarm.

The Umzat shrieked and trilled from below and behind her. Dammit, she didn't have time for this. She spun and a fresh wave of Void had reformed. The battle had moved toward the temples once more. Her dwindling stores of Duine'at would not take her far. She hoped Noor's foraging was turning up successful, even though it disturbed her to her core. Reminded her of her own competing needs and desires.

The void below broke through the ranks. There was no time to be delicate. She sent a wave of psychic energy down upon them, all friend and foe alike. Not a wave, but a crashing flood. There would be no dancing around the damage like the Void were prone to do. There would be destruction. The thing Galas, no, Prima-Caz, was good at.

A sour smile turned up the corners of her lips. And then that tingle of alarm went up her back again. She looked about, but there was no threat to be seen. But then she turned and saw what she hadn't guessed at before. The Void had drawn her attention away while others formed up behind her. She pulled at the Heretic's well of power, but again, it eluded her grasp. She was too depleted already?!?

The mech lurched beneath her and she struggled to keep her footing and then something black shot through the air. A bird. No, a crow. It raced toward one of the Savages lurching up the temple steps and then at the last moment turned into the form of a man.

"What the..." she started to ask but then one of the creatures blipped closer and she was forced to use some of her last remaining Duine'at to blast it with an energetic pulse. Her A'ta faded, and she viewed her homeworld through human eyes once more. She touched the talisman, but it too was depleted as well.

The man slashed at another creature with a staff and then all Galas could see was the deep, lightless Void and glowing red eyes of her enemy.

She may not have magic, but she had talons and teeth as well.

The creature slashed, and she stepped inside its reach, slipping behind its back as the two toppled over the edge. She sank her claws in deep, brought her teeth down on its neck as she ripped her hands apart and the thing exploded in a flash of blinding light and then stars shot through her sight as she hit the temple steps, toppling end over end.

Galas came to her senses, and she was sprawled over the corpse of Makrit, its neck and torso in ribbons of oozing black. Her hunger kicked up instantly, even as she held back the urge to vomit. She was so weak, but she sensed that this creature had been dead too long. What life force was left had turned and would only make her sicker if she consumed it.

She dragged herself farther along the ground before realizing she'd fallen, not just to the temple grounds but down one of the environmental shafts. The inside of the mech was dark, but she could see well enough with her borrowed Chareth-Ul senses. It'd be better, of course, if she could ascend and use her third eye but, that was out of the question until she could feed.

She sniffed the air, and her stomach growled. The carnage was less rancid up ahead. She pulled herself along the floor through filth and dismembered appendages. Oh, how the mighty had fallen. A creature skittered from under an Umzat body and Galas seized, cracking it in half and gorging on its insides. There was a time and place for propriety, and this wasn't it. It was a drop in a bucket, but it was something. A few dozen of those and she could maybe walk again.

Then the mech lurched beneath her. She flew up into the air and then came crashing down on the floor with a pained grunt. Explosions from far on the other side rattled through walls and floor. So this was how she was going to die. She'd thought that thought so many times before, but this one seemed final. This really did seem like it.

Galas heard a noise up ahead and prayed that maybe there was a flyer that had merely been wounded but it wasn't so. A dark shape slid into the long corridor just a dozen meters away. It looked one way and then its gaze came to rest on her.

She froze. The creature glitched a few meters closer, and she knew she couldn't fight back. At least this would be quick. The hallway lurched again, and she recognized the movement this time. The Heretic was moving. If she was atop the temple right now, she'd be maneuvering it to rest on its haunches while she figured out where the rest of the Gold Line bombs, for lack of a better word, were located. Spell bombs? She didn't know. She had absolutely no idea what kind of witchcraft they'd come up with to sabotage the massive mech in order to blow the Chronoshield and the Void portal apart.

A thought occurred to her in the last fleeting moments of her life, *the reactors*. Let the rest of the ship tear itself apart, but if they could just isolate the reactors ... She hoped Noor could figure that out. Or maybe that random guy that showed up. Maybe him.

She realized it might have been the mage, just as the Void creature blipped forward and slashed. She rolled, pulling the severed carapace of a flyer between her and the creature's massive taloned hand. The force swatted her across the hall and into the wall, knocking the wind out of her.

The creature shrieked and was about to lunge when the whole space started twisting away. They both rose into the air as the corridor tipped further and further downward. They crashed to the floor and started sliding. She and the Void Savage collided with clots of shells that hadn't succumbed yet to gravity and tumbled along. The good news was that the creature was unable to get a footing. It swiped at her but with little effect. She lost the shell but collided with still more debris as the mech continued to fall at an arrested rate.

She had no idea what was going to happen when they finally came to rest. Another explosion ravaged the mech but from ahead. Galas watched in horror as a ball of brilliant light grew in the distance. "Oh shit," she said as she bashed into still more bodies.

In desperation, she held them close and twisted her body away from the blast.

It ripped past them, an infernal wave that felt like hitting the ground from way too high up. For a second, her fall was stopped. She smelled burned flesh and feared it was her own. The good news was that the Savage was nowhere to be seen. The bad news was now Galas was staring down a corridor that had turned into a shaft, without a bottom. And where it had disappeared into darkness, now she could see darkness, but within that darkness was land and water lit up by flaming debris. And it was coming up fast.

So, this ... is how I die? she wondered, but then the mech stopped short and she shot down the shaft and out into the chill night air.

It was peaceful, she thought. The wind buffeting as it rushed past, the river reflecting the fire-lit clouds above that little bridge she was probably going to flatten herself on.

Or maybe not. Maybe she'd just pulverize herself into the river, which from this height would be the equivalent of hitting the pavement of the bridge. Either way. At least now, she finally knew how she was going to die.

She wondered who would greet her first in death. Drakas, her blademate whom she'd failed to honor by following through with their suicide pact? Maybe Sun-Thurr, who she'd bludgeoned with a homemade boulder flail attached to her power armor and then finally crushed with her boot-mounted repulsors. Or would it be Kada of the Gold Line? That would be a sweet reunion...

The water rushed up to meet her, and she closed her eyes. *Hello, old friends ... did you miss me?*

CHAPTER 39

THE ANCIENT

Epriot Prime, Outer Orbit, *The Tahlah*

Commander Thelos held the last image of shimmering foliage in his mind—waves of gray bloomed brilliant green before bursting into orange and red, finally slipping into gray once more. Magnificent flocks skated above the canopy while the howls and cries of living creatures echoed from within the great tree. His home. His greater self.

This might be the last time he'd see the Gefkarri Pentarch like this. He allowed himself one moment longer before returning his mind to the mission and readying himself for the launch into the freezing darkness of space.

The launch tube portal sealed, and he heard the mechanism charging behind him.

There must be a more elegant way to do this, he thought, suddenly concerned about this one tiny aspect of the operation. This had been a foregone conclusion for the many months prior to finally arriving here, the outer orbit of Epriot Prime.

Thelos waited, siphoning off fear and trepidation to the collective in order to maintain optimal preparedness for the launch.

Any second now, he thought as he waited for the charge cycle to complete. This was it. the Ahead Team, a million strong, was mostly away. The first contingent was just now breaching the debris cloud caused by those buffoons, the Delvadr. He didn't know why they needed them, other than having more bodies to soak up damage before his Ironwood Shock Troops arrived. It'd make little difference though.

Besides, in forty years they'd accomplished nothing but the near-extermination of the species that they now knew to be of utmost importance in the battle to come. The humans. The Pan Arcanum. What a wonderful new toy to play with.

He was looking forward to testing out their capabilities once they'd gained control of New Varhus and the Spires by ousting the backstabbing Chareth-Ul. They'd be brought back into alignment with the greater cause, but he and the Ironwood would relish that correction.

Images filtered into the collective eye of the first wave of soldiers entering the debris belt. Casualties were horrific, as expected. Still, a substantial number of troops were getting through, and, as of yet, no reprisal from the Arcfire.

Intel received was proving accurate. The Arcfire was unmanned. Still, the ahead team would continue as planned and the flagship would move in closer to support. No sense risking the greater being unnecessarily.

Retainers released. Thelos's tube dropped into place. The firing sequence lights on his HUD lit up a low green, then brighter, and then, just as he anticipated, the last light indicator before firing, he heard the whoosh of the charge dissipating behind him.

"What's the matter? Why isn't the tube firing?" he asked the launch officer, suddenly even more concerned now that there appeared to be an actual system failure.

"I don't know. Checking now." The officer replied, a tinge of terror in his voice as the ranking officer's deployment was being delayed by technical difficulties.

"Allay your concerns, Somos. Just get it right," he thought to the man through short-distance telepathy. The soldier's emotional signature diminished significantly.

Thelos settled back to wait when a new presence entered his awareness. At first, it was a faint smell of old wood, wet and well-layered, with bios established for millennia. And then a twinge of recognition tickled his spine. His own emotional level spiked before he could export the excess.

The Ancient.

The Ancient

"Eldest," he spoke into the psychic space, now thick with the heady cocktail that was the presence of the oldest of the species. An original aspect of the greater Gefkarri before the split, so long ago that no one truly knew when it had occurred. Thelos had an audience with the Pentarch himself. Fifth of the original thirteen.

Thelos offered his deference, and the Ancient swept it aside with little regard.

"Commander."

"Yes."

"You will now be a vessel for my presence."

The lights on the HUD lit up as the charge returned and before he could acknowledge the command, the propulsion tube exploded with energy and Thelos shot out into the freezing cold and blinding light of space.

"Next stop, the debris field of Epriot Prime," he thought from the background of his own mind.

End

BOOK CLUB QUESTIONS

1. Galas, after defeating one enemy, finds that there are even greater enemies joining the fight. What would you do when you found this out? Have you had similar experiences in your life? What did you do then?

2. D'avry launches off into the unforgiving void of space, only to find his magic abilities fading. Have you ever attempted to face your fears only to find the strength, ability, or support you counted on to do so disappear? What would you have done in D'avry's shoes, er, boots?

3. Seda seems to have an unhealthy interest in and commitment to D'avry. What do you think this is about?

4. After initially assuming that his ancestors have no impact or nothing of value to say to him, Jinnbo gets a chance to speak with all of his ancestors. Would you like to have such an opportunity, or do you feel much the same way that Jinnbo did initially?

5. Wahr-Zen informs Galas she was chosen by the Deathhounds because she was exceptionally destructive and lacked morality. How do you think Galas felt being lauded by her enemy as a pinnacle of their values?

6. The Chareth-Ul doomed their planet in two significant ways. What were they, and do you see any parallels to our own journey as a species?

7. Seraf seems ambivalent about finally getting the opportunity to meet her mother. This is probably just a defense mechanism against being hurt again, but do you think her wariness is warranted?

8. Near the end of the story, the human remnant, through the aid of Seda, forms a collective consciousness of their own. Does this idea frighten you, or does it seem like the inevitable outcome of humanity's journey? Or both?

AUTHOR BIO

Eric's base camp is at the foot of the oft-smoldering Sierra Nevada in NorCal where he enjoys surfing, snowboarding & mountain biking with his wife and three adult sons. You can check out excerpts for upcoming projects at his author page: enlard-author.weebly.com.

On his nightstand, The Hitchhiker's Guide to the Galaxy by Douglas Adams, The Martian by Andy Weir, any one of the Muderbot Diaries books by Martha Wells or the Arcane Casebook series by Dan Willis. There's some Stephen King stuff too.

Discover more at
4HorsemenPublications.com

10% off using HORSEMEN10